Award-winning author **Louisa George** has been an
avid reader her whole life. In between chapters she's
managed to train as a nurse, marry her doctor hero and
have two sons. Now she writes chapters of her own
in the medical romance, contemporary romance and
women's fiction genres. Louisa's books have variously
been nominated for the coveted RITA® Award and the
New Zealand Koru Award, and have been translated into
twelve languages. She lives in Auckland, New Zealand.

Alison Roberts is a New Zealander, currently lucky
enough to be living in the South of France. She is also
lucky enough to write for the Mills & Boon Medical
Romance line. A primary school teacher in a former life,
she is now a qualified paramedic. She loves to travel
and dance, drink champagne, and spend time with her
daughter and her friends.

ER DOC TO MISTLETOE BRIDE

LOUISA GEORGE

CHRISTMAS MIRACLE AT THE CASTLE

ALISON ROBERTS

MILLS & BOON

First Published in Great Britain 2021
by Mills & Boon, an imprint of HarperCollins*Publishers* Ltd,
1 London Bridge Street, London, SE1 9GF

www.harpercollins.co.uk

HarperCollins*Publishers*
1st Floor, Watermarque Building,
Ringsend Road, Dublin 4, Ireland

ISBN: 978-0-263-29782-9

11/21

MIX
Paper from
responsible sources
FSC® C007454

This book is produced from independently certified FSC™ paper
to ensure responsible forest management.
For more information visit www.harpercollins.co.uk/green.

Printed and Bound in Spain using 100% Renewable Electricity
at CPI Black Print, Barcelona

ER DOC TO MISTLETOE BRIDE

LOUISA GEORGE

MILLS & BOON

To the Waipu Ocean Diving Sistahs…
Thank you for teaching this old dog
a) amazing new tricks, and
b) that whatever I'm doing, I must always finish in style. ;-)
This book wouldn't exist without you.
Thanks for the brainstorming, the love and the laughter. xxx

CHAPTER ONE

As a successful ER doctor who'd won scores of grants and awards, Rachel Tait prided herself on never making mistakes in her job. Unfortunately, she couldn't be quite so glib about her personal life.

She stared out of the taxi at the snowy landscape of Sainte Colette unfolding before her: the laughing children throwing snowballs, the pack of huskies pulling a sled carrying a clearly besotted couple, the snow-covered mountains and the blackest night sky lit with thousands of stars, the cute Swiss-style chalets and the twinkling lights strewn across the resort's reception façade and threaded through tree branches.

It looked like something out of a movie set.

And she had to admit it was also looking very much like another personal mistake she'd spend the next four months regretting.

Why had she chosen somewhere so very *Christmassy* to spend Christmas?

Why hadn't she chosen Australia, or the Maldives…? Or somewhere where they didn't celebrate Christmas at all? Surely that would have been a better idea than this?

Lesson learnt. Taking the first job offered to her just so that she could escape Leeds General Hospital hadn't been her finest decision-making moment.

Objectively, she could see Sainte Colette was enchanting. And bitterly cold. Perhaps, she laughed to herself,
she could actually *become* the Ice Queen she'd so often
been accused of being. Hopefully, the cold would be contagious and she'd be able to freeze her heart, too, and
prevent it from ever getting hurt again.

She shook herself. She'd come here to forget, not to
remember.

After paying the driver she looped her handbag across
her body, hefted one hold-all under one arm, hauled another up on to her left shoulder, gripped the wheelie-
suitcase handle, then wondered what to do with the skis...

She'd come here to forget, but the memories still hit
her with force, and all she could see was the long stretch
of aisle ahead of her. Still felt the kick in her heart.

She swallowed.

Still saw the apologetic look on the vicar's face as
she walked towards him...the embarrassed best man...

'Puis je vous aider avec vos bagages?'

What to do with the skis? She put the bags back down
on the icy ground and looked for a ski rack she could
leave them in while she checked in. There. To the right
of the entrance. She left her bags while she stashed her
skis, then retraced her steps for her luggage. Hefted two
bags on to her shoulders and dipped to grasp the suitcase
handle. She felt like a packhorse.

'Vos bagages, mademoiselle?'

The grip of her father's hand on her arm as the truth
had finally dawned...made so much worse because it had
taken a lot of organising for her parents to attend such an
event together. Humiliation instead of joy on what should
have been the happiest day of her life....

And now she was here. To forget.

It was proving to be a lot harder than she'd thought.

'Ahem. *Puis je vous aider?*'

She was vaguely aware of a deeply resonant voice saying something in French and looked up into soft, dark-brown eyes. A man, behind the reception desk, was staring at her as if she had two heads. What had he said? *Can I help you?* 'Oh. Right. Check-in. Yes.'

The man nodded. *'Bonsoir, mademoiselle. Bienvenue à Sainte Colette.'*

She was in France, she needed to practise her language skills. Okay. Yes. She'd rehearsed this. What was it? *I'd like the keys to my bedroom.* She cleared her throat and said, rather more slowly than she'd have liked, *'Oui. Bonsoir. Je... Je souhaiterais récupérer les clés de ma chambre.'*

'Of course.' He understood! She'd clearly nailed it. A smile hovered around the corners of his mouth. The dark eyes shifted down to the screen. 'Please, just one moment, Miss…?'

Rachel leaned against the reception counter. 'Dr. *Docteur.*'

'I beg your pardon. Dr…?' He wasn't wearing a name badge but, despite the smile, had that air of authority that, in her experience, only existed in high-end establishments such as the Sainte Colette ski resort.

Handsome, in a super-clichéd kind of way. All nice eyes and swept-back dark hair. Stubbled jaw. Sexy-as-hell accent that tugged at her gut.

Not that she was noticing men these days, or ever again. One broken heart per lifetime was quite enough. She met his arrogant air with one of her own and tried to remember what *I am called* was in French. 'Er… *Je m'appelle* Dr Rachel Tait.'

What had she done with the email the ski resort owner

had sent her with her orientation instructions? She dug into her handbag for her phone. 'I'm here... *J'ai...*'

She'd practised this, too, but the three-hour journey winding up into the mountains had made her nauseous and sleepy. Speaking a foreign language was a stretch right now.

The man smiled at her, probably out of pity for her woeful accent. 'I speak English if that would be easier.'

Thank God. It dawned on her that the last three things he'd said had been in English and she hadn't even noticed. She'd been thinking about being jilted at the altar. Why had she dragged her depressing past along with her? It was weighing heavier on her than the three bags plus skis. She was supposed to be healing, not moping.

She looked at the man and nodded. 'Much easier. Yes. Thank you. Good.'

'Welcome to Sainte Colette.' He handed her a swipe card in a little cardboard holder. 'Here is the key to your chalet. Number twelve. Behind this building, round the corner to the left. I will call Frederik to assist you.'

Tempting. In her haste to leave the country she hadn't given much thought to what she'd need for four months in the French Alps, so she'd pretty much packed the entire contents of her wardrobe. Juggling three bags and skis had been difficult to say the least.

And the truth was, she desperately wanted someone to help her, just once in her life, and to be able to drop the *I'm fine* pretence she'd been putting on since that hot July day...since as long as she could remember, in fact. Her heart ached to say yes to his offer, but she didn't have the energy to make niceties with someone she didn't know, and she firmly believed that if she said she was fine enough times then she would start to believe it. 'No need. I'm fine.'

The man looked surprised by her rejection. 'But—'

'I can manage, thank you,' she cut him off as weariness seeped into her bones. The bag on her left shoulder was pinching the skin on her neck. The other holdall was balanced between her knees and the reception-counter strut. She wasn't sure she could hold it in that position for much longer. Plus, she needed to pee.

'We have welcome drinks in the bar—'

'No. I've been travelling for what feels like days. I'm going straight to bed.' Welcome drinks? Did he think she was a guest? She hated small talk and couldn't think of anything worse than enforced mixing and mingling. All she wanted was to soak in the spa bath she'd been promised in the room spec, have an early night and be fresh for her first day tomorrow. Then she could meet, and hopefully impress, her new boss and get on with her job.

The man with no name badge nodded. 'I'd like to—'

'No.' She held up her hand and enunciated a little more slowly. Even though his spoken English was impeccable, maybe he had trouble understanding it? 'Thank you. I can manage my bags.'

More surprise flickered across his eyes as he appraised her, then he gave one of those shrugs that told her he didn't much care. And she realised, close-up, just how gorgeous he was.

His eyes met hers and she saw gold in the brown. A tenacious strength. They really were quite alluring. He had a presence of calm control…quite the opposite of how she felt right now, being scrutinised by him.

His reply was as slow as her words had been. 'As. You. Wish. Dr Tait.'

'Good.' She bent to allow the heavy holdall balancing on her knees to slide to the floor as she signed the registration forms he'd pushed across the desk. 'Do you have milk?'

'Milk?' He frowned.

'In the chalets. For tea.'

A hoity eyebrow rose. 'Of course. In the fridge.'

'Not the long-life stuff, it makes tea taste horrible. Proper milk? Low fat, if possible.'

A sharp nod. 'I will have some brought to your chalet.'

'Please ask them to knock and leave it outside. I don't want to be disturbed.' Also known as, expecting to be shoulder deep in a deliciously warm bubble bath. 'Oh. And can you contact Matthieu LeFevre and tell him the new resort doctor has arrived? I'm expecting to meet him at eight a.m. sharp tomorrow. I'll need a tour of the facilities.'

She turned and scanned her bags. What else did she need? Anything?

Oh, she hated starting somewhere new. She liked to be in control, to be confident of her surroundings and space. She didn't like surprises or uncertainty. No. She couldn't think of anything else.

She nodded to the man, ignoring the flicker of attraction prickling over her skin as he gave a curt nod in return, shifted the bag on her left shoulder to stop the neck-pinch and went to retrieve her skis. Determined not to make any more mistakes before the four months were through.

Matthieu watched the new doctor disappear into the darkness outside and shook his head. Truthfully, he was lost for words and that didn't happen very often.

The automatic glass doors swished open again and he saw the lone figure heft her bags on to her shoulders and simultaneously drop a ski, the slump of her back as she bent down, overburdened with bags, to pick the ski up, only to have the holdall on her left shoulder drop to the ground. Watched as Frederik ran to help and saw the hand she raised to stop him.

What the hell? There was independence and then there was stubbornness. Matt dashed outside. 'Dr Tait, please let us help.'

'I'll just leave the skis here.' She brushed a wisp of her dark-auburn bobbed hair back from her flushed face as she propped the skis back against the rack. 'I'll pop back for them later.'

'I can—'

'Please.' Her grey eyes grew wide and she shook her head vehemently. 'I can manage.'

He froze and caught her gaze. She meant it. She absolutely didn't want help or conversation or company. Which was an issue in his resort, with a culture that focused on open, positive and, above all, friendly communication. But, given the strained look on her face, he doubted she'd want to hear that right now.

'As you wish.' Sighing, Matt went back inside and called the hotel bar. 'Louis? Matt here. Cancel the welcome drinks for the new doctor. Sorry for all the trouble you went to.'

'Aaargh. Don't tell me he's not coming?' A frustrated sigh that matched Matt's own. Louis was the resort events co-ordinator, bar manager and Matt's number two in command, and equally committed to Sainte Colette being a success. He was also Matt's best friend of about thirty-two of his thirty-four years. 'What are we going to do? We can't run a place this size and not have a medic.'

'Oh, *she's* here all right. She just doesn't want drinks. Or a welcome, as far as I can see.'

'Well, she's here, that's something. We can do the drinks another time.' His friend's voice relaxed. 'What's she like?'

Difficult sprang to mind. Frosty. And also beautiful. She'd certainly made an impression. 'I'm wondering whether I should have interviewed her personally instead of letting the agency deal with it, but I was juggling a few things at the time. I'm not sure how she's going to cope with the clients we have here.'

'She's forgotten to pack her kid gloves, right?'

'They pay enough to be treated well. And they expect it.' His heart sank as he thought about her easy dismissal of him and his staff, her offhand manner and invisible but palpable keep-out sign on her forehead. Rich guests had very particular demands and needs. Sometimes, outrageously so—which was something he tried hard not to encourage and didn't pander to, if possible. But, even so, they did deserve civility. 'I'm going to have to talk to her about it first thing tomorrow. We can't have her upsetting people. Trust me, I am not looking forward to having that conversation.'

'Tough love, right?'

'Something like that.' And just like that Matt was thrown back to the last time he'd had to exercise tough love. But it hadn't been with a client or a colleague, it had been with his mother. His gut clenched at the memories and how spectacularly he'd failed.

'Give her a chance, Mattie. She might settle in okay.'

'And she might not. I can't take that risk. Best nip it in the bud at the beginning. I'm going to have to say something.' No matter how much he didn't want to.

'Good luck with that.' Louis laughed. But then he hadn't met the formidable Dr Tait. 'And I meant, what's she *like*, like? Hot?'

'Cold.' But he paused as he remembered the fleeting wistfulness in her large grey eyes when he'd offered help for her bags. And how quickly that wistfulness had been erased. The no-nonsense auburn bobbed hairstyle that framed a pretty face. The determined, fixed jaw.

He'd also noticed the sensuous mouth and form-fitting clothes wrapped around a very attractive body.

And, call him a pushover, but he kept going back to that micro-flicker of vulnerability before she'd slammed the shutters down. He'd been instantly intrigued.

But after tomorrow's difficult conversation with her, any lingering, inconvenient attraction to her would no doubt be extinguished.

Aargh… He scrubbed his hand across his head as more frustration rattled through him… *What the hell?* He hated to see someone struggle. He ended the chat with Louis, waited until Zoe, their usual evening receptionist, returned from her break, then he tugged on his gloves and went outside to deliver her skis to her chalet.

Whether she wanted him to or not.

CHAPTER TWO

THE FIRST THING Rachel noticed when she opened the heavy curtains the next morning was the vista of deep, indigo-blue lake and vertiginous snowy mountains that her bedroom window looked out on to. It was picture-postcard beautiful and made her heart sigh after a lifetime of living in a city. Breathtaking didn't go far enough—it was simply stunning.

The second thing she noticed was the silence.

She couldn't remember the last time she'd heard…well, nothing. The ER department was never quiet; there were always patients, monitors, chatter. Her little Leeds apartment gave on to a main road—all the better for quick and easy access to work—and between traffic sounds, footfall and birdsong there was always noise. To hear nothing at all was disorienting to say the least. Stillness was foreign to her because, even though her body and environment might be still, her brain never was. There was always some challenge to work out: a difficult fracture, a strange illness, an elusive diagnosis. She liked solving problems.

And she loved this cosy chalet. A one-bedroomed A-frame house hewn out of pale wood. Plaid sofas in the living area and a little dining space with table and two chairs, a roomy bedroom with a comfortable mattress and pillows and the crispest linens, fresh flowers in a vase on the wood table. Scandinavian-inspired decor with everything she could need, including fresh milk and a place for her boots and skis by the front door.

Skis that had been left by an unknown deliverer, although she would have bet money it had been the insufferably over-helpful man from reception last night.

She remembered his soulful dark eyes and the disappointment that had flickered in them when she'd refused his help. No matter. One thing Rachel Tait did not need was a kind man's help. Although…the smile had been warm and friendly and she didn't mind admitting he'd been great eye candy.

And very off limits.

Relationships with colleagues were definitely not going to happen again. She knew that road led straight to heartache. She could look, but absolutely not touch.

She stretched and inhaled the fresh air, feeling a lot more positive than when she'd arrived. Today was the first day in her new job. A new challenge. The job she'd taken because…

She slammed those thoughts back and hurried to shower, dress quickly in lots of layers and head over to the restaurant for breakfast.

She hadn't really noticed the hotel lobby when she'd been here last night but, along with everything she'd learned so far about Sainte Colette, there'd been no lack of attention to detail when it came to decor and atmosphere. It was modern and airy, but inviting with opulent touches: thick faux-fur throws over deep, inviting couches, a massive, crackling open fire, freshly baked cookies that infused the air with a sweet cinnamon scent. Swathes of tinsel hung from wooden rafters. Fairy lights twinkled in rivulets down slate walls. So far, so Christ-massy, although no tree.

She was standing open-mouthed, staring at the extravagant glittering chandelier hanging in the centre of the foyer when she heard a voice behind her.

'Dr Tait. Good morning.' The man from last night. Yesterday, he'd been dressed in a pale blue polo shirt with the resort logo on it, but today he wore a slim-fitting navy-blue padded jacket over a cream merino base layer and narrow-legged black ski pants. He was also not behind the desk, but walking towards her. 'I hope you slept well?'

'Not really, but then I never do the first night in a new place.' How had she not noticed how tall he was? Or how strikingly good looking? *Look, don't touch.* 'Was it you who left my skis outside my chalet?'

He nodded. 'It was.'

As she'd guessed. Insufferably helpful.

And even though she'd been irked because he hadn't done as she'd asked, it had been a kind thing to do. 'Okay. Well, thank you for that.' But now she felt beholden to him, too. She rummaged in her bag for some cash and thrust it at him. 'Okay. Well, thank you.'

He frowned, but didn't take the coins. 'For what?'

'It's a tip.' Was he new? Or did they not tip in France? She thrust them at him again. 'For helping me.'

'Really. No need.' He blinked. 'I'm—'

'I insist,' she interjected and put the money into his hand. But maybe they didn't tip. Oh, dear. Was that insulting? In some cultures it was. He looked so bemused she changed the subject. 'Can you tell me where the restaurant is, please?'

'This way.' Still holding the coins, he walked her across the tiled floor to the Montagne room and pulled out a plush chair for her to sit facing a huge picture window with the same view as her bedroom. The table was set for two people with steaming pots of, she imagined, coffee or hot chocolate.

'Thank you.' She sat down and poured delicious-smelling coffee into a cup. 'Now, could you find um…?' She took out her phone to check the name. 'Matthieu LeFevre? I need to speak to him.'

'The boss? Sure.' But instead of turning away to go find the owner of Sainte Colette resort, he slid into the chair opposite and put the coins on the table.

Rachel sat back, shocked. 'Excuse me. What are you doing?'

'I am Matthieu LeFevre.' With a smug self-satisfied smile, he stuck out his hand. 'Good to be properly introduced at last, Dr Tait.'

No! It couldn't be. This man owned Sainte Colette? The one from the reception desk? Who'd carried her skis in the snow? Whom she'd just thrust money at?

She'd been expecting an older man, a businessman. Not *this* man?

Earth, swallow me up now.

Then it occurred to her that he must have misunderstood her. 'I mean the *owner*…' She checked her phone again. 'Yes. LeFevre. I need to speak with him.'

'Still me.' He nodded. 'Everyone calls me Matt.'

Her stomach tightened. 'You own this resort?'

'Yes. Is that a problem?'

Inconvenient. Especially when she'd thought he was eye candy. And kind. She couldn't do kind or attraction to someone she worked with. To anyone, really, but definitely not a colleague. 'You're so…it's unexpected. I imagined someone older.'

'I'm thirty-four.' His eyes sparkled in amusement. 'How old is old enough, in your opinion, to own a business?'

'I...um.' He was right, of course, but he was also clearly enjoying her embarrassment. 'Why didn't you say something before? Last night? Earlier?' She stared at the still-outstretched hand and shook it, but her heart wasn't in it. The coins glinted, mocking her. 'Is this some sort of game? Embarrass the new staff? A silly induction by baptism of fire? Make a fool out of me?'

'No.' His smile faded instantly. 'That was not the plan. Not at all.'

'I am not a fool, Mr LeFevre. You could at least have introduced yourself last night.'

'I tried.' He shifted in his seat. 'But you didn't give me the time of day. I offered to carry your bags, but you refused. I suggested one of my staff help you to your chalet and you snapped. I invited you to the drinks I'd arranged to welcome you, so you could meet the rest of the staff and be properly introduced to everyone. Including myself.'

She'd been exhausted, distracted by her reasons for coming here, second-guessing whether it had been a good idea. Clearly, it hadn't. 'At any point you could have said something.'

'What would that have achieved? I would have embarrassed you, which I did not want to do, but would it have changed your attitude?'

'My attitude?' Shock ricocheted through her. No. She could not be attracted to this man.

'This is my resort, Dr Tait, and I am very careful of its reputation.' He didn't match her tone, keeping his soft and low. But there was steel there, too. He was a man who liked to be in control. 'If you're going to be rude to my staff, I have to worry that you'll also be rude to my guests.'

'I treat everyone the same.'

'Then we're in big trouble. At Sainte Colette we pride ourselves on warm hospitality.' He put emphasis on *warm* as he steepled his fingers in a headteacher kind of way.

She leaned forward and matched his disapproving gaze with one of her own. 'And I treat everyone professionally. I apologise that I didn't feel like having drinks with strangers when I'd had a long journey and was exhausted. But trust me, I will treat my patients with the respect they deserve.'

Yes. Big mistake to come here. She hadn't even started the job and she was clashing already. This man certainly brought out her combative side. How had she thought he was eye candy?

So, he was a good-looking guy. So, he had a mesmerising smile when he flashed it, extremely expressive, and deep brown eyes.

What the hell had she been thinking?

But she'd signed a contract, so she was going to go through with it. Unlike other people, Rachel Tait did not renege on her promises. 'I can assure you, I have been commended many times on my efficiency and accuracy in diagnosis.'

He tapped his fingertips together. 'And your bedside manner?'

'I worked in a busy emergency department—there isn't much time for a bedside manner when you're doing CPR.' But his words rattled her. She'd never had a patient or colleague complain about her manner, but...

Cold. Aloof. Sure, that's what her ex had flung at her, just to make himself feel better after he'd called off their wedding. She preferred independent, self-reliant. She was practical, in control, she didn't need warm fuzzies. Apparently, being able to think unemotionally and cope level-headedly was a crime.

Her throat felt suddenly tight. She took a sip of water. 'This isn't exactly the kind of start I was hoping for.'

'Me neither.' Mr LeFevre exhaled deeply and fixed his mouth into a smile that didn't reach anywhere near his eyes. 'I truly hope we've just started off on the wrong foot. I understand you were tired after your journey and I apologise if you feel the victim of a joke.'

'Not a victim, not at all.' *Never.* She sat up straight. 'Now, would you, please, give me directions to the medical centre? I think it's about time I started work.'

He frowned. 'But you haven't eaten.'

'I'm not hungry.' She picked up her cup and willed her hands not to shake. 'Coffee will suffice.'

The sooner she got out of his way the better.

'As you know, it's a slope-side resort with ski-in, ski-out facilities. Most people tend to chairlift up and ski home, but you can come back down on the chairlift, too. The medical rooms are at the top of the main chairlift, next to our Michelin-starred restaurant, shop and hire facilities. Please, come this way.' Matt walked the new doctor to the chairlift outside the reception area. He'd been initially relieved to see she'd dressed appropriately for the conditions, but that relief had been replaced by another bout of frustration with her frostiness. What was it with this woman? She pressed all his buttons.

He usually got on with everyone. He always had. Made damn sure he did. But Rachel Tait? Prickly, brittle and downright rude.

She'd better be a damn fine doctor.

But he needed to make this work and he believed everyone deserved a fair chance, at least for now. Further down the track he'd review her professionalism.

He waited for her to follow him on to the chairlift, then tugged the safety bar down in front of them. He watched as she settled into her seat, seemingly completely unfazed by the process. Her hair was held back by knitted blush-coloured earmuffs which made her look younger than he'd thought she was. He pinned her the good side of thirty, unlike him. She was dressed well for the conditions in a pink gilet with fur trim, over a long-sleeved merino jumper. She'd slipped on a pale pink ski jacket just before they'd clambered on to the lift and her trousers looked warm. She also carried a backpack and he guessed she'd brought her own preferred medical equipment with her. At least she'd got the practical things right.

He drew his gaze away from her profile—which, despite everything, he had to admit was pretty good to look at—and filled her in on the job details. 'There's a small medical practice in Sainte Colette village down the mountain we can use, but when an injury is too serious, we transfer them to hospital. Sometimes, an injury may not be life-threatening, but needs immediate attention up here. We prefer to have our guests attended to wherever and whenever they need it.'

'Excellent.' A sharp nod. 'And staff?'

'We have a nurse, a part-time physiotherapist and first-aid-trained ski patrollers. We're trialling drone surveillance, too, to give us a better overview of the harder to reach off-piste areas. Some of the staff form the mountain search-and-rescue team.'

'Good.'

'It also helps if our medics are proficient skiers, in case we need to get them to the patient before transporting them on the ski mobile.'

'I am proficient.' Her breath plumed out in the frigid air. The chairlift jerked and swung in the wind, but she showed absolutely no discomfort or unease, only the frost she'd been showing since she'd arrived. 'I discussed all this with the agency.'

'Yes, I know, but I wanted to check you'd be safe. Where did you learn?'

'France, Italy, Austria, USA. Basically, I spent every Christmas and February half-term holidays on a ski slope somewhere.'

'Wow. Okay. That's a lot of skiing.'

'Yes.' She nodded and he tried to read between the lines. Most people gushed about the beautiful scenery or the rush of the downhill or reminisced about their favourite or challenging runs, talked about the après-ski, the fun, they shared stories, compared resorts. But Rachel wasn't illustrating her memories.

He got that. Sometimes you didn't want to relive your past, but this was only a getting-to-know-you conversation. Maybe Rachel Tait didn't get to know people. Again, could be an issue with the celebrities who came here expecting personal service. 'Perhaps you'd like to join our staff ski group? We close the lifts at four-thirty, five days a week, but on Tuesdays and Thursdays we close at four and let our off-duty staff have time to enjoy a quiet resort and empty trails.'

'I'm happy to just explore on my days off. I can do more in a day than thirty minutes.' Her eyebrows rose at his expression. She raised her hand. 'I like to keep my personal time...personal.'

'I see.' Maybe she didn't play well with others.

'But I do work well in a team, if that's what you're concerned about.' Her chin rose and she stared out at the mountain range, away from eye contact.

He supposed it was refreshing to be able to be so blunt and know exactly what you wanted and didn't want. Not trying to be a people-pleaser like he was. But her forthrightness intrigued him. She wore it like a barrier along with the *keep out* sign he'd noticed last night.

His mind slid back to that one softening glimpse she'd given him. There was more to Rachel Tait than her hard veneer. Question was, did he care enough to find it?

At this point, the jury was still out. He spent all day, every day, dealing with demanding guests and knew from other, too-personal, experience that trying to find what made other people tick could lead to pain. He didn't have the energy to go deep digging into his staff's psyches, too.

The chairlift slowed, they dismounted on to hard, packed snow and made their way to the cluster of buildings off to the right, to be met by Alfonse, their head chef, running out of the medical room and almost careening into them. One of his hands was wrapped in a red towel and he was pale, gritting his teeth. He spoke in rapid French. 'Where the hell are the medics?'

'The medical centre doesn't open for another twenty minutes. What's wrong?'

'My hand.' He lifted it for Matt to see and he realised that the towel wasn't actually red, but was white stained with blood. A lot of blood. He beckoned Rachel closer. 'This is the new doctor. She'll take a look. Rachel…'

'What's happened?' She looked from Alfonse and back to Matt. 'We'd better get the medical centre open.'

As they rushed into the medical rooms Matt translated Alfonse's French. 'Carving knife slipped and cut across his palm. He says it's deep.'

'Okay.' She nodded, completely devoid of emotion as

they settled their patient on to the gurney in the treatment room. 'Let's see what you've done.'

She took Alfonse's hand and slowly unwrapped the towel. The cut was indeed deep, showing things underneath the skin that no one should ever see. Matt swallowed and glanced at her expression. She remained impassive but said, 'Impressive work, Alfonse. It's deep and going to need some stitches. Looks like you might be off work for a few days.'

Matt was about to translate, but his chef nodded and replied in English, 'Just as we're starting the busy season.'

'That's for Mr LeFevre to worry about, not you. Your job is to heal.' She started opening drawers and cupboards, putting various things on to a silver trolley. 'Do you have keys for the meds cupboard, Mr LeFevre? I need some local anaesthetic.'

He dragged the master keys from his pocket and opened the cupboard.

'Now, while I'm drawing this up, I'd like you to put pressure on the wound.' Her eyes met his. Steady. Cool grey. *'Please.'*

He knew that was a nod to their earlier conversation and he felt a smile forming. She'd heard him and was trying to be polite. That was something at least.

'Okay, Alfonse. This is going to sting a little, then your palm will start to feel numb.' She took his hand and rested it on the trolley, inserting the needle.

There was a sudden groan and Alfonse slumped forward, sending the trolley flying sideways. Without missing a beat Rachel stopped the trolley with her hip, caught their patient in her arms and gently laid him back on the gurney. 'Mr LeFevre, lower the headrest. He's fainted.

We need to get him stable and safe. And put a pillow under his knees—'

Just as Matt was lifting Alfonse's leg the phone rang. She nodded for Matt to answer it, obviously used to having colleagues do the minor stuff. He was okay with that, but he sighed at the message. Another injury. Never mind that he had other work to do. 'A what? Yes, the new doctor is here. Bring them down.'

Pausing from taking Alfonse's pulse, she looked over at him. 'What is it?'

He regarded the unconscious patient and the blood now dripping into a kidney dish. 'One of the ski patrol team has rolled a snowmobile and hurt his ankle. They're bringing him in now.'

'We don't have room in here for more than one patient. There's no privacy. When he gets here, put him in the physio room. *Please.*'

He'd only brought Rachel up here for a quick tour. 'When the nurse gets here, she can do it. I've got a meeting—'

The door flew open and one of the guests, Bianca, a supermodel known only by her first name, rushed in with blood gushing from a gash under her eye. 'Stupid bloody people should watch where they're going when they're carrying skis.'

Matt's heart rate doubled. He couldn't remember a day when they'd had more than a handful of medical issues over eight hours. The medical centre hadn't officially opened, yet they already had a queue.

Where was the nurse? Thank God Rachel was here.

She blinked up at him, entirely calm. 'Grab some gauze and press it on the wound.' Then she turned to Bianca and gave the world's most famous face a nod with no hint of recognition. 'I'm afraid there'll be a bit of a wait.

You'll have to sit out in the office until I'm done here. Hold the gauze on the cut until I come through, okay?'

'Why can't you do it now?' The model bristled. 'How long will I have to wait?'

'As long as it takes. I have to prioritise by severity of emergency.' No apology, but also enough authority for Bianca to take note. Rachel returned her attention to Alfonse.

'I'm doing a magazine shoot tomorrow. I can't do it with a swollen eye.' Bianca had edged towards the door, but had stopped to examine her reflection in a mirror over the washbasin. 'Will I need plastic surgery?'

Rachel raised her head from assessing Alfonse and gave the model a brief incredulous look that said, *Why are you still here?* But then her expression smoothed. 'I'll examine it thoroughly when I come through to the other room. They'll have great make-up to cover it, I'm sure. Now please, wait next door.'

Matt was impressed. Instead of snapping, as he might have done under the circumstances, Rachel's tone was firm and polite, but also authoritative.

'All the make-up in the world won't cover up this swelling.' Bianca blinked back tears as her lips formed a pout and Matt wondered if she'd ever been asked to wait for anything in her life before. Supermodel she might have been, but Alfonse needed privacy and Rachel needed space. He stepped in. 'Come with me, Bianca. Let's get that gauze on it.'

Rachel looked up from taking the blood pressure on a now semi-conscious Alfonse. 'Actually, put ice on, too, if you have some.'

'Yeah. I think we have enough ice, thanks.' He grinned and she followed his gaze outside to the snow.

'Yes. Of course.' But then she seemed to realise he was

trying to make a joke and her lips curled upwards into a smile. 'Ha! Fill your boots…or rather, a plastic bag.'

For a moment he was struck dumb. Not just because she smiled and he hadn't seen her do that before, but because her whole face transformed. The ever-present two lines on her forehead smoothed away to nothing. Her eyes lit up, turning from guarded grey to a glittering silver. And her mouth…

God. That mouth was divine. It was like looking at a different woman. Another softer, prettier, enchanting woman. His body prickled and the strangest thought slid into his head. How would she react to a kiss…?

She was looking at him, too, her gaze snagged on his. Those beguiling eyes misted, as if she'd been struck by the same crazy idea as his, then she looked completely shocked before she erased all emotion from her face. She turned her attention back to Alfonse and the heat he'd felt dissipated.

He'd been imagining it, right? That brief connection? He snapped back to reality. The supermodel was staring at him with frank displeasure and the doctor's cheeks had turned a shade of bright red. *Not good.*

'Okay, Bianca. Let's go sort out that cut.'

Rattled by the sudden rush of desire, he ushered the world's second-most beautiful woman out of the room.

And left number one to deal with his injured chef.

CHAPTER THREE

TEN HOURS LATER Rachel stared at the pictures on her digital tablet on the table in front of her and pressed her hand to her heart, trying to stop it beating so fast. As if that was going to work.

She blinked quickly to stop the tears from dripping on the tablecloth. *You can't cry in a restaurant, you daft thing.* She sniffed. Used the starched white napkin to dab her eyes. *Stupid. Getting emotional over him.*

Maybe it was the drain of the first day at work, getting to know where everything was kept, meeting new colleagues. Maybe it had come from the start of the day and that brutal conversation with Matthieu about her manner. The embarrassment about the tip.

Whatever it was, something was making her feel more wobbly than usual.

She stared at the photo and wondered why it made her feel so wretched when she knew she was better off without David. But she knew why; here he was with another woman on his arm, flaunting their mutual adoration for the world to see, the other woman being a colleague and friend of them both. He'd moved on. She felt betrayed.

No emotions, remember? Where's that Ice Queen spirit you've been chasing since the break-up?

She cleared her throat, sat up straighter. Anyway...

she'd moved on, too. Here she was, in beautiful Sainte Colette. She was almost tempted to put up a photo of herself at the ski resort, but that would only be sour grapes. She knew she was okay and that was all that mattered.

'Good evening, Dr Tait.'

Damn.

She flicked off the social media page and turned towards the voice. Matthieu LeFevre.

Because the first person you want to see when you feel wobbly is the boss who already thinks you're unsuitable for the job.

'Good evening,' she replied in French. 'Call me Rachel, please.'

Had he seen what she was looking at? Irritation shivered down her spine, along with something else. For a moment, in the medical room this morning, something weird had happened. She'd looked up at him and been unable to look away. Something about the way he was looking at her, the way the golden mountain light through the window had illuminated his face, he'd looked simply beautiful. Astonishing.

She'd been captured by his gaze. It had heated her from the top of her head right down to her toes. Hot enough to melt all that ice he'd been talking about. For a nano-second she'd slid into the feeling, then had quickly remembered she was very definitely never mixing work with pleasure again, plus they had a room full of patients. That was so not the kind of professional she was.

'Good evening, *Rachel*.' He leaned on the chair opposite her, slipping back into English, and glanced at her tablet. 'How is your evening going?'

'Perfectly fine, thank you.' She swallowed away the tight knot in her throat and nodded. One day she would encounter this man and be perfectly serene instead of mixing him up with staff or being caught in an emotional state over her ex. To deflect the conversation from herself she gestured towards her empty plate. 'The lamb was delicious.'

'I would hope so. We don't win awards by serving bad food.' Without being invited, he pulled the chair out and sat opposite her. He was so damned sure of himself it bordered on offensive. 'I wanted to catch up with you to find out how the rest of your day went.'

'It was fine. A handful of the usual twists and sprains as you'd expect here. A concussion. A couple of cuts and bruises. Three evacs from the slopes which I triaged and sent to hospital: a dislocated shoulder, an open tibula shaft fracture and a probable ACL tear. Nothing I couldn't handle.' Like him, she was sure of her work. Extremely.

An eyebrow rose. 'Excellent. Both Suzanne and Eric said you found your way around easily.'

'Suzanne is an excellent nurse and Eric is a very experienced physiotherapist. I think we'll make a good team.'

'I hope so. The morning was a real baptism by fire, but you handled it well.'

'That was nothing compared to Leeds Emergency Department on a Saturday night. You don't get a chance to catch your breath. You roll from a road traffic accident, to a stabbing, to a birth, then a drug overdose. Everything and anything.' She realised she was burbling on. He wouldn't care what Leeds ER was like. She reminded herself of his words at breakfast. 'How was my bedside manner? Did I pass?'

If he noted the renewed frostiness in her voice, he didn't show it. 'The way you dealt with Bianca was exceptional. Firm but fair.'

'The same way I deal with everyone in the ER, although I note she wasn't happy with the wait. But you have to prioritise by need, not by who can ask the loudest. Bianca's need was not as great as Alfonse's even though she thought it was. Is she famous? Only, judging by the way the team reacted to her later, I got the impression everyone knew who she was.'

'You really don't know?' He leaned back in his chair and regarded her.

'No. Why?'

'She's one of the most famous women in the world. On the cover of most magazines.'

'I don't read them. I don't have time for that.' Even tonight she'd only taken a brief break from reading up on some papers about anaesthetic developments in trauma settings and opened her social media pages to see what her friends had been up to back in Leeds. 'She is very beautiful.'

'And, because of your suturing skill, she will remain so.'

And remain self-absorbed, too, because, it appeared, no one ever said no to the woman. 'Cosmetic appearance is always a high consideration with facial lacerations, but I also have to think about wound management, infection risk and any deeper tissue or bone injuries that may also have occurred. Or should I put appearance higher up the list just because someone is pretty?'

'Of course not. However, you need to know that most of our guests are on the front of magazines for one reason or another. Either beautiful or rich. Or both.'

She shook her head. 'Is that supposed to impress me?'

He visibly bristled at that suggestion. But there he was, sitting opposite her in a dark grey business suit that looked as if it had cost a fortune. And also made him look seriously sexy…and sexily serious.

Oh, dear. Had she really just thought her boss was sexy? Twice?

No. No. No.

'Like you, I aim to treat everyone the same.' He regarded her steadily. 'But wealth and beauty impress a lot of people. Clearly, not you.'

'Why should it?' She clamped down on the swell of a sudden desire-fuelled panic. 'We all work hard in our chosen fields. Why does being on the cover of a magazine make someone more important?'

'Actually, it doesn't. Not at all. No more important than the chefs and the housekeepers and the lifties. But celebrities are my core clientele because it's the world I walked in for a while. I know what they like, what they expect, et cetera. They also pay the bills so I can pay my staff.'

She glanced round at the luxurious touches in the room. The dark wood walls, crisp white linens and sparkling tableware. The ever-attentive waiting staff, the plush decor of gold-coloured velvet curtains and matching upholstery. The hushed tones, the emphasis on exemplary service.

Embodied by this man and yet, if what he was saying was true…it was just a job. Business. Yet, she could see he carried the weight of it all.

Who was he?

It wasn't her usual style to encourage conversation, but something about him made her want to know more. About his business, of course, her place of work. And not for any other reason. 'So, you're on the rich list, too?'

'Not quite.' He laughed wryly. 'Actually, not at all. But I get by and things here are going from strength to strength. Third season in and we're doing better than last year, which did better than the year before. But there's always room for growth. I'm not going to rest until the resort has reached its full potential.'

'How do you know so many rich people? I mean, some of my colleagues are doing okay, but not enough to afford a ski resort with its own lake and chairlifts, and probably not enough to even holiday here.'

'My previous business was a tour guide agency for celebrities, based in Paris. I employed people that took actors, musicians, models, to wherever they wanted to go. I made the whole thing happen: sourced the exclusive accommodations, researched the best local activities, kept everything moving so the celebrities didn't have to make any decisions they didn't want to make. When I came back here, I thought this old place had potential and I put what I knew, together with a business proposal, to an old friend. He gave me some backing which helped secure a loan. And here we are.'

'So, you gave up basically full-time holidaying to come and work here. Why?'

'Hey, it wasn't a holiday for me. I spent most of my time in the office doing all the co-ordinating, smoothing things over for my teams on the ground. Although, it did have some perks—I got to know people in the entertainment industry, got invited to parties, vacations on yachts, film festivals. All very attractive to a twenty-something from the countryside.'

'You clearly enjoyed it.' He was grinning at the memories and that did something fizzy to her gut. She wasn't sure she liked the fizz…it made her feel edgy and she liked to be in control. 'Why give it all up?'

Why did she care?

She didn't. She just wanted background information on her boss.

'I was born in the village of Sainte Colette and grew

up around here, skiing and hiking in the mountains and swimming in the lake. Back then, the Sainte Colette resort barely existed—just a few basic ski huts used by the locals and a rudimentary lift. It was a good place to grow up, but, like everyone, I dreamt of escaping. I took a chance I was offered and stayed away for a few years. But then…' His eyes darkened as his words slowed. He shifted in his seat and didn't meet her eyes. 'It was the right time to come home.'

Home. She wondered how that felt. To have one place where you felt completely secure.

But Matt looked away and for the first time since she'd met him she saw shutters slide up. Then he pushed his chair back and stood, giving her a quick sharp bow, abruptly saying, 'I have taken up enough of your time, Rachel. Good evening.'

So, whatever Matt's reasons were for giving up the globetrotting lifestyle, he wasn't going to share them with her. Which, of course, as a scientist who liked getting to the bottom of puzzles and challenges, made her want to know even more.

But she'd be mortified if he pushed her for personal information, so she let it go, let him go. Leaving her with a lot more questions than answers.

He was rattled.

She'd looked at him with those piercing eyes and asked him why he'd come home and he'd almost told her. Almost spilled his guts to frosty Rachel Tait. And then what?

Watch her trample all over his past? No, thanks.

Their conversation last night had started hesitantly and with difficulty, as every conversation with her seemed to, but when she forgot about being frosty, he found her questions intelligent, her conversation interesting. Until she strayed too close to his personal life.

His thoughts seemed to return to her too frequently and he couldn't understand why. Sure, she was different to every woman he'd ever dated—not that he had a type as such. But he usually went for someone fun loving, chatty and sociable like him. Rachel wasn't bubbly and outgoing, she was reserved and independent to the point of appearing to be indifferent. She certainly wasn't a team player as far as he could see.

'Boss? You okay?' Cody, one of his team, shouted over the roar of the snowmobile engine, bringing Matt back to the present. En route to an evac on the Home Run.

He gave Cody a thumbs up. 'Great.'

Not great, when he should have been looking for the injured party instead of being intrigued and distracted by a colleague. The snowmobiles bumped up the nursery slope and underneath the chairlifts, slowly climbing their way up the mountain.

Further up, sitting on the ground, was a little girl with a pale, tear-stained face, her little chest rising and falling rapidly as she silently sobbed. Her father was sitting next to her, waving to them as they approached.

Matt jumped down from the snowmobile and recognised the man immediately. 'Michael. Hello.'

The man peered up, ashen-faced, but as soon as he saw Matt he relaxed. 'Matt. Thank God.'

'What's happened?' Matt put his hand on the man's shoulder in a gesture of solidarity, knowing too well, from personal experience, how worrying about someone you cared for ate away at you. Guilt that you couldn't help, couldn't fix them, did that, too. Then he crouched down to look at the little girl. 'Isla, sweetie. What have you done?'

'Snowboarder took her out. Damned idiot.' Michael shook his head, distress swirling in his eyes, his voice barbed and angry. 'They should be banned from the mountain.'

'Accidents happen, no matter how experienced.' Matt nodded, well aware that Michael's anxiety fuelled his words. That, and the fact he was renowned in the film world as a genius director, but outspoken and difficult to work with.

Michael smoothed his daughter's hair down. 'She says her knee hurts.'

'Okay. We just need to check her over to make sure she hasn't injured her neck or back, then we'll shoot down to the medical centre for the doc to take a look. Won't take a minute.'

'But...' Michael's jaw tightened and he looked as if he was about to complain about something, but he nodded. 'Please hurry. She's cold. We both are.'

'I know. But I'm not prepared to take any risks. I have to assess her first. We'll be as quick as we can.' Matt nodded to his colleague. 'Cody, grab some emergency blankets, please.'

Between them Matt and Cody wrapped their clients up in the foil thermal blankets and Matt spoke above the crinkle-crackle noise that was made every time one of them moved. 'Should have you both warmed up in no time.'

Michael shook his head as he looked at Isla's tear-stained face. 'My wife is going to kill me.'

So, it wasn't just his child he was concerned about. Matt sighed. 'It was an accident. She'll understand.'

'You think?' Michael raised his eyebrows, his tone turning tense. 'She's going to blame me. She always does.'

Matt glanced at the little girl who was staring up at

her father and his heart went out to her. He really hoped she wasn't going to start blaming herself for whatever was going down in her parents' marriage.

'Hey, it was just an accident, sweetie.' He gave her a smile, then lifted her gently on to the snowmobile and headed back to the medical room. Wondering how his new doctor would react to a concerned father who had a reputation for outbursts and expected everyone to do his bidding.

That said, it would be a good opportunity to see her professionalism and tact in action when pushed. Because he had no doubt that Michael's good behaviour was starting to fray.

He wheeled the stretcher through to the medical room and found Rachel in the office.

She jumped up as soon as she saw him, her cheeks flushing. 'Matt? You're doing the evacuations today?'

He nodded. 'We have a roster. Management are on it, too. We all pitch in.'

'I didn't realise.' She focused on the girl. 'Hello there. Been in the wars?'

'We've just picked this little one up on the Home Run. She got in the way of a snowboarder who took her out. She's complaining of a sore knee. No other obvious injuries.'

'Ouchy.' Rachel winced and gave the little girl an empathetic smile. 'What's your name, honey?'

'Isla,' Michael butted in and added with emphasis, 'Isla MacKenzie.'

It astounded Matt that Rachel didn't know the girl's name, although why would she if she didn't read the gossip pages? But this girl was one of the most famous kids in America, if not the world. Everyone had watched the social media posts sent live from her mother's hospital bed five years ago as she gave birth. There'd even been lucrative betting on the name choice.

'Hey, Isla.' Rachel tilted the girl's chin to look into her face. 'My name's Rachel and I'm a doctor. I just want to have a look at your leg so we can work out how to fix it. You want to come sit on here?' She patted the gurney and Matt lifted the little one over on to it. Rachel glanced up at him. 'Thanks, Matt.'

The tone was a form of dismissal, but he decided to hang around a few moments longer to ensure they could all cope with Isla's situation. Michael was fractious at the best of times and, showing no flicker of recognition, Rachel clearly didn't know she was dealing with a famous film director who was used to being surrounded by *yes* people. Rachel was definitely not a yes person. Neither was Matt—boundaries were important, after all. But if they could get through this and still have a paying guest that would be good.

She bent to talk to Isla as the door flew open and Bianca bowled in.

Déjà vu.

Rachel glanced over to her. 'Ah, yes. Your suture-check. Could you please wait outside? We're just dealing with an emergency.'

'But—' The model ran over to the gurney.

Rachel sighed and her tone was one of frustration. 'Bianca, please. Not again. This is a medical room, you have to wait your turn.'

'And this is my daughter.'

'Ah.' Rachel's eyes widened as she looked at mother, then daughter, and then nodded. 'Sorry. I didn't realise.'

'Where have you been? Under a rock?' Bianca threw

back at her, then whirled round to Michael, who had taken a seat close to Isla's head. 'What the hell happened?'

The film director raised his eyes from the phone he was scrolling on. 'She got taken out by some lunatic on a snowboard.'

Bianca gripped her daughter's ski jacket lapel as she scanned the little face. 'She looks okay. No damage to her beautiful face.' She pinched the little girl's cheek gently.

'It's her leg that hurts,' Michael deadpanned.

A roll of those famous large hazel eyes. 'I thought you said you could manage.'

'I can manage. It's snow, Bianca. People have accidents all the time.'

'I bet you weren't watching her properly.'

'At least I was with her. I wasn't swanning about having my picture taken.'

Matt stepped forward, about to ask them to quieten down, but was beaten to it by Rachel who glared at them. 'Quiet, please. I am trying to do an examination here. Of your injured daughter.' She turned her back to the bickering adults, almost as if shielding her patient from them, then she unbuckled Isla's ski boot Velcro. 'Let's just take this off first, honey. I'll go slowly, but tell me the moment it hurts.'

Bianca's voice rose. 'It's my *job,* Michael. It's why we're here.'

'Oh.' Michael's voice took on a sarcastic tone. 'And I thought we were here for some family time. Silly me.'

Matt watched as Rachel's shoulders tensed, but she continued to carefully slide Isla's boot from her foot while the little girl looked from her mother to her father and back again as if she were watching a tennis match. Worse, she didn't even look as if this was anything out of the ordinary. As if this happened every day.

Rachel's voice was calm and reassuring as she said, 'Good girl. My, you're brave. Can you point to where it hurts?'

'My knee.' Isla pointed.

'You okay if I take a look now? I'll try not to tickle.'

The little girl nodded, but her bottom lip began to tremble. 'It hurts.'

'I know, honey.' Rachel stroked the girl's hair. She was different today. Softer. Was it because of their conversation last night? But Matt doubted she'd change her approach because of a word from him. 'If you like, we can give you some painkillers. I'll check with your parents, first. Then, if I can have a quick look at your knee, I'll know how to fix it, okay?'

'What exactly are you going to give her?' Bianca's tone was accusatory.

Rachel blinked. 'Just some painkillers.'

'Yes.'

'No.'

Both parents answered at once.

'No.' Bianca shook her head vociferously. 'We eat clean and we don't do drugs of any kind. Ever. Do you have arnica?'

'For a ruptured tendon? That's ridic…' Rachel caught Matt's gaze and clamped her mouth shut. He just knew she'd been about to say ridiculous which would have inflamed an already volatile situation.

Instead, she smiled…and it almost looked genuine. 'I completely understand your concerns and I never suggest giving drugs to a child unless they need them. But, you can see she's in a lot of pain and it really will help.'

Silence hung thick and heavy.

Rachel looked at them one at a time. Waiting. 'The sooner we give them, the quicker they'll work.'

'Okay, but she's allergic to nuts and eggs, so you can't just give her anything.' Bianca threw her husband a sarcastic look. 'I bet you've forgotten that little fact about your daughter?'

'Of course not. I was just about to mention it. We went for lunch today and she survived, didn't she?' He snarled. 'Daddy managed.'

'Oh. You didn't wait for me so we could eat together? Gee, thanks.' Bianca folded her arms across her chest. 'So much for *family* time.'

'I can't help it if you're always working.'

'Says the guy who's always away working on a film.'

'You say that as if it's a bad thing. My films are important.' Michael's chest puffed out a little. 'They win awards. They're intelligent and considered.'

'Oh, please.' The model's hands rose in exasperation. 'Don't go on about your social justice campaigns again. Give us all a break.'

Matt couldn't and wouldn't take any more of this.

This was why he tried not to get personally involved with the clients. Why he'd chosen to head up the office in Paris instead of going on all those tours, because there was something about their outrageous demands that triggered something deep inside him. He wouldn't pander to their whims and definitely not to the detriment of a child.

That poor kid shouldn't have to listen to this. Rachel couldn't do her work properly.

He had to do something. 'Enough!'

'Stop!' Rachel ordered at the same time, putting her hand up to silence them all. Her tone gave them absolutely no question as to who was in charge here. 'I'm trying to assess this child. She's in pain and you're making it worse. Can you stop this bickering and please take her into consideration? She is the most important person in the room right now. Not any of you.'

They all stared at her, mouths open.

'If you can't speak nicely to each other, one of you will have to wait outside,' she continued, as she marched both Michael and Bianca towards the door, herding them along with her hands and then added quietly, 'I won't ask Isla to choose which parent gets to stay because that's not fair on her. So, be grown-ups and decide. Quickly.'

Whoa. He hadn't expected that. Matt gave her a mental fist bump while simultaneously wincing at how she was speaking to his paying guests. He admired her strength and forthrightness. And the way she was looking at the little girl, with such empathy and concern, made his heart hurt. She was like a mama bear protecting her young. Her grey eyes sparkled with fury and a gauntlet. Steel. Polished silver. Magnificent.

He looked at the two superstars who now turned to him with fire in their eyes and wondered what it would take to smooth this over for everyone. And whether he even wanted to.

'Are you going to let her speak to us like that?' Michael huffed.

Rachel had been firm, but they had been downright crass to argue like that in an emergency situation concerning their five-year-old child. Matt kept his voice low. 'I won't tolerate a challenge to my medical team. Any of my team, for that matter. This is a medical room and we need peace and quiet. One of you can stay in here, the other will have to wait outside.'

Michael frowned. 'But—'

'One of you.' With a heavy heart he envisaged his bottom line dropping because of this, but what was money compared to Isla's safety and upholding his team's respect? 'Or both of you. Feel free to leave.'

Bianca glared at her husband and shrugged. 'Okay. I'll go.'

Even that backdown seemed like point scoring. She pulled a mobile phone from her pocket and held it in front of Isla. 'Can I just…take a quick snap. Isles, baby, look up at Mommy. There. Let's see how many likes you get for a poorly leg. That'll make everything better.'

'Leave. Now.' Rachel's tone was dangerous and, even from this distance, he could see she was trembling.

The supermodel bristled. 'What? How dare—'

Rachel held her hand up again, caught Matt's eye again and added, *'Please.'*

Once Bianca had left the room Rachel's shoulders relaxed and she breathed out, put her focus firmly and completely on the child and restarted her assessment.

And Matt just stood there, lost for words. He'd thought she was cool and offhand and rude, but the way she guarded that child was *personal.* It was the closest he'd got to seeing real emotion from her.

Was this the real Rachel Tait? Fierce and raw and strong?

He wasn't sure, but it felt as though he'd got her all wrong.

CHAPTER FOUR

SHE WANTED TO SCREAM.

She wanted to shout and stamp her feet. To put her fingers in her ears, as she had so many times when she'd been Isla's age, and pretend she couldn't hear the constant slurs, attacks and bickering. Pretend the world she lived in was happy and bright and not exploding into ugliness.

But she was a doctor now and these weren't her parents. She had to be professional and responsible and act like a grown-up, too. She'd thought she'd dealt with all that years ago, but watching that little girl's impassive face while her parents had argued around her had brought the memories rolling back, hitting Rachel square in the chest.

She hated emotions. They got in the way. They whipped the ground from under her feet and made her see things subjectively instead of objectively. And she couldn't do that. Would not allow that.

Having put Isla's leg into a temporary splint and checked Bianca's sutures, she sent them all away to get a scan on the knee. Then she breathed out and took a moment to centre herself by looking out of the window on to the ski field. The sky was a brilliant blue and there wasn't a cloud anywhere. She could hear laughter and chatter…

'Well, that was intense.'

Matthieu.

Her spine prickled.

She'd watched him walk the guests out, but he must have come back into the room. No doubt he was about to reprimand her for what she'd said and done. There was no way she could let him see her discombobulated.

She took one more deep calming breath, then turned to him. Ready. Her voice completely steady. 'A couple of things.'

He stepped back, frowning. 'Okay.'

'I don't like feeling as if I'm constantly being judged by you. Being careful about what I say or do in case my bedside manner doesn't make the grade.'

'I'm not judging you.' His hands rose in a gesture of submission.

'It feels as if you are. Every time I speak to a patient or staff member you look as if you're holding your breath, waiting for me to mess up. I get it. It's your business and you want it to be successful. You think I'm a loose cannon or just downright rude. But the medical room is my domain, Mr LeFevre. I get to set the tone. I've dealt with many patients in many different scenarios. I know that tensions run high and I expect that. I expect to have anxious and worried parents. It's only natural.' Natural to most parents, anyway. 'But that poor girl. Her parents were horrible. Clearly, point scoring is a game to them. Being discreet isn't. Putting their child first isn't. Taking photos to post on social media? Really? Hoping to get more likes? I'm speechless.'

'Clearly, you're not.' The corners of his mouth twitched, but he wrestled them back into a serious line. 'Isla MacKenzie is a social media phenomenon on her own. She has only ever known her parents as ultra-famous. A film director father who had a string of high-profile flings before settling down with a world-famous supermodel. Little Isla was probably the most anticipated birth after the royal family's babies.'

'I don't care. She's five years old.' Rachel took another breath. 'You know what? I realise now that I don't treat everyone the same. That girl needed extra care because her parents weren't going to give it to her. And I'm not going to apologise for what I said to them. I don't care how much money they have or who they are, she needed someone to be her advocate, because clearly neither of them are up to the job.'

'That's what made the difference, then. The child.' He said it so quietly she thought she might have misheard. Then he smiled. 'So, Dr Rachel Tait does have a heart after all.'

Her stomach did a weird flippy thing at that smile.

Which was ridiculous. Because Matthieu LeFevre could not make her stomach flip. No one could.

'A heart?' *The Ice Queen?* 'Don't count on it. But did you see her face? Nothing. No emotion except for the pain from her injury. She was completely inured to the fact her parents were fighting. She's used to it. I bet they don't show that side of themselves on social media.' Rachel picked up the cup with the remains of the coffee she'd made before Isla had come into the medical centre and realised her hand was shaking again.

She put her coffee cup down. She really did need to get on top of this. 'They didn't care about her leg. They cared about yelling at each other, at winning the blame game or scoring points. She doesn't deserve to be ignored, Matthieu. She's a little girl. Not an adult's chattel to be argued over.'

She blinked and for one awful moment she thought she was going to cry, but she cleared her throat and shrugged back on that mask of professionalism and resolve that meant she would not show her emotions. To him, or anyone else.

Why was it starting to happen now? This trickle of feelings leaking out of her?

Sure, she'd borne witness to plenty of disagreeing parents, but the fighting today was exactly the kind of thing she'd been through. Petty. Point scoring. As she'd listened to those adults arguing, something had triggered inside her. '*So much for family time!*' one of them had yelled. That had been the only thing she'd yearned for and yet whenever she was in the same room as both her parents she'd been forgotten altogether. Just like Isla.

She shook her head, swallowing back all the emotions. Shoving them deep down inside her and closing the lid, the way she'd done ever since she'd been younger than that little girl.

'Are you done?' Matthieu folded his arms and gave her a look that she couldn't read. It felt as if he was sympathising with her. Which was totally at odds with what she'd been expecting from Mr Business Owner.

She met his eye. Lifted her chin. 'With what?'

'With railing at me. I'm not the one who treated her like that. I asked them to leave, remember?'

'I am not railing.' She cleared her throat. Okay, she was railing at him. And it wasn't his fault.

'You could have been more tactful, but you're right. We can't allow that sort of behaviour in a medical setting.' His eyes roved her face and she saw concern there, which felt personal. 'This has really got to you, Rachel.'

'I'm fine.' She did not need anyone to be concerned about her.

'Here we go with that again. *I'm fine. I'm fine.* It's okay to be affected by things. You're not a machine.'

'No, not completely.' She threw him what she hoped was a high-beam grin. 'But it's an aspiration.'

'I don't understand you. Are you afraid of feelings, or admitting you're feeling something?'

Panic rushed through her, tightening her gut. 'I don't need to feel. I don't want to feel. I just want to do my job.'

'You do it very well.' Shaking his head, he looked out of the window. For a couple of beats he was silent then he turned back to her, eyes shining. 'I know…come outside.'

'Why?'

'After that little debacle I need some air and I think maybe you do, too.'

'I can't just leave the medical centre.' She couldn't shake the feeling that the way he'd looked at her had been personal. As if he cared…the way a friend might care for another friend. Or something…

Since her wedding fiasco she'd withdrawn into herself and neglected her friends. Not that work had given her much time for a social life and she'd always struggled to open up to people—and she would never have talked about her disastrous walk of shame back down the aisle—but she and David had had a core group of people they'd had drinks with every now and then. Friends? She'd always hoped so, but not recently. Which was her fault, she knew.

Basically, it had been hard to face them unless through the veil of work where she'd revelled in being busy, so she didn't have to talk to them.

And now David was sharing photos of him all loved-up with one of their friends.

'Suzanne and Eric are in the office.' Matthieu shrugged nonchalantly. 'Just give me five minutes. I think it'll do you good.'

'No—'

'Look, I'm not a doctor but I do know this place has magical healing powers. So, come on. Five minutes.' He took her ski jacket from the hook and held it out to her. It looked as if she didn't have any choice, so she shrugged on the jacket and stepped out into the icy air.

They trudged along the snow, past the restaurant and people sitting out in the sunshine laughing and chatting. Then up the hill, which was slow going in thick snow.

When they got far above the buildings, to the edge of the mountain, they stopped at a fence line and gazed down the valley to the lake and beyond, to a little cluster of red-roofed buildings that made up Sainte Colette village. Majestic pine trees bordered the mountainside and jet boats skimmed along the water, leaving little white trails behind them. Everything looked fresh and clean and bright, like a piece of art that had just been painted.

The sounds from the resort faded away, along with the tension that had sunk into her bones. She leaned her elbows on the fence and hauled cool air into her lungs.

Matthieu settled next to her. Close enough that she could breathe in the tang of masculine scent. He smelt wonderful and it made her feel even more off balance than she had in the medical centre.

Not inhaling too deeply, she looked out at the lake. 'It must have been amazing to grow up with this view to drink in every day,'

'It makes everything feel better, right?' A pause. Something flickered across his eyes, then it was gone. That darkness she'd seen last night, fleeting, then wiped clear. 'Almost.'

'What do you mean? Almost?'

He hauled back on his beautiful smile, but she could see it had taken some effort. 'Not everything can be fixed, Rachel. But it certainly helps to have something picturesque to look at.'

She looked up and regarded his profile. Tall and broad. Fit. Strong jaw, aquiline nose. Long black eyelashes framing deep brown eyes. He was a handsome man, objectively speaking. Beautiful. She wanted to look away, but couldn't bring herself to.

And, yes, weirdly, looking at him helped ease this tightness in her chest. 'What happened to you?'

'Ah, you know... Nothing.'

She didn't want to pry...hell, she'd hate it if anyone probed her too hard about her past, but she wanted to help. It felt, with Matthieu, as if they'd started out on the wrong foot, skipped normal conversation and jumped quickly to intense. Or maybe it was just the whole Isla thing had made her a bit more sensitive today. 'Hey, I'm sure it's not nothing. It's obviously important to you.'

'It's in the past.' He shrugged. 'Families are complicated.'

'Amen to that.' She paused, waiting for him to fill the silence, knowing from professional experience that many people didn't sit in absolute quiet well.

He clasped his hands together as he leaned his elbows on the fence, not looking at her. And, as she'd hoped, he filled the gap. 'My mother lived here her whole life, she loved it. She said she needed the peace and I dare say it was better for her than a city. She...she wasn't well.'

'I'm sorry.'

'It's okay. She died a couple of years ago.'

Rachel did the maths. *It was time to come home.* 'She's the reason you came home?'

'Yes.'

She sighed, impressed that he would do such a thing and yet sad for him at the same time. 'I don't know where my mother is half the time, never mind giving up my career to look after her.'

'Really?' He turned to her and his eyes had taken on such a wealth of sadness she wanted to soothe it away. 'You don't know where your mother is? Don't you talk to her? Message? Visit?'

'Not much. Like you said, it can be complicated. We're not close,' she clarified, her voice flattening the way her mood did when she thought of her parents. 'Or my dad. They've both got other families now.'

'Even so. You should see them before it's too late. You don't know what's around the corner.'

'It's fine.' She couldn't bear to see the incomprehension in his eyes. Is that what had happened to his mother? Something out of the blue? She couldn't ask him for more details because it would look like prying. But then she realised she'd used her well-worn phrase again and suddenly felt a need to explain why she must seem so cold. Why that was important she wasn't sure, but it was important. 'Honestly, it really is fine. We were never a close-knit unit and my parents split up when I was ten years old.'

He gave her a sad smile. 'That would have been hard on you.'

'It was, but it was better than them arguing all the time.' She drew her eyes away from him, because she was scared she was giving too much away.

But he gently pressed her. 'Like Michael and Bianca?'

'Kind of. Their bickering earlier just triggered something inside me.' She looked out at the view and took deep breaths, letting the beauty ease her soul as she tried to make sense of the jumble of emotions in her chest.

Matthieu sighed. 'No one wants to relive things like that. How are they now? Your parents?'

'The divorce was very bitter and still is.' She turned back to him. 'But I've dealt with it. Honestly.'

At least, she thought she'd dealt with it, until today. Worse, she could feel him looking at her, pitying her, assessing her and she knew he could see more than she allowed anyone else to see. There was just something about him that made her feel seen.

'Tant pis.' He kept on looking at her, his forehead furrowed. 'I am so sorry, Rachel. I brought you outside to feel better, not worse.'

'It doesn't make me feel bad, I'm just sad you lost someone you loved.'

'Me too. It was difficult.' He shook his head and for a few moments the silence descended again. But then his expression brightened. 'So...what was the other thing?'

'What do you mean?' She noted he'd deflected the conversation back to her. Clearly, his mother had suffered in some way and he had, too. But, like her, he didn't want to talk about it.

Some things were best left unsaid. She knew all about that.

He smiled at her confusion. 'You said you had a couple of things to talk to me about.'

'Did I?' The anger from before had steamed out of her and she wanted to learn more about this man, about his mother and how a bond could be so strong between two people that they'd give up everything the way he had.

But this wasn't the time. And she wasn't sure it would be wise getting to know him better. Or for him to know more about her. 'Oh. Yes. That. I guess I need to thank you for not bawling me out in front of Michael and Bianca. Thank you for your support.'

'I wanted to speak up sooner, but I also didn't want to step in because you're right, that room is your domain.

And you rule it like a queen.' His eyes crinkled at the sides. He had such nice eyes. Trusting. Warm. Kind. They lit up as he spoke. 'But I couldn't stand by and let them speak to you or Isla like that. I do have a line that I draw between professional and acceptable and it takes a lot to make me step over it, but today I did.'

'I don't think I helped, though, with my outburst.' She snorted. 'I think my line is a lot more defined than yours. Or I'm a lot closer to it.'

'Not all the guests are like Michael and Bianca.'

'Good, because I don't think I can hold my tongue for four months. I think I'd explode.'

'Isn't that what you just did?' He laughed and made an explosive gesture with his fingers. 'Boom! Run for cover, Dr Tait is blowing up.'

'Trust me, you haven't seen anything yet.' She laughed too, feeling a little freer than she'd felt for a while, also feeling a lot closer to someone than she'd felt for a long time, too. He'd taken the trouble to ask her questions without sounding too intrusive, to listen to her, and she couldn't help telling him things she normally preferred to keep hidden.

Although, that was probably not a good thing.

You're cold and aloof and you don't let people get close.

For good reason.

But Matthieu's eyes twinkled. 'Is that a promise, Dr Tait?'

'You'll have to wait and see.' Wait…was that…was that *flirting*? 'Er…maybe.'

His smile grew. 'Well, I definitely can't wait.'

The laughter stalled in her chest. Had he edged closer? Was she imagining it? Or had she moved?

Either way, he was closer. She could feel his warmth,

his breath whispering on her skin. His scent wound round her, like a magic spell pulling her closer to him.

Since the break-up she'd thrown herself into work and closed herself off from everyone, away from prying eyes and more pain. She didn't discuss her personal life, she didn't talk about her past and she most certainly didn't do flirting.

But clearly her body did trembling and fizzing. And there was an ache deep inside her that she didn't think would go unless…unless she did something really stupid, like touch him.

His gaze caught hers. For a moment the beautiful backdrop faded from view and Matthieu LeFevre was the only thing she was aware of. Just here, in this moment.

No past. No pain. Just a man who somehow drew her out of her self-imposed prison where she felt safe and comfortable. His deep brown eyes that she could get seriously lost in. And that mouth she suddenly wanted to kiss.

What the hell?

That mouth shaped up into a heart-melting smile.

She swallowed back the panic rising in her throat and turned to go, but her hand brushed against his.

'Wait… Rachel…' The way he said her name… *Ray Shell*…so soft and exotic and sexy, had her keening towards him.

His fingers curled into hers and the panic mingled with the fizz that started in her stomach and spread through her, making her limbs tremble and her heart race. The sensation of his skin on hers sent ripples of heat through her. But the ache didn't go. If anything, it got worse. Until the only thing she could think about was gripping those fingers and holding on. Holding him.

Is this the line, too? Professional and personal?

She could not cross it. She could not get close to him.

Not to anyone. She slipped her hand from his. 'I have to get back.'

And put some distance between herself and this man who made her feel things she didn't want to feel.

CHAPTER FIVE

HE'D HELD HER hand like a smitten teenager. Grabbed on to it like a lifeline, propelled by some kind of force he'd had no control over.

He didn't get it. What was it about Rachel Tait that made him want to break down her barriers and get closer to her? She was like a complex challenge he needed to work out.

He'd managed to keep out of her way for the last few days, burying himself in his work to avoid her, but he just couldn't get her out of his head.

He sat at the bar, nursing his beer, trying to concentrate on a conversation about Christmas festivities.

'The big Christmas tree for reception is arriving next week,' Louis informed him.

'It's already a week late. We should never have paid in advance.'

'I know, they've been promising delivery for days. We'll use a different supplier next year.' Louis gave an apologetic shrug, then ran his finger down the meeting agenda in his open planner. 'And we're decided about Christmas Day, then? A later breakfast window so families can spend family time together in their chalets, then Father Christmas after lunch once they've all come back from the mountain. I've hired the suit, so we just need to make sure it fits you.'

This was a part of the holidays Matt always loved— probably more than the kids, if he was honest. Just seeing their faces when he entered the lobby was pure magic. He knew, well enough, the ache of a difficult Christmas and if he could help make a child's day happier then he'd done his job.

He patted his belly. 'Better get some padding for it then. Where's that orange and cardamom cake you usually put out for après-ski?'

'In the fridge, help yourself. But, mate, if I had a decent pack like yours, I wouldn't be eating cake. The women love it just as it is.' Louis looked down at his own stomach, as flat as Matt's, and sighed. 'Man, I need to get some exercise.'

'You ski most days, lug crates of bottles around, carry wood. You're doing okay.' In fact, Louis was impressively fit.

'That's not the kind of exercise I mean.' His friend's eyes widened. 'Hey, we should have a night out. Get away from here where we're all about work. I can't remember when either of us last had a day off. We deserve to have some fun, maybe meet some women.' He swayed his hips suggestively. 'Have some more fun…'

Matt laughed at his friend's hopeful expression. 'Aren't we supposed to be talking about Christmas plans?'

'Yes. But I've briefly diverged on to weekend plans. Come on, Mattie. You haven't been out much since your mum died. Two years. It's time.'

And yet he didn't feel as though he'd been losing out. Which was weird, because he'd loved his old life. He'd spent most of his twenties partying, travelling the world, having a good time—a wild time even, hooking up, but he didn't much feel like playing those games any more. 'We've got too much to do here. Maybe, in the new year, we could take a trip over to Geneva or down to Nice?'

'Okay…but don't blame me if the women think you're old and boring.' Louis winked.

'At thirty-four? I prefer mature and wise. And, after this season, hopefully rich, too,' Matt shot back with a laugh. 'Believe me, I'm fine.'

He realised he was using the same words as Rachel. He meant them—did she? Was she truly fine being on her own? Dealing with everything with no support? Maybe she had support he didn't know about.

Maybe she was married or engaged or otherwise committed.

He'd held her hand.

And he was allowing her back into his head again. Why was he attracted to the woman with the biggest 'no entry' sign on her forehead?

He gave his friend a wry smile. 'Can we focus back on the meeting and not my shortfalls as your wingman?'

'Of which there are many…' Louis grinned. 'One, you always get the most beautiful ones—'

Matt coughed. 'The meeting…?'

'Okay. We'll do your shortfalls later. But open a bottle, we may be there some time,' Louis warned through his evil grin. 'After you've done your *Ho-ho-ho* routine— probably meaning some poor kids will be in therapy for years—we'll put on the staff ski show. Then in the evening we'll just serve a buffet.' Louis checked things off against his list. 'I think that's all for Christmas Day. The plans are all set up for New Year's Eve. The band have confirmed and the ticket sales are going well.'

'Excellent. Right, back to work.'

'Yes, boss.' Louis gave him a swift jokey salute. 'Oh,

and we need to reschedule the welcome drinks for the new doctor. She's been here a week and we still haven't organised anything.'

And just like that, she was at the front of his mind again. Along with the sharp tang of desire that seemed to kick into action whenever she was near. 'I don't think she's keen.'

'Not keen for a party? Who is this woman?'

Rachel Tait. An enigma. 'It's her call. Not everyone's a party animal like you, Louis—'

Fast footsteps thumping down the tiled corridor had them both turning towards the door.

'Hey, boss! Can you help?' It was Frederik, breathless and red-faced. 'We've got a collapse in reception.'

'Did you call Rachel? The doctor?' Matt asked Fred as they ran towards the lobby. 'Get her down here to help.'

'We tried her cell, but she's not answering.'

'She must be somewhere. Try the restaurant.'

'Tried that. I was coming from there when I saw you in the bar.' Poor Fred was trying to keep up and failing. 'Sorry, boss.'

'I saw her heading out with skis a few hours ago,' Louis said. 'Around lunchtime.'

Matt glanced out the huge picture window that ran along the corridor and out to the dark night. 'And she's not back yet?'

'Search me.' Louis shrugged. 'What about Suzanne and Eric?'

'They went home, back down the mountain.'

'Looks like it's just us, then,' Louis said. 'The A Team.'

'Totally, we'll deal with it.' As head of the first-aid responder team, Matt was prepared for pretty much any emergency they had, but he'd have preferred some proper medical back-up, too.

They turned the corner to see a body on the floor in the recovery position and a woman Matt knew was Rita Marsh, a TV soap opera actress, kneeling next to him. As he got closer he could see her body was rigid with panic while her son's seventeen-year-old body jerked and twitched.

Thankfully, Zoe was keeping onlookers at bay. There was nothing worse than having gawkers in situations like this.

Rita looked up as they approached, the agony of worry etched across her face. 'Please help us. Zane's diabetic. His sugars are very low.' She showed them a small hand-held monitor. Sure enough, the readout showed life-threatening blood sugar scores.

'Get a privacy screen,' Matt called to Zoe, then knelt down next to the boy, checked his safety, made sure his airway was clear and that he was securely on his side. He turned to the mum. 'Do you have any glucagon?'

She looked blankly at him. 'What?'

'The sugar injections. Perhaps you were given some from the hospital or your doctor?'

'Oh, yes. Sorry, yes, we do. And insulin, too. It's all so new to us, you see. He was only diagnosed a few weeks ago and we've been in shock really. He was so sick and I thought he was getting better...' She rummaged in her ski jacket pocket and pulled out a bag of jelly sweets. 'We've got some sweets. I don't know... I don't know what to do. I can't remember what they told us.'

Matt's heart went out to her, she was clearly terrified and racked with guilt and anxiety. He made sure his voice was gentle. 'I can't give them to him while he's like this, he could choke if he can't swallow properly.'

'Oh. Yes.' She nodded. 'But the injection pen thing is back at the chalet. In his toiletries bag.'

It would have been much better if Zane had it with him, but that was a conversation they'd need to have later. Matt looked at Louis, who was talking in reassuring whispers to Zane. They always made a good tag team in situations like this and Matt thanked his lucky stars that Louis had done the same first-aid courses he had. 'Louis, go to chalet four. Grab Zane's wash bag and bring it back. Run.'

Then to Fred. 'Call the helicopter, explain the situation. Severe hypoglycaemia in a seventeen-year-old.'

Zoe slid over a screen on wheels, as fat tears slid down Rita's face. 'We should carry it with us, I know. But I thought he had it, he thought I had it. I wanted him to take responsibility for looking after his meds.' A choked sob. 'But he's still a child really and he's dealing with all the new things he needs to know about the condition.'

'It's a lot to understand and a new diabetic has to learn to be guided by how they're feeling as well as by the blood glucose readings. Add in extra exercise and that can cause a drop in sugar levels, too. He probably isn't at that point of understanding and recognising the changes yet. That's why you have to do frequent blood sugar readings.' Matt put his palm on her arm to comfort her while he watched the boy's face. He was pale and his breathing was raspy.

They needed to get the glucagon in, and quick, because if they didn't Zane could slip into a coma. Then he'd definitely need more help than Matt was able or trained to give. *Where was Rachel?*

Why wasn't she back yet? Was she okay? Was she lost? It was dark outside and no one had seen her since lunchtime. His gut tightened with a gnawing stab of worry. Something he hadn't felt in a couple of years, but was all too familiar.

He pushed it away and asked Rita, 'How long has Zane been like this?'

'Five minutes? I don't know. He said he wasn't feeling great as we came off the mountain, then he started mumbling odd things that didn't make sense. I asked if he felt it was his blood sugar, but he just snapped at me. Then he collapsed.' She stroked her son's hair. 'This is all my fault. I should have watched him better.'

'It's no one's fault. Honestly. It's a tricky thing to negotiate, particularly at the beginning.'

Fred ran back over. 'Heli's on its way with the paramedics. ETA ten minutes.'

He was swiftly followed by Louis who rushed in carrying a large leather wash bag. 'Here we go.'

'Thanks.' Matt grabbed the bag and found the orange emergency glucagon set. Clicking it open, he primed the syringe, reconstituted the little vial of powder, then jabbed the needle into the boy's deltoid muscle on his arm. 'It should only take a few minutes to work.'

'Thank God. Thank God.' Rita grasped Matt's hand as more tears spilled down her cheeks.

'But he's not going to feel great when he comes round.' Matt tried to be gentle while preparing her at the same time. 'He might vomit and he'll be groggy, but even so, he's going to need more sugar intake in the first instance. I'll get some juice organised.'

They watched and waited. Matt hoped they hadn't been too late, knowing that Zane's life could still be in danger. With all situations like this he felt as if he was holding his breath, wondering if there was anything more he should be doing, knowing he didn't have the resources or skills for much more—unless he needed the defibrillator unit.

He hoped like hell it wouldn't come to that.

Slowly, the twitching stopped and then Zane lay still, his breathing coming back to normal as the paramedics ran into the lobby. Rita's tears hadn't stopped and now they started to flow uncontrollably.

'Thank you, Mr LeFevre.' She wrapped Matt in a warm, shaky hug. 'Thank you so much.'

See, Rachel? They aren't all like Michael and Bianca.

He wanted her to be here to see the gratitude and warmth. He wanted her to be here. That sent a warning alarm shuddering through his body. Maybe a night out with Louis was what he needed after all.

Once he'd handed the boy over into the paramedics' care, Matt was finally able to breathe out. Within minutes patient and parent were safely ensconced in the helicopter on the way to hospital and he retreated to the bar for a steadying drink and a debrief with Louis.

They'd managed to save the boy's life without her. But where the hell was Rachel?

Gulping down the last of his beer, he jumped off the bar stool and went to the restaurant to see if she'd somehow bypassed them, but she wasn't there. He went to her chalet, but it was in darkness and no one answered his knocking. She still wasn't answering her phone. Maybe she'd gone down to the village on the shuttle bus? But the bus driver didn't recall dropping her off.

He tried her phone again. Still no answer.

Now he was starting to get concerned. What if she'd hurt herself?

What if she'd got lost?

CHAPTER SIX

IT WAS DARK now and the trail was lit only by the stars, a full moon and the soft glow from Rachel's head torch. But the snow reflected all available light and she could easily make out the twists and turns ahead and any bumps or crevasses to avoid.

It had been a couple of years since she'd skied and she'd felt rusty at first, but now she was totally into the groove with the wind in her hair and the cold air blasting her cheeks. Flying faster and faster down the mountain, she felt wonderfully, masterfully, fabulously free.

A loud beat blared in her headphones. *God,* she loved eighties rock music. All that angst and emotion, the awesome anthems. She joined in, singing at the top of her voice, as she whooshed through the snow and really did feel as if she was free falling through the night.

At a crossroads of two tracks she paused to get her bearings. Far below, to the left, the resort lights twinkled and winked. It looked like a pretty Christmas card and she knew the calm and comfort it held for everyone, staff and visitors alike. She felt a sudden warmth in her chest.

Home? No. She had her little flat in Leeds waiting for her…to sell, probably, given she didn't want to go back to work in that city while David was there.

So, Sainte Colette was her place, for now.

To the right, and much further away, the village lights glittered. A huge dark expanse—the lake, she imagined, loomed in between.

Which brought her right back to Matthieu and those moments by the fence the other day. His skin touching hers. The ripple of want that had slid through her. The want she'd been trying to get rid of ever since and that had prompted today's adventure to get Matthieu out of her head.

Hence the skiing. Purging her thoughts with loud music. Pushing her body to the limits with black runs that challenged her experience and took all her focus and concentration to get down.

One stop. One little stop, one moment's lapse and he'd come tumbling back into her thoughts again. She could only thank her lucky stars she hadn't bumped into him in the last few days because she just knew she'd die of embarrassment. Well…actually, she'd made sure she hadn't crossed paths with him, avoiding him any time she'd got a glimpse of that body, easy to do as he was head and shoulders above anyone else and instantly recognisable in a group.

Fancy grasping his hand like that.

Fancy wanting to kiss him.

What had she been thinking?

Nothing. That was the problem. She'd been led by her body's instinctive tug towards him. So acute she'd not been able to stop herself.

So, she'd stayed away from anywhere he might be. Turned her thoughts to anything but him.

Trouble was, no amount of avoiding him would stop the chatter in her head. Where exactly was that line he talked about? Was it talking? Flirting? Touching? More?

Did she want to cross it? Did he?

Aargh! Why did relationships—*people*—have to be so damned complicated? Give her science and predictable outcomes any day.

Turning the music up extra loud so she couldn't hear any more of her thoughts, she set off down the hill, setting her sights on the resort, a hot spa bath with a soothing glass of red wine and an early night.

No stopping at the restaurant on her way through, she'd make do with cheese and biscuits in her chalet.

No popping into reception. No buying a drink at the bar.

No hankering for a chat with Mr LeFevre.

A Matthieu-free zone.

That's what she needed.

He heard her before he saw her. The trudge of ski boots through the darkness. A hum…was it a hum or a wail? No, she was humming a song he thought he might recognise, but wasn't sure. She was woefully out of tune.

His brisk heart slowed. The alarm abated. She was okay.

She walked round the corner, her head bobbing to a tune he could almost hear through her headphones it was so loud. Her gaze was down, so she didn't see him. But he could see she was smiling.

The automatic light on the lintel jumped into action and she was lit by a warm golden glow. Once again, he was spellbound by her beauty. She was, unusually for her, utterly calm, her cheeks pink from exercise. Her eyes glittered—he knew exactly how that ski high felt, but his breath whooshed out of him as concern and relief took over in equal measure. 'Rachel. Hey.'

'Whoa! Matthieu?' She lumbered towards him, her gait rocky in her ski boots. Her expression had gone from pure joy to alert, personal to professional as if a switch had been flipped. 'You nearly gave me a heart attack. What's wrong? What's happened?'

She was clearly okay—more than okay, in fact. Looked as though his concern was an overreaction and now he was standing here like an idiot. He stuck to work issues. 'I thought you should know one of the guests had a seizure in reception.'

She breathed out plumes of air. 'Oh, dear. Are they okay?'

'I think so. He's gone in the helicopter to the hospital at Bourg St Maurice.'

'Okay.' She rested her skis in the rack outside her front door. 'You'd better come in.'

She swiped her key card into the lock, then lumbered into her chalet, stopping in the hallway to undo the Velcro on each ski boot and slipping her feet out. Then she hung her jacket up on the hook by the door and he followed suit with his.

The chalet was neat and tidy with no personal items anywhere, just a closed laptop on the small dining table. But the whole place smelt of her—a flowery, light perfume at odds with her strong and vivid personality. It made him feel almost light-headed to be enveloped in her scent.

She walked him through to the kitchen and flicked the kettle on. 'Right. Talk me through it.'

She clearly thought his alarm had just been about the patient and not about her. Which was a lucky escape for him. The last thing he needed was someone else to worry about.

But he knew it was guilt that fed his concern, because what if something had really happened to her and he hadn't been able to help her, or find her in time? The way he'd spectacularly failed before.

The thought that he was starting to care for Rachel spooked him. He hardly knew her, but he was strangely drawn to her. Which had to stop. He needed to dial back his reactions. Flick the same switch she had, from personal to professional.

Work. Think about work.

'Zane's a newly diagnosed diabetic and his blood sugar reading was very low. His mother was with him and had a glucagon injection that we gave him. We protected his airway and called the helicopter to take them to hospital.'

'Okay. Good.' Rachel took off her knitted headband and shook her hair loose. It skimmed her jawline, framing her face perfectly. 'You know a lot about it.'

'I'm a trained first aider, I need to know about these things.' And after looking after his mother most of his life he was invested in first aid. Not that he needed to tell Rachel that.

She nodded. 'You did the right thing. Completely. Sorry I wasn't around to help.'

'We called you a million times.'

'Did you? I didn't hear my phone.' She looked behind her at the looming shadow dotted with the little golden lights of the piste-grooming machines, her eyes dreamy. 'I was on the slopes.'

'On your own?'

Her forehead creased and her eyes narrowed. 'Yes?'

'In the dark?' It shouldn't matter who she skied with or when. She was a competent skier who knew the risks. Only, he owned the resort and if anything happened to her it was his business.

But it wasn't his business he was thinking about right now. It was her.

He imagined her lying on the snow damaged from a fall.

He imagined her lying in his bed.

This was crazy. And totally inappropriate.

Now he couldn't *not* think about her in his bed. Hot desire prickled through him and he almost wished he had kissed her back there on the mountain, then at least he could have expunged some of this need. Although he doubted he'd erase that need completely.

Her eyes were still dreamy as she spoke, her head clearly somewhere on the mountain. 'I had my head torch, so I was fine. It was fun up there for the sunset.' Her face lit up. 'The colours were amazing. Beautiful.'

He imagined seeing Sainte Colette through new eyes and agreed it would be magical. But to him, although it was his home, it had undertones of pain, too. And guilt. Along with immense gratitude for all the good times he'd experienced, despite the bad. So, yes, home.

She put a teabag into a mug, then looked up at him, her eyes asking a question. *You want a drink?*

And spend more time here, with her? Tempting. But that would only deepen his attraction to her.

He shook his head. He was just going to give her some advice that he hoped he could dress up as a suggestion, then go. 'Look, there are some challenging trails up there. You might want to join the staff ski group tomorrow.'

'Oh, I don't know.' A shrug.

'They're a friendly bunch, it's a good way to meet the other staff.' He remembered she'd said she preferred to ski on her own and waited for her refusal, but she just smiled.

'Friends?' She thought for a moment, then nodded. 'Maybe.'

It was probably as good as he was going to get from

her. 'Okay. Well, I should get going. Just wanted to give you a heads up about Zane for when he gets back from the hospital. In case either he or his mum needs to chat to someone who knows what they're talking about.'

'Great. Thanks. If you see him, tell him to pop by any time.'

'I will.' He turned to go, but she said,

'Matthieu…'

He whirled round. 'Yes?'

'About the other day…' There was a glimpse of softness there. Wanting.

He couldn't deny there'd been a connection up on the mountain. But did Rachel want more? What was she going to say? That she wanted to take things further? Did he?

In the past he'd only ever kept things light with women. Having his mother fill his spare time with her needs gave him precious little emotional space for anyone else. Now he was free to do whatever he wanted, but the thought of deep and meaningful gave him hives. Find happiness? When his mother never had? When the thought of him being too late to save her still haunted him?

He scuffed his hand across his hair. 'It was an intense conversation.'

'It was. Yes. That's what it was.' She exhaled, as if she'd been holding her breath waiting for his answer.

'And people do things, reach out. At times like that.' He was trying to convince himself, as much as her, that it hadn't meant anything more than a friendly hand squeeze. 'It won't happen again.'

'No. It won't.' She nodded sharply, then walked through to the front door and opened it, expecting him to leave. She was clearly used to people doing her bidding. He swallowed as something akin to disappointment

ran through him. He hadn't realised just how much he'd
been hoping for her to want more. Which clearly meant
he did. And now he was being rejected. Okay. He could
deal with that.

Looked as though he didn't have a choice.

And it was weird, because he usually only hooked up
with women who thought the same way he did. But something about Rachel made him crave more of her company.

As he tugged his jacket on, she said, 'You did well
today with the diabetic patient.'

'I know.' Stupid thing was, even after her rejection, he
still wanted to kiss her. 'Goodnight, Rachel.'

'Goodnight.'

He stepped out into the icy night, looking back one
last time.

She raised her hand in a small wave. 'Matthieu?'

Her voice was soft. Her pupils were dilated and he saw
raw need there, too. It fuelled his arousal. He couldn't
look away. In spite of everything he still wanted to kiss
that pouting, sensual mouth. What would she taste like?
Hot and spicy, he thought, just like her personality.

His heart jittered. 'Yes?'

He wondered whether she'd invite him back in,
whether he'd agree. But she gave him a wavering smile.
Something was making her back off and he was pretty
sure it wasn't him.

'Thanks for checking on me,' she said gently, and he
knew she'd worked out—or guessed—the real reason he'd
been waiting for her: to make sure she was safe. 'But I
can look after myself.'

Then she closed the door, leaving him hot and cold
and very confused.

CHAPTER SEVEN

EVEN THOUGH SHE liked being on her own, Rachel had to admit there was safety in numbers. Especially when Matthieu was close by.

The feelings he stoked in her were too intense for her to be alone with him again—she just knew she wouldn't be able to hide them next time. But she'd heeded his message and come along to the staff ski session.

She also had to admit that skiing in a group was fun, too, despite her earlier reservations. Five of them had met at the chairlift: Sonia from the restaurant, Louis the bar manager, Zoe from reception, herself and…of course, Mr Resort himself. She'd thought perhaps he'd come to assess her skiing skills, but, apparently, he came on these jaunts most Tuesday and Thursday afternoons just to hang out with his friends, who also just happened to be staff, too. It turned out that he employed half the village and they all thought he was a local hero for turning a struggling economy into a booming one and for bringing famous celebrities to their part of the world.

A hero? She had to admit there was a lot of good in him.

They'd taken her out on to the back trails where few tourists went and kept together as a close group. It had been wonderful to ski through unmarked snow, weaving through pine forests and look across deep valleys into neighbouring ski fields and resorts, but now they were racing down some tricky black runs on their way home and she had to concentrate hard.

Rachel followed them, happy to be the last, knowing she didn't have their skills, but glad she could keep up. Almost.

'Not bad!' Louis shouted as she reached them, breathless, looking down the hill to the resort buildings far below. A small round of applause came from the group with cheers of, *'You did well!' 'You made it!' 'Go girl!'*

'Thanks.' She caught her breath and did a jokey bow. 'I'm a bit slow, but getting there.'

She caught Matthieu's eye and he gave her a look that told her he was impressed by her skiing prowess and he was glad she'd come along. There was something exciting about his brief smile that made her feel as if they shared a secret. It slid into her chest, making her feel warm and seen. She hadn't realised before how little she'd felt seen by anyone recently. Or maybe it had been that she'd chosen not to be...she wasn't sure.

Zoe raised her ski pole and pointed off to the side where the snow had been packed into little humps and bumps. 'Mogul run?'

'Why not?' Rachel grinned. It looked far harder than what she was used to, but she'd come to realise that these guys would talk her down, pointing out the easiest way through while coaxing her to try some of the more technical bits.

And that was exactly what they did, with whoops of encouragement. If she'd been on her own, she'd have avoided all of it, but with this group she was learning, growing. And they were all light-hearted and fun, too.

She made it safely down the moguls and they only had

a couple more runs left before they reached the resort. She swished up to the back of the group and gulped in air, to find they were deep in discussion about some sort of show they were going to do for the guests.

'On Christmas Day,' Sonia explained, 'the boss dresses up as Father Christmas and we dress as his helpers and elves, reindeer, fairies, that sort of thing. And we do a skiing display down the Home Run. The kids love it.'

'The adults do, too,' Louis added with a cheeky smile. 'The ladies in particular. We're very…popular.'

Rachel ignored Louis's comment, even though she imagined anyone would love to watch Matthieu's skills.

She looked at 'the boss' and grinned. 'Father Christmas?'

He shrugged but smiled. 'What can I say?'

'I don't know?' She laughed. 'Ho-ho-ho?'

'Good one.' He guffawed, then pushed off on his right leg, then his left, and before she could say Rudolph he was skiing flat-out towards a rail. He jumped up on to it, gliding along on one ski, then he did a star jump off and something she'd only ever seen a gymnast do before that involved a sideways twist in the air, before disappearing over the edge.

With whoops and cheers the others followed one by one, doing somersaults, star jumps and twists.

'You can do this,' Rachel told herself and pushed off on her left ski, but when she got to the rail, she lost her nerve. *Hot damn.* She couldn't go back up the hill without a lot of bother so that was it. Her one chance at doing something daring.

Disappointed with herself she inched alongside the rail to the edge of the jump and saw them, below, waving at her. It was a long way down.

Thank God she hadn't actually caught the rail because

she had no idea how she would have landed without making a fool of herself in front of them. In front of Matthieu.

She'd been a fool too many times before. The altar sprang to mind.

She raised her poles and waved back, but shook her head. 'I'm good, but I'm not that good! See you at the bottom!'

By the time she got down to the next run the others had all skied off, but Matthieu was waiting for her.

Her heart gave a little jolt as she skied up to him and she hoped he'd interpret her heating cheeks for exhilaration and the icy blast. He hadn't admitted that he'd been concerned about not being able to get hold of her yesterday, but he hadn't denied it either. Just the thought of someone caring enough to worry about her gave her an extra layer of warmth.

Warmth that her body interpreted as something hotter, judging by the tingles in her traitorous body. She couldn't deny she was attracted to him, but she was not going to act on it. They'd agreed. 'You should have gone with the rest, I'm fine to get down by myself,' she said.

'No one's left behind, Rachel. That's a rule of ours.' He grinned. 'Thought you might have given the rail a go?'

'Hey, I know my limits. But that was brilliant. You're all awesome.'

'You're not bad yourself.' He nodded. 'I'm happier now I've actually seen you ski. You can join the search-and-rescue team if you want.'

High praise indeed. Her belly filled with heat. 'I'd love to.'

'Excellent. I'll put you on the roster. You coming for a drink?' His eyes roved her face, and he must have seen the hesitation in her eyes because he quickly added, 'We usually stop in for one after these sessions. You're welcome to join us.'

'No, thanks.' She searched her mind for an excuse, because just thinking about the altar had made her jittery about giving too much of herself away. 'I really need to send some emails.'

He regarded her for a moment, then nodded. 'Okay. Another time, maybe?'

He didn't press her or try to convince her but then, why would he after what she'd said to him yesterday? She shut people out the moment they got close. But it was for the best. Short-term pain for long-term gain.

She had no desire to be hurt again.

A few days and another group ski session later Rachel was sitting in her usual place in the restaurant. It had been a good day. The patients hadn't been too taxing, but challenging enough. She'd even had a quick drink with the ski group which had been fun, but they'd all dispersed and she was grateful for some alone time.

Mainly because of the picture she was looking at right now.

David and Vicky at the annual hospital ball, an event she and her ex had attended together for the last two years. She swallowed back a lump in her raw throat and, despite herself, enlarged the photo so she could see them more easily. Dressed in glamorous evening clothes, they looked absolutely besotted with each other in front of the huge Christmas tree in the hotel foyer. A place she and David had stood for photos. She still had them, on her tablet. Somewhere.

All those photos of their trips away, their little engagement party. David had been the one person she'd ever felt close to. The only person she'd allowed herself to open to…and apparently even that hadn't been enough. She'd tried…tried so hard, but some things you kept private, right? You didn't need to tell everybody everything. Maybe she should have?

And… *Oh!* Her heart squeezed as she enlarged the photo even more and, yes, on Vicky's left ring finger was a huge sparkling diamond. They'd got engaged? So soon? How so? How could two people fall for each other so quickly? Unless…

'There's no one else. It's not that,' he'd said, but *It's not me, it's you* was what he'd meant. Or had Vicky been waiting in the wings? Their friend…her friend really. At least Rachel had thought they were friends.

She didn't even want to think about that. One betrayal was bad enough. And she couldn't remember a time when David had ever looked at her like that, with such adoration—

'Nice-looking couple.'

'Oh!' Her heart jerked in surprise at the voice.

Matthieu, of course. She'd been so absorbed in the photo she hadn't heard him approach. She turned the tablet over so he couldn't peer too closely—not that he could miss it; she'd enlarged it to about ten times its normal size.

She cleared her throat. 'Were you looking for me? Is something wrong?'

'Not at all. I do a round of the bar and restaurant every night before I finish work, just to make sure everything is running smoothly.' He glanced back at the tablet. 'Friends of yours?'

'My ex, actually.' The words tumbled out before she could stop them. 'And his new girlfriend. *Fiancée.* Well, it looks like they're engaged. Which is quite sudden given we only broke up a few months ago.'

Hot damn. Why had she just told him that? But she'd been so taken aback by him being there and so derailed by the picture she'd blurted it all out.

He was going to think she was a complete flake.

'Ouch.' He grimaced and put his hand on his heart. 'That must sting.'

Sting, yes. That's how she felt. An acute stab of pain. She thought about saying *I'm fine*, but had come to know that Matthieu wouldn't accept that from her. *What to say?*

He kept on looking at her, expecting more from her. *Oh, what the hell.* She'd already been caught looking at the photos, she should probably elaborate a little more as to why an engagement could be hurtful. 'We were supposed to be getting married last July.'

'Ah.' He looked at her sympathetically. 'It's never easy.'

'On the contrary. It's getting easier by the day.'

'And yet you're still looking at the photographs.'

'I know. Stupid. But I just came across them on a mutual friend's post.' The stabbing pain was easing a little and she realised she hadn't even thought about David for a few days, until now. She didn't want him to intrude on this special place. He was her past, she needed to move on. She sat up straighter and gave Matthieu a smile she hoped was reassuringly bright. 'It was just a surprise to see them together, that's all.'

'Of course. I imagine you gave him hell?'

'For falling in love with someone else? No! What he does is none of my business.' Despite the heartache.

Two years gone, just like that. All that feeling of being part of something bigger than herself, all the belonging she'd yearned for, had thought she'd achieved, had come to nothing but hurt.

Being single could be lonely at times, but if it meant she didn't have to go through that again, then she would remain steadfastly on her own. She pushed her hair back from her face and smiled. 'Ah, well. You live and learn, right?'

'You sure do.' Matthieu gave her such an understanding smile in return she wondered if he'd ever had his heart broken. She doubted that. From what she'd heard from Louis about their past escapades, she doubted either Matthieu or the bar manager had ever loved and lost. They were all about the fun.

But he tilted his head to one side. 'Rachel, can you do me a favour?'

'Of course.'

'I've got an errand to run in the village and I need someone to give me a hand.' He lifted a large cloth sack that bulged at odd angles. 'Louis is busy, Zoe can't leave reception, it's Fred's day off. Angela—'

She shoved the tablet into her bag and stood up. 'What is it? Father Christmas duties already?'

He laughed. 'Kind of. But you'll need a warm jacket, gloves and scarf. Meet me at reception in about five minutes?'

Intrigue wound through her.

Intrigue and something altogether unexpected... excitement.

CHAPTER EIGHT

SHE WAS BACK there in four minutes.

She followed him across the car park and over the road to a building she'd seen, but not investigated yet. Round the back she discovered a low wooden sled complete with cushions and a rug.

Frantic barking came from behind a large wooden door which Matthieu creaked open to reveal a huge barn and six beautiful husky dogs. He was immediately bombarded by them all vying for his attention, jumping and barking in excitement. He laughed at their antics and gave each of them a good rub and stroke. 'The dogs need a run and I have to send some packages from *la poste* for my guests, so I thought we could do both at the same time.'

She looked at her watch and realised it was close to seven-thirty. 'Won't the post office be closed this late?'

'Natalie's an old friend of mine. She won't mind if we call by. Come in.' He beckoned to her. 'They won't hurt you.'

'Are you sure?' But she couldn't help laughing as one of the pups, with the most adorable golden eyes, jumped up and gently nuzzled her hip.

'I think you've got an admirer, Rachel. That's Loki.'

'As in Thor's Loki?'

'Yes. That's Thor there. And Freya, Sif, Fulla…' He

made a strange half-whistling, half-clicking noise and they all gathered round him...except one. Matthieu laughed and click-whistled again. 'This is Odin. He's younger than the rest and still in training.'

'Cool names.'

'Louis is a bit of a mythology geek. We're doing Norse at the moment, but I think we're going Greek soon. He said he wants an Apollo next.'

'Perfect.' She laughed. 'They're all Louis's dogs?'

'They're our dogs.' At her frown he explained, 'We've been friends a long time. We grew up together, worked in the agency together and then he came back here a couple of years after me.'

Her heart warmed as they raced around her legs. 'They're absolutely gorgeous. Do they mind about pulling the sled? Is it hard for them?'

'Not at all. They're bred to work and to run.' He crouched down and nuzzled Odin's snout. 'They're strong and smart and they love it. That one's Freya. She's Odin's mum.'

'Hey, gorgeous girl.' She bent and rubbed Freya's ears, then laughed as the dog nuzzled her, making her lose her balance. 'Hey. Hey. Yes. I know you love me already.' Now sprawled on the floor, she scrubbed Freya's fur and got face-licks in return. 'Hey! Yes, yes.'

'Freya,' Matthieu snapped and the dog stopped licking and sat completely still, looking up adoringly at Matthieu.

Rachel hauled herself upright and sat on the ground, recovering from near death by licking. 'I didn't realise both dogs and bitches pull the sleds.'

'Huskies are bred for speed and agility. Gender doesn't come into it. The clever ones go at the front to lead. Freya's a leader.' He smiled as the dog put her paw on

Rachel's knee and cocked her head to one side. 'She has very good taste.'

'She just wants a cuddle.' Once again, she was suffused with heat at his words. He gave a lot of compliments and she wasn't sure how to take them. She grabbed the chance to deflect as Freya tugged at Rachel's coat sleeve. 'I think she wants me to come with her.'

Sure enough, Freya led her outside to the sled. 'Okay, so how does this work?'

Matthieu started to clip the dogs on to harnesses at the front of the sled. They were so clever they knew exactly which order they were to line up in and where to stand. Except Odin, who kept wandering off, only to be called back by Matthieu who never lost his patience. 'You sit on the sled and I stand on the back to steer.'

The fleeting image of them both wrapped up under the rug dissolved as quickly as the spike of desire. 'Why do you need me?'

He motioned for her to sit, pulled the rug over her legs and then gave her the bag to hold. 'You have the most important job. Some of these packages could be fragile and are probably very expensive. I don't want them to fall off and break.'

'Noted. I'll keep tight hold.' She knew he was making up an excuse to distract her from the photo. They both did, but she went with it because…huskies.

And because… Matthieu, she had to admit. How could she not like a man who loved dogs?

David didn't like pets at all.

She really needed to stop thinking about the man who had destroyed her heart and her faith in love.

Matthieu did the click-whistle thing again and the dogs started to run. And…wow!

Just, wow.

The sled breezed across the snow so quickly it almost stripped her breath. The terrain had looked to be all downhill, but it actually undulated in a gradual slow descent. She kept a tight hold on the bag with one hand and a hold on her beanie with the other and the whole time she grinned and screamed in delight.

All too soon, they came to a stop in a chocolate box village with a little square flanked with ancient plane trees and grey stone buildings; she could see a *tabac*, a post office, a greengrocer, a *boulangerie* and a bar on the corner. The bar was bustling with wrapped-up customers sitting outside, beneath fairy lights and heaters.

Matthieu stepped off his spot behind her, anchored the sled in the snow, petted all the dogs, then came over to her. 'Did you have fun?'

'The best. Wow. That was amazing.'

'You look…elated.'

'I didn't think they'd go so fast.' Heart still pounding, she took out her phone and snapped a couple of photos of the dogs.

'Quick, let's take another.' He grabbed her phone and took a picture of her on the sled. 'Smile, Rachel.'

'My face hurts with all the smiling. The dogs, the sled…this place.' *You.* He looked adorable all wrapped up in his scarf and hat with a nose pink from the cold. Her heart stuttered. He really was an extraordinary man to be doing this for her.

But it was one thing to think someone was adorable and another altogether to act on those feelings.

She looked away and started to get out of the sled.

'Wait.' He crouched next to her, cuddled in and took a snap of them together, cheek to cheek. 'Put that on the internet. That'll show him.'

Matthieu's skin against hers sent shivers of need spiralling through her, but the mention of her ex was enough to chase them away. 'Don't be silly. He won't care.'

'But you do.'

'I do not.' She grabbed for her phone, but he held it away, laughing. His laugh curled around her, making her laugh, too, when once she would have cried over her failed relationship. But, truthfully, she drank him in: his smiling face and kind eyes, his fun-loving streak, his carefree nature. To look for the fun in things was infectious and liberating and so new to her that, after a lifetime of running away from pain, of working so hard and applying her serious work ethic to every aspect of her life, she wanted to chase that fun so hard.

'Honestly, Rachel, you shouldn't give a damn what he thinks.' Matthieu held her gaze. He was close enough she could smell his scent. To see the snowflake crystals land on his nose and upper lip and melt clean away on contact. He really did have the most gorgeous mouth… 'And he's a crazy fool to have let you go.'

Especially when he said things like that. In that French accent that almost brought her to her knees. If she hadn't already been sitting down…

'He didn't let me go. He dumped me at the altar.' Damn. She couldn't believe she'd just admitted that to him. Words had just tumbled out, again. Now he was going to think she was dump-worthy. Instead of kiss-worthy.

Did she want to be kiss-worthy to Matthieu?

But he blinked, his arm still outstretched, his expression one of shock and anger. 'He did…*what*?'

Uh-uh. This was exactly why she kept her thoughts and feelings to herself. So she wouldn't have to relive her most embarrassing and hurtful moments. But she'd started, so she had to tell him the rest. 'He told his best friend to let me know he was sorry, but he couldn't marry me. He said I was too… I was too…'

'Too…? What?' Matthieu encouraged her with his eyes to continue, but she could also see his ire growing, too, on her behalf. His expression of support was like a sucker-punch of heat to her chest.

'Hard to get to know…we'd been going out for two bloody years and now he decides he doesn't know me? I'm cold, apparently. Aloof.'

And she'd tried to be that ever since. Doubled down on it. Keeping everyone at arm's length the way she'd learnt growing up, because that way she wouldn't get hurt again. But Matthieu…he was sorely testing her resolve.

'He actually said that? You? Dr Blow-Up? Isla's advocate? Lover of huskies? Cold?' Matthieu smiled and shook his head. 'Private, yes. And there's nothing wrong with that. Not everyone wants to live their lives on social media. Independent, definitely. But clearly, he hasn't seen you stand up for an injured child or roll on the floor with a puppy. Even so…even if he thought those things of you, to leave you at a church on your wedding day is unforgivable.'

'I hadn't seen it coming, so it was a shock. Sure, we were in a routine, but he called it a rut, like a weight on his shoulders he couldn't carry any more. He said I was too closed off, but I tried, I really tried to be part of a couple. I'm just not one to wear my heart on my sleeve and say how I'm feeling, it's just not who I am.'

'Can I ask…' he pulled an apologetic face '…why would he propose to you if he didn't think he knew you?'

Her cheeks heated. She swallowed. *God,* this was embarrassing. 'I asked him.'

'Ah.'

'Yes. *Ah*. It was leap year. And I thought it was what he wanted. Turns out it was, just not with me.'

Matthieu groaned. 'He's crazy.'

'I must be to have proposed, right? We were on holiday in Crete and it had been a good day; we'd swum in the sea, done some sightseeing—nothing mind-blowing, but it had been easy, you know? Everything seemed to slot into place. At least, I thought it had. I was content.'

After seeing her parents' passion turn to hate she'd steered away from extreme emotions. Hadn't wanted or looked for an all-consuming big love because she knew how that ended.

'I said it would be nice if every day was like this and he agreed. And then I said, "So marry me, David."'

'That would have taken some guts, Rachel.'

She laughed. 'On paper he was perfect. Steady and reliable and the opposite of what I'd grown up with. I wanted stability, I guess, and thought he'd give me that. I felt like I belonged, finally. That I was part of something that wasn't just my team of one. Something…content.'

'What did he say when you proposed?'

'He looked at me open-mouthed for a few moments, making me feel like an idiot, and then eventually nodded. I'd thought it was the surprise that made him hesitate, but apparently he'd been too worried to say no in case I got upset.'

'Leaving you at the altar isn't upsetting?'

'He said he'd been trying to tell me for weeks, but thought that he might just have pre-wedding jitters. He realised on the day that he couldn't go through with it. And now I'm seeing pictures of him and Vicky. Our friend. Engaged.'

'You know her, too?'

'She was in our friendship group. More my friend than

his, or so I thought. Problem was, we worked together and shared the same friends and colleagues…when you work weird shifts it's hard to make friends outside work and you just sort of form a team who you socialise with, too.' That's what she'd hoped for, anyway. 'So, everyone we knew, knew about what had happened. That he didn't want me. That I wasn't good enough. Just not… enough for him.'

She laughed, but it was empty, wondering why the hell she was telling this guy all about the previous guy who'd discarded her. 'The two weeks we were supposed to be on honeymoon we spent separating our things and looking for a place for him to move into, speaking only through text messages. I couldn't bring myself to talk to him. I had nothing to say.'

'God, Rachel, that's cruel.' Matthieu's gaze had softened. He was looking at her as if none of this made sense.

That made two of them. At least, it hadn't made any sense to her at the time, but now she was starting to see that her tendency to keep things close to her chest could be seen as aloof and cold. The way she always told everyone she was fine didn't invite anyone in. In fact, Matthieu had said as much on that first morning and opened her eyes to how she came across to other people.

Why she was baring her soul to him like this she didn't know, except that the words were pouring out of her and he was interested, seemed almost invested.

Although she was probably scaring him off.

'We still worked in the same department most days and it was stifling. I love my job. I live for my work and I got to the point where I didn't want to go in. That's when I knew I had to leave. And that's why I came here. I needed to get away from it all.'

She blew out the pain of embarrassment and hurt. Her

breath plumed in the cold air, mingling with Matthieu's. She watched as the vapour wisps curled together and then faded into nothing right in front of them. Gone. She sent all her sadness that, way too, out into the atmosphere to disappear. Gone. All the hurt from that day. Gone.

'You have some unfinished business, then?' he said.

'No. God, no. David knows what I think of him.' The love she'd felt for him had turned into something a lot uglier and messier. But now she just didn't want to think about her ex at all.

Matthieu laughed. Actually laughed. 'Poor guy.'

And for the first time in what felt like for ever, Rachel gave a hearty laugh, too. 'He's probably quaking in his boots, waiting for me to unleash.'

'Don't give him the satisfaction.'

'I have no plans to. I just want to forget him. Forget her. Forget them.' Surprisingly, after talking about it, her chest felt lighter. Her heart felt lighter. She knew she had a lot more work to do, but right now she was free from five months' worth of heartache. She'd escaped Leeds and all those repressed emotions that she'd swallowed so she wouldn't blow up in front of her friends...and here she could breathe and be free. She had everything to look forward to.

The thirty years' worth of another kind of heartache was going to take a bit longer to breathe out—another time.

Heck, she was in France with a gorgeous man and six adorable dogs. Suddenly, she was acutely aware of the press of Matthieu's thigh against hers, of the rise and fall of his chest. Of his strength and heat.

'You know what? To hell with all that. It's all in the past.' She was determined to let it stay there. 'Look at me. I'm here, on a freaking husky sled. It's magical. Beautiful. Wonderful. I'm not going to let anyone ruin this moment. But please give me the phone, my whole life's in there.'

'Only if you promise to upload that photo of us to that stupid website. Show him that you've moved on. A picture with a sexy Frenchman might help, yes?' Matthieu made a pretence of preening.

'Sexy?' She laughed. 'You have one seriously big ego, Matthieu LeFevre.'

'And…? What's the problem?' He winked, getting up to give each of the dogs a treat. Walking along the line, then back to the sled. 'I haven't had any complaints so far.'

'Honestly…' she tutted, playing along. 'I bet *most* women hang off every word you say.' She emphasised most, making the point that she wouldn't be one of them.

'It's a drag…but…yes.' His grin stretched. 'Seriously, who could keep away from me and six gorgeous huskies?' He nuzzled Odin's neck and fluttered his eyelashes at her. 'Look at this one. How could you resist those puppy eyes?'

'You use your dogs to score dates?' Giggling, she bugged her eyes back at him in mock horror. 'Matthieu, I'm shocked.'

'Actually, I've only just thought about it. But it's an excellent idea. Thanks for the tip.'

'Oh, you know me. Such a successful love life. Any time you want advice, I'm…your…girl.'

Her words slowed as she realised Matthieu's grin had slipped. He had completely stilled and was looking at her with such sexual hunger it made her insides liquid. And she knew, she just *knew* he'd brought her here on the sled because he wanted to make her happy. And that made him the sexiest man she'd ever met.

Their gazes tangled and the atmosphere seemed to charge with a delicious sexual tension.

He reached a gloved palm to her cheek and stroked her skin. She curled into his touch, wanting and wishing to press her mouth to his. To press her body against his.

'Dr Tait, has anyone ever told you how pretty you are when you smile?'

Her throat worked, but she wasn't sure she could find words.

'No,' she managed. 'Never.'

He ran a finger over her lip, making her shiver with anticipation. 'Beautiful.'

'You know that line we talked about?' She barely recognised her own voice, it was so sex-fuelled and cracked with need.

'The other day?' His eyes twinkled and he twisted his whole body to face her. 'Yes.'

She couldn't believe she was saying this, but she had to. 'Do you ever cross it on a personal level?'

His other palm cupped her cheek and he encouraged her to stand up. 'I haven't, to date.'

'You want to make an exception?' she said. This was the kicker...had what she told him put him off?

His face inched closer, she could see snowflakes on his eyelashes and that made her heart melt just a bit more. 'Will it make things awkward, Rachel?'

'I don't know.' She pressed her hand to his cheek, too. 'Probably.'

'This is just to get your ex back, yes? Get him out of your system?' The way he looked at her told her that was an excuse, not a reason. He wanted this as much as she did. His eyes had become very serious indeed and blazed with heat.

'I don't know. I just... I just have to...' *Kiss you.*

'Say it, Rachel. Tell me what you want.'

Ray Shell. Ray Shell. Way to make an ice queen melt.

But this was exactly what she couldn't do. Sure, in her working life she could command the whole ER to do her bidding. But this…? Asking for things she wanted? How many times had she done that growing up and been ignored? To the point she'd learnt not to ask at all.

But it was clear he wasn't going to respond until she said the words. What was the worst that could happen? She'd already been rejected in the worst possible way. All Matthieu could do was walk away and, judging by the way he was looking at her, she didn't think he'd do that right now. 'I want to kiss you, Matthieu.'

'The feeling is very, *very* mutual.' He stepped closer until his body pressed against hers.

'Are you sure, after everything I just told you?'

'Why would that put me off? You were being honest. I like that.' He pressed her against the trunk of an ancient plane tree, caught her bottom lip between his teeth and smiled. 'Very cold. But heating up nicely.'

Then he slid his mouth over hers.

CHAPTER NINE

OH, SHE WAS COLD, all right.

But not in the way her ex had meant. Her lips were like ice from the whip of freezing air. Her cheeks were so cold he felt it through his gloves.

But her mouth… God, her mouth was hot and wet and divine.

She tasted of fresh snow mixed with the Chablis she'd been drinking earlier, of renewal and excitement, and he felt it emanating through her.

She tasted, quite simply, exquisite. But she was holding back…wanting it, but hesitant. Keeping herself in control, apart in some way. Knowing her the way he did, she was probably telling herself it was just *fine*.

Which made him smile inside. Because he knew she was a whole lot more than fine right now. He also knew this was probably the most insane thing he'd ever done, because Rachel had just come out of a relationship that had broken her heart. She needed to heal. Needed more than he could give her. But, like her, he just wanted one kiss. One taste. If nothing else than to erase the spectre of her ex from her head.

No, if nothing else…just to taste her. Over and over.

He pulled away slightly and looked at her. Her eyes were wide open, but her dark pupils were huge and misted. He laughed, kissed her cheek, her nose, then one eyelid and the other, forcing them closed, hoping she'd relax. 'You are exquisite, Rachel.'

'Say it again.' Eyes still closed, she curled into his palm on her cheek. 'Say my name.'

'Rachel.' He licked her bottom lip. Then her top one. *'Je veux t'embrasser partout,'* he whispered into her mouth.

'Kiss me all over? *God*, Matthieu…' He saw the moment she finally let herself fall. Her eyes had shuttered closed, but he could see the heat and desire in her features, in the pink stain on her cheeks, the way she tilted her head. The puckering of those lips, the swallow in her throat.

The kiss deepened and he felt her soften against him as if she was breathing out and finally letting the control slip. She circled her hands round his shoulders and tugged him closer until he could feel the press of her breasts against his chest. The hitch of her breathing.

As her tongue slid into his mouth fresh arousal shot through him, hot and tight. Deep in his belly. Hard in his groin. Prickling over his skin and under his skin, in his chest, in his bones. He felt the need for her *everywhere*.

He'd had a glimpse of the real Rachel Tait, the heart of her, and now he wanted to see through to her core. He wanted her open, he wanted her falling apart with him rocking deep inside her.

'Matthieu. I need…this.' She moaned and her hands cupped his backside, tugging him closer and closer.

Whoever said this woman was cold had absolutely no idea. She just needed time and the right kind of kissing.

Woof! Woof!

The dogs! *Damn.*

The barking brought him crash-landing back to reality.

They were in his village—everyone knew him. He'd always kept his liaisons out of their glare—mainly to protect his mother—but now the local gossip machine would whirr into action.

Hell, he half expected a round of applause from the crowd over at the bar, until he realised they were hidden by the tree trunk.

He tugged away from her, reluctant to let her go now she'd finally opened up enough for a kiss, however brief, but knowing it was the right thing to do.

Desire had made him rash, letting his body lead. But they'd been reckless kissing out here. Kissing at all. Now he had to let things cool.

She looked thoroughly dazed and thoroughly kissed. He pushed a stray lock of hair back under her beanie and couldn't stop the smile. 'Has he gone?'

'Who?' She smiled back up at him, but he could feel her trembling against him. He was shaken up, too. He'd never had a kiss like that. Full, giving, open.

'We should probably head back, but let's drop the bag off to Natalie first,' he said. Then he gave the dogs another treat and tied the sled off on the tree trunk.

Maybe real life would set his brain straight.

But, of course, it didn't. All he could think about was the way she'd looked at him when he'd licked her bottom lip—as if she wanted to eat him. He'd never seen a woman so hungry for a kiss. For *his* kiss.

He tried to bury those thoughts as they talked with Natalie. And he wondered if Rachel was thinking the same…that it had been a mistake. She was gracious and friendly with Natalie. Quiet on the ride home, no screeching at the speed, no huge smiles.

She seemed to have turned in on herself—not actively

blocking him or pushing him away, but not allowing him in either—and she wasn't pursuing any deeper conversation than polite, which he should have been grateful for, because he didn't want deep. Sure, he knew the value of community and friendship, but anything more intimate? He'd never been able to go there. And wasn't about to start.

Once the dogs had been fed, watered and put back into their kennels. she hugged her arms round her chest. 'I should go. It's late.'

He secured Odin's kennel, then turned to her. 'Let me walk you back to your chalet.'

'I'm fine—' She smiled, rolled her eyes, then corrected herself. 'I mean… I know my way.'

He couldn't read her. Didn't know what she was thinking.

The last thing he wanted was to have to second-guess someone else. He'd done that all his life with his mother: watching her moods, interpreting her expressions, assessing, guarding, preparing himself for whatever she was going to throw at him, which was always unpredictable. What he needed was transparent. What he liked was easy.

'Are you okay, Rachel? You haven't said much since… the village.'

'It's been a long time since I did anything like that.' She sighed. 'And I'm naturally a quiet person. I do a lot of thinking and not so much talking. But the thing is, I need my space. I need to— Look, Matthieu, I'm not looking for a relationship right now.'

'Of course. Me neither.' Rachel was a special woman and he was intrigued and turned on by her. But that was where it had to stop. He nodded his assent, then kissed both of her cheeks in as platonic a way as he could muster. 'Goodnight, Rachel.'

She squeezed his hand. 'Thank you for the adventure. It was a lot of fun.'

'No problem. I enjoyed it, too. Very much.' He nodded then turned away.

Truth was, Matt knew it was a lot more than fun. But, no matter what his sensible brain was telling him, he ached to do it again.

Rachel closed the front door of her chalet and leaned back against the wood, her heart jittering and her insides tightening at the memory of his mouth on hers. Had she just made another of her catastrophic mistakes?

Probably. But it had been one of her better ones. Her best worst mistake?

'Oh, God.' She put her head in her hands, her cheeks burning at the mortification and wonder of it. She'd kissed him. She couldn't stop the giggle bursting out of her. Since when had she ever giggled?

He'd wanted to kiss her all over.

Yes, please. It had been a wonderful kiss, but a crazy idea. It was right they'd agreed not to take it any further.

She had barely slept for reliving his touch, his taste, and she got up the next morning feeling two-parts groggy and one-part still excited.

Had she ever thought about David like this? Lain awake and yearned for him? Overly excited at the prospect of seeing him again? She didn't think so, couldn't remember ever having this washing machine churn in her stomach. Their relationship had always been just, well…nice enough, satisfactory. Their sex life had been perfunctory and she'd been okay with that, not expecting or wanting big passion like her parents.

David had been serious, like her. Practical, like her.

Then he'd gone and fallen hopelessly in love with someone else. It didn't seem fair that he got to do the dumping *and* the falling in love.

A long day off stretched before her.

She had made some breakfast, read her emails, then looked round her little chalet for something to do. She'd felt on edge, jittery, as if she needed some serious exercise to get rid of the excess energy coursing through her.

She couldn't just sit around here replaying that kiss, so she went out to see the dogs, gave them each a pat and cuddle and found some treats that she sneaked in to them. Then she wandered through the resort, looked in the high-end shops at things she didn't want to buy. Had a coffee and pastry in a cafe. Then… What to do?

Normally she'd have read a book, but today restlessness ate at her until she couldn't take it any longer. She couldn't wait until four o'clock before she did some exercise, she needed to do some now.

She rushed back to her chalet, dressed for skiing, then climbed on to the chairlift, pausing to tell the liftie, 'In case anyone asks, I'm going up to the top trails. I have my personal locator beacon in case of emergency and I'll be back for the staff ski session at four.'

He saluted as the chairlift cranked up speed. 'Got you, Doc. Have fun.'

'I will!' Then she clutched the safety bar, remembering, too late, the headphones that she'd last seen on the dining table in her chalet.

Looks like I'm going to have to listen to my thoughts, then.

Not great. The last thing she needed was to relive that kiss all over again.

She set off along a route the group had skied the other

day, but things were different today; the sky was filled with clouds, the visibility wasn't as good, the snow was hard and icy. She knew she'd have to keep her wits about her.

Cold. Aloof.
Ray Shell.
Ice Queen.
Lover of huskies.
Isla's advocate.
Kisser of Matthieu.
Ray Shell.

It started to snow, thick white flakes falling fast all around her. She skied through them, catching them on her tongue and laughing. Glad to be so free and having some space and time on her own and, yet, strangely alone. She'd come to enjoy skiing in a group, the laughter and challenges and just the…friendship. Should she have waited until four o'clock? Should she have invited someone to come with her? Zoe? Matthieu?

They all seemed to like her, too, even though she kept them all at a distance by design.

What had she missed by being so closed off? Should she talk more? Was that the problem? Is that what people in successful relationships did? They talked. Not argued like her parents. They communicated. Could she do that? Apparently not enough, as far as David was concerned. Even Matthieu had mentioned her silence last night.

After that kiss.

Shoot! Her foot skidded on the ice and she careened sideways, her body twisting until she was facing directly down the mountain. It was steep. But she could manage. She let the momentum take her straight down until she gathered enough control to put pressure on her inner ski and turn swiftly and in control.

Her heart slowed. Good. Right. No more Matthieu thoughts because they seemed to sap her attention. The snow was falling faster now, coating the track with fresh powder, shrouding her in a cloak of white.

She skied across the mountain to a trail she hadn't seen before. It had a gentle descent, meandering through the trees, and looked to be heading towards the resort buildings. She took it, easing her way down a picturesque track flanked by pine trees.

It reminded her of last night on the sled. The cute dogs with quaint names.

And then the kiss.

It had been so good to be in Matthieu's arms. She'd felt as if she'd come home, so wanted. Desired. He'd pushed her to open up and she'd felt so free. More, he'd seen her as someone more than a jilted woman. More than a doctor. And he'd treated her with such care.

She'd wavered about him walking her home. Debated in her head about inviting him in to her chalet. She hadn't known what to do, so she'd panicked—

Ugh. Her foot struck something hard and suddenly she was flying through the air.

No! She tried to right herself, but landed hard and off balance, the impact on slippery ice flinging her forward, her left ski breaking loose and skittering to the edge of the mountain…disappearing over the edge…

She watched it go as she tumbled over and over, hitting small rocks, the impacted snow. She couldn't stop… didn't stop, in free fall down the deceptively steep hill, putting one hand out to slow her fall, one hand on her helmet to protect her head. There were trees in front of her, trees everywhere, and she was flying, tumbling towards them. Too fast.

Please. Stop. Please.

She held her breath, closed her eyes. Braced for impact, hoping this would be survivable, but knowing there was a chance it wouldn't be. Isla's little impassive face flittered through her mind, then Odin's. Then Matthieu's.

Matthieu, I'm sorry...

Suddenly she came to a crashing halt as her back collided hard with a tree trunk. For a few moments she lay there dazed, unsure which way was up. Numb to everything apart from the fact she was still alive.

Stupid. Stupid. Stupid.

A searing pain radiated up her right leg. Her back stung from the impact. She sat up, a little dizzy and shocked at how quickly things had turned bad.

Mooning over a man.

'Get up. Get up and go home, girl,' she told herself as adrenalin kicked in, making her more alert, but shaky. 'Get up, already.' She hauled herself upright and tugged up her salopettes. Her right knee was red and raw and swelling up. *Damn.*

What to do? More to the point, where was she? The falling snow was so thick it felt as if she was in a cloud, unable to see much beyond her outstretched hand.

She looked around, trying to get her bearings. There was no track here, she'd skidded off it, leaving a trail of tiny, fluffy snowballs and grit in her wake. Her one ski was cracked, but still attached to her boot. She flicked it off. One ski was no use. Hopping all the way back down the mountain would take hours and she'd risk hypothermia, but it was her only option. But which way? Where was the track?

If she set off the locator beacon, she'd bring the whole search and rescue team out to her...she didn't need that. They didn't need that...this wasn't a real emergency. She was just a little...dazed. Perhaps a bit lost. In a bit of pain.

A lot of pain.

She just needed to know where she was. She took out her phone to look at the GPS map. The screen was cracked. No signal. She peered closer. All she could see were a few jagged coloured lines. She jabbed at the screen—no response. The fall must have broken it.

Hell.

She remembered veering off the track further up, so she'd walk back up and find it. That would be the only way she'd get her bearings. *Right. A plan. Good.*

She peered up the hill, which seemed a lot steeper than she'd originally thought. A lot of up. But that was the only way she'd find her way home.

Back to Matthieu.

Her stomach flipped. Matthieu.

Yes. Thinking about him gave her the impetus to move. She didn't know where she was, but she was pretty certain up was the way to go. Yes. That's where she'd go.

Having retrieved, thankfully, both her poles, she put herself perpendicular to the mountain and kick-stepped and limped her way up the ice, inch by inch, using the poles as walking sticks until she reached the point where she thought her ski and backpack had flown over the edge. There, below, a pink-tipped ski stuck out of the snow and her backpack was further down.

There was no way she'd get down there, so it was back towards the trail.

Come on, girl. You've got this.

As the ascent levelled out, she hopped slowly through the ever-falling snow until she found something that resembled the track—she just couldn't see where it led and it was completely deserted. But she set her stall on the resort being eastwards and downwards, so started to trudge, trying to ignore the pain in her back and her leg.

She sang. 'Living on a Prayer'. 'Stairway to Heaven'. 'Bohemian Rhapsody'. 'Eye of the Tiger'. 'Total Eclipse of the Heart'.

Then she ran out of songs and energy.

No point bringing snacks if they're in a backpack out of reach. Just need a rest.

Tired and thirsty, she slumped down on to the snow and sat for a few moments, easing the ache in her back. Taking a breath. Everything hurt now: her lungs, her back, her knee, her head. Exhaustion swamped her.

Surely it couldn't be too far? It wasn't dark yet, although the visibility was still very poor.

It would have been good to have someone with her right now. They could have laughed this whole episode off, then trudge-hopped down to the resort for après-ski. That would have taken her mind off the pain and the cold that seeped through her salopettes and under her skin.

If I ever get out of here alive, I'm going to make sure I have more fun.

She would keep on kissing Matthieu.

She would invite him in. Yes. She'd invite him in. Because to deny herself some pleasure of the Matthieu variety had been pretty darned stupid. He hadn't been asking for for ever, he'd just asked to walk her home. Instead of curling into her shell, instead of not taking a risk, she should have said, *hell, yes!*

The thought of kissing Matthieu gave her an incentive to carry on. She forced herself to stand up again and started walking when something caught her eye. A silver bird shimmered above her in a brief break in the clouds. She lifted her hand to shield her eyes. It wasn't a bird. Was it a bird?

Had she hit her head? Her back hurt with every step, but she was convinced it was just bruised. She knew she hadn't hit her head. She looked skywards again. The silver bird had disappeared.

She looked ahead of her and realised the path was no longer there. Panic wormed into her gut. She was lost and she was all alone.

Again.

CHAPTER TEN

'SHE'S ABOUT FIFTY metres off Heaven's Gate. Just past the copse, to the left. Looks like she's lost her skis.' Cody expertly landed the drone and looked over at Matt, grimacing. 'She doesn't look in great shape.'

'Let's go get her,' Matt snapped at his colleague and tried to control the emotions swirling inside him. 'Come on, man. Hurry up.'

'On it.' Cody jumped on to the back of the evac snowmobile as Matt gunned the engine, then they sped off up the mountain towards the Heaven's Gate track.

The returning cloud cover had hit fifteen-hundred metres and as they climbed to the higher altitude it was like riding through soup. What the hell had she been doing skiing out here in this weather? They'd closed the ski fields an hour ago because the conditions were so dangerous. His gut clenched as he fought back rising concern. What if something bad had happened to her? What was he going to find up there on the mountain?

God, no. Please.

He slammed thoughts of that day two years ago. Whatever he found, he'd deal with it. And deal with the fallout later.

Weird thing was, he'd done countless evacs like this

and not once had he had this tight panic in his gut. Memories of last night's kiss added heat to it.

Yes. He was a mess.

He peered through the falling flakes. Everything was whited out. 'Can you see anything?' he called to Cody.

'Literally nothing. Visibility's probably five metres, if we're lucky.'

They rode along the track to the end. Nothing. Not even footprints. Everything was covered in fresh snow.

'Damn it.' Matt hit the handlebar with his palm. 'Let's circle round and try again.'

They did another loop and his heart dimmed like the fading daylight. She wasn't here. 'One more go-round? Then we'll widen the search.'

'Wait. There. There!' Cody nudged him and pointed to their right. 'Is that her? Can you see something pink?'

Matt willed his eyes to focus. Was there something?

A movement caught his eye. He steered closer. Something…? Her ski jacket?

'Rachel? Rachel!' he shouted into the blinding whiteness.

They sat in silence, craning their necks to listen. Nothing.

'Rachel?'

Nothing.

And then…

'Matthieu?' Faint. 'Matthieu?'

All the air whooshed out of his lungs and his body relaxed. She was talking—that had to be a good sign. 'Hold on! We're coming to get you.'

He jumped off the snowmobile and ran towards a bundle on the ground.

Please be okay. Please be okay.

Memories of another day, another woman swamped him. That time he hadn't been so lucky.

She was slumped over, cheeks pink with cold, lips a funny shade of grey. 'Rachel. Rachel.'

'Matthieu?' She started to sit up, but slumped back down again. 'Oh.'

The panic had hitched a ride with all the air from Matt's lungs, replaced by relief and an overwhelming feeling of…what, he wasn't sure. All he knew was that he was beyond glad to have found her. He managed to control himself enough not to wrap her in his arms in front of Cody. Instead, he crouched down to assess her. She looked frozen through, but was conscious, so that was something. 'Hey there. What's happened?'

Her forehead scrunched into a frown, but there was a brittle, false brightness in her voice. 'I was…exploring.'

'And how was that going for you?' He gestured to their environs. 'Making your own path down, instead of following a perfectly decent one just a few metres over there?'

'Ah, that's where it is.' She blinked and smiled weakly. 'I like making my own path, right? You know that.'

So, they were going to play the *pretend everything's okay* game. Frustration swelled in his chest, tingeing the initial relief that they'd found her alive. He wanted to shake her and kiss her at the same time. Then he remembered she'd insisted on having space. He edged away a little, not wanting to overwhelm her. 'Where are your skis?'

'One went over the mountainside when I took a bit of a tumble and I'm sensible enough not to go down a sheer cliff to retrieve it. I couldn't manage to ski without it and I couldn't carry the other one. So, I'm walking. I was walking, but…' She stretched her leg out and grimaced. She'd taken her boot off for some reason.

'What's happened to your leg?'

'Oh, it's probably nothing.' Although she wasn't able to hide the wince. 'I just bent it a bit in the tumble. It'll be fine. I've just been putting ice on it while I rested for a minute.'

'You must be totally freezing, then.'

'It is a bit chilly. Thank goodness for ski wear.' She was at least able to answer him coherently. But the risk of hypothermia was increasing the longer they stayed up here. She hugged her jacket close to her. 'Um… Can I hitch a ride down?'

'Rachel, we came to get you,' he explained, as gently as he could. 'I think you might have some hypothermia.' Confusion was a symptom.

Although, really, he was the mixed-up person here. Relieved and frustrated and just plain glad to see her. He fought the desire to stroke her cheek, knowing she wouldn't want such a display in front of one of their work colleagues. Knowing it was better for both of them if they stuck to last night's agreement. 'We thought you might be lost. We closed the ski field ages ago because the conditions quickly deteriorated and it was too dangerous to be up the mountain. Didn't you hear the siren?'

'I was singing.' As if that was the most natural thing to do in a snowstorm.

'Of course you were.' He imagined her bobbing her head and singing out of tune like the other day and smiled. 'We put up a drone and saw you wandering up here.'

'A drone? Oh. Yes. Of course. The bird.' For a moment she pressed her lips together and he could have sworn he saw tears swim in her eyes, but if they were, she soon blinked them away. 'Were you looking for me? You didn't have to, I'm fine.'

'So why are you sitting down in the snow in the middle of nowhere?'

'I heard you calling so I stopped walking. If you're waiting…or hoping, for someone to find you, the most important thing is to stay where you are. I heard the engine and then your voices and stayed put.'

'Good. But what about your locator beacon? Why didn't you use it?'

'I was just about to.' She shrugged and shivered. 'But then you appeared, as if I'd conjured you up.'

Now it was his turn to press his lips together, although it was more a case of trying not to curse at her. Setting off the beacon would have brought them to her earlier. But he knew hypothermia slowed thought processes, too. He wrapped her in a thermal blanket. 'Let's get you on to the snowmobile.'

'Yes, please.' She went to stand, but grimaced and closed her eyes. Her hand went to her back and she rubbed. He watched as she literally smoothed her expression from one of pain to one of light-heartedness. 'Just give me a moment.'

'Wait.' He leaned over her, halting her movements. 'Have you hurt your back, too? What's happened?'

'Just a little bump. It's stiffened up since I stopped moving.'

'What about now?' He ran his fingers down her spine, checked her limbs. Checked her neck.

But she shook away from him. 'I've just been walking up the mountain, Matthieu. Neither my back or neck are broken, I promise. I can—'

'Cody…give me a hand.' He looped his arm under her armpit and Cody did the same on the other side and they helped her stand. She straightened, then bent, then finally straightened. Pain ran across her features.

He was surprised when she didn't refuse his help and took his outstretched arm to enable her to climb on to the snowmobile. Ice had formed on the strands of hair sticking out from her helmet. He lay her on the stretcher and tucked the silver emergency blanket round her. And then layered up another blanket and tightened the tarp cover over her. 'Warm enough?'

Her eyes had fluttered closed and she gave him a grateful smile. 'I will be now.'

'I promise the first thing I'll do back at base is make you my famous *chocolat chaud*.'

'Yes, please. That sounds perfect.' She didn't open her eyes, but this time her smile was full and genuine. She looked almost peaceful lying there, except for the wince of pain that drew little frown lines on her forehead. He imagined her asleep in his bed. Waking up to her. She was so beautiful. So frustratingly gorgeous.

And so out of reach.

Regardless, his heart gave a little stretch. 'You gave me a fright, Rachel.'

'I'm sorry for worrying you.' Opening her eyes, she put a hand to his face. 'Thank you for coming to get me.'

'Don't thank me until we've got you back to base.'

Why the hell had she been skiing on her own in these conditions?

But he knew her well enough that she would do what she wanted—she was her own woman and that was what he liked about her. But that independence also came with side-effects. He wasn't sure how to navigate that.

His mother had been all about emotion…dark, tragic, painful emotion that had leached out of her all the time. Tears. Angry outbursts. Highs. Lows.

Rachel was the opposite. She kept it all inside her. It would take a special kind of guy to tease her out of herself, to get her to share. He wondered if he could be that man. If he even wanted to be.

No.

Everything in him shied away from deep personal connections. But something about Rachel pierced his own emotional walls. He couldn't reconcile the concern, the raw panic he'd felt when they couldn't find her. Didn't want to care that much for someone again, only to lose them.

But he gently tucked the silver blanket around her some more. Then, without second-guessing himself, he leaned in and pressed a kiss to her forehead. 'You're safe now.'

'I am. I was… I have to admit… I was starting to panic a bit.' She blinked at him, giddiness swimming in her eyes. 'Thank God for drones. I love the ski patrol. I love hot chocolate. And I love you, Matthieu LeFevre.'

What? Matt's chest hurt. He did not know what to say to that. Because he knew she didn't mean it and, stupidly, foolishly, he wanted her to. Wondered what it would take for her to actually mean it, to feel it. Knowing also that she wouldn't let herself slide into that feeling, not after what she'd been through with her ex.

'Aww, get a room, you two.' Cody laughed.

'Oh, I love you, too, Cody.' She grinned. 'My knights in shining salopettes.'

'She's clearly hypothermic and doesn't know what she's saying.' Matt knew she was just plain grateful, but he couldn't shake the weird feeling in his chest that was at once weighty and light. And it scared the hell out of him. 'Crazy to be out here on her own. Isn't that right, Rachel?'

She smiled up at him, her eyes a little bit wild. 'I think I got lost.'

'You think…?' He didn't know whether to laugh or cry.

Then there was nothing left to say as they sped down to the medical centre.

Rachel wasn't sure which hurt most: the pain in her bones or the sting of embarrassment at being the patient and adding to the workload of her colleagues.

'Honestly, please don't fuss. I'm fine,' she told Suzanne as the nurse examined her knee.

'I'm not fussing, I'm assessing. Take these painkillers.' Suzanne handed Rachel a plastic pot of two white tablets and a glass of water, then looked at the bruising blooming across her knee. 'You need a scan of that injury.'

'I know.' Rachel's heart sank at the prospect of time off work. 'I'll sort it out tomorrow. Let's just put a brace on tonight and leave it at that.'

'If you're sure? I'll pop this on, then say goodnight.' Suzanne slipped a black brace over the swollen knee, secured it with Velcro, then waved goodbye.

'Okay. That feels better already.' Rachel hopped down from the gurney and wiggled her toes, half glad she was now alone with Matthieu and yet half anxious. Because, after their kiss last night, everything was muddied.

He'd been by her side the whole time, looking after her, cajoling and being kind, but she could feel tension radiating from him as he'd gradually emotionally retreated from her since they'd arrived at the medical centre.

She imbued her voice with a brightness she didn't feel. 'The support really helps.'

'I'll run you down to the resort on the snowmobile so you can get a proper shoe for the other foot.' Matthieu held her coat out for her to slide her arms in, but kept his distance at the same time. 'Then, I'll drive you to Bourg

St Maurice hospital. I'll call ahead and let them know we're on our way.'

'Honestly, not tonight. I just want to get warm and dry and have a rest. The scan can wait until tomorrow.' The pain was so intense she just wanted to lie down and she didn't want to take up any more of Matthieu's time. 'It won't affect the management plan to wait until the morning.'

He frowned. 'Surely the sooner you get it fixed the better?'

'Tomorrow will be fine. I'll just go soak in my spa bath.'

'On your own?'

'Matthieu?' That was unexpected. Her eyes darted from him to Suzanne's disappearing form. Had she heard? Was he really suggesting…?

He saw her reaction and then his eyes misted. 'I mean, you shouldn't be on your own.'

'I'll be okay. The painkillers should kick in soon.' But thoughts of her and Matthieu relaxing in the spa bath had taken centre-stage in her brain. Her knight in lashings of bubble bath, although a happier Matthieu than this withdrawn one in front of her.

He huffed out a breath. For some reason his emotional distance was sliding into frustration. 'Rachel, you're obviously in a lot of pain. I can't allow you to be on your own when you're like this. What if you have an emergency during the night? Internal bleeding?' He stared at her. 'Would you allow someone to be on their own… like this?' He gesticulated to her knee and then her back.

'There's no internal bleeding. I'm quite sure of that.'

'You have X-ray eyes?'

'No. But—' She started to hop, but a searing pain in

her back made her stop. Take a breath. Grip the side of the gurney.

'You expect to be able to do everything for yourself when you can't even walk a few steps?'

'I'll manage. I'm strong.' She could do this on her own. She'd managed well enough on her own for most of her life. She didn't need help.

He opened the door and she hopped through it, biting her lip against the pain. 'Go on, then.'

'Okay.' If he didn't believe in her, then she would show him she could do this.

She took a deep breath and put her weight on her foot. Then stopped. Used her good leg to lead instead. But she didn't get further than the doorway before she had to stop. She leaned against the doorjamb, looking at the distance that stretched between her and the chairlift. This morning she could have done it in a few strides without even thinking, now it was an interminable distance.

It wasn't just her knee and her back, it felt as if everything hurt and as if someone had siphoned every ounce of energy from her body. She'd spent everything she had climbing back up that hill. Basically, she was exhausted. Done.

And from a medical perspective she shouldn't really use her bad leg, so perhaps an evening with help would allow her to rest and start to heal. She looked up to see him watching her with a stony expression, and barely had the energy to form words. 'Okay, you have a point, I may need some help for tonight. But where do you expect me to go?'

'Well done. I know it would have cost you a lot to say that.' He pressed his lips together as he thought. 'I'll call Suzanne. You could stay at hers.'

He tapped his phone, spoke, then clicked off and shook his head. 'She's unavailable tonight. I'll call Zoe.'

He clearly didn't want to offer his place and she couldn't blame him after the weirdness that followed the kiss. And she sure as hell wasn't going to suggest it and risk his rejection.

So much for all those promises she'd made to herself on the mountain. *She would let him in. She'd do more kissing. Great.* She hadn't accounted for *him* not wanting more kissing.

And yet, why hadn't it? It wasn't as if she had a slew of men wanting her.

But there'd been a connection between them.

He shook his head again and finished the call. 'She's busy, too. There's nothing for it. You'll have to stay with me.' He didn't look happy about the prospect.

'I'm sure I'll be okay in my own place—'

'Rachel. No.' He raised his hand the way she'd done to quieten Bianca. It worked. She closed her mouth. 'I'll send Fred over to get some of your things. My place is bigger; I have three bedrooms, unlike your one-bedroomed chalet. We'll be able to give each other the space we need.'

Space? Judging by the way he was looking at her, she'd clearly upset him. How could she fix it? Her parents would have shouted at each other. David would have slunk away and sulked…as would she in days past.

But Matthieu? He pushed her to open up. Showing her there could be another way. Making her want to find that way.

Inviting someone in meant you accepted them, warts and all. It also meant talking instead of arguing. Understanding instead of jumping to conclusions.

He slid an arm under her shoulders to steady her as she hopped and she said, 'Matthieu, are you angry with me?'

He breathed out. 'To be honest, Rachel, I don't know.'

'Okay.' An ache swirled into her chest. 'Is it because I won't get the scan tonight? Because I fell? Because I went skiing on my own? Or am I missing something?'

'Because…' He stopped walking and stared at her, as if trying to weigh up what to say. Eventually, he shook his head in what looked like defeat and exasperation. 'Because you got hurt.'

'You're cross because I fell over? That doesn't make sense, Matthieu.'

'Probably not.' He turned away from her. 'I'm dealing with it.'

She put her hand on his shoulder and turned him to face her. Not knowing if doing something so intimate was the right way to go but doing it anyway. God, they'd kissed yesterday and now they couldn't speak to each other properly. 'Matthieu, please. Talk to me. What's going on?'

Talk to me? A phrase she'd had thrown at her enough in the past because she *never* talked about things. And yet here she was, pushing him for more.

He grimaced as if this conversation was costing him. 'I'm trying to stay calm, Rachel. You're in pain, you don't need me unloading on you as well.'

'I think I'd prefer it if you got it out of your system so we can move on. Tell me what the issue is. I hate tension.'

He looked away, then back at her, and shrugged wearily. 'The weather turned bad, but you didn't come back to base. You didn't use your locator beacon. You won't get a scan today. You don't want to stay with someone overnight for your own safety…'

She wasn't sure who was the most rattled. Him, because he clearly cared and didn't want to. Or her, because the emotion in his eyes connected deeply with something inside her. 'Hey, I told someone where I was going and what time to expect me back. I'm strong and fit and a damned good skier, as you know. If I'd really been in trouble, I'd have set off the locator beacon—'

'You weren't in trouble?' His voice rose and his eyes blazed. 'Out there, on your own, in a blizzard. Lost and in pain? What do you call a real emergency, Rachel? *Death?* Are you so independent that you're too proud to ask for help?' He shook his head. '*I'm* responsible for things that happen around here.'

'You're not responsible for me. No one is but me.' She glared back. But he cared enough to worry about her. That thought flooded her with warmth. 'I didn't think I needed rescuing. Please don't try to rescue me, Matthieu. I can look after myself.' That was it, she realised. He couldn't help but rescue people…after all those years with his mum when he hadn't been able to save her. Whether he realised it or not, he was still trying to save those he cared about.

He bristled, shoulders bunching. 'Why won't you let people help you?'

'I will absolutely admit if I'm in the wrong and am more than happy to accept responsibility for things I say and do. I was coming round to the fact that I was getting out of my depth and I, honestly, was about to set off the beacon just before you arrived.'

'But you didn't.' He threw his hands in the air.

'Because you arrived. Look, I'm independent, but I'm not stupid. I know what's within my capabilities and what isn't.' Then a thought struck her. She'd been so happy to be finally warm, and safe and looking forward to hot chocolate, that she'd said the first thing that had come into her head. Which was unusual for her, she was usually very careful about her word choices. But she'd said it. It was out there now. Even if she didn't feel it, it was a big, stupid, thing to say. 'Are you also angry because I said…um…that I love you?'

'Not at all.' His eyes widened and his throat worked. He looked totally blindsided. The playboy ensnared. He was a rescuer, but he didn't want to be shackled. 'It was obvious you were just grateful to us.'

'Exactly. I didn't mean…you know…that I *love* you, love you.'

'I know…' He breathed out, looking a lot brighter, a glimmer of a smile played on his lips. 'Cody's going to be heartbroken.'

'I somehow doubt that. And you promised me hot chocolate. Which, I might add—' she wanted so much to get back on a happier footing with him '—you still haven't produced.'

'Ah. Yes.' He relaxed just a little more. 'Medical treatment beats hot drinks every time. Give me ten minutes and you'll have one in your hand.' He helped her on to the back of the snowmobile, taking care to position her sore leg properly. 'You might want to hold on. Well, you might not want to, but you probably should.'

And there it was—neither of them knew where they stood or what the other person was really thinking and wanting. The accumulation of uncertainty, fear and total exhaustion was causing a major communication breakdown.

He climbed up in front of her and she snaked her arms round his waist, feeling the stretch and glide of his muscles as he steered down to the chalets. Remembering that the last time she'd had her arms around him, he'd been kissing her senseless.

Just how was she going to get back to that?

CHAPTER ELEVEN

HIS LODGE WAS annexed at the side of the hotel complex. A huge three-bedroomed space with high wooden ceilings and whitewashed walls. Matthieu helped her along the corridor to a large open-plan lounge and sat her on a window seat in front of a window that looked out on to the resort and beyond. The clouds had cleared and the sun was setting, staining the sky with glorious soft peach and apricot hues.

She breathed in the view and smiled, trying to break the tension, digging deep inside her to make a first move to make things better between them. 'This weather is crazy. One minute you can't see anything, the next we have this.'

'It keeps us on our toes.' He turned to go, but she caught his fingers and he swivelled back to her, frowning. 'What is it, Rachel?'

Here goes nothing.

She squeezed his hand. 'Look, Matthieu. I'm sorry for today. Thank you for bringing me here and looking after me.'

'It's okay.' An eyebrow rose. 'It's my job.'

'It's above and beyond your job. So, again, thank you.'

'Not a problem.' But he hadn't let go of her hand and that gave her some hope.

Should she? Could she? She'd believed she could up there in the cold—it had been the only thing keeping her going. She couldn't stall now and let herself down. 'I was thinking, up on the mountain…'

His eyes narrowed. 'Sounds serious.'

'Actually, no. Not serious at all. I don't want to do anything serious ever again—not in my personal life anyway. I gave two years of my life to David only to learn that I'm not good at being part of a couple.' She took a breath. 'But I do want to have more fun and I think… what I hear about you and what I know about you…is that you like fun, too…'

'Louis been shooting his mouth off again?' His eyes glittered. But he was intrigued, she could see.

'It's common knowledge that you're…' She smiled. Knowing Matthieu wasn't wanting to commit to anyone made her feel a whole lot better about this. 'Let's just say, you're not ready to settle down yet.'

'No.' His eyes narrowed and he looked confused.

She could almost see his thought processes trying to join the dots. 'So, can we please forget today and rewind?'

'That depends.' His twinkling eyes narrowed. 'To when?'

'Back…on the sled. We were laughing then. And…' She held his gaze, feeling the most vulnerable and yet most alive she'd ever felt. 'Against the tree.'

His eyebrows shot up and his lips twitched. 'You want to kiss me again, Rachel?'

She was known for being forthright so here it was. Here *she* was. Asking for something she wanted. 'Yes. Yes, Matthieu, I'd like that very much.'

He sat on the edge of the banquette and took her hand,

mock shock in his eyes. 'What? Even though you don't *love* me, love me?'

He smiled. No, grinned. A beautiful grin that lit up his whole face.

A mirroring smile glowed deep inside her and she almost forgot her pain. 'Even though I don't love you, Matthieu. I am more than happy to kiss you. Lots. If you want the same.'

'What about your space?'

'There was enough space on that mountain to last me a long time.' She flashed what she hoped was a rueful smile. 'Can we start over? I hate this tension between us.'

'Me, too.' He looked down and stroked her hand for a moment, then looked back up at her. 'I'll go make that hot chocolate I promised you.'

Her heart clutched and she started to panic. He hadn't actually agreed to anything more. Had she just made a huge fool of herself? 'Are you escaping?'

He shook his head. 'Thinking.'

'You have to think about it?' Embarrassment spread through her. 'That is not a good sign.'

'Trust me, making you my famous hot chocolate is the biggest compliment you can get.' He leaned close and whispered, 'I don't need to think about it, Rachel. I was just planning where to start.'

Need rippled through her, pooling low and deep in her belly. 'And that is…?'

'You're still in pain and you've had quite an ordeal. Comfort first.' He brushed his fingers over her forehead, tucking some stray strands behind her ear, so gentle it made her heart squeeze and her stomach tighten with heat. Then he pressed his lips to her cheek.

'Wait.' She turned so her mouth was inches from

his. 'Matthieu, I know exactly what's going to make me feel better.'

Then she reached her palm behind his head and drew him closer to take his mouth for one of those kisses they'd been talking about for too long.

She felt his smile against her lips and the deep rumble of his laugh vibrating through her as he cupped her face and kissed her. Finally. Perfectly.

This kiss was gentle and exploring, his caress tender and caring, like a magic balm of heat and pleasure, stroking and stroking. She didn't know if it was the painkillers kicking in, or just the delicious pleasure of tasting Matthieu again, but all her aches seem to dissolve and she felt light and dizzy. Her skin prickled with shivers of excitement and her gut contracted with longing. She wound her arms round his neck, pressing her breasts against his chest, wanting his languid heat to reach every part of her.

Was this crazy? To want a man so much? To crave someone's touch? To dream about him? To let thoughts of him steer her off her path and down a mountain? Was she going crazy?

If so, she welcomed every wild thought running through her head right now: kissing, undressing, making love. Everything she'd been through today was worth this and every nerve ending tingled as she slid her hands over his shoulders, exploring hard muscles that held her in place, that she clung to.

But eventually he pulled away, tracing kisses along her collarbone like promises. 'It's been a hell of a day. You must be exhausted, Rachel.'

'I'll never be too tired for kissing.' She rested her head on his shoulder, her limbs liquid and her head a whirl of possibilities and wishes. She felt weirdly wired and yet sublimely relaxed. 'But I am...yes, actually shattered.'

'Not too tired for hot chocolate?' He kissed her again, lightly on the lips.

'After kissing, that's number two on my wish list right now.'

'*Mon plaisir.*' He dipped a kiss on her nose, then disappeared into the kitchen.

It was actually *her* pleasure. How was it that he could make her feel so breathy and light? So warm and yet excited with just a kiss?

How had she never felt like this kissing anyone else?

While he pottered in the kitchen, she took a moment to scan the room. She'd been expecting a typical man cave, all minimal monochrome, but this room was decorated in the same style as the rest of the hotel and chalets, in sumptuous warm shades and with luxurious fabrics. Mementoes from travels dotted shelves: exquisite hand-carved boxes and top-end Russian stacking dolls.

The walls held huge black and white photographs of cities—New York, Hong Kong, Singapore, Tokyo taken from arty angles—and had a signature at the bottom that she recognised as Matthieu's name. So, he was a man with an eye for the artistic as well as a businessman and all-round sporty outdoor guy.

'Is there no end to your talents?' she asked, pointing to the New York photo, as he brought through a tray with a silver jug that was like a teapot but taller, two steaming white porcelain mugs of delicious-smelling hot chocolate and a plate of bread and cheese. Her stomach growled, but his enigmatic smile made her hungry for something altogether different.

'The photos? I was just indulging my famous ego by blowing them up so big.' He handed her a mug and some food, then settled opposite her on the window seat, leaning back against the wall as he cut off a wedge of cheese and ate. 'You like them?'

'They're fabulous. Do you miss your old life?'

'Not at all. Although, I do miss the free travel. That was definitely a perk. Have you travelled much?'

'Oh… I guess so. I went away every school holiday. America, Thailand, Croatia, Greece… Lots.'

He tilted his head and smiled. 'Very lucky.'

'Kind of.' She silently mused over her difficult childhood and then remembered that she'd promised herself she'd be more open. She had to try to let him in and that meant letting something of herself out into the world. 'I suppose that sounds ungrateful, but after the divorce my parents played this sort of one-upmanship game— although neither admitted they did it.'

'What kind of game?'

'Who could take Rachel on the best holidays, hence the numerous ski vacations, too. Who could buy me the best presents. Basically, who was the best parent. But then they'd spend all holiday complaining about what the other parent had done or not done or said… In the end I used to beg to go to the kids' club each day just to get away from it all.' She laughed, although it wasn't funny. It never had been. She'd just wanted to stop being the thing they argued over, in front of, and about.

Matthieu's smile disappeared. 'For a few moments there I was jealous, but that sounds terrible.'

'It was. Not all kids' clubs are made equal. But I generally made some friends and hung out with children my own age, and if it was one of the awful clubs, I'd bury myself in a book. I did a lot of reading back then. The librarian at my local library said she'd never known anyone read so many books.' She dug deep for a smile. 'My parents did the same with birthday and Christmas presents, too: who spent the most, who bought the best present. Funny thing was, neither of them ever bought what I actually wanted.'

He sat forward, interested. 'Which was?'

'Ballet lessons. One of the series I loved reading the most was about a ballet boarding school. Oh, I dreamt about that place. Begged both parents to let me have lessons but, because I spent a week with Mum and a week with Dad, they couldn't agree on where I should go to dance school. Too close to Dad's and Mum would freak about how difficult it all was, too close to Mum's and Dad would complain about the traffic. It was just another thing for them to argue about. All well and good to be seen to give me the best, but another thing to actually give what I asked for. In the end I gave up asking. It was probably for the best. I mean, look at me.' She raised her braced knee. 'I'm a klutz. Do I look like I'd make a good ballerina?'

'Not unless it was a ballet about a hospital emergency department, *chérie*.' He laughed as he slid his hand over her leg as if it was the most natural thing in the world to do. It felt comfortable. Intimate. 'But it can't have been easy growing up in an environment like that. I can see why you'd withdraw into yourself if people were arguing around you.'

'They never stopped. They had a very volatile relationship…they loved hard and argued hard. I learnt to keep my own counsel from a very young age. I learnt how to entertain myself, to keep out of the way. I also learnt not to ask for anything, because I knew from experience that I wouldn't get it.'

'And you grew to depend only on yourself. I see that.'

'Apparently, it can be problematic.' She huffed out a breath, thinking suddenly of David, wishing she hadn't.

But the more she thought about her failed relationship, the more she realised David hadn't been the only villain in the piece. She'd never told him the things she'd just told Matthieu…silly hopes and dreams. Never really opened her heart to him. Matthieu made it easy to talk about things. He didn't judge. He empathised. He made her feel…safe.

'Oh, I don't know. You made your needs very clear just now.' Grinning, Matthieu leaned forward and put his lips to hers. 'You don't ever need to ask for kisses again. Just take them, Rachel. Whenever you want.'

She palmed his cheeks and stole another kiss. 'I'm going to hold you to that.'

'Good.' He gently lifted her sore leg and rested it on a cushion on his thigh. 'You need to keep it elevated.'

'Thank you, *Dr* LeFevre.' She laughed as he tickled her toes. Then she sipped the hot chocolate he'd laced with marshmallows and possibly some kind of liqueur. It was like no other hot chocolate she'd ever experienced. Along with the rich chocolatey taste there was a pop of something citrusy and something else…a deep, lush undertone that made her think of ice-cream, which was ridiculous because this was warm and lined her throat like velvet. She took another sip. Then another. 'This is incredible. I feel five hundred per cent better already.'

'I know. It makes everything better.'

'What's in it? I've got to make this at home.'

'I can't tell you.' He shook his head dramatically, grinning and tapping the side of his nose. 'Secret recipe.'

'There's something alcoholic in here, isn't there?'

'With you on painkillers? No way.' He frowned, but laughed, too. 'You're safe to drink it.'

'Secret recipe? Come on, Matthieu.' She nudged him

with her foot. 'You have to tell me. I want to recreate this myself. It's like nectar from the gods. Heaven in a cup.'

'It's out of my hands.' He shrugged, palms upwards. 'Handed down from my mother and her mother before her. I'm sworn to secrecy.'

'It's divine. Really.' She drained her cup, hoping for a refill. Then realised he was looking over at a photograph in a silver frame on the coffee table. A young woman with a small boy on her knee. The boy was definitely Matthieu aged about four years old…an impish face and mischievous grin. The woman was looking directly into the camera and laughing. Carefree. She had the same large dark eyes as her son, the same-shaped mouth. 'She's beautiful. Your mother?'

'Yes.' He blinked and smiled softly. She liked that he loved his mum and felt a pang of envy. They'd clearly been close. She'd always wanted that kind of relationship with her parents and it still hurt that she couldn't have it.

'You miss her?'

'Of course.' But there was something else in his eyes.

'Matthieu…' With her heart in her throat, she touched his arm. 'You said she'd been sick. Was it cancer?'

He shook his head. 'She wasn't well her whole life, Rachel. One way or another. The kind of sickness that is unpredictable. Hard to have, hard to live with. She had bipolar disorder and depression. We had manic ups and very bad lows.'

We. He took it on board as his own issue to deal with too. 'Did she…?'

She didn't want to say the words in case she was jumping to conclusions or to hurt him too much by bringing up memories.

'Take her own life? Yes.' His eyes had darkened, his

face hollowed out. He looked desperately sad and she found herself feeling the same. 'This time, I was too late.'

'You found her?' *This time.* Which meant there'd been other times, too. Her hand went to her chest—how utterly unbearable.

'Yes. I'd only left her for a few hours to come up here and sort some things out. She'd waved me off and told me she was fine. She hadn't been great, you know? But I'd left her before, many times…' His throat worked and he looked desolate. 'She'd taken pills, a bottle of cognac. There was nothing I could do.'

'God, Matthieu, that's awful. No wonder you're so protective.' This explained why he felt responsible for everyone, needed to keep them safe…even though he tried to keep away, he couldn't help himself. She was beginning to understand.

He rubbed his jaw. 'I should have stopped her. I should have known.'

'You can't believe that any of it was your fault.'

'I should have known things weren't going well. I learnt early on to read her micro expressions.' He shook his head. 'So I could tell what mood she was in. What kind of a day it was going to be. Whether she needed help or not. She'd be fine for a while—months at a time—take her tablets and everything would be happy. But then she'd stop taking the meds because she felt okay and said she didn't need them. Trust me, she was not okay.'

'I can't imagine how that was for you.'

'As a five-year-old you want routine. As an eight-year-old you want her to get help. As a teenager you don't want anyone to see or know about it—cruel, I know, but it was how I felt. Christmases were unpredictable. One year I'd be overwhelmed by expensive gifts she couldn't afford.

Another year she'd be so debilitated we wouldn't have presents or even food.'

He hauled in a breath.

'But we got by. I helped… I hope I helped. As I moved into my early twenties she was doing well. She had a boyfriend, he was kind and he helped her with her meds. Things were straightened out for a year. Two. Three. When I got the job offer in Paris I turned it down at first, but she heard about it from Louis's parents and insisted I take it. A job of a lifetime, she'd said.'

'She was right.'

'Yes. I had friends here who kept an eye on her and, of course, I spoke to her every day and came back most weekends and holidays. But she'd get angry with me for coming home all the time. Told me I didn't trust her. And she'd been okay, you know? Taking her tablets regularly, looking after herself. So, I started to travel a bit more. Relax.'

He looked down at his hands. 'Then the relationship with Gilbert ended and she started to decline. She stopped talking to me, refused to see anyone, so I came home. She was in a bad state, but I managed to get her some medical help and she was okay. For the year I was with her she was okay. Then one day she wasn't.' He paused, grief sliding into every hollow in his face. 'I hadn't seen the signs, I didn't know.'

'Sometimes there aren't any signs, Matthieu.'

'I should have known.' Guilt bit at his features. 'I was always alert around her. I found her twice already, hell… I should have seen it coming.'

'It wasn't your fault. You have to know that.'

He shrugged as if he heard her, but didn't agree. 'Now I'm on my own. I have no one to be responsible for, no one to worry about. And thank God for that.'

'And that's why you couldn't commit to a relationship, isn't it? Because you had to always think about your mum, about coming home.'

'No… It's because I didn't have space for anyone else. I didn't want…*don't* want to carry that responsibility for someone else ever again.' He stared out of the window for a few beats, then turned to her with a wry smile. 'Good job we're just about the fun, right?'

She laughed and stroked his arm. 'Maybe…the better you get to know someone, the more fun you can have.'

She couldn't believe she was saying this…feeling this. Because she'd been trying hard not to let anyone know her at all. But with Matthieu that was getting harder and harder every moment she spent with him. There was something about him that made it impossible not to talk, to share, to open up. His gentle questions, his interest and genuine concern. And she felt the more they shared the better it would get.

Wow. Maybe this was Rachel Tait finally learning how to get close to someone. Talking. Sharing. Being honest and admitting how she felt about things instead of bottling them up. It was liberating and wonderful and yet wildly exposing.

But safe. Always safe, even in her most vulnerable moments. She knew Matthieu treasured her…it was evident in the way he looked at her, his touch. That he accepted her, faults and all.

'I'm sure we can have lots of fun getting to know each other. Especially physically…' Matthieu laughed as he kissed her again, but then grimaced. 'I'm sorry. You didn't need to hear all that. It's not something I generally speak about…although, of course, it's no secret. Everyone in the village knew her and knew our story. They collectively kept an eye on me growing up…so Louis tells me. Because she couldn't always do that. Sometimes, like the difficult Christmases, they'd drop off food and small gifts. When I think back, there were other gestures, too—tickets to a football game, toys they were "throwing out" and did I want them?'

'They love you, that's obvious.'

He blinked. 'I owe them a lot.'

'Hence the resort and the jobs for locals.'

'That's part of my motivation, yes. Funny thing is, I tried to hide it all. Thought I'd covered it all up, but her problems were well known. Nothing's private here. Not even pain.'

'It's a pain shared, though. That's got to help, even just a little bit, to know that someone else—a whole village— cares about you?' Even though he'd had a deeply personal loss he'd had a community round him. God, if only she'd had that and had someone else help carry her load.

But then, looking back, she'd collapsed in on herself and not reached out. Maybe she should take a leaf out of Matthieu's book and try to do that more?

And risk rejection? Like David? Like her father? Her mother?

And yet, find the right people, dare to share and you have a home. A place where you belong.

Where did she belong?

Nowhere.

Matthieu stroked her hand. 'That's enough about me.'

'Thank you for telling me.' It was all so sad and yet the simple act of talking and listening had brought them closer. They'd both suffered trauma, but had dealt with it differently. She was amazed at his strength and his capacity to give so much. There was no doubt he had adored his mother.

There was also no doubt as to why he didn't commit

to anyone else. He needed to be free from having to think about someone else. Who could blame him?

He was a good man. Quite possibly the nicest man she'd ever met. He genuinely cared about people, about making them comfortable and relaxed. He was kind... he'd taken her on the sled just to make her smile. He took time to help people. And yet he'd been through so much sadness it made her heart hurt for him.

For a few moments they sat in peaceful silence, hugging their mugs to their chests and admiring the view. She didn't feel a need to fill the space.

Eventually, he turned to her and stroked his fingers on her cheek. 'Hey. You look beat. Early night?'

He clearly wasn't about to make a move and that was okay. She didn't think it was the right time for anything even more intense, so she decided to leave him with his memories and thoughts. She hefted her sore leg to the floor and stood up, gripping the banquette cushion for balance. 'Yes, but first I'm going for a bath. Wish me luck.'

'Hey...' He caught her hand. 'You okay?'

She cupped his face. 'I'm fine, Matthieu.'

'Fine?' His eyes narrowed in a warning and she laughed, knowing exactly what he meant.

'By which I mean, thank you, you've been amazing. My stomach is full, my heart is full. But my leg and back are painful. I think a long soak would be a very good thing.'

'Of course. Take this with you.' He poured more chocolate from the silver jug into her mug and gave it to her. 'If you need any more, just shout.'

She hugged the cup close to her chest. 'A girl could get used to this kind of treatment.'

'Hey, please don't go throwing yourself at trees just to get the chance for hot chocolate in the bath. Just ask next time, okay?' Then he stood and wrapped her in his arms and held her. Just held her there and she held on, too.

A girl could get used *to this*, she thought.

But it probably wasn't the best idea she'd had.

CHAPTER TWELVE

WELL, HE'D PROBABLY blown it.

They were supposed to be having fun and no doubt he'd scared her off with his tales.

But, despite what she thought, she wasn't closed off, she was quiet, thoughtful. Reluctant to share, but when she did, she had so much to contribute.

And was sexy as hell. And wanted no strings.

She was perfect.

He cleared up the tray, finished getting the guest room ready, then flicked through his music app for something she might like… He smiled, probably not the time for bellowing God-awful songs from the eighties—

'Aaargh!'

A crash. In the bathroom. Something breaking. A splash.

His heartrate tripled as he ran to the closed bathroom door. What was he going to find? Images flashed through his head…images he wanted to forget but were branded on to his brain. 'Rachel! Rachel! Are you okay?'

'Don't come in!' She sounded anxious, but also as though she was laughing, too.

Was she hysterical? 'Rachel! What's happened?'

'Just don't. I'm…it's okay. I'm just—ow!' She cursed. There was more squeaking and splashing and more groans and he couldn't bear to wait any longer. He pushed the door open a crack. 'Can I—?'

A pause. Then… 'Okay. But don't look.'

He shoved the door wide and stopped, trying not to look, but catching a glimpse. Adrenalin slowing, then ramping. 'What the hell? Rachel?'

'Don't look!' She was immersed in the water, completely covered by bubbles, her hair plastered to her head in wet tendrils, bubbles caught on her head and shoulders, on her eyelids and chin. The spa jets were firing at full speed, creating even more bubbles that were scooting over the edge of the tub and on to the floor. 'I slipped getting in, trying to protect my knee. And got a total dunking under the water and knocked the mug on to the floor with my good foot. I'm so sorry, Matthieu. I hope it wasn't a good one.'

'It wasn't.' He looked to where she was pointing, to a puddle of hot chocolate and broken porcelain, and raised his hand. 'Don't get out. You'll cut yourself.'

'Honestly, don't worry.' She bit her lip and then grimaced. 'I was going to clear it up when I got out. I was hoping you hadn't heard me, and I could get away with hiding the pieces underneath in the rubbish bin.'

'Hiding the evidence? I'd have caught you eventually.' She was smiling ruefully and he shook his head in mock frustration. 'And doing it with a bad foot? Hopping on a wet floor would be even more dangerous.'

He dashed to the kitchen for a dustpan and kitchen roll and started to clear the mess up, all the while acutely aware of her sinking under the water, washing her hair, sluicing the shampoo off. Doing something else splashy, which he assumed was washing.

Far more aware of her than he should have been.

She was naked. Wet. Covered in bubbles. She wanted to kiss him.

His whole body burned for her.

He couldn't remember a time when he'd wanted someone this much. Not kissing her before had almost killed him, but he'd wanted to give her time. Give himself time to think about her offer.

God, since when did he have to think about kissing someone who was offering it?

But this was Rachel, and he was drawn to her in a way he'd never been drawn to a woman before. He didn't know what to do with the feelings in his chest every time he looked at her. She'd had a rough life with her parents and her douchebag ex. She needed more than he could give. And she wanted to give so much too, he could see.

He saw it in her eyes. Saw everything in her eyes. The vulnerability she tried to hide. The pain of her past. The simmering need that turned her irises from soft grey to shimmering silver. And he felt an answering need deep inside himself. A burning, burnished golden desire, bright and hot, that flickered into life whenever she was around and a good amount of time when she wasn't as his thoughts strayed to her, over and over.

She was naked. Two feet away from him.

This was pure torture.

After a few minutes he heard, 'Matthieu—can you pass me a towel for my hair?'

'Sure.' Trying to stay calm, he grabbed a hand towel and, without looking at her, shoved it behind him.

'Um...' She laughed. 'Matthieu... I'm over here.'

'Where?' He turned to find her reclining at the opposite end of the bath and was paralysed by the sight of her bare skin, the regal neck, the smooth décolletage and soft swell of her breasts peeking out above the water. No more bubbles.

He handed her the towel and turned away. No way should he be looking at her like that. 'Right, I'm going. Call if you need more help.'

'Will do. Oh? Oh, God.'

'What is it?' He found himself turning back to her.

Her mouth formed a horrified 'O' as she covered her breasts with an arm before sliding further under the water. 'I thought...where have all the bubbles gone?'

'That happens...with shampoo and soap...it's the cationic and anionic charges...positive and negative... makes the bubbles collapse...' He'd looked away again, but couldn't shake the memory of that creamy skin, the dark nipples. Hot arrows of need shot through him. *God.* She was divine.

Not touching her was killing him.

'Ouch. This bath is so not comfortable with a bad back.' She sat up sharply and lent forward, her back to him.

And he was just about to leave, he really was, but his eyes fixed on her spine at her groan. His gut lurched at the sight. '*Dieu,* Rachel. Your back is a map of bruises.'

'Is it? It's pretty sore. Where? Can you check, please? Is it bad?' She reached her arm round to her back. 'Lower rib?' Can you point to where it's worse? See if that's where the pain's coming from.'

He swallowed back his desire—the woman needed his help—and gently grazed her bruised skin with his fingertip, trying not to hurt her. 'Here?'

She flinched. 'Ouch. Yes.'

He thought about pressing his lips to that very spot, or

any part of her—*all* of her—but clamped down on those thoughts, too. *'Je suis désolé.'*

'Don't be sorry. It wasn't your fault. Is it really bad? Where?'

'It's very bruised. I think I can see Italy there and… um… Australia.' At her bidding he ran his fingers down the pearls of her spine, chasing drips of water, tracing down to the small of her back and then up again, dipping carefully over black and blue smudges. 'Russia's kind of warped and I think Spain's melted into Morocco.'

'That can't be good.' She shivered, and her skin erupted in goosebumps, but she didn't move away. 'Whatever river your fingers are tracing is making me ticklish.'

'Rachel—' He swallowed again. This was probably completely inappropriate. But he was human and she was gorgeous. *But broken.* In too many ways. With some sense seeping back into his brain, he edged back from her. 'Sorry. Look, the guest room's down the hall on the left. I'll see you in the morning.'

'Matthieu…wait.' Her hand slid over his, catching his fingers the way she had earlier, a grip that was firm and yet soft. Warm skin, a flutter of fingertips, that had him imagining those hands on the rest of his body.

'Yes?' He met her eyes to study her expression. Was she going to ask him to join her? Tell him to get the hell out?

She pulled a face. 'I think I'm going to need help to get out. It's just… I can't take weight on my bad foot and I should probably have had a shower, but I do love bubbles and the spa jets are amazing.'

'Call me when you need me.'

The spa jets whirred off. 'Matthieu.' Her voice was cracked and sex-laden. There was a moment when it felt as if the atmosphere hung around them, imbued with frank desire.

'Yes?' His voice sounded rough and thick in the muggy, too-bright bathroom.

Her eyes snagged his and she looked at him, so flagrantly in need of kissing that it almost took his breath away. 'I need you.'

With those three words something inside him burst into flames. The air crackled around them so thick he could almost touch it.

'Sure thing.' Reining in his desire—at least, trying to—he grabbed a towel and held it up for her to step into, but of course, climbing out of a bath with one working foot was a lot harder than climbing in. She cursed and wobbled and gripped his arm and eventually, she was out, wrapped in a towel and squeaky clean.

She looked so beautiful, her cheeks all pink with the heat, her eyes glittering with water drops, and she must have seen whatever was in his eyes because she sighed on a secretive smile. 'About that map. If Russia was here…' she took his hand and guided it behind her to her ribs '… following a line of latitude…then Canada must be…' she slid his hand across her ribs to the curve of her breast '…about here?'

'I don't need a damned geography lesson,' he growled into her damp hair, struggling to control his overactive libido. Then, unable to stop himself, he pressed her against the wall and palmed her damp breast. 'I know exactly where I want to be.'

With a strangled moan Rachel lifted her mouth to his and kissed him, hard. She couldn't wait any longer. Wouldn't wait. *Take it*, he'd said. Now she was going to hold him to his word.

He tasted of the sultry hot chocolate and his own Matthieu tang of spice and heat. So intoxicating she wanted to drown in him. His fingertips down her spine, the way he looked at her, made her hungry for him. Desperate.

His tongue slid into her mouth, taking the kiss deeper and more frantic, and before she could stop or think she was peeling his sweater and T-shirt off in a rush of need and urgency.

She ran her hands over his back, down his chest, feeling the way his muscles moved as he pressed her against the wall. The toned biceps that held her there. The strong thigh muscles pressing against her legs. The hard swell against her thigh. Taking his mouth again, she wriggled closer so she could feel him press at her core.

She wanted his mouth on her, everywhere. His hands touching her everywhere. She wanted him deep inside her.

This need for him, shocking and bright and raw, made no sense and yet it made perfect sense. It was everything. He was everything.

But there was so much about him she still didn't know, so much she *did* know that she was attracted to. So much he'd endured, taken on as his burden just to help ease his mother's suffering. Then built the resort as a gift of gratitude to those who had helped him.

And as he'd trusted her with his story she'd wanted to cry with him, to ease his pain...wanted to stop him from walking into that room where his mother was, a full body block so she could have taken those shockwaves of grief for him. She'd burned with sadness and yet saw, *felt* the hidden light inside him that drove him to fight for those he loved.

And she'd wanted that light to burn for her, too. She still did.

Her towel slipped…or had she let it slip? She didn't know. But here she was, naked, in front of him. Enjoying, relishing, the way he looked at her with raw need and promise in his gaze.

Doing this was crazy…inviting rejection. She didn't open herself up like this, she closed herself off. Kept herself safe. But something about the way he was looking at her spurred her on. Made her feel special, sexy. Wanted. Safe. *That* was intoxicating.

He bent down and slid his hands under her knees and whipped her into his arms. She laughed. 'Whoa, caveman. I can walk.'

A deep rumble of laughter burst from his throat as he kicked her discarded brace out of the way. 'Actually, *chérie*, you can't.'

Then he strode…fast…into his bedroom.

She'd imagined this moment countless times over the last few days, imagined the way his bedroom would be, the way he'd look at her, the way she'd feel, but none of her imaginings had come close to the reality.

His room was lit by two nightlights that cast a dreamy sheen over the room. Her eyes fixed on his, her mouth on his, she didn't spare any glances at the decor. Didn't care. His sheets were cool and soft. The mattress giving just enough as he laid her down as if she were something precious.

Sliding his hands out from under her, he lay down next to her, his top half gloriously naked, smooth skin defining hard abs.

The look on his face as he traced his fingers between her breasts undid her completely. That was something she hadn't anticipated. Such hunger. Raw emotion. As if he was close to the edge and didn't know whether to cling on tight or let go and let himself fall. As if she was the only person in the world who would catch him.

Biting her lip, her breath coming in short gasps, she ran fingertips down his belly, over his jeans zipper where she cupped his erection. The light in his eyes ignited. He caught her fingers in his hand the way she did to him. 'Wait, Rachel...'

'No. Can't wait.' She tugged at him, pulled him down over her so she could feel the beautiful weight, the press, the heat, the length of him. 'Waited too long. The water almost went cold while you cleared up the mess. And I waited and waited for you.'

He grinned, sexy as hell. 'I didn't know if you wanted me to join you, or just act as your chambermaid.'

'I wanted you to join me about three hours ago. Yesterday. Last week.' She kissed his jaw, his cheek, his mouth, knowing she'd never have enough of his taste.

He laughed. 'We've got all night, *chérie*.'

'Then let's make every minute count, *chéri*.' She parroted his word, feeling his laughter rumble through her, and she couldn't help but laugh, too. This was insane and yet so completely right.

She stroked his erection again, slipping her hand into the space between denim and skin, felt the twitch of his body away and also toward her fingers, felt the shudder of his groan against her cheek. And his hand gripping hers, taking it from his jeans. 'No. Rachel. Wait.'

Ray Shell.

'If you could just say my name again and again that would make me happy for ever. I don't think I need anything else.'

'We'll see about that.' He grinned, then nuzzled against her throat. 'Rachel. *Rachel.*'

'*God,* Matthieu.' She giggled. Undone, unwrapped and unravelled. 'Yes. Anything. Yes. *Yes.*'

He kissed down to her breasts, sucking in first one nipple, then the second, making her arch against him, the sensation of teeth and wet against her tender skin making her dizzy with desire. Then his mouth went lower, a dazzling tease of nips and kisses to her belly, lower…to her thigh, her inner thigh.

He pushed her legs apart and kissed between her legs, sending jolts of heat spiralling through her. His tongue and his fingers explored her, slipping inside her, and all she knew was this moment, the sensuous pleasure of his hands, his mouth.

And then he slowed the pace, teasing her, making her think about begging. Rachel Tait didn't beg. Rachel Tait didn't ask for anything, she took it. She didn't call out. She didn't show her emotions. She didn't do needy. She didn't do desperate. She kept everything inside, in a tight knot. But Matthieu made her feel everything, want everything.

But he waited. Then he teased some more and she squirmed against his hand. Then he waited again, hot breath on her thigh, pleasure–pain rasp of his stubble on her skin, the pressure of his fingers against her most sensitive parts.

'Matthieu.' She half laughed, half sobbed his name, desperate now.

'What do you want? Say it.'

Her fingers tightened in his hair. 'Don't stop.'

But he'd already stopped and she was going out of her mind with need. Then he teased again. 'Tell me what you want, Rachel.'

Rachel Tait didn't beg.

Not until she screamed, '*Please.* Matthieu. *Please.* More.'

'*Mon plaisir*, Rachel.'

Nothing had ever felt this good. She felt him murmur her name against her skin once, twice, as he slid his fingers deep into her and then she was slipping, rising, flying, moaning, gripping his hair as he brought her to the edge, then took her over. And over. And over. Shattering her into pieces only he would be able to fit together again.

For a few moments she lay there, trying to breathe, to force air into a body that shook. She suddenly felt weirdly emotional and blinked back tears that had sprung from nowhere. 'What are you doing to me, Matthieu?' she asked him, again half laughing, half sobbing. All his.

'Hopefully something good?' He kissed his way back up her body, but when he saw her face his smile dropped. He kissed a rogue tear slipping down her cheek. 'What's happened? What's wrong?'

'Nothing at all. Everything is perfect.' It was. Like nothing she'd ever imagined. This feeling in her heart, through her body, dizzy with release and also more greedy need. She breathed against his chest, inhaling his scent that drove her crazy, then she looked up at him and traced the lips that had given her so much pleasure. 'Stupid tears. I don't know why this is happening.'

'What are you feeling? Tell me.' He stroked her face so tenderly it made more tears spring.

What was happening? How did something so amazing make her want to cry?

Speaking her truth about deep, personal things was new territory. She never did that, preferring to keep deeply private things close to her chest.

But she found her voice through a thick, full throat, not sure if she even knew the words to describe this emotion. Or had the wherewithal to say those words out loud.

But she tried, because he asked. And she trusted him not to reject her. She trusted him.

Wow. That was a first for the Ice Queen. 'I feel… like…something new. Someone new. Someone…free, like a bird. Or freer, at least. I'm not making sense. You can't ask me questions like that after you've done such amazing things to me. I'm having trouble saying anything at all.'

He laughed. 'My free bird. I think I understand.' Then he took her hand and placed it over his heart. 'Fly high, *chérie*. Enjoy the ride.'

'Oui. Bien sur.' Of course, she'd enjoy the ride if he was her travelling companion. 'And…*merci,* Matthieu. *Merci pour tout.'* For everything he'd done, he'd said, for the way he made her feel.

'Good effort.' He blinked, smiling at her French. 'As I've said many times, it's my pleasure…to give you pleasure.'

Then he cupped her face and kissed her. His tongue dancing with hers in sultry circles that hypnotised her, stoked the heat inside her, until she couldn't think straight, didn't know her own name.

The kiss changed, slowed, softened into a caress she felt in every part of her. A prayer. Worship. Tender. Her body trapped by his arms, her heart captured by his soul.

Breathless, he pulled away, eyes smudged with desire. 'And your leg? Your back?'

'Shoot!' She clamped her hand over her mouth. 'I'd forgotten about them. Or at least, the pain doesn't seem so bad when you're having an orgasm.'

'Or the drugs are working.' Grinning, he stroked her nipple, then he bent and sucked it in, making her squirm in delight. 'We haven't even started yet.'

'That is very good news. Because I want you, Matthieu.' She pulled him to face her again. 'And I want you to feel the way I just did.'

'Pretty sure I already do. I almost lost it just watching you come.'

'I want to watch you come, too.' She laughed, surprised to be talking like this. David never talked like this. They only ever had sex in the dark, in a sort of hushed reverence. She'd thought that was all she needed. Believed it was enough. How wrong she'd been.

She snapped her eyes closed for a second and refused to allow any more thoughts of him into her head. Then she tiptoed her fingertips down Matthieu's stomach. 'But I think it'll only work if I wasn't the only one naked.'

'Ah. Yes.' He looked down at his jeans and his hand went to his zip, but she stopped him. 'Let me.'

'Be my guest.' Laughing, he lay back, arms behind his head, a very smug expression on his face, and she loved that he was playful and fun and yet could be serious and deep. She sat up and tugged at his zip, inching it slowly down, watching him watching her. In control, but hanging on by a thread. Knowing she turned him on made her feel the sexiest she'd ever felt.

She helped him wriggle out of his jeans and then his boxers, and he was so hard and yet silky soft to her touch. She took him in her hands and stroked. Slowly. He groaned, his laughter dying and his eyes misting. His back arched at each stroke. '*Mon Dieu*, Rachel. You make me want so much. I want to be inside you. Deep inside.'

'Yes.' Nothing else mattered now. She would ask, she would tell, she would take. She would beg for more of this, more of him. '*Please*, Matthieu.'

'*Attends*. Wait.' He touched her hand. 'You'll have to let go. Condom,' he clarified.

'Gotcha.' It was too long since she'd done this. Laughing, she shifted sideways while he rolled to the edge of the bed, magicked a condom from somewhere and sheathed.

Within seconds he was back, tucking her underneath him, his gaze a burnished gold of intent and desire. He lowered his head and sealed his mouth over hers in a kiss that was carnal and feral and possessive. His erection nudged at her centre and she writhed her hips against his in anticipation and encouragement.

But he paused, running his palms over her forehead, smoothing her hair. 'Rachel, are you sure about this?'

'Never been more sure about anything. Please, Matthieu.' She angled her hips and then, yes! He was pushing into her, filling her, stroke after slow, sensuous stroke. Sensations rippled through her: his mouth on hers, his stubble on her jaw, the long thick glide of him inside her, the heat. His taste.

She'd been wrong before; nothing had ever felt *this* good.

Something flickered in his eyes as he held her gaze, something he didn't say, but she felt deep inside her soul. Something pure and new. Then he groaned into her hair, 'Rachel... Rachel...' and his rhythm kicked up. She met him beat for beat, thrust for thrust, angling her hips so he could go deeper.

'Matthieu...' She clung to him, fingers digging deep into his shoulders, pinning him there, part of her. And he clung to her, his hands clasping her arms.

'Rachel...' He drove into her harder and faster and she felt herself losing her grip on control, spiralling higher and higher. Then he called her name one more time before she felt his final thrust, a ripple deep, deep inside her as he found his release.

For a few moments he held her close as he hauled in

breath after breath. Then he finally relaxed and slid sideways, his arms never letting go of her.

She lay still, not wanting to move, never wanting to leave this bed again. Completely spent, she breathed out and smiled, feeling sleepy and relaxed and utterly, thoroughly sated. 'That was amazing. I don't think I've ever felt like this before.'

'Then you've been doing it wrong.' He winked, but something about the mist in his eyes made her think none of this was a joke to him. 'Next time, I want to undress you. That's part of the fun.'

Next time. 'Do you want me to get dressed now, so you can strip me later?'

'No.' He hauled her tighter against him. 'Do not get dressed again. Ever.'

'I'm going to get pretty cold up that mountain, naked.'

'Hush.' He put his finger to her mouth. 'Don't talk about work. Or about anything out there. Out there does not exist. What do you need, here, right now?'

I need kissing. I need someone to talk to and to listen. Someone to care. I don't want to be on my own any more. I need this.

She realised then that she needed understanding and connection. And she got it from Matthieu.

I need you.

Tears filled her eyes. She'd never felt as if she'd needed anyone before. Not like this. Not this gnawing ache of anticipation and joy. It meant something, she knew. And yet she didn't want to know, didn't want to push it into more than it could be.

She kissed him languidly, pressing herself against him. 'I need more sex, please.' But then stifled a yawn as fatigue bled into her bones. 'Oops…sorry. I think I might need a little nap first.'

'Then sleep, Rachel.' He ran his hand down her spine and kissed her throat, her neck, her shoulder. 'You need rest, *chérie*. You've had a big day.'

Not just a big day. A big revelation. She'd been trying to hide from him, trying to keep herself safe and intact, closed off and aloof. But he'd broken her open with a kiss, shattered her with sex and seen through to her core. No...worse, *more*, she'd taken him by the hand and willingly shown him, told him. Begged and demanded. And she didn't care.

There were no regrets, not for this.

CHAPTER THIRTEEN

'MATTHIEU…'

He wasn't sure if he was dreaming or if this was real, but Rachel Tait was in his bed and her hand was stroking down his bare thigh.

Reality check.

It wasn't a dream. She was still here, tucked into the crook of his arm. He fitted himself against her soft curves, warm skin. '*Chérie*…you okay? Any pain?'

'A little. My knee's throbbing, but I'm okay. Are you?'

'Yes,' he groaned into hair that smelt of the resort verbena shampoo and tickled his nose. It was the best he'd felt in his whole life. She hadn't moved into the spare room as he'd thought she might, she'd settled against him and fallen asleep. First time he was glad a woman had stayed over. First time he'd wanted one to. It was now three forty-five, they were enveloped in a soupy darkness. There was no noise, no light. It felt as if the whole world was comprised of just the two of them. 'Never felt better.'

'Good.' A pause. Then she laughed. 'Everything feels different here.'

'In what way?'

'It's like my senses are on full alert. The sun is brighter. The snow is whiter. The sky is so beautiful and it is very, very dark in this room. So dark I can almost grasp it.'

'You want me to put a light on?'

'No. It's just disorientating.' Her bottom snuggled against his groin. 'Or maybe it's this situation that's got me a bit off balance.'

'Me, too.' But to make sure she knew it was a good off balance he squeezed her tight and kissed her neck. 'We've applied to get dark sky reserve recognition. Come look outside.'

After activating a wall light with his phone app, he handed her a robe, then opened the heavy curtains. Rachel slipped the robe over her shoulders and he helped her hop across the carpet to the window where she leaned against him, craning her neck to peer out at the creamy purple trail of the Milky Way. 'Wow. It's amazing.'

'Wait.' He turned off the light with the app and then held her close. 'Look at all those stars, all those planets out there. Pretty special, eh? Stretched across the globe… the Earth's roof holding us all safe. If ever I'm travelling and I see this, I feel right at home.'

She sighed. 'To be honest, I've never really felt like I've had a proper home. I might give this a go when I'm back in my apartment. It might make me feel as if I do belong somewhere. Unfortunately, we don't have dark skies like this where I live in Leeds, there's too much light pollution.'

But he was stuck on her previous words. 'No home? Mine was difficult…tragic even, but it was still my home. I can't imagine how it feels to not have a special place.'

'I'm working on it. I have plans. I'm going to sell the flat I shared with David, then I'll buy something just for me. Finally. Growing up, I had two homes. Just two houses really, because neither of them felt like a place where I could properly relax. Although, things got a little better when Mum and Dad eventually split up.'

'The arguing was hard to live with?'

She nodded. 'The silences, too. I hated them, because they meant my parents were simmering and it would only be a matter of time before the explosion. And there was always an explosion, Matthieu.' She shuddered. 'Silence is scary.'

'I understand. It was all or nothing with my mum, too. Silences were the worst because I never knew what she was doing…' He switched off the flashing images running through his head. 'Or had…done.' Three times she'd tried to take her own life over the years and he'd found her each time.

That was the reason he didn't believe in all that love stuff. Love hadn't been enough to stop his mother killing herself. It hadn't been enough to keep her in this world, in *his* world. For him. Love hadn't stopped his heart shattering. It had just made everything worse.

'I can't imagine, Matthieu. I just can't. But I want you to know that I'm so sorry.' She stroked his cheek. 'I wish there was something I could do to help.'

'It's done, Rachel. I just live with it. I try to remember the best times.' Because remembering that day, reliving it over and over, would bring him to his knees.

'I'm so glad you had some good times.' She smoothed his hair and smiled. 'I want you to have so many more. I want you to have the very best full life. That way you live for her, too.'

She understood. Sure, she didn't know what it felt like to lose a parent, but she knew what it was like to live with that fear that the world was going to implode at any moment. She wanted to help. Just knowing that was like liquid heat in his chest. He cupped her face and kissed her, soft and slow. 'Thank you.'

They stood together in the dark, staring up at the endless sky, and he felt it might be the right time to ask her, 'You really aren't close to either of your parents? Tell me some more, please. I want to know *you*.'

He made sure to put the emphasis on you and she blinked up at him. 'Are you sure?'

'Of course. I've made love to you, shared my bed with you, I want to know who the real Rachel Tait is and that means knowing more about your past.'

Her smile told him she was being brave, but she clearly didn't want to go there. 'It's not something I talk about. I never even told David. People don't understand.'

'Try me. I've told you everything about me and my *maman*.' There wasn't much to tell. He'd tried to save her and he'd failed.

'Okay…' She gave him a wobbly smile. 'The thing you have to understand is that they met and married within a few weeks. One of those passionate all-consuming loves, but it quickly withered and then their hate was all consuming, too. Powerful, destructive. There were affairs, reconciliations. Crockery thrown against the wall. Rage. Then one day I begged them to just stop, told them I couldn't take it any more and I made my dad leave. He got remarried first. In some ways it was a relief to have him focus on someone else, although it didn't stop the arguing. At that point it felt like he'd given up on the one-upmanship thing and now I was just a problem he didn't want to be around.'

'Never.' Matthieu's grip on her tightened. He ached to show her just how much she mattered.

'Mum met and married Ken when I was sixteen. She was so besotted with him I sort of faded from her life.

Until my wedding, of course. They both insisted on coming to that, even though I knew it was going to be a war zone. I made them promise not to speak to each other. I was so nervous about the whole thing. Mainly…if I'm honest, about making them proud of me. Being happy for *me*. Seeing me for who I am. Not a problem to be argued over. It felt, when Dad walked me up the aisle, that I'd finally got that father–daughter thing going… You know, the one where there's an inseparable bond, where he'll fight anyone on your behalf? The one where you're always his little girl and he means it, truly means it, instead of using it as ammunition to get his own way. Well, of course you don't know because you're not a woman.'

'I get the drift.' He'd wanted that parent–child bond, too. Had it for a while with his mum, but she'd become so ill he'd ended up looking after her.

Rachel's shoulders bunched forward. 'Then David did his disappearing act and I was left looking like an idiot.'

'What did they say? Please tell me they were supportive.'

'Dad was furious and said he'd been humiliated in front of everyone…as if it was all about him and not my life that had been ruined. He certainly did fight for me. He roared, making everything worse, but he took it as a sign to leave early and get back to his wife…who'd refused to come to the wedding because my mum was going to be there. I don't think I'll see him again for a long time.' She breathed in and then exhaled deeply, as if trying to stay in control, but her shaking hands gave her away. 'Mum was a little more supportive. In as much as, after the initial shock and three stiff whiskies, she said it was a shame, but I was lucky to escape someone who didn't love me.'

'She was right about that.' It astounded him that anyone could not see Rachel. That she had to wish for affection.

'True. Then she added that I would be better on my own because that's what I've always been. That she'd marvelled at how much time I could spend in my room, just reading and ignoring the world.' She bit her bottom lip at the memory. 'Like she wasn't the reason for it in the first place. And that perhaps I should be more giving in my relationships and then people would like me more. Then she left. She didn't hug me or help me, she just looked at me as if she'd expected it all along—that I was my father's daughter.'

A vice tightened around Matthieu's chest. She looked so sad he wanted to do something, anything, to erase that pain. To rail at her parents for making her feel this way. He tipped her chin to look into her eyes. 'How did you react? Please tell me you did your famous Dr Blowout?'

'There was no point. They don't want to hear what I have to say. I did what I always do and pushed the disappointment down inside me. Gave her a kiss and waved her off, promising her I was okay. Because it looked like that was what she needed to hear. I saved my anger for my texts to David.'

'I can't even compute this.'

'It's what happens.' Her shrug and acceptance made his heart twist.

'No, it isn't.'

'It's what happens to me. I'm used to it. I deal with it. That whole wedding disaster just proved that I can't rely on anyone. I'm on my own. That's okay. It has to be, otherwise I'll lose myself. I can't be the wreck I was back then. Sobbing in sluice rooms, hurting so much. So damned much. I'd thought we were a team, you know? I thought we belonged...no, I thought *I* belonged. But I don't. So, I have to be a team of one.' She stared up at him, eyes shining. 'You know, when I was falling down the mountain and I thought I was going to die I saw Isla's face, Odin's, too, and yours, Matthieu. But not my parents' faces. Or even David's. That must tell you a lot. I've left them behind, they're no longer part of me or my life.'

She'd thought about him in extremis. About her life here and not about what she'd endured before. He tried not to read too much into that. Had she pushed her traumas so far down she believed she'd dealt with them? Because she was fooling herself. Even he could see they marred her thoughts and actions still. Everyone she'd loved had let her down. God knew what it was going to take for her to truly trust again.

He knew he couldn't change what had happened to her, but he wanted to make her feel better now. He wanted to show Rachel that she mattered, that he saw her, that he knew her. That her present and her future needn't be marred by her past.

But then, what did he know about that? His past coloured everything he did. So, he was probably setting them both up to fail, but he wanted, so badly, to try. For her.

He stroked her cheek. 'You can rely on me, Rachel Tait.'

'Oh, Matthieu. You're a good man and I know you mean it.' Her smile was genuine and warm and she covered his hand. 'But I don't want to rely on anyone, can't you see? I've learnt that there's no point setting yourself on a course for heartbreak. We've only got ourselves, in the end, right? That's why we just need to have some fun. Nothing heavy.'

He had a bad feeling that heavy was exactly the route he was taking, whether either of them wanted it or not.

'Sounds like we've both got pretty messed-up family history, *chérie*.'

'Doesn't everyone?' She laughed. 'And it's up to us to survive it. I used to put on my headphones and listen to loud music so I couldn't hear them fight. Then dance round my bedroom until I felt better.'

'The terrible music you were listening to when you were skiing that first time?' At her bugged eyes he said with a grin, 'I heard you. I think the whole resort heard you.'

'Good, I hope they smiled. Better still, joined in. But, Matthieu, how can you say that? Eighties rock anthems are not terrible, they saved my life. Or my sanity at least.' She raised her hands above her head and rocked from side to side, dancing to a beat only she could hear. 'You should try it. Pass me my phone. I'll find some music and I'll show you.'

'Mine's here.'

She scrolled through his music app and grinned. 'Come on, raise your hands... Ready? Final Countdown! Now, sing as loudly as you can.'

He almost did, but couldn't quite bring himself to do it. Besides, he was far too busy watching her. 'It's the middle of the night, Rachel.'

'So? We're far enough away from anyone. No one will hear.'

'And I'm stone-cold sober. Men only dance when they're drunk.' Not that he hadn't frequented clubs, only he'd been happier to watch from the sidelines—basically, the bar—and let the celebs and his friends strut their stuff on the dance floor.

'Ha! No way.' She laughed. 'Real men dance sober, too. And I've got a busted knee and a very sore back, but I'm determined not to let that stop me having fun.'

'Still…' He held his hand up for a definite no.

'Oh. You probably know the singers? You probably went on holiday with them and think I'm the very opposite of cool.' She grinned. 'My love for ballet turned into a love for music. The louder the better as far as I'm concerned and for dancing any old way. My kind of dancing. And I don't care.'

She really didn't, he could see that. She didn't try to be anyone she wasn't. She didn't crave fame or wealth, she just wanted to be accepted for who she was. That would be enough for her.

Thing was, Matthieu didn't just accept her, he wanted her…with a force he'd never felt before. As if he'd die if he didn't sink into her again and pretty damned soon. But he held it together. 'No, I didn't holiday with the band. And I don't want you to be cool. I prefer you hot and getting hotter.'

'Then warm me up, Matthieu.' She put her arms round his neck and swayed with him—standing on her one good leg, singing the words and wriggling her hips until he couldn't do anything but join in.

She did this to fill the gaps, to cover the silence. She danced to a song no one else could hear. She entertained herself, shut out the world. Chose to be alone, whereas he surrounded himself with people, friends, women, work. But, in the end he and Rachel were the same: two people trying to deal with the past in any way they knew how. Trying to find meaning and get through.

Hell, getting through would be a lot better if he did it with Rachel Tait, especially if they spent their time doing this.

He swayed with her, twirled her round…or rather, helped her hop in a circle. Sang what scant lyrics he knew…not loudly to start with, but as embarrassment slunk away he raised his voice and he had to admit she was right; it did make everything better.

She laughed, encouraging him along, and he felt the ache in his chest start to loosen, the slip and slide of her mouth against his as she sang the words between snatched kisses. The play of her hands in his. This serious, beautiful, buttoned-up doctor was also a spirited woman who had so much to give, was sexier than hell and drove him crazy with desire.

He watched her flipping her hair from side to side, the graceful way she moved her hips, the swish of her perfect breasts in her too-big-for-her robe and was utterly transfixed. Enchanted. *Captured.* His heart, his body. He was hers. Completely.

He pulled her to him and kissed her and she gyrated against him, making him hard and hot. Harder and hotter than ever before. And before he could stop himself, he was pulling her down on to the bed, sheathed and sliding into her.

'Yes, Matthieu. Yes. Yes.' Her kisses became frantic and intense, her moans the only soundtrack he could hear. She grasped at his skin, fingernails digging deep into his shoulders. He thrust inside her over and over, driven by a wild unstoppable need, sinking deeper and harder, feeling her tighten around him, holding him there. Every stroke melded his heart to her. Every kiss forged their connection tighter and stronger.

She moaned, moving her hips with his, never once breaking eye contact. He threaded his fingers into hers, arms above her head, his gaze latched tight to hers. Those grey eyes holding a glimmer of trust and a lot of want. And something else, too, something he didn't want to put a name to.

Then she said his name on a sob, and he found his release…and it felt as if something inside him broke open, all the heavy and all the light mingling together, all the stars in the sky, the whole Milky Way, bunching tight in his heart, in a Rachel-shaped space.

CHAPTER FOURTEEN

He was gone by the time she woke up.

She blinked into a room filled with sunlight. He'd opened the curtains, left a tray with hot chocolate and croissants. Sent a text:

Call me when you wake up and I'll come over to help you. xx

Not that any of that made up for his absence because she missed him already. He'd taken her to heights she'd never known existed before, kissed her in a way she'd never been kissed. And she really, *really* wanted to do it all again.

But it did give her time to think.

Last night—this morning—had been more intense than anything she'd ever experienced. She'd decided to be fun and to seduce him, yet he'd teased her history from her bit by painful bit, like picking petals from an ox-eye daisy. Tug and release. Tug and release, on and on, until there was nothing about her he didn't know. She'd exposed her past like a raw nerve.

She'd expected him…okay, she hadn't known what to expect from him, because she'd never said words like *humiliation* or *belong* about herself before, never admitted to wanting to be a daddy's girl, so she'd thought he might be shocked, but not *moved*. He'd looked as if he was living her pain. And while it had felt wonderful to have someone share the hurt, she didn't want to expect that from him, to think that could be something permanent in her life.

She wanted sex, yes—and lots more with Matthieu—but preferably not with the accompaniment of equilibrium-knocking emotions that she had spent her life trying to avoid. She was a grown woman, a medical professional and that was who she wanted to convey to everyone and especially to Matthieu. Not someone looking to belong to anyone. She was done with all that.

Had been done with that.

After showering and dressing she used her ski poles to help her hop over to reception to organise a taxi to take her for her scan. But she stopped short as her eyes were drawn to the biggest fir tree she'd ever seen and to the beautiful man dressing it with Christmas decorations.

He grinned as she hopped over, striding to greet her with a kiss on each cheek. 'Good morning, Rachel.'

Her heart danced and her body keened towards him, which she was fairly sure was obvious to anyone who looked at her, so she quickly scanned the room to make sure no one was listening, but they were all engrossed in their own jobs. She felt weirdly shy around him, not knowing how to be that professional woman when the second she was in his company she just wanted to step into his embrace and stay there. 'Hi, Matthieu. How's the medical centre going?'

He kept his hand on her arm. Protective. Possessive. 'Suzanne's coping and Eric is coming in early to cover for you.'

'I feel so bad not being up there pulling my weight.'

'We can work something out. Scan first. Wait—' He dashed across the reception hall, grabbed her a chair, then made her sit in it. 'How do you feel?'

'Truthfully? Like I was broken into pieces and then put back together.' She smiled up at him, because she couldn't help herself. But *broken*? She never said things like that. She needed to stop thinking like that.

But he didn't seem put off by her gushing, he just grinned and stroked his thumb over her mouth. Their secret shining in his eyes. 'A good sleep can do that.'

So can good sex.

'Thanks for letting me have a lie-in.'

'You were exhausted.' His smile told her that he knew exactly why and he very much wanted to share his bed with her again. 'You should have called. I'd have come over to get you.'

And let him see her struggle? No way. Being looked after last night was enough of a dent to her ego. She was a capable woman and wanted him to see her as one. 'I'm fine. I can do this weird shuffle-hop thing with the help of two poles and some decent painkillers. I was just about to organise transport to the hospital for the scan.'

He frowned. 'I'll take you.'

'Honestly, I can manage.' She looked up at the half-dressed Christmas tree. Hundreds of little silver lights flickered behind glittery baubles in myriad colours. 'It looks like you're busy.'

'A little. But if you help me, we can finish it quickly, then I'll drive you into town.' He handed her a gold bauble. 'Find a place for this, please.'

'Bossy.' She laughed. 'Where?'

'Anywhere you want. You choose.'

'Be careful what you wish for. The only bonus of living in two houses was that I always had two Christmas trees to dress. So, you've asked an expert.' She hung the bauble on the tree as warmth spread through her. This was so domesticated and so intimate.

And there...right there, her thoughts started to co-alesce. It was *too intimate*. Starting to feel like a real re-lationship. One with expectations and plans. Hopes and dreams. Taking someone into account, second-guessing what they were feeling and wanting. Changing herself to fit into what they wanted. She could too easily fall into that trap again and then where would she be? Back to hurting again.

So many warning alarms rang in her head, but when she looked up at him and saw him beaming down at her she took a deep breath. She was overreacting. After their special night together she was imbuing the whole thing with the issues she'd inherited from her previous break-up. Matthieu wasn't asking for anything more. He was just asking her to hang a bauble on a tree.

She pushed it on to a branch. 'I like symmetry. Bau-bles matching on each side.'

'I like a big mess of colour.' He strung gold tinsel across the boughs of the tree, then stuck a red bauble next to her gold one. Too close in her opinion. 'We didn't have a tree every year—most years, in fact. But Louis's house always had the biggest and brightest tree in the village, so I used to go over there and help them dress theirs. It almost made up for it.'

She immediately squished her need to match the bau-bles and let him carry on making a mess even though it made her shudder, just a little. 'Kids continually amaze me. They always find a way to happiness.'

'There's a lesson there. Let's grab some now.' Wink-ing, he came over and crouched down in front of her. It was only then that she realised he'd placed the chair in the corner of the room, out of direct line of sight of anyone. He kissed her full on the lips, then held both her hands. 'I didn't intend for you to end up in my bed when I invited you to stay in my house. But I'm very glad you were there.'

She palmed his cheek, acutely aware they were at work, but choosing to grab a bit of that elusive happiness while she had the chance. She pressed her lips to his again. 'Are you worried about the line we crossed?'

'Not at all. I'm sure we can keep our night together out of the spotlight. I just don't want you to think I was taking advantage of the situation.'

She laughed as she stroked his inner thigh. Yes, this was fine. The man just wanted sex. She could do that. *Wanted* to do that. 'I like to think I seduced you, Matthieu.'

His eyes met hers, suffused with heat. 'And you're doing it again.'

'Just…taking advantage of the situation.' She chuckled, as a matching heat seeped through her. 'It would be rude not to—'

'Matthieu! Matthieu!' A little voice had them jumping apart and turning round.

Rachel craned her neck round the tree to see Isla in a wheelchair being pushed by her father.

Matthieu's eyebrows rose as he quickly squeezed Rachel's hands and let go, then strode to talk to the little girl. He crouched down by the side of her chair giving her a high-five. '*Coucou, Isla.*'

'*Coucou*, Matthieu. *Coucou*, Rachel.'

'Hi, there.' She looked from one to the other. '*Coucou?*'

'It means hi,' Isla chirped. 'Matthieu taught me. And

Joy...eux Noel means Happy Christmas.' Stumbling over the words she looked at the boss with the kind of adoration Rachel was used to seeing whenever people looked at Matthieu. And her heart tripped again.

Trying to keep things polite although still feeling quite impolite towards him, she nodded to Michael, then beamed at the little girl, raising her leg to show her the knee brace. 'Snap!'

Isla's eyes widened. 'You, too? Did you get knocked over by a snowboarder?'

'No. It was my own silly fault. I fell over and slid down a mountain.' Her eyes darted to Matthieu and she saw the smile on his lips.

Isla nodded seriously. 'Did Matthieu rescue you on the snowmobile?'

'He did.' The whole of Rachel's body blushed as she thought about all the things that had happened between him picking her up off the mountain and now. Hot chocolate kisses, a bathroom seduction, letting him in to her darkest thoughts, naked dancing... All of it filling her up, but as she watched him and ached to be touched by him again, she had a bad feeling it wasn't enough. Would one night with him be enough? Ten nights? A hundred?

Then she filed all those thoughts away and focused on her patient. 'How's your knee doing, sweetie?'

'Sore. But we're watching lots of movies and Daddy gives me ice-cream and tells me not to tell Mom. And Mom gives me pizza and tells me not to tell Daddy.' Isla grinned as if she'd won the lottery.

But discomfort wormed through Rachel's gut as she glanced at Michael and frowned in question. Had they not learned anything?

His thin mouth broke into a smile. 'It's okay, honestly. Things are good. We had a long chat after you highlighted how we were behaving. Then we cancelled all our commitments over the holidays and decided to stay here for some real family time. Just the three of us. The parent treats play-off is just a game now.'

Rachel would have preferred no play-offs, but she couldn't help smiling, knowing they'd tried to make things better for Isla. But her heart ached, too, wishing she'd had parents who'd been so committed to making things work, or to something even resembling a civilised divorce instead of a battlefield. 'I'm so glad things are working out.'

'Us, too. Thanks for giving us a reality check. Bianca will be along in a minute. We're heading into town.'

'Hey, Isla, want to help with the tree?' Matthieu handed the little girl a bauble almost as big as her hand, then lifted her up so she could hang it high. Then another and another until the bauble box was empty and there was a gaudy mismatch of colour covering the branches. Rachel's hands itched to put it into some kind of symmetry, but she understood she had to let that go.

She'd let go of a lot of things these past few weeks.

Eventually, Matthieu put Isla back down on the ground. 'There you go, sugar. Every time you come past the tree you can see your beautiful handiwork.'

Rachel was entranced just watching him. The cute faces he pulled to make Isla laugh, the gentle voice, the tender way he helped her hang the decorations. He was a kind, generous man who'd been through so much pain, yet just wanted to make people smile. He deserved so much happiness.

Her eyes pricked. Something hot slid into her chest, like a weird yearning. A need that actually hurt. Was it Isla? Sure, she was as cute as a button. Rachel hadn't ever thought about having kids...at least not since the break-up with David. Of course, they'd idly talked about having them at some point, but there'd never been a plan. And she hadn't realised how much she ached for them. She should have realised that when she'd fallen head over heels for Odin.

Or was it Matthieu she ached for? Matthieu and a child? A family?

No. No, she couldn't be so far down the line with him that she was envisioning a future. She couldn't do that to herself. Couldn't let all that resolve go along with everything else. Her heart fluttered in panic as reality dawned: she was way down the line already.

The real problem was, he wasn't asking for more, but she was wanting it.

What was she going to do? She had to pull back, find herself again. Find the bricks of her wall that he'd carefully smashed down kiss by kiss and reconstruct it again, tight and tall around her heart.

'Just gorgeous, Iles. But don't be too long now.' Bianca's voice behind her was filled with softness, in such a contrast to her highly strung tone last week, and, turning to look at her, Rachel saw the transformation in the model's features from pinched and tense to radiant and happy. 'Don't forget we're heading to the hospital for a check-up for that knee.'

Rachel grabbed the opportunity to have some space from Matthieu. 'Oh? Could I please hitch a ride?'

'Why? Have you hurt yourself, too?' Bianca looked her up and down.

'Knee. Yes. Yes, please, a ride to the hospital would be great.'

Had she really just asked these people for a lift? But they were her ticket out of here so she could have some breathing space. She turned to Matthieu, hoping he wasn't going to insist he take her instead. 'Is that okay?'

She realised, too, that she'd asked him instead of telling him, taking him into account even when she was trying to get distance.

'Of course.' He nodded and smiled, but his eyes were filled with questions. 'I've a million things to do. Let me know what the verdict is? Maybe we could have a chat later?'

'Sure.' She smiled, then turned away.

Not even sure what to say.

'The ligament's not torn, but it is badly sprained. Aargh!' Hands fisting, Rachel hopped back and forth on her crutches across her chalet lounge floor, her mouth a taut line. 'I'm so sorry, Matthieu. I know this is going to be a big hassle for you and the team.'

'We'll work something out.' Matthieu bit down on his own frustration that she hadn't been in contact with him for hours and also that the resort now had a less than ideal staffing situation. The latter he could deal with, the former suggested he needed to take a chill pill. She was her own woman. She could go into town and have a scan without him.

Even so, the fact she'd dumped him for a ride with Bianca rankled. Because, more than anything, Rachel didn't like Bianca, and she'd just spent the night with him. *Tant pis.*

She grimaced. 'But I came here to work up the mountain and now I can't even leave the resort without help. I hate letting you down. And being dependent on someone else.'

'You don't say?' He reached for her arm and pulled her

down on to his knee on the couch. 'You have to rest and elevate your leg. It isn't going to heal if you keep using it.'

'I know.' She slumped against him, staring wistfully out of the window. 'I should be up there with Suzanne and Eric.'

'They can manage. You can do remote consultations.'

'Sure. We did a lot of video consults when that virus hit a couple of years ago. It's not quite the same though, is it?'

'The same as hands on? Not at all. We like hands on, right?' He leaned in for a kiss. Was it his imagination, or did she tug away far too soon? Probably his imagination. 'I've taken the liberty of setting you up in the office at my lodge. It has the best Wi-Fi in the resort and lots of room for you to have a proper set-up with a desktop computer, large monitor and headset. Trying to fit anything on this tiny dining table would be challenging.'

'Oh. I see. Well… I think it would be better if it was in my space, to be honest.' She pointed to the too-small table. 'I'll make it work.'

'If you like.'

She nodded. 'I just prefer—'

'Your own space.'

'Is that such a bad thing?' She looked spooked. She'd looked spooked earlier, too. Something had shaken her, something to do with Isla. Or was it their night together?

But even though she was probably right—space was a good thing—he liked being around her. Liked having someone to care about, someone to care for him. Liked waking up to her. Talking to her. Sharing. Which was a whole new thing for him and it was all down to Rachel.

But he knew better than to let things get too cosy. 'No, you're right, of course.'

'I'm sorry. I'm tired.' She looked at him for a moment

and he saw a hundred different emotions pass through her gaze before she ran her palm over her forehead and sighed. 'And in pain, to be honest, and frustrated that I can't do my job. And I feel guilty that I've let you down.'

'No. Don't ever feel guilty. It was an accident.' He knew guilt coloured everything. She didn't need to add that to her pain and exhaustion. He circled his hands round her waist and pulled her closer. Feeling the hot press of her body against his, the softening of her muscles as she relaxed against him. Eventually. But he did notice the hesitation that hadn't been there last night. 'Get some rest, *chérie*. Have a break and don't put too much pressure on yourself.'

She placed her hands on his chest as if she was about to push away from him, but she didn't. 'I have to work.'

'You have to rest. Damn it, Rachel. Just for an hour or so. You need time out.' He gently slid her off his knee on to the chair and stood up. This was getting them nowhere. 'I'll leave you to it. I'll see you later.'

He started towards the door, but heard her voice behind him. 'No. Wait.'

'What?'

'Look, last night was great. I loved it. But I don't want anyone here to know about it. Not Louis or anyone. I had enough trouble in my last job trying to pick apart my work and my private life.'

'Of course.'

'And I'm not looking for anything serious...you know that. This morning I had a wobble because the whole Christmas tree thing was lovely. And I was still feeling all sexy from our night together and I started to feel...' Her cheeks turned a dark shade of red. 'I don't know... You're fun to be around, Matthieu. But you listen, too.

And you're great with kids. It felt cosy by the tree and I decided I shouldn't get used to feeling cosy.'

That word again. That feeling of letting your guard down. 'Things did get intense last night. It was fun, though.'

'Yes. And basically, I just can't seem to stop wanting you.' She ran her fingertips along his jaw. 'What I'm trying to say is, other than that I'm an idiot—'

'You're all about the sex?' He laughed.

'Yes. Yes.' Her shoulders sagged with relief. 'I'm not looking for anything more.'

'Excellent. We're a good match then.' His brain was already working on a rerun of last night, his body more than prepared. Although...even though he agreed with her, he felt deflated, too. Part of him wanted...what did he want? More. Deeper. Which was ridiculous, because he was already embroiled too deeply in this.

'I'm so glad you understand.' She kissed him and this time there was no hesitation.

When she eventually pulled away, he stepped his fingertips over her collarbone. 'I chose the beds for these chalets. I know they're plenty big enough for two.'

She laughed and rubbed her head against his chest. 'What are you thinking, Matthieu?'

'Whether I can take you up on that offer to strip you naked. Help you relax.' He smoothed his hand over her breast and saw heat mist her gaze.

But she leaned away from him, a small frown forming over her eyes. 'But work...?'

'But first...?' His other hand slid up to her cheek, cupping her face.

'Matthieu.' Her mouth curved into a very sexy smile. 'What are you doing to me?'

'Something good, I hope.' He laughed. 'Let me take care of you.'

'I don't even know what that feels like.' She blinked up at him, eyes glistening.

Her words were like a knife in his gut. She'd had to look after herself, even after the break-up. Or maybe she'd pushed too many people away. People who didn't understand her the way he did. What she needed was time and space and encouragement. He would give her all of those things if it meant he got to know her better. What turned her on, what made her smile. He'd tried hard not to get involved, but he kept coming back for more.

He stroked her hair. 'It's a lot like last night. But way more sex. Let me show you.'

Her hand covered his. 'And then?'

There was so much he could say, so much he could offer, but they'd just agreed this was sex and fun and temporary. 'Then I'll bring the computer over and you can work.'

'Okay.' She licked his bottom lip then sucked it into her mouth. 'That's a very good plan.'

'I'm a planner, what can I say?' He laughed and pulled her closer, put his lips to that tender spot just below her ear. 'I have so much planned for you in the bedroom, too.'

'Matthieu… I can't…think… Yes, please…' Her hands were on each side of his face and she kissed him as if her life depended on it. Kissed him and kissed him until he was left in no doubt about what she wanted from him. At least for now.

And that's what they'd agreed: now was all that mattered.

CHAPTER FIFTEEN

'HE LOST CONTROL and hit a tree. Head injury. Nasty cut on his forehead.' Matthieu's voice was crackly, and the image kept shorting out, but she could just make out a prone young man, very still with his eyes closed. An open wound oozed blood on to the fresh snow.

'Is he conscious?' Rachel watched the monitor, controlling her frustration that she couldn't be there doing the first responder assessment on the injured snowboarder, having to make do with a screen and a dodgy cellphone network. But it was better than nothing, and this set-up had served them well for the last couple of weeks. On good days Matthieu drove her up to the medical centre on the snowmobile, but this morning she'd had a knee check-up in town, so she'd stayed at the hotel.

It wasn't perfect—she couldn't fully do what she needed to do, but they improvised. Like this: talking them through serious incidents while co-ordinating the emergency response. With a lot of resting with her leg elevated in between.

Matthieu held the digital tablet so she could see the patient. 'He was responding when we got here, but he's deteriorating quickly.'

Not good. 'If you talk to him, does he open his eyes?'

'Justin? Justin?' Matthieu tapped their patient's face. 'Justin, can you hear me? No.'

'Can you squeeze his nail bed for me? One of his fingers? Any one.'

Matthieu did as she asked. Then shook his head. 'Nothing. But he's maintaining his own airway.'

'Okay.' That was something. Rachel started to tap the landline phone to put a call through for an emergency evacuation. 'It's important we get him out of there as quickly as we can.'

'We'll put a collar on and keep him warm.' Matthieu put his hands at each side of Justin's neck, waiting for Cody to slide the collar on.

'Can you cover that wound up, too, please?' Rachel thought about what more she could do all the way down here. 'Is he with friends or family?'

'No one around but him. But he's holidaying with a group. I don't know where they are. Lucky one of the crew found him.'

God, she wished she was up there helping. Sitting here was driving her insane. 'Leave his helmet on, too. I'm phoning for the air ambulance. What's your location?'

'Just off Heaven's Gate. Near where we found you. I'll text through the GPS co-ordinates.'

'Okay. It can be treacherous up there. Be careful.'

'Thanks, Rachel.' Matthieu looked up into the monitor and smiled. For a brief moment he held her gaze, then he focused back on the injured boarder.

With that one look, her chest heated. Her body heated. Even though this working situation was frustrating, he'd made it as easy as possible for her to contribute. And he'd certainly made her evenings interesting. They'd fallen into a routine of one night at her chalet and one night at his lodge. Their secret. And it had been perfect: fun, sexy, giving and taking.

She smiled back, hoping it was reassuring, but understanding that he knew the dangers up there as well as she did. 'I'll let you know ETA.'

'Great. Looks like the weather's closing in.'

Which would mean delays. 'I'll tell them to get a hurry on.'

'Thanks. Over.' She called it in and waited for the helicopter response. Then took a deep breath before she conveyed her news to Matthieu. 'They said they'd try to reach you, but the potential for icing is high.'

'They can't fly in thick snow. Freezing precipitation stops the blades working. But…we need them here. Quickly. It's not just the head injury I'm worried about, it's frostbite and hypothermia.'

'I'll let them know.'

Then she waited. And waited.

She watched more heavy clouds roll in. Broke the news to Matthieu that the chopper had returned to base, so he and Cody had called extra help to bring blankets and for help lifting Justin if needs be. Eventually, unable to wait any more, they carefully manoeuvred him on to the snowmobile and drove him slowly to the medical centre. Time chugged round from lunchtime to early afternoon. Matthieu's reports were more and more demanding.

'We need an evacuation now. We need the chopper now. Tell them, Rachel. Tell them to hurry.'

Then she heard the welcome sound of helicopter rotors and looked out to a clearing sky. 'They're here, Matthieu,' she told him. 'How's he doing?'

'Not good.' His tone was flat. 'He's warm and safe, but that's the best we can do.'

* * *

When he arrived back at the hotel with Cody an hour later, they both looked frozen through and ashen. She ushered them into her chalet and gave them hot drinks, wrapped them in thick wool blankets…wanting to wrap Matthieu into her arms, too, but holding back. 'How was he?'

'He was in a bad way, Rachel. He was still breathing when the helicopter took off, but I don't know if he'll make it.' Matthieu shrugged. He was so pale and cold it made Rachel's heart twist. 'On Christmas Eve, too. I'll inform his family and arrange for them to get here as soon as I can. We managed to catch up with his friends on our way down the mountain. They've gone to the hospital.'

'Is he a local?' She prayed he wasn't, because she knew the delayed evacuation would have serious impact on Justin's condition. Even worse if he was Matthieu's friend. She knew he still carried guilt over not being able to save his mother and someone else dying on his watch would weigh heavily on him.

He smiled softly. 'Justin is a very famous American singer and songwriter, with a string of hits and lots of awards.'

'So, his family will have a long way to travel before they can see him.'

Matthieu nodded. Having got used to her inability to recognise a star, he never mentioned his surprise now. 'I'll get them here as quickly as I can.'

Cody stood. 'I'm heading for a shower, then a drink in the bar. Fancy joining me for a beer?'

'Sure. I need something strong after that.' Matthieu stood, too, folding the blanket neatly and putting it on the couch. 'I need to debrief the staff anyway. But first I have to make those calls.'

'You coming, too, Doc?' Cody hovered at the door. 'It's always better to deal with things like this as a team.'

'Yes. Thanks, I will.' She liked that he thought she was part of their team even though she couldn't do her job as well as she might. 'I'll call the hospital for an update first.' Which of course was only a little elaboration. She just wanted some alone time with Matthieu.

After watching Cody go, she gave Matthieu a hug. 'You okay?'

He was still cold. He looked haunted, his features hollowed out. 'I hate it when we can't help them.'

'You did help. You kept him warm and safe. That's all anyone could do until the chopper arrived. You may have saved his life.' It wasn't that she'd got used to it in her line of work…losing anyone was hard…but it was something she did experience in the emergency room. What amazed her was that Matthieu was okay about admitting these things. Usually, in this situation she'd just tell everyone she was fine and bury those feelings deep, but here he was saying them out loud. Just being his amazing self, he'd taught her a lot about her own issues.

He raised his palms. 'It could all be too late. I would have flown that damned helicopter myself if I could have.'

'You did what you could. It's not your fault that the weather closed in.' She put her arms around his neck and held him, wishing she could take away his pain. Knowing that today's helplessness mingled with memories of him finding his mum. 'You did your best, Matthieu. That's all anyone can ever ask of you.'

'What if it isn't enough? What if I could have done more? What if I should have tried harder?' Doubt swamped his features. But she knew what he was really asking. Had he done enough for his mother? Had he missed anything? Could he have saved her?

She didn't know the answer to that, but she believed, beyond a shadow of a doubt, that there was nothing more Matthieu could have done to save the life of someone so determined to end it. So, she held him tight and whispered, 'One thing I've learnt in the ER is that sometimes bad things happen and we can't stop them, no matter how hard we try. You can't blame yourself when you absolutely do your best and when someone's too far gone to save them. You, Matthieu LeFevre, care enough to try... harder than anyone else. This is not your fault. You are enough. You are enough.'

He held on, too, silent and drawn. Her heart ached for him and she wanted, so much, to be able to carry his pain, carry all of the team's pain.

No. Carry Matthieu's pain.

The last few weeks she'd learnt so much from him: how to relax more, how to share, how to give. How to receive more, too. How to be a friend, a lover. How to care for someone. Properly care. Put their needs ahead of your own. Like Matthieu did, continually for other people. For her.

The connection between them had tightened and something had bloomed inside her, something deep and resonant and strong.

And as she held him, her heart swelled with so many more complex emotions. Sexual desire, sure. That was always present when she was with Matthieu. But this desire...this need to erase his pain and to wish him only the most wonderful of lives, this ache she carried when he wasn't around, the excitement when he was. It threatened to overwhelm her.

It was like nothing she'd experienced before. It was pure and bright and possessive and passionate. It was raw and savage, yet soft and yielding. She hadn't felt it for her ex. Not like this…so *much* of it all the time.

Matthieu nuzzled against her neck, still holding her as if she was his lifeline. 'Thank you, Rachel. I needed that. I needed you. I hope that's okay?'

'Of course. I want you to talk to me about these things. Don't ever feel you can't.' But she wasn't sure how to deal with being needed and how that made her light up inside. She wanted to hold him for ever, never wanted this closeness to end. Even though she knew it would, because something this good never lasted. 'Just…tell me you don't blame yourself. Please.'

He blinked. Then looked away. She pulled him to look at her. His pain torturing her. 'Listen to me. It wasn't your fault. You fought and you fought. You can't save everyone, Matthieu, hard as that is. And you can't lose yourself in the aftermath. It's not fair to spend the rest of your life feeling guilty for something you couldn't stop happening. Sadly…oh, so sadly, it was going to happen anyway. You'd say that to Cody, you'd say it to me, or Louis, and you have to say it to yourself. So, say it.'

Moments passed. He swallowed. Blinked. Then fixed on her gaze. 'It…wasn't my fault.'

'Oh, Matthieu.' She hugged him, her throat a raw mess of unshed tears. 'I'm so proud of you.'

Eventually, he unfolded himself from her arms and stroked her cheek. Back to his wonderful, commanding self. 'It's Christmas Eve, we need some festive cheer.'

'You go. I'll be over in a minute.' She tried to breathe out. Tried to calm herself. Because she knew what this was, this muddle of extreme emotion. And it was wondrous and yet terrifying at the same time.

She'd fallen in love with him. Or at least, was falling hard and fast and irrevocably.

And that wasn't just one of those silly personal mistakes she kept on making, it was a monumental disaster.

The bar was decorated with so much tinsel and twinkling Christmas lights it made Rachel blink and wish she'd put her sunglasses on. The log fire crackled and hissed in the corner, laughter emanated from groups huddled around tables. Christmas songs played in the background and there was a fizzy feeling in the air, of excitement and anticipation. A typical Christmas Eve.

She found Matthieu and the others sitting around a large table in the far corner, out of the way of the paying guests. She dug deep for a smile. 'Hey.'

'Doc! Come sit down. Here's a glass of your favourite.' Zoe scooted up to make space for Rachel who hop-shuffled into the seat between the receptionist and Matthieu. A glass of merlot sat in front of her on the table.

'Wow. Love the service. Thank you.'

Zoe, Matthieu, Louis and two of the lift hands all began jeering as Cody tried to extricate a wooden brick from the middle of a tower on the table.

'Hey. Any news on Justin?' Matthieu said quietly. As always, his manner with her was friendly, but not too intimate, when they were in company. Truth was, she didn't want to sit so close to him now she'd had her revelation and actually acknowledged her feelings.

She refused to love him. She refused to love anyone. And even if she had developed feelings, she would bury them deep inside her and pretend they weren't there. 'They've managed to stabilise him and he's having brain scans at the moment. They'll have more news for us tomorrow. I'll chase it up in the morning.'

'Thanks.'

'You want to have a general debrief?'

'That's what I'd planned.' Matthieu looked round the laughing group. 'But not at the moment. Cody was the one most shaken up and he seems okay. If he brings it up we can talk it through. Let him have fun for now.'

'Okay. Hopefully, we'll be able to give him good news tomorrow.'

'In the meantime, we put on a happy face for the guests and staff for Christmas Day, too.' He looked troubled, but determined not to let it overtake him. 'You want to join in Jenga?'

'Yes!' Louis clapped, clearly having already had a fair amount of Christmas spirit. 'You can be on our team, Rach.'

'No.' Zoe held up her hand. 'She's sitting next to me, she can be on my team.'

'Hey, don't fight over me.' Rachel's chest glowed.

Despite her misgivings about her feelings for Matthieu she found herself laughing, feeling valued and part of something. This was what she wanted, right? To be part of the team. Having friends. Not to have fallen in love with Matthieu thrown into the mix.

He was so close, she could feel the brush of his arm against hers and even now ached for his hands on her. She closed her eyes briefly, pushing it all further down inside. 'Looks like the teams have even numbers at the moment. I'll join in next round.'

She watched as they all took turns to tease out a brick, the emotional fallout of Justin's accident easing a little with the camaraderie. Another round of drinks was bought, another game of Jenga played. This time she did join in and enjoyed the banter, even if her team, consisting of herself, Zoe and Matthieu, lost.

Then the hum of conversation settled as they dived into a new round of drinks. Presently, Cody asked, 'So, are we all set for tomorrow? Fancy dress outfits sorted? All our elves and fairies present and correct? How's Santa feeling? Going to be up all night?'

Matthieu blinked. 'Making presents, you mean?'

'Sure.' Louis winked. 'If that's what you want to call it.'

'Everything is wrapped and ready.' Matthieu shook his head, frowning, but ignoring the innuendo. 'Some of the kids get a bit shy in the spotlight, so I'm going to need some help with handing the gifts out.'

'Oh? Aren't you Santa's little helper, Rachel?' Louis laughed, his eyes wide and bright.

A hum of unease settled across Rachel's chest, but she ignored it. Louis was always making silly comments. But Zoe was laughing, Cody, too.

'I... Um... I...' Her eyes darted to Matthieu for clues on how to respond, but he didn't look at her. She looked back to the others, feeling just as shy as those little kids, with the glare of everyone's gazes on her. 'Happy to help you all out. Any time.' She put emphasis on the *all*.

'But especially Mattie.' Louis laughed. 'Come on, seriously? Did you think we didn't know? It's great news. It's about time Mattie found someone.'

Zoe nudged her. 'It's lovely. Matt deserves some happiness after everything he's been through. We're so pleased for you both.'

'Cheers to the lovebirds.' Cody grinned and raised his glass at them in salutation.

So much for having a secret. Everyone knew.

Rachel's world tilted, the ground beneath her quick-sand-soft. She felt completely exposed. As if she'd just walked across the bar naked. As if they could all see her hopes and dreams written on her face and knew her deepest wishes. As if they could see the light she had for Matthieu that was burning brighter and brighter every second she spent with him. And that they knew…because everyone could see, everyone knew, that it was all out of reach for her. She wasn't enough. She was fooling herself that she could have what she wanted.

Because why would she get it now, when she'd never had it before?

They were laughing. Matthieu was silent. He didn't look at her, but he didn't say anything to contradict Louis either. He just let the comments hang.

So much for being part of a team and having friends. These people weren't her friends, they were his friends. This was his team. Had been before she arrived and would be after she left. She was reliving everything she'd run away from. Worse, their secret felt tarnished, sullied.

And the sad truth was, she loved him and she couldn't bury that any more. It kept bubbling up inside her and threatening to show itself in her mannerisms, her tone, her gaze. It was ever present. All. The. Time.

When would she ever learn?

Her hands felt clammy and her breath caught in her tight chest. The walls were pressing in on her, faces, too…the same way they had when she'd walked down the aisle without a husband.

She had to get out. Air. Space.

'Um. Right. That's me done.' Her cheeks burned as she jumped up and started to shuffle out in front of a baffled-looking Zoe. 'I'm going to get an early night.'

'But you haven't finished your drink.' Zoe tapped Rachel's hand.

'I'm done. Thanks.' And she was. Completely done. This thing was done. It had to be. She didn't want to be gossip, or the subject of innuendo. She didn't want complications at work. She didn't want to be in love with Matthieu, or with anyone. She didn't want to be wanting permanent or for ever with someone when it was never going to happen.

Tears stung her eyes as she hopped on her crutches towards the exit, ungainly and uncoordinated, wishing she could run, instead of limping off with all these eyes watching her.

Wishing she hadn't let herself fall so hard in so many ways.

Wishing she'd never met Matthieu LeFevre, never mind lost her heart to him.

CHAPTER SIXTEEN

HE FOUND HER in the barn, sitting on the dusty floor wrapped around Odin and he knew, just by her slumped posture, that he should have left her alone. But he'd been compelled to come find her.

'*Coucou*, Rachel.'

'Matthieu.' Her flat tone was enough warning for more anxiety to slither into his chest. Bloody Louis. A best friend knew when to joke and when to shut up. But then, Louis didn't know anything, he just thought he did. He didn't know about the deal Matthieu had with Rachel. That it was all about the sex. And that it was so much more than that.

She'd pushed him so hard into a corner that he'd had to face the fact he'd been letting guilt run his life. She'd held him as if he mattered. He'd trusted her with his fears. He'd relished her kisses and lovemaking.

Simply, being with her was the best thing in his life.

And feeling that scared the life out of him.

He slid down the wall and sat next to her, his heart a mangled mess, because here he was, trying to read her micro expressions all over again. Wanting to read her mind, to be wrapped in her, in his sheets, rather than watching her wrap herself round his dog like it was some sort of shield. 'You hot-footed it out of the bar and I went to look for you. I figured if you weren't in your chalet, you'd be here with pretty boy. I just want to make sure you're okay.' He didn't even have to explain why. He'd seen the humiliation on her face.

She looked at him, eyes the colour of molten pewter shining with tears. 'Not okay at all.'

'What? No *I'm fine*?' As a joke it was lame, but it gave him an insight into her psyche. She could tell him her feelings now, that was good. Even if those feelings were used against him.

'I'm not fine, Matthieu.' Her voice snapped on *fine* so he put his hand on her arm, just wanting to touch her and help soothe whatever it was that hurt.

'What's wrong?'

She hugged Odin to her chest. 'Everyone was laughing. They all know about us.'

'They just think they do.'

Her eyes blazed now. 'You didn't say anything to shut them up.'

'What could I say? You asked me not to say anything to them about it. I couldn't deny or admit anything.' He'd been stuck between a rock and a hard place, so he'd held back. 'Besides, it's not the worst thing in the world if people know we've got something going on. They were happy for us.'

'I've been here before, remember? I know what the fallout is like. Gossip, innuendo. Talk. When it ends there'll be the dissection of whose friend is whose. And, when it comes down to it, they're all yours. And I'll be alone. Again. Which is fine when I choose it, but not when I have it thrust on me because of a break-up. I like these people, Matthieu. I like this team. I don't want to be marginalised or looking on social media to see what kind of fun you're having without me.' She shook her head vehemently. 'We should never have started this.'

'But we did and we could just carry on having fun and to hell with everyone else.' But he didn't feel as though it was just fun—she was right, it was more than that. It was everything. Intimate, sexy…terrifying.

'It's…the thing is…' She took a deep breath, her bottom lip wavering on the inhale. 'Oh, Matthieu, I've done something really stupid.'

'I doubt that very much. What did you do?'

'You really don't want to know.' She shook her head and nuzzled Odin's fur, looking forlorn and wretched.

His heart pumped like a rifle shot. He wasn't sure he did want to know, but he needed to hear. 'Try me?'

Another deep breath. 'Despite what we agreed, I know deep in my heart that I do want to be an us. I want the team to know that we're doing…whatever it is we're doing, because I want it to last. I don't want to sneak around, I want to stay around and that's crazy. We agreed. I agreed. This…' She pointed to her heart. 'This is not me. None of it makes sense. And yet it makes complete sense.' Shock ran through her gaze. 'I've fallen for you, Matthieu. I didn't want to, I tried not to, but there it is. Give me a bit longer here and I have a bad feeling I might fall in love with you.'

'Okay.' He thought of all the things he could reply, but they bundled up in his chest.

'And I don't want to. I can't. I just can't.' She gently moved Odin from her legs and clambered to standing, favouring her bad leg, putting her hand on the wall to steady herself. 'It's too hard. Too quick. Too much. I like you too much.'

She loved him, but didn't want to.

Now he wished he hadn't got her to open up. He didn't want love. He didn't want to love anyone.

And he had a bad feeling he was already halfway there, too. And then what? Heartache. Disaster. She'd leave. Trash his heart. Everyone left, one way or another.

He stood, too, trying to settle his tumultuous thoughts, having given up on settling his emotions. 'We agreed it wouldn't get serious.'

Pointless words when his body was aching for her. When the centre of his chest felt as if it was on fire.

'I know.' She smiled sadly and it damned near pierced his heart. 'Silly me. But I couldn't help it. You're so thoughtful and kind. And you kiss…well, you kiss so well. And you listen and you see me. And I thought I could lock my feelings away like I've always done, but I can't stop them coming to the surface. And I don't want them to. I don't want to feel them. I want to be the Ice Queen. Untouchable. I like living like that. Not like this. With too much inside.' She hugged her arms round her chest. 'We need to stop it all and go back to just working together. I'm sorry, Matthieu.'

'You want me to forget the last few weeks and you want me to be okay about it?' He didn't know how to navigate this. Couldn't reconcile this feeling inside him. He should have been relieved, but he felt broken, as if his chest was imploding.

Her eyes closed for a second and she looked as if she was struggling to hold herself together. 'You don't get a choice.'

Yeah. Figured. His life on repeat.

But she was right about falling in love; that could never happen. He'd avoided it for the last few years, giving relationships a wide berth, not allowing anyone to get close. So why he'd let his guard down with Rachel Tait he didn't know. She was so locked up, almost impenetrable. Worse, she didn't *want* to love him.

Maybe that had been the challenge?

Whatever, it didn't matter why he'd let his guard down he had, over and over and now she'd said she could fall in love with him and that fleetingly had made everything brighter. Because he knew those fledgling emotions were seeded inside him, too.

Before he could stop himself, the words tumbled out on one last high of hope. 'What if...what if we tried to navigate a way through this?'

'How?' Desolation flickered in her expression. 'How do we do this without getting closer?'

'I don't know. I just know we can't give up.'

'I just did, Matthieu.'

'We can work it out.' He didn't want to sound desperate, but maybe he could convince her? To what? To stay just to make him feel better? He didn't want that.

'I can't do it.' She shook her head. 'I told you. I can't be part of a couple.'

'You just weren't good at being part of a couple with David.'

'I'm sorry.' She leaned in and kissed his cheek, then slid her arms into her crutches and worked her way towards the door.

'But Rachel... Rachel!' He strode towards her, but she tugged the door open and slipped out into the freezing night.

'Don't follow me, Matthieu, please. I can manage.'

The familiar cloak of hopelessness fitted itself around him. 'But—'

'No.' She pressed her lips together, but he could see her

mouth trembling as if she was holding in a sob. 'Please. Matthieu. Please don't touch me. I'm *fine*.'

And with that he knew he'd lost her.

She hadn't made another mistake, she hadn't. Cutting things off with Matthieu was the best idea.

She'd never wanted a big love and now…she had a bad feeling she'd found one and it was just what she'd imagined. It hurt. Physically hurt. So damned much.

Tears kept welling up and as soon as she fisted them away more came. She couldn't stop them no matter how much she told herself she'd done the right thing. Her body disagreed. Her heart was staging its own revolution.

She hobbled back to the chalet, hoping he wasn't following her, but wishing he was. Wishing he'd try to convince her to go back to his bed. Crazy.

This falling in love thing made no sense. Every step she took away from him made her heart splinter just a little bit more. The crazier thing was, he'd looked at her as if he felt the same way. As if he wanted her as much as she wanted him. *We can work it out.*

She'd almost wavered then. Almost said yes, let's try.

But it wouldn't work out. It had never worked out, not with her parents, not with David, so why would Matthieu be any different? She'd be left with a broken heart. Just like every time she'd tried to love someone.

And this time she didn't know if she'd have the strength to fix it.

It looked as though this Christmas was going to be one of the difficult ones. He'd thought he'd seen the back of those when his mother died, but, no. Here he was, Father

Christmas, feeling the least Christmassy he'd ever felt. Feeling more alone than he'd ever felt.

Next year he'd go to the beach, somewhere exotic, and get very drunk.

Sure, the hotel lounge looked amazing. The ice swan centrepiece on the table was magnificent. The tree was magical. The long lunch had been delicious and he'd been surrounded by friends. It was the kind of Christmas he'd always dreamed of. Only, two people were missing.

One he'd never get back, he would only ever have memories, but the other woman was just…absent. God knew where she was. At least with an injured knee she wouldn't be solo skiing.

Over the last few hours he'd gone over and over what they'd shared together, the things she'd said in the barn. And the things she hadn't said. He knew it had taken so much for her to admit her feelings and he'd been too stupid or scared to accept them warmheartedly. He didn't want to love or be loved. Love wasn't enough.

But he did want her.

'*Père Noël!*' A chorus of screeches.

For now, the fate of Christmas was solely in his hands.

He walked towards the group of children sitting by the tree, the sack of bulging gifts over his shoulder, not feeling at all in the mood, but when he saw the pure joy on their faces he hauled on a grin of his own.

'*Père Noël!*'

Cheering, the kids gathered round and he tried his best to be the Father Christmas they wanted. It didn't take long to hand out the gifts and soon he had the last one in his hands. He sought out the recipient. 'And last, but not at all least, Isla!'

'*Merci,* Matthieu,' she whispered, taking the present in both hands and rewarding him with a huge smile.

'Ahem… *Père Noël*, please.' He winked, really feel-ing the smile he was giving her instead of just faking it.

'I know it's you, Matthieu.' She laughed and hopped back to her mother's open arms. The little unit of three seemed genuinely happy.

He looked at Michael and Bianca. Against so many odds and dealing with two super-egos they'd found a way to make things work, thanks to Rachel. By not accept-ing anything but what the little girl deserved she'd made a huge change in Isla's life and in her parents' marriage.

Pain sliced through him. He wished she was here to see this, to be part of this.

He missed her more than he'd thought possible. An ache he knew would never ease. A future he hadn't known he'd wanted had been snatched away from him. A future with her in it and possibly some kids of their own. Hell, he hadn't ever thought about it and he missed it already.

She'd be a fierce and protective mother, a challenging wife…in a good way…pushing them to strive for the best they could be. She would love hard.

Love.

He'd believed for so long that love was the problem; he'd rejected intimacy because love hadn't worked for him. It hadn't stopped his mother taking her life and it couldn't bring her back. It had just caused him a life-time of pain.

But his mother had made the choice she'd made. He hadn't been able to stop her and guilt for his failure was the burden he carried. But Rachel was right; he'd saved her twice and fought for her for thirty-one years. He'd done his best to love her and she'd known she was loved until the very end. She'd been so determined, and so unhappy, that there'd always been the chance he wouldn't save her. Sometimes you just can't. Maybe she'd hung around a few extra years just to make sure he'd be okay. And he had been, with the help of his friends and this community.

Love.

Rachel told him that was what Sainte Colette had given him. It had helped him thrive and nurtured him. Looking back, that's what he'd tried to give them in return, by setting up this resort to give them jobs and a future. It occurred to him…no, it hit him with a force, that love had brought so many positives into his life. And he'd embraced it for a community, but hadn't thought he deserved it, or had been too damned scared to take it for himself. He'd closed himself off from intimacy out of fear. But he knew, rationally, that whatever had been going on with his mother hadn't been because he wasn't enough, it had been because she was ill and couldn't see a way through.

He'd poured all his love for his mother into this place and into his friends. Maybe now it was time to pour all his love into himself. Into a relationship?

To save himself and forge a new future.

There was only one person he wanted to share that with.

He realised then what he'd known all along, but had refused to acknowledge: he didn't just want a future without Rachel in it. He loved her.

He loved her. Yeah. That was a low blow given she didn't want him. Didn't want to love him.

But maybe, if they could put the fear aside and just talked, if he told Rachel what he felt instead of hiding from it, just maybe they could find a way.

He tugged on his ski boots, promising himself he'd find her as soon as the ski show was over.

She didn't want him to save her, but he might just have to try to save himself and convince her to come along for the ride.

CHAPTER SEVENTEEN

HER HEART WAS breaking so badly she'd hidden away from the festivities, but she wanted to see the show.

With the aid of Bianca and Michael she'd hobbled on to the chairlift and up to the ski field and now stood with them and Isla whooping as elves, fairies, angels and reindeer skied down the slopes doing acrobatics that seemed to defy gravity, to a soundtrack of Christmas songs blaring through loudspeakers. Rachel looked around and saw the magic in everyone's faces and wished she could feel it for herself.

But she was too sad right now. Maybe next year, on a beach, a cocktail in her hand, she'd celebrate Christmas, but not today. Not when her heart hurt so much.

Next to her Bianca and Michael shared a kiss, then a hug with their daughter. They looked happy. Really, genuinely happy. And she hoped it would last.

She hadn't ever wanted what her parents had had, that destructive force and passion, she'd been happy just to be part of something. To share a kiss on Christmas Day with someone who mattered, with someone who cared for her. Someone who thought she mattered too.

Poor David. She'd thought he was the answer. Thought jumping into a marriage with him would protect her from all that hurt, that she'd be content to be content. He clearly hadn't been. He'd wanted more...and who could blame him in the end? Because deep, caring, proper big love was wonderful. It was everything.

Until it ended.

She'd ended it with Matthieu because it had been growing, deepening, becoming a big love for her and she hadn't been able to trust her judgement a second time. Neither of them had wanted more, so it had only been a matter of time before Matthieu ended it anyway. That's what she told herself.

A jingle of bells had her scanning the slopes and she held her breath, waiting for Matthieu to appear. Then there he was, dressed in his red suit and white beard, flying through the air to raucous cheers and applause.

She watched as he whooshed down the hill, then on to the rail for a jump. She held her breath again as he soared high, doing the splits mid-air, then landing.

Wobbled. Righted himself. *No.*

He wobbled again, then slid sideways, falling, tumbling down the hill towards the barrier.

Everyone stopped talking. All she could hear was the tinny music and the sound of her heart rushing in her ears. He was falling and falling and falling. Then he stopped.

Get up. Get the hell up.

But he didn't move.

Come on, Matthieu. Please.

Nothing.

No. Matthieu. Please. No.

We can work it out. He'd given her a lifeline with those words, a chance to talk things through. To be honest about what they wanted and felt. To be together. To trust each other with secrets and pain and to help each other heal. And she'd been so scared by what she was feeling she'd panicked. Rejected him.

He still didn't move.

Matthieu.

Ray Shell.

All the love and truth she'd been hiding from hit her then like a thunderbolt. What if she never got the chance to tell him properly how she felt? What if it was too late? What if all her second-guessing had stopped her having the best thing she could ever have in her life? Matthieu LeFevre. Her big love of a lifetime.

No. She couldn't lose him. Wouldn't.

'Matthieu! No!' She pushed her way through the crowd, wincing at every painful step as she hobbled across the snow. When she reached him, he was being attended to by an elf and a reindeer she recognised as Cody. 'Let me through. Please.'

She fell to her knees and touched his face, then closed her eyes and pressed her mouth to his. Felt the shudder of breath against her lips. But he didn't kiss her back. 'Are you okay? Please be okay.'

'Hey, there.' Blue eyes blinked up at her. His hand went to her trembling lips, but she grasped his fingers.

It was fear, she knew. For both of them. Fear of getting hurt. Fear of rejection. Fear of letting someone in. But hell, if he could fly down that mountain without a second thought and trust that he would land well, surely he could take a chance on her? Trust her?

But she knew that saying she loved him wasn't enough, he needed to see it in action to believe it. Never mind that she had an audience, if she didn't do it now, she'd regret it. This was her one chance to tell him how she really felt and if he rejected her again then she'd take it.

One chance.

So, here she was. Thinking about opening her heart to him, putting herself on the line the way she had with David. Asking. Reaching. Saying the words. The last time had been the biggest mistake of her life. But this was different, because Matthieu was different.

She took a steadying breath. 'Matthieu, I need you to listen. I was hurt very badly. I didn't want to fall for anyone else. I didn't want to open my heart. I wanted to close myself off, stay apart, be an ice queen. I've always been scared to show my emotions because no one ever seemed to care, but I can't control them with you. I love you so, so much. And I know you're…hesitant, but can we try? At least…' she suddenly felt shy '… I'd like to try.'

But he shook his head, his hand limp in hers.

He didn't want her.

Blue eyes.

Matthieu's eyes were brown. Weren't they? Maybe she'd been wrong.

'Ahem.' Someone tapped her shoulder.

She put her hand up. 'Please. Wait. Can't you see I'm trying to—?'

'Kiss my staff?'

That voice. *Matthieu.* She looked down at Father Christmas. Two Matthieus? 'What? But…?'

Looking decidedly un-Father Christmassy in his resort salopettes, he helped her to stand up. 'I had to do a few things, then took an urgent call from Justin's mother, so Louis took my place.'

'Oh.' She'd just sworn her love to his best friend.

Great.

Her heart thundered against her ribcage. 'How's Justin doing?'

Not on Christmas Day. Please, not on Christmas Day.

'He's opened his eyes. He's moving his arms and legs.

He has a long way to go, but it looks like he's going to be okay.'

Her heart went into free fall. 'Oh, thank goodness. That's excellent. I'm so relieved.'

'Me, too.' He was laughing, his eyes glittering. 'Now, I want to know why you're kissing my staff in front of the whole resort?'

'I thought it was you. I wanted you to know how I feel.'

'Can I get up now? I'm getting cold,' Louis grumbled and Matthieu helped him stand up. 'Are you okay?'

'I will be when I've watched this.' Louis slapped his friend on the back. 'Go on, mate. You've been a real pain for the last few hours. Don't let her get away. Don't mess this up.'

'I don't intend to.' He took her hands and, in front of the whole community who had gathered round he said, 'Rachel, you said you loved me.'

'Yes. I do. More than anything.'

'You've said it before.'

She smiled, remembering. 'This time I mean it. Really mean it. I *love you*, love you, Matthieu. I didn't want to, but I couldn't help it. Now I want everyone to know. I love you.'

He nodded, his eyes shimmering. 'And I'm an idiot. I think everyone will agree?'

Jeers erupted from the crowd.

'A scared idiot, too. I didn't think much of love, to be honest. It didn't help my mum and it just smashed my heart. So, I did what you did, Rachel. When it came to relationships, I locked those smashed pieces away. But then you came along, and you challenged me in so many ways. You cared for me, hurt for me. And you've started to put those pieces back together.'

Her throat was raw. 'Matthieu—'

'But then I felt so *much* for you I panicked. I thought I could lock everything up again, but I can't.'

Rachel pressed her lips together, holding back a sob. 'We've both been hurt before, Matthieu. It's hard to let ourselves fall into something like this.'

'We get to choose, though. We decide if we want to let someone in. And I choose you, Rachel Tait.'

She couldn't believe it. He hadn't fought for her, for them, last night. But even if he had she wouldn't have wanted to hear it. She'd set her mind on leaving.

But now he was saying these words. Words she'd never thought she'd hear from anyone. She could see the love and the trust in his eyes. 'I choose you, too.'

He reached into his pocket and pulled out a little box. 'I have a gift for you. To show you that I want you to have everything you ever wanted. To show you how much I care…no…how much I love you, Rachel, and want to keep on loving you.'

'Is it…? No.' She shook her head. A proposal was too soon. She wasn't sure she even wanted a wedding after her last disastrous attempt. 'What…?'

He pushed the box closer. 'Open it. I think you'll understand.'

Heart thundering, she took the box and opened it. Inside, a pair of crystal and silver ballet shoe earrings twinkled and sparkled. She gasped, understanding exactly. He couldn't give her her childhood dream, but he could give her the next best thing.

Her throat felt tight, but her chest felt blown wide open. He listened. He saw her. He loved her. 'Oh, Matthieu, they're beautiful.'

'Like you.' He kissed her cheek. 'I want you to know I hold your dreams and will help you chase them. I believe in you and I want to hold your heart and your hand for ever.'

'Oh, Matthieu.' The last vestiges of fear melted away. 'Thank you.'

'And I know you were badly let down when you should have been happiest. I want you to know, I will never let you down.'

Her wedding day? 'It's too early to talk about things like that.'

'My love will last for ever, Rachel. I'll wait until you're ready.' He closed his hand over hers. 'I promise with all my heart.'

'Thank you. Thank you so much. But I don't have anything to give you.'

'I can think of a few things.' He laughed and drew her closer. 'How about coming over to my place and having our own Christmas celebration. Just the two of us?'

'Definitely.' She leaned in, trying to shut out all the cheers and applause. He chose her. She let the words settle in her heart. This amazing man chose *her*.

Then he kissed her, and the rest of the world melted away...and she knew it would be the first of many happy Christmases together.

EPILOGUE

One year later...

'THIS HAS BEEN the best Christmas ever.' Matthieu wrapped Rachel in a hug and kissed her neck. The show had gone well, no one had fallen this time, the guests were happy, the evening was just theirs to enjoy.

She looked out of the lodge window and sighed, knowing she'd never get tired of this view. Then leaned into her husband, definitely never getting tired of that view either. She twisted her shiny new wedding ring round her finger and hugged him close. In the end she hadn't wanted to wait and their wedding last month had been a simple ceremony with no aisle, no parents and no surprises. 'Best year ever.'

And going to get better...

He squeezed her gently. 'Okay. Sit down, we've done all the hard work. It's time to relax.'

'Wait—' She felt him slip away from her and heard the pop of a champagne bottle cork.

Aargh. Too late. 'Um...can I have hot chocolate instead?'

'No bubbles?' Frowning, he poured out a glass for one, then put a pan on the stovetop and poured milk into it, discreetly adding the secret ingredients that he still refused to divulge.

'Not today, thanks.'

Not for nine months, actually...

'You feeling okay?' His smile turned into a concerned frown.

'I'm—'

'Fine?' He laughed. Then he peered at her. 'Not fine? What's wrong, *chérie*?'

She was more than fine. Damned fine. The finest she'd ever felt in her whole life. She tried to hide her excitement but couldn't. 'I have a present for you.'

'But you gave me my gifts this morning.'

'One more.' She reached to the back of their little Christmas tree and pulled out a box she'd hidden. 'Happy Christmas, darling.'

He looked at her, eyes narrowing. 'But? What—?'

'Open it.' Her heart was thumping.

He tore the wrapping paper off and opened the box, pulling out the tiniest pair of ski boots ever made. 'What's this? These are baby size.'

Her heart swelled. 'We're going to need them.'

'What?' His eyes shone as reality dawned and he pressed his palm to her non-bump. 'Wow. A baby? A dad? Me?'

'Yes, Matthieu. And you'll be amazing at it.'

He kissed her long and hard. 'Our baby is going to have the best parents in the world. I love you, Rachel Tait.'

After their dysfunctional childhoods they deserved a proper family. One filled with love and not fear. With understanding, not one-upmanship. With an abundance of health and happiness.

She put her hand over his, over her stomach. 'I love you, too. Or should it be, I love you two?'

He nuzzled her hair. 'Really, truly the best Christmas ever.'

And only going to get better.

Just the three of them and a whole lot of love.

* * * * *

CHRISTMAS MIRACLE
AT THE CASTLE

ALISON ROBERTS

MILLS & BOON

For Becky
With so much love and happy memories
of magical Christmas moments. xxx

CHAPTER ONE

THERE WAS NO doubt about it—this was going to be the best Christmas *ever*.

The sheer joy of seeing the first, fat flakes of snow drifting down onto the high street in Inverness, Scotland, stopped Dr Abby Hawkins in her tracks. With a level of excitement that was probably more appropriate for one of her small patients in a paediatric ward, she tilted her face to stare up at the slate-grey sky. She had the presence of mind to behave well enough not to poke out her tongue, but she did hold out her gloved hands, palm upwards, hoping to catch some flakes that way. She knew she was creating a bit of an obstacle on one side of a footpath crowded with Christmas shoppers, but it was simply irresistible to savour this moment of pure magic.

'Never seen snow before, lassie?'

Abby's head swerved fast enough for her to identify that the speaker was the driver of a taxi amongst traffic that had ground to a halt beside her.

'Not for Christmas,' she told the taxi driver. It felt as if she were smiling from ear to ear. 'Not in New Zealand.'

'You're a long way from home, then.' The traffic was lurching back into motion so he began sliding his window shut. 'Aye, well…you'd best make the most of it. Might be pretty enough now but it'll turn to slush. It always does…'

The window closed with an audible clunk and the wave over his shoulder as he departed looked more like a gesture of dismissal, but Abby wasn't about to let that kind of attitude from a Christmas Grinch spoil the moment. Nothing could spoil this. The snow was falling more thickly and it was beginning to coat things, like the shiny red top of a mail box nearby and Abby couldn't remember the last time she'd felt quite *this* excited.

She'd been spot on to choose to come to the north of Scotland, thinking that it would offer her the best chance to have a white Christmas for the first time in her life. No, that wasn't quite true, was it? The choice had really been made well before she'd thought of that particular bonus. In fact, she'd been so captured by the unusual advertisement she'd seen in the professional careers opportunities section of *The Lancet* that she would have applied even if it had been a Christmas camp set in the middle of the Sahara Desert with zero chance of experiencing a decent snowfall.

Because Christmas was all about children and these were special kids that were being treated to a fantasy Christmas. Kids that had congenital heart problems, family circumstances that ranged from difficult to appalling and, as if that weren't already a heart wrenching situation, they were also sick enough to need expert medical staff available twenty-four-seven. It was a marriage made in heaven. Abby not only adored being with children, she had just spent a year in London, completing a year of specialist paediatric cardiology training and she was taking a short break to think about exactly what she wanted in her next position. She also adored everything to do with Christmas and, as if that combination weren't perfect enough, this unexpected five-day gig was happening in a castle that looked as if it had come straight out of a fairy tale with its stone walls and turrets, a lake and a forest in its extensive estate and a dramatic backdrop of rugged looking mountains.

Abby had forgotten all about the grumpy, Grinchy taxi driver as she ducked across the road, heading for a pharmacy. She couldn't be happier. Except that she'd accidentally left her toilet bag behind in the B&B she'd stayed in last night to break the long journey and she couldn't turn up at the castle and ask to be provided with shampoo and toothpaste and makeup and even a hairbrush, could she? There were other things she only realised she needed to add to her basket as she spotted them on the shelves and some things that had definitely not been left behind in her toilet bag—like the wearable decoration of a small elf, his legs forming part of the headband's curve. His arms were outstretched, he had a huge grin on his face and there was a real bell on top of his hat that would jingle merrily when the wearer moved their head. The children she would be caring for would love that, wouldn't they?

Never mind the kids… Abby loved it herself. She had long suspected that there was a part of her that had never quite grown up but that was often a good thing in her line of work, because she could explain things to older children in a way they could understand and she had a knack of finding ways to distract any child or baby from a frightening or unpleasant medical intervention, and even make them laugh sometimes. It was always more noticeable at this time of year, of course, because she could so easily tap into the magic of Christmas with all the joy of a child.

And it was going to be on a totally different level this time. So different, it felt…huge. As if being accepted for this position was an honour. That she was privileged to be part of something that would be creating a memory like no other for these children and the people who loved them. After reading up on the information she'd been provided with, Abby knew that for some of the children coming to this Christmas camp at the castle, it was a miracle that they were actually having another Christmas. Most would be coming with carers or parents and siblings—the people who were living with the fear that serious illness could bring so they deserved to share a very special celebration. It was enough to mean Abby needed to swallow a rather large lump in her throat. She couldn't wait to meet Margaret McKendry, who must be a rather special woman having apparently been making this happen for twenty-five years now. She couldn't wait to meet the children and the rest of the team who would be caring for them and she was hanging out for a first glimpse of the castle.

She just couldn't wait, full stop. Abby was itching to get back on the road that led to the village of Kirkwood and on to Ravenswood Castle as soon as possible so her heart sank a little as she saw the length of the queue to get to the check-out counter. She had no choice than to take her place at the back, however, and wait patiently behind a tall man in a black woollen beanie hat and puffer anorak, who was focused intently on the screen of the phone he was holding.

There was no doubt about it. This was shaping up to be the worst Christmas ever and that was saying something when Euan McKendry had learned to dread the festive season so many years ago he'd barely been in his teens.

The meteorological website he was scanning was forecasting heavy snow showers for the next twenty-four to thirty-six hours. It would clear by Christmas Eve but, by then, there would probably be snow drifts deep enough to bury cars and/or people. It would be bitterly cold and he would, as always, be sleeping in that turret that had drafts whistling through the gaps around those mullioned windows.

One of these days, Euan promised himself, he would go and spend Christmas on the beach. In Australia. Or New Zealand. Somewhere he could soak up the sun and have a barbecued Christmas dinner of steak or prawns, perhaps, instead of turkey and bread sauce. He could swim in the surf, feel the sand between his bare toes and not have a care in the world. One day, he wouldn't have to steel his heart to cope with all the sad memories or having his heartstrings pulled as tightly as piano wire by the stories and personalities of not only sick but disadvantaged children.

But it wouldn't be this year. Not when this could be the last Christmas camp that his grandmother, Maggie, would be well enough to host in the astonishing castle that was her home and she had told him how much she needed him to be there.

'Just one more time, Euan. It's the twenty-fifth anniversary of that first time. Please come...this is for Fiona, after all...it's always been for Fiona and, if this is going to be the last time, I want it to be absolutely the best ever.'

No... Euan tried to stave off the inevitable pull back in time. He wasn't going to start thinking about the younger sister he'd lost so long ago. He wasn't even going to dwell on the fact that his beloved grandmother was awaiting results on a biopsy that probably wouldn't come until after Christmas now but the surgeon had warned her the news might not be good. If it was an ovarian cancer, it was well advanced and the prognosis was poor.

'If this is going to be the last time...'

Euan could actually hear the echo of his gran's voice in

his head from that phone call last night and, if he wasn't careful, he might end up standing in this queue—waiting to pick up the prescription pain medication he'd decided to add to his medical kit at the last minute—with tears running down his face. And he wasn't about to let that happen. He hadn't let it happen in twenty-five years. He might not have inherited Maggie's remarkable ability to face the hardest parts of life with a dogged determination to find something to be thankful for, that silver lining she insisted was there somewhere, even in the darkest of clouds, but he could do what he was very, very good at doing. He could keep that door in his heart firmly locked and avoid the kind of emotions he never wanted to grapple with again.

It might have been difficult to distract himself completely from the worry of what those biopsy results would show, or the fact that he was adding a powerful analgesic to his kit because his gran might be in a lot more pain than she was admitting to, if he hadn't been actually jolted hard enough to prevent him thinking about anything other than what was happening in this moment.

Someone had pushed him from behind, hard enough to make him almost lose his balance. His phone flew from his hand to land with an ominous crash on the tiled floor of this old pharmacy. There was a much louder crash at the same time.

'Oh… I'm *so* sorry…'

Euan ignored the woman directly behind him in the queue because he was scanning the whole scene, automatically assessing where his attention was needed first. Further back in the queue, a man was standing with his fists raised.

'This is a *queue*. You don't push in, mate,' he was shouting. 'Got it?'

Another man was on the floor, sitting amongst a pile of hair products that had fallen off the shelf he'd obviously been pushed into. No wonder other people had hastily tried to get out of the way of the falling containers and boxes so it was no fault of the woman with the unusual accent that she'd bumped into him so abruptly. It possibly wasn't the fault of the man who was now picking himself up from the floor, either. Maybe he'd only wanted to get to the other side of the queue to buy some shampoo but fortunately he wasn't about to engage with the angry customer protecting his place in the line. He got up and headed for the door as stressed looking pharmacy staff were rushing in to clear the mess.

Euan shook his head in bemusement, swore under his breath and bent to retrieve his phone, which had been stopped from sliding further away by a basket someone had put down on the floor. He wasn't surprised to see the deep, jagged crack on the screen of his phone after how loud the impact had been but his heart sank a little further. There was no chance he could get that fixed before heading out of Inverness so it would be a pain to use the device for at least a week. At the same moment he was noting what was going to be a serious nuisance, something in his peripheral vision caught his attention and it instantly added insult to injury. On the top of that almost full basket was one of those ridiculous bits of Christmas nonsense that people made a point of putting on their heads, like reindeer horns, or miniature Santa hats. This had to be the worst example he'd ever seen— a stupidly grinning elf who had his arms outstretched as if he was ready to hug anyone and everyone.

It was so horrible that, as Euan straightened again, he couldn't help looking behind him at the person who was about to purchase it. The same person who'd just apologised for shoving him in the back. He knew that he might not be disguising how he felt about someone who would choose to buy such an idiotic stuffed toy to wear on their head but he didn't care. Maybe he would be doing her a favour and she'd decide to leave it behind. His look, which was admittedly probably more like a glare, clearly surprised the woman but it was backfiring badly for Euan because *he* was even more surprised.

Gobsmacked, in fact.

He was staring at what had to be the most beautiful woman he'd ever seen in his life.

Huge, blue eyes framed by a tangle of dark lashes. A generous mouth that had clearly been designed with laughter and smiling in mind and her lips were clearly on the brink of curling right now, because she was not only gorgeous but she appeared to be quite possibly the *happiest* woman Euan had ever seen and that glow was only enhanced by her long, long blonde hair that fell in soft waves from beneath her red woollen hat. The hat didn't look quite right, did it? A shining halo might have been more appropriate because, whoever this was, she looked like a Christmas angel that had suddenly come to life.

Good grief…

She was definitely smiling at him now.

And, dammit, but it was making her look even more beautiful. Even happier.

'Is your phone okay?'

'No.' The word came out as a growl. 'The screen's broken.'

'Oh, no… I'm so sorry. I didn't mean to land on you like that, honestly. I got shoved as well.'

Euan was finding it impossible to look away and he could feel his forehead creasing into a frown. 'What are you?' he asked. 'American?'

'No.' The smile widened. 'You're way off. Wrong side of the world, even. I'm a Kiwi.' She tilted her head to look past him and then raised an eyebrow. 'Queue's moving. If you leave a gap, someone else might try and push in and I think there are a few people around here who might be grumpy enough already.' She was shaking her head sadly. 'I really don't understand it.'

Having to take a step closer to the cashier meant that Euan had to look away and he had no intention of looking back. Or of continuing this conversation with a complete stranger. He could still hear her voice behind him, however, and he knew perfectly well that she wasn't speaking to anyone else.

'I mean, it's *Christmas*… How can anyone be so grumpy when it's the most exciting time of the year? I *love* Christmas. And it's *snowing*…'

Okay, the sheer joy in her voice was threatening to tip him over the brink. Euan turned his head. 'And you think that's a *good* thing?'

Those blue, blue eyes widened. 'It's going to be a white Christmas. I've dreamed of having one ever since I was a little kid. We might have Christmas in summer in New Zealand, but we all know a *real* Christmas has snow. And holly with red berries and robins and mistletoe and—'

'And people who are freezing because they can't afford to heat their houses and roads that become inaccessible because of the snow, which can mean that people who get sick or have an accident might actually die before help can arrive.'

The woman's jaw dropped. 'Wow…and I thought the taxi driver was enough of a Grinch. Phew…' She gave her head a tiny shake, which made that tumble of golden curls shimmer under the bright, overhead lighting. 'Is it a Scottish thing to hate Christmas in general or just a white one in particular?'

For a crazy moment, Euan was almost tempted to tell this stranger exactly why Christmas was overwhelmingly difficult for him, on a purely personal basis that had nothing to do with his nationality or the weather. But, even if she wanted to listen, which was highly unlikely given how it might tarnish that glow of happiness, these were things he never said aloud. To anyone. He did his best not to even think about them. That he'd been pushed too close to that locked place he managed to avoid for the vast majority of the year created a knee jerk defensive reaction.

'Christmas is nothing more than a charade,' he snapped. 'It's fake. As far as I'm concerned it's a promise that life is full of good things when, in reality, that promise gets broken far more often than not. The expectation that kids are going to get everything their hearts desire, that families are going to have a wonderful time cooped up together, that there'll be a feast on every table or maybe even that there's going to be some damned miracle that will suddenly make life perfect, well…'

Well…life's not like that, is it? And, making the most of every Christmas because it might well be the last for someone you love more than anyone else on earth is nothing but a recipe for heartbreak that will haunt you for the rest of your life and be at its worst every single time that one day of the year is approaching…

Not that he said that out loud, of course. Good grief… where was this all coming from, anyway? Euan had never bothered analysing exactly why he still dreaded Christmas so much because that was nothing more than a key to open that locked place where disturbing emotional stuff got relegated. Maybe his cracked phone had been the last straw. Or, more likely, that stupid elf headband.

Whatever the cause, he was appalled by the fact that he was dumping it all on a happy tourist who had every right to enjoy her Christmas as much as she wanted to.

'Sorry,' he muttered, turning back to find he had a space in front of him again. That he could actually get close enough to ask to speak to the pharmacist who would have his prescription for controlled drugs ready for him to sign out. He flicked a glance over his shoulder and even managed an apologetic half smile.

'Have a great Christmas,' he added. 'Take no notice of me.'

Take no notice?

As if…

Abby might have been getting a totally unexpected lecture about the dark side of Christmas, but that accent was *gorgeous*.

This man might win the prize for being the biggest Grinch she'd ever met in her life, but he was also…undeniably gorgeous.

Tall. Not traditionally handsome, perhaps, but he had an astonishingly compelling face. His eyes were as grey as storm clouds about to break and his features were certainly not soft. He was craggy, that was the word. Interesting. It was impossible not to notice those deep lines from his nose to the corners of his mouth and around his eyes when he frowned. And he looked as if he might frown rather a lot, in fact, but even this man's grumpiness was kind of sexy. Imagine if someone could make him smile? That reluctant tilt of his lips as he'd wished her a happy Christmas, just before he'd walked off gave Abby the feeling that a real smile would melt her on the spot.

Not that she'd ever find out. She was watching the Grinch as he got to the counter, only realising now that he didn't appear to have anything in his hands to pay for. He spoke to the cashier, who nodded and pointed him towards a hatch that opened to the prescription part of the pharmacy. A nod then summoned Abby to the counter. She began emptying the numerous items from her basket, starting with the elf headband that was on top.

Okay, it was a ridiculous accessory, especially for an adult to wear. For someone who hated Christmas as much as the intriguing man she'd just encountered, it was probably symbolic of everything that was wrong about Christmas, like hyped-up expectations and promises that got broken. Outrageous enough to be like a red rag to a bull, even. As she was a naturally empathetic person, it took some effort to push aside a curious voice in the back of her mind that was asking why he might feel so strongly about the season. What could have happened that was so awful?

Abby managed to silence the voice by the counter argument that no reason could be enough to justify spoiling the happiness of other people. Especially children. Most especially the kind of sick children that needed every extra bit of joy that came their way. The kind of children that Abby was lucky enough to be about to spend her Christmas with. And…and it was going to be a *white* Christmas. Abby beamed at the cashier as she handed over the headband. As soon as it was rung up, she took the price sticker off it and put it on her head, over her hat.

She looked sideways as she continued unloading her basket, rather hoping that that Grinch would notice what felt rather like an act of defiance. A public affirmation that, even if it made her look silly, she was going to spread as much joy as she could in the next few days. But the man wasn't at the hatch any longer. She could only

see his back, as he walked out of the pharmacy with a
paper carrier bag in his hand.

It was still early afternoon by the time Abby drove out
of Inverness and headed north to the village of Kirkwood. Her sat nav had estimated the journey time at forty
minutes but it was clearly going to take longer because
daylight seemed to be fading already and it was gloomy
enough to make the whirling snowflakes look like glitter
in her headlights, which was distracting enough to make
unfamiliar, winding roads quite a challenge.

Abby was more than up for the challenge. Growing
up on a high-country New Zealand farm and learning
to drive through rocky rivers and steep gullies, she had
the skills to cope with anything so she was actually enjoying this. Having to focus was a bonus, because she
could forget about the fact that the only two people she'd
spoken to since she arrived in Scotland had been determined to rain on her Christmas parade. At least she could
be sure that nobody like that would be a part of where
she was heading.

This Margaret McKendry, the woman who owned the
amazing castle, had to be as much of a fan of Christmas
as Abby was, to go to what had to be an enormous effort to create something so special for sick children. A
Christmas fairy, in fact, who was waving her wand to
make a dream come true and provide joyous moments to
people who deserved them more than most.

A large Christmas tree was lit up in the central square
of Kirkwood village, there were decorations hanging
over the streets and the shops looked busy. The snow
was falling much more slowly by the time Abby was
through the village and, while surfaces like hedges and
footpaths were smudged and white, the roads were still

clear enough to be safe. A helpful sign told her she was taking the correct turn off to get to Ravenswood Castle and, only minutes later, Abby found her breath completely stolen away as she got her first glimpse of the castle's turrets at the end of a long, treelined driveway. It was dark enough for it to be no more than a silhouette, but as she drove closer lights from many windows twinkled through softly drifting snowflakes and, when she got close enough for the stone walls to be towering above her, Abby could see fairy lights around the arch shaped windows and framing the rather intimidatingly grand main entrance.

She was holding her breath as she climbed the steps and lifted the lion's head knocker to tap on the massive, wooden door. She had a smile on her face, ready to greet the person who opened the door. A butler, perhaps? Or a housekeeper? Maybe it would be Mrs McKendry herself? Abby's smile widened as the door slowly swung open. She couldn't wait to tell anyone she met how excited she was to be here.

A heartbeat later, however, that smile was fading from her face so fast it was gone by the time Abby could take a new breath.

'I don't believe this,' she said. 'What the hell are *you* doing *here*?'

'I could ask you the same thing,' the Grinch said. 'Except I might do it a tad more politely.'

'Who is it, Euan?' The voice from further behind the door was coming closer. 'Oh, I do hope it's our other doctor. She's due to arrive about now and I can't wait to meet her.' The door was pulled from the man's hand. 'Oh, for heaven's sake, don't leave the poor girl standing out in the snow.'

The woman was tiny. No more than five feet tall and

she had a pixie cut of pure, white hair over a well-wrinkled face, but the first impression was not one of frailty—quite the opposite.

'I'm Margaret McKendry,' the woman said. 'But please call me Maggie.' Her smile was so welcoming Abby felt as if she were turning up at her own grandmother's house. 'You must be Abby. You're just how I imagined you'd look after we spoke on the phone.'

'Abby Hawkins.' She nodded. 'And I'm so happy to meet you, Maggie.'

'Come in, come in.' Maggie kept talking as Abby stepped inside, coming uncomfortably close to the man she knew was glaring at her. 'We've got a fire going in the drawing room and we'll get you something to eat. Are your keys still in your car?'

'Yes. I've got some bags to get out of the back.'

'Euan can park your car,' Maggie said. 'He'll get your bags and take them up to your bedroom.' She turned to the Grinch. 'I'm putting Abby in the blue room, next to you.'

He actually closed his eyes, Abby noticed, and let out a slow breath, as though he was trying to keep his temper? Or maybe preparing himself to face something unimaginably unpleasant. It was only then that she remembered she was still wearing the silly elf headband. Embarrassed, she snatched it off, but it was clearly too late to appease him in any way. For the second time in little more than an hour, he was turning to walk away from her.

Except he wasn't going to disappear this time, was he? Abby turned back to Maggie and the question in her eyes must have been obvious.

'Oh, I'm sorry, pet.' Maggie stepped forward to push the enormous door shut. 'I didn't introduce you properly.

That's Euan, my grandson. He's also the other doctor who's here to care for the children.'

Was it her imagination or was there a gleam of mischief in the older woman's glance as she led Abby across the elaborately tiled floor of an enormous foyer? Her eyes widened as she walked past a trio of what looked like genuine suits of medieval armour. Maggie led her through open double doors into a long, wide room that was filled with light and warmth. A tall Christmas tree stood to one side of an open fireplace wreathed in twinkling lights and covered in a bright rainbow of decorations but Abby wasn't distracted this time. Maggie didn't catch her gaze as she kept walking towards several couches arranged in front of the roaring fire.

She smiled as she sat down, her hand gesture an invitation for Abby to follow suit. 'Don't be fooled by that grumpiness,' she said. 'My Euan's got a heart of gold and I'm sure the two of you will get along like a house on fire.' The tone of her voice was perfectly serene but Abby was suddenly quite sure that Maggie was aware of a lot more than she was letting on.

Like a house on fire might be an apt simile, Abby thought, her heart sinking along with her body as she sat down on the squashy, feather-filled cushions of the couch opposite Maggie. A catastrophic house fire, perhaps, where there was the very real possibility that someone might not survive?

Abby had the horrible feeling that what might not survive was going to be the magical Christmas experience she had been so excited to be a part of. She might have to work very hard—for everybody, including herself—to make sure it was not going to be ruined by a real life Grinch.

At least Maggie was adorable and Abby had no doubt

that she'd be on her side of the creating Christmas joy equation. She smiled back at the Grinch's grandmother.

'Don't worry,' she said. 'I've had experience with grumpy men before so I know not to take it personally. You never know, he might find himself enjoying Christmas whether he likes it or not.'

CHAPTER TWO

IT BEGGARED BELIEF, that was what it did.

Euan McKendry climbed the majestically sweeping staircase that led from the main entrance foyer to the first floor of this wing where there were some of the nicest bedrooms in Ravenswood Castle. They all had en suite bathrooms, some had sitting rooms or walk-in wardrobes and one of them—his—had a round wall where it fitted inside one of the larger front turrets of this extraordinary dwelling that dated back to the seventeenth century.

He was carrying a small suitcase in one hand and a large carrier bag in the other. A bag that was heavy enough to have made him glance at the contents to spot toiletries like bottles of shampoo and conditioner. So now, he was off to deposit these belongings in the bedroom that was next door to his turret room and he had a mental image of Dr Abby Hawkins standing in her shower washing that impressive mane of blonde waves. Naked. With soap bubbles sliding down her skin. The thought that she would be singing was a growl in his head and he let it become even more annoying. No doubt she would be singing *Christmas* carols…

It wasn't that he hadn't known Maggie had engaged another doctor to help with the camp. She always did and he'd spoken to his grandmother only a few days ago to hear how thrilled she was with the latest response to her annual advertisement in a prestigious medical journal.

'This one is perfect. The best I've ever found, I think. A paediatrician who's just finished postgraduate training in congenital heart disease, would you believe?'

Right now, Euan would believe anything. If someone had told him in that pharmacy that the Christmas angel come to life who'd almost knocked him over would be landing on his doorstep straight after he'd arrived at his childhood home, he would have laughed it off by saying something like, *Och aye, and pigs might fly*. But, if he'd had any idea at all that she was going to be participating in one of Maggie's fantasy holidays for sick kids, he would never have dreamed of unleashing his opinions about the seasonal festivities. Because Gammy had more than enough to worry about at the moment and the absolute last thing Euan would want was for her to have her heart broken by hearing how much he hated this time of year.

He opened the door of the blue room to see it had been beautifully prepared for a guest. There were fresh flowers in a vase on the dressing table, a stack of fluffy, clean towels on a chair by the bathroom door and the ornately carved four-poster bed had a corner of the thick duvet turned back invitingly to reveal the classic white linen with beautifully embroidered borders.

Not that he was about to allow himself to imagine that bed being occupied. Or think about what Abby Hawkins might wear to sleep in. Even acknowledging how attractive this young doctor was would probably add an unacceptable level of tension to an already difficult few days. Just her presence in the house had ramped up that tension very noticeably so he needed to talk to her in private as soon as possible. To beg her, if that was what it took, not to pass on a single word of what he'd said about Christmas to anyone, but most especially not to Maggie.

Euan left Abby's bags just inside the room and closed the door again. The lighting in this wide hallway came from pairs of glass lamps shaped like flames on long metal torch handles that crossed. A soft light that threw shadows on the heavily framed portraits of bygone generations and made the polish on dark floorboards gleam on either side of the carpet runner. As he walked back to the main staircase, one side of the hallway became a balustrade between pillars that provided a stunning view of the staircase and the foyer below. He could see the open doors of the drawing room as he headed down and knew that was where Abby would be but, for a heartbeat, any plan he was forming to find an excuse to speak to her alone was sabotaged by the kind of ghost that always lay in wait for him here.

He actually turned his head and looked up, as if he could see the small face, peering through the rails of the balustrade, watching him. Waiting for him to go up and read that favourite bedtime story for the umpteenth time, already overjoyed by the prospect. Such a delicate little face with those wispy golden red curls and blue eyes the colour of new denim jeans. A smile that could light up an entire room, even as big as some of the rooms in this castle.

Fiona.

The little sister who'd come into his life when he was seven years old, just weeks after his father had died, which could have contributed to the fierce need to protect her that he'd had from that first captivating moment he'd seen her, along with a love that was so big he'd been sure it could conquer anything. That he'd always be able to keep her safe. He could step into his father's shoes and take care of his whole family. Grandmother, mother and now this precious baby.

The lump in his throat was all too familiar as Euan blinked away the ghost. He knew that he could swallow it, but he also knew that it would sit in his gut and be joined by others to create a weight heavy enough to be physically as well as emotionally painful. It was the same every year but it was going to be worse this time because there was no getting away from the worry about his grandmother's health. That he might have to face up to the reality of losing the last member of his family sooner, rather than later.

He couldn't allow her to be upset by Abby saying anything. This had to be the best year ever. Because it was not only for Fiona, the camp had been the heart and soul of Maggie's life for the last twenty-five years and, while Euan might have been totally unable to protect his family the way he'd wanted to, that love for three generations of McKendry women had never faded.

The glow of happiness he could see on Maggie's face when he entered the drawing room gave his heart a squeeze so tight he had to catch his breath.

'You'll never guess what Abby's just told me,' she said.

'Ahh…' She certainly wouldn't be looking this happy if Abby had told her what Euan was desperately hoping she would keep to herself. 'Nope. I give up. I can't guess.'

'She grew up on a farm. She can drive a tractor and she just told me that using a chainsaw is one of her splinter skills.' Maggie's glance towards Abby was full of admiration. 'You'll have to do the Christmas tree hunt together. Abby's going to be such a great role model for our girls.'

Euan headed for an empty couch. 'Somehow that doesn't surprise me.'

'Why not?' Abby was watching him as he sat down.

Because she was too good to be true? Some kind of cross between a Christmas angel and Superwoman? Euan shrugged rather than admit that out loud. 'Maybe we expect people from Australia and New Zealand to be good at anything to do with the land.'

'Oh…like we expect every Scotsman to be good at playing the bagpipes?'

Maggie laughed. 'Euan *is* very good at playing the bagpipes, as it happens. Wait till you hear some of the Christmas carols he plays up on the ramparts.'

Abby's eyes were dancing. 'Does he wear a kilt, too?'

'But of course.'

'I can't wait.' Abby was grinning now. 'Christmas carols are one of my favourite things.'

The mischievous look she was giving Euan made him wonder what she was about to say concerning men in kilts but, instead, she sighed happily. '"The Little Drummer Boy" is one of the carols I love the most.'

'Not in my current repertoire,' Euan said. 'Sorry.'

'Perhaps you could dust it off,' Maggie suggested. 'It's one of my favourites too. Now… I've asked Catherine to bring us some afternoon tea but do either of you need a rest before we get busy? I'd like us to have a chat about all the children we're expecting to arrive tomorrow and go over our timetable so it might take a wee while.'

'I'm fine,' Abby said. 'I can't wait to get started and I had a bit of a break in Inverness.'

Her face was giving nothing away. And, if she wasn't going to confess she'd already met him in the pharmacy, she probably wasn't about to tell Maggie what he'd said about Christmas being nothing more than a sham and broken promises. The way she was looking as innocent as you'd expect an angel to look made Euan think that she must be very good at keeping secrets and he should be feeling relieved about that but, oddly, it was almost disappointing.

As if she'd dismissed meeting him as too unimportant to bother remembering.

He could feel himself frowning. 'I'm fine too,' he said. 'But what about you, Gammy? Do *you* need a rest?' He knew he was searching her face, looking for any signs of her being in pain or fatigued.

Maggie ignored him, helped by Abby's surprised query.

'Gammy?' The word came out with a gurgle of laughter.

Maggie laughed again, too. 'That was Fiona's doing. Euan's wee sister. She couldn't say "Grandma" when she was little so she called me "Gammy". Like a wonky leg. Euan thought it was hilarious, of course—as any nine-year-old would, so he started using it as well.' Maggie shook her head. 'And here he is, a grown man of thirty-six and he's still using it.'

'It's adorable.'

Euan was on the receiving end of that mischievous look again. Combined with the tilt of Abby's lips it felt as if he was being teased. Or charmed, perhaps? It was a relief when Catherine the cook came into the room, wheeling a tea trolley.

'I've got you some of my best shortbread,' she announced after greeting Abby with a smile. 'And mince pies and teatime scones with jam and cream. You'll no' go hungry here, lassie, not while I'm in charge of our kitchens. Coffee or tea?'

'Tea would be wonderful, thank you. And that shortbread looks amazing.' It seemed to be a big decision whether to choose a Christmas tree shaped biscuit or a star. She chose the star. 'Very Christmassy.'

Maggie accepted a proffered cup. 'I do believe we've found someone who loves Christmas as much as I do, Cath.'

'I find that hard to believe.' The cook shook her head but she was smiling. 'But then, we all love Christmas here.' She handed Euan a cup. 'It's good to see you back again, laddie.'

'It's good to be here, Cath,' Euan said. He could feel Abby's gaze on him and he knew what she was thinking—that this castle was about to put on a Yuletide extravaganza that was everything he'd told Abby he deplored about Christmas. But he knew his words would sound genuine because they *were*. Never mind how he felt about Christmas or the responsibility of caring for sick children, he was back in a part of the world he loved the most, with the person he loved the most.

He was home, that was what it was.

And, no matter how difficult it might be, home was the place you were meant to be for Christmas.

They didn't know, did they?

Did nobody here know how much Euan McKendry hated Christmas? It made Abby feel a little uncomfortable but it was hardly her place to spill a secret like this. Especially not in front of the man's grandmother, who clearly doted on him. Even the castle cook was obviously very fond of this 'laddie' and Abby wasn't about to upset a woman who had a supply of the best, melt-in-the-mouth shortbread she'd ever tasted in her life.

When the afternoon tea trolley had been taken out, Maggie produced document folders that she handed to both Euan and Abby.

'Let's have a quick look at the medical records for the children coming this year first,' she suggested. 'I know you and Abby will need to discuss the medical side of things between yourselves but it would be helpful if you could flag anything that stands out in the way of any more supplies I might need to order in the next few days before the Christmas shut down. Like extra oxygen?'

Euan was nodding as he opened the folder and then Abby saw him smile for the first time.

'Milo's coming again.'

It was a real smile. And Abby had been right to imagine the effect it might have on her. The way it changed and softened his face did make her melt inside. She could feel the tingle right down to the tips of her toes and it was impossible to look away.

'Isn't it wonderful?' Maggie was beaming again. 'It wouldn't really feel like Christmas without Milo here, would it?' She turned to Abby. 'This is his third Christmas at the castle. His mum, Louise, told me they start counting the days right after his birthday in August. He's just the happiest wee boy on the planet. You'll love him as much as we do.'

Having managed to look away from Euan to listen to Maggie, Abby opened her folder to stop her gaze going straight back to him. The first set of medical records in the file told her that Milo was a six-year-old boy with Down's syndrome and he'd been born with a partial atrioventricular septal defect and an abnormality of his aortic valve.

'Surgery to repair the AVSD at eighteen months old,' she murmured as she speed-read. 'With what looks like a few complications post-surgery.'

'He had a tough time.' Euan's tone was neutral. 'And more surgery, including a mitral valve replacement at three years old. The latest procedure was a balloon dilation last year when his aortic stenosis became symptomatic. He was also given up for adoption at birth because the parents turned their backs on what they deemed to be a "defective" child.'

'Oh...that poor baby...' Abby was appalled. 'I can't believe there are still people like that in the world.'

'Fortunately, there are the people who *aren't* like that,' Maggie said quietly. 'And Louise is one of them. She was still single at forty and knew her chances of having a baby were disappearing fast. She was overjoyed to be allowed to adopt Milo and she's been totally devoted to him ever since. She's an expert in baby sign language, which is Milo's main form of communication. And she's coming with him to camp, of course.'

'I'll look forward to meeting them.' Maybe Milo would be a fan of the elf headband that was lying on the couch beside her. 'I've been trying to learn a bit of baby sign language myself in the last few months.'

'We'll talk about his management later,' Euan said. 'I see there's a note about a recent episode of him being short of breath. With his history of aortic stenosis, we'll need to keep an eye on him.'

Euan was already turning a page to the next set of notes but Abby's brain had briefly veered off on a tangent. There was a dedicated clinic somewhere in the castle and she was going to be working closely with this man for the next few days. What was that going to be like, she wondered, given that she could still feel the odd tingle that had reached her toes when she'd seen him smile?

He really was a seriously attractive man.

Apart from hating Christmas but, in a weird way, that made him even more attractive. Because he was totally different from any man Abby had ever been interested in in the past. Perhaps even a polar opposite of herself? Was this like the way 'bad' boys were so attractive to the girls who would never dream of breaking any rules?

'Leah's our oldest camper this year.' Maggie's voice brought Abby smartly back to the job at hand. 'She's twelve years old and is just over a year past her heart transplant for HLHS. She was chosen for the camp because she needs to build some confidence.'

'I can imagine...' Euan was shaking his head as he scanned the file. 'She's spent a lot of her life in hospital, hasn't she? Multiple arrests and having to be put on bypass more than once. She's lucky to have made it to a transplant.'

'I've been involved with the treatment of quite a few children with hypoplastic left heart syndrome over the last year,' Abby said. 'Despite the increase in survival rates it's still the most severe and life-threatening form of congenital heart disease.'

'You'll find that the majority of children who are chosen to come to our camps have HLHS,' Maggie told her.

'Oh? Is there a reason for that?'

Instead of answering her, Maggie shifted her gaze to Euan, her eyebrows raised, as if she was inviting him to answer Abby's query. There was a frisson of something in the room that felt tense, as well—as if the explanation was significant—but Euan simply shrugged.

'As you say, hypoplastic left heart syndrome is one of the more challenging forms of CHD. Add in difficult family circumstances and they're the kind of kids the associations put forward for a special treat like our Christmas camps.' He cleared his throat as he turned another page. 'Ben's a good example,' he continued briskly. 'Six years old. He had in-utero surgery to correct an aortic stenosis at twenty-two weeks and four open-heart surgeries for his HLHS by the age of three. He has some developmental delays and difficulty with spatial tasks. His grandmother is coming as his carer because his mother has just had a new baby and there are also older siblings to care for.'

Abby could still feel that tension in the room. Maybe it was the way Maggie was still watching her grandson, her brow furrowed in what looked like concern. Sadness, even? She only looked away when someone came through the doors of the drawing room.

'Sorry to interrupt, Mrs McKendry, but there's a phone call for you. They say it's urgent.'

Maggie got to her feet with a speed and grace that belied her years. 'Thanks, Ruth. I'll come right now.' She looked over her shoulder as she began walking out of the room. 'Ruth's one of our volunteers from the village,' she told Abby. 'She helps with the admin side of the camps. I'll introduce you to everybody later but I'd better take this call, I think. I do hope it's not someone who's too unwell to come to camp.'

For a long moment after Maggie had disappeared, there was such a deep silence that the crackle of flames in the fireplace sounded loud. Abby pretended to be reading the notes on her lap but the words were not sinking in. She was too aware of Euan sitting on the other couch. Was he, too, pretending to read? She sneaked a peek only to find that he was staring at *her* and, to her dismay, Abby could feel heat flooding into her cheeks. She was *blushing*? Maybe she was mortified because that look was making her feel as if she was the last person on earth Euan would want to be looking at.

'What?' she found herself asking. 'Is it a problem that I'm here? Do you need to have a look at my CV to check my qualifications?'

'Of course not. My grandmother is more than capable of choosing the best medical backup to keep the children on her camps as safe as possible.' He closed his eyes as he rubbed his forehead with his fingertips. 'You're just the last person I expected to see here after…you know… the way we met.'

'I bet I was even more surprised,' Abby said. 'When you can't wait to get to a place that sets out to make Christmas as magical as possible, the absolute last person you'd expect to find there is someone who hates everything to do with the season.'

The way Euan's eyes snapped open as he threw such a swift, almost fearful, glance over his shoulder made Abby bite her lip.

'Don't worry,' she said. 'I'm trying to forget I heard it in the first place so I'm not likely to say anything to anyone else.'

'Thank you,' Euan said slowly. Then he sighed. 'My only excuse for such an inappropriate outburst to a complete stranger is that I'm finding this a somewhat stressful time. Maggie's not going to tell you that she's unwell but she's waiting for some biopsy results on an abdominal growth that could be serious.'

Abby put her hand to her mouth. 'Oh… I had no idea. I'm so sorry to hear that.'

'We might not know before Christmas but that's enough for her to be dealing with and the distraction of the celebrations is probably a good thing so I don't want her to know…ah…about my stress levels.'

'No… I understand.' Which wasn't entirely true. There was more to it, Abby thought, but it really wasn't any of her business, was it? 'Look, I think your gran is an amazing woman with what she's doing for these children and I'm only here to do whatever I can to help in any way. It doesn't have to be simply medical. I'm up for participating in any of the activities.' She smiled at Euan. 'Especially if I get to play with a chainsaw, although...' She turned her head. Up close she could see that the bright array of decorations on the tree beside the fire were tiny toys made of wood, like soldiers and teddy bears and rocking horses. 'This is already a gorgeous Christmas tree. Where's another one going to go?'

'We have the biggest one outside, for when the village children come to the camp's Christmas party. There'll be another one in the foyer and we have little ones in everybody's rooms. Santa leaves a few surprises under those ones during the night.'

Maggie had come back into the room in time to hear his last words.

'Speaking of surprises,' she said, 'it looks like we might have an extra camper coming. A little CHD girl called Lucy and her brother Liam. That was someone from Social Services on the phone—Judith—who had my number because she visited once with another child, a few years ago. She's so upset about the situation these children are in, she's prepared to give up her own Christmas to bring them here as their carer.'

'Have we got room?' Euan was eyeing the files yet to be opened. 'We seem to have our usual tally of campers already.' The moment's silence in response made him expel his breath in a huff. 'Silly question. Of course we've got room.'

He was smiling again. This time, Abby intercepted the look he was giving Maggie. A look of fond tolerance. Understanding. A bone-deep love that was almost fierce in its intensity. It wasn't just her toes that tingled this time. Abby could feel such a tight squeeze on her heart that it took her breath away. She wondered if Maggie was feeling what she would feel if someone looked at *her* like that.

As if she was the luckiest woman in the world…

CHAPTER THREE

GETTING FAMILIAR WITH the general background of the children they would be caring for this year was the easy bit. Discussing their medical needs in more detail with Abby would not be a problem, either. Euan was quite sure she would be impressed with the extra equipment they had available in the castle's clinic specifically to identify the first signs that a heart was failing to cope with its task of pumping oxygenated blood to the whole body. They had the ability to monitor levels of oxygen saturation in the blood, heart rhythms and rates, blood pressure, and smart, digital scales that could distinguish whether fluid retention was contributing to weight. If a higher degree of assessment was needed, they had a very good relationship with the cardiology department at the main regional hospital in Inverness where cardiac ultrasound equipment was available to check on heart function with an echocardiogram.

What wasn't so easy were all the other bits that had nothing to do with the medical care of these children.

The Christmas stuff.

Euan would have simply excused himself from the room while Abby was becoming progressively more thrilled with the timetable for the next few days except that he'd heard the catch in Maggie's voice when she was starting to tell her more about the camp and the activities that were on offer. She was in pain, he was sure of it.

'You have a petting farm? Oh, wow...'

'It's not huge. A couple of donkeys, who have suitably Christmas names of Joseph and Mary.' Maggie's face lit up. 'Mary's pregnant but donkey foals can take anywhere from eleven to fourteen and a half months to appear so we don't know yet when it will arrive. We have a few bottle-raised sheep as well and a cow. And there are our ancient Clydesdales that are long retired but can pull the sleigh. They wear reindeer antlers that I had specially made to attach to their bridles a very long time ago. Twenty-five years ago, in fact.'

She was avoiding catching Euan's gaze. Because they both knew that those antlers had been made for that very first time there was more than one child with severe heart disease at the castle for Christmas. The year that Fiona's very best friend, Jamie, had come to stay. Four-year-old Fi had actually burst into tears of joy on that sleigh ride. At eleven, Euan had been far too grown-up to cry but he could still remember the way it had felt as if a giant hand had taken hold of his heart and squished it. How happy he'd been to see his beloved baby sister so happy.

Even the echo of that squeeze gave him another one of those lumps that had to be swallowed. It wasn't helping that Abby was looking more and more as though *she* was about to burst into tears of joy. Or that Maggie clearly needed a painkiller. He could see the way her fingers were digging into the upholstery on the arm of the couch.

'Are you all right, Gammy?'

'Never better.' Maggie gave him a bright smile. 'You know I'm never happier than when I've got someone to plan Christmas celebrations with.'

'That's not what I was asking. When did you last have a dose of your medication?'

Maggie's gaze slid instantly away from his. 'With my cup of tea. You were too busy scoffing Cath's shortbread to notice.'

'Has Graham been to check on you today?'

'Why would he? None of the children have arrived yet.' Maggie sent an apologetic glance in Abby's direction. 'Graham's our local GP. He likes to get involved with camp in case we need any backup.'

'To see you,' Euan said. 'Maybe I'll ring and have a word.'

'Don't you go making extra work for him when it's not needed.' Again, it was Abby who was given an explanation. 'He's been trying to retire for years but it's not easy to attract doctors to a little village like Kirkwood. And I'm fine, Euan.'

Her tone was telling him in no uncertain terms that the matter was not up for further discussion. Or maybe it was a warning that it could be taken in another direction—the one where he was disappointing the whole village by choosing to be a GP at pretty much the opposite end of the United Kingdom. It was fair enough if Maggie didn't want to talk about her health concerns in front of Abby. And Euan certainly didn't want to discuss why he'd made his career choices but he was also determined that Maggie was not going to spend the next few days in more pain than she needed to be in. It was more than half an hour since they'd had that afternoon tea so the analgesics should be reaching peak effect soon.

And, while he would much prefer to remove himself from hearing about the kind of frivolous seasonal activities both these women clearly revelled in, he wanted to keep a close eye on his grandmother for a little while longer. He would notice the slightest body language like a grimace or stiffness that could indicate inadequate pain relief and he could talk to Maggie quietly later on and persuade her to try something a bit stronger.

Maggie had turned her attention back to Abby. 'So, we have a lot of indoor activities for the children. You might have noticed already how short our days are this far north. We don't have much more than six hours of daylight at this time of year.'

'I know, it's crazy, isn't it? Here it is not even four o'clock and it looks like the middle of the night out there.'

When Abby swung her head to look towards the wall of arched windows that looked out on the entranceway to the castle, it made the length of her hair ripple as it fell over her shoulder. She was sitting close enough to the fire to be catching the glow of flames and the chandelier above her head seemed to be adding another sparkle to that amazing shade of gold. Euan couldn't take his eyes off her.

'But I love it,' Abby added. 'It makes everything brighter, like the lights on Christmas trees and even the flames in a fire look warmer. And we can wear woolly hats and mittens and have all the wonderful, hot comfort food like roast potatoes and gravy. It never feels quite right when it's bright sunshine and scorchingly hot.'

Euan closed his eyes in a long blink. How good would that be? To spend Christmas Day just lying on a beach and soaking up the sun without a care in the world? So why did listening to Abby talk about a frozen, dark Christmas Day make it seem so damned inviting? As if it were the best thing in the world?

It wasn't.

It was an ordeal that you had to get through every year, for the sake of other people who actually believed that it could somehow create some kind of a miracle. Euan wasn't seeing any signs that Maggie was suffering. Quite the opposite—she was clearly enjoying this discussion with Abby—but it was getting rapidly more annoying for him to sit here and listen. He didn't want to hear about exciting outdoor expeditions to cut down pine trees, build snowmen, or go ice skating on the lake. He was even less interested in the craft sessions to make Christmas decorations or bake Christmas cookies and as for the letter writing session to tell Father Christmas what they were wishing for the most...

Okay, that did it. He *really* had to get out of here. Euan propelled himself to his feet swiftly enough to startle both Maggie and Abby.

'I've got to go.' The words came out in a snap that he knew sounded rude so Euan tried to excuse his abrupt exit. 'There's...ah...'

What? Something he needed to do? Someone to see? Ghosts to escape from? He shook his head, words failing him, so he just lifted his hand by way of farewell and walked away.

He couldn't get away fast enough, could he?

And this was getting ridiculous. Euan McKendry seemed to have already made it a habit to walk out on her but Abby found her heart sinking again as she watched the way Euan McKendry straightened his back and walked away so decisively this time. She'd been right in thinking that it was going to be hard work not allowing him to dampen the joy of Christmas.

Maggie hadn't been watching her grandson leave the room, however, because Abby found that she was the focus of the older woman's gaze when she turned back.

'I know...' She dug deep to find a cheerful smile.

'He's got a heart of gold. He's just one of those clas-sically grumpy Scotsmen that I'm sure isn't actually a genuine stereotype?'

She expected Maggie to smile back, so they could brush off the effect of Euan's brisk-enough-to-be-rude exit and get back to talking about Christmas but, instead, she was looking almost as if she might be about to cry?

'There's something you should probably know,' she said quietly.

Uh, oh…after many years of being part of often very intense medical situations, Abby knew what it was like to both hear and deliver significant information that could change someone's life. Whatever it was that Maggie was about to tell her was clearly going to change at least the next few days of her own life. She said nothing and just sat very still to listen carefully.

'I thought Euan might say something when you asked why most of the children who come here have HLHS.'

Abby nodded. She remembered that frisson of some-thing tense in the room.

'It's what his wee sister, Fiona, was born with. Just a short time after his daddy had been killed in an accident on the farm. Euan was just a bairn—seven years old.'

'Oh…' Abby caught her lip between her teeth. 'That's tragic…' Had it happened at Christmas time? Was that why Euan hated the season so much?

'Aye…' Maggie pressed a finger to the bridge of her nose and it looked like a well-practised way to stem any unwanted tears. 'But the baby saved Euan from thinking it was the end of the world. I've never seen a child fall in love with a baby like that. He adored her.'

It was already plain to see how much Euan loved his grandma so Abby could easily picture him besotted with a sister so much younger than himself. How precious that little life would have seemed when it was hanging in the balance so soon after losing his dad.

'She was the happiest wee girl,' Maggie said. 'Despite everything she had to go through. Or maybe because of it. And she had so much love to give. It was because she wanted her best friend, Jamie—another heart baby—to visit, that Camp Christmas started in the first place. It grew a bit every year after that.'

Abby knew the statistics. That first camp had been a very long time ago and very few children with such a serious congenital heart condition made it to adulthood but she didn't want to ask any of the questions that were springing to mind, like how old Fiona had been when she died and whose idea had it been to keep the camp running afterwards when it must have been such a sad reminder of their loss?

Maggie obviously saw something in her face because her face softened. 'Ask Euan,' she told her. 'I've no business to be telling a story that's his as much as mine if he doesn't want it to be told. I just wanted you to know enough to understand why he is like he is.' Her breath came out in a sigh. 'This is a hard time of year for him.'

'I understand,' Abby said softly.

Maggie got to her feet—a clear indication that this conversation was over but a smile on her face to soften the dismissal. 'Let me show you to your room. You'll need time to settle in before dinner and I have some organising to do to get ready for the unexpected addition to our numbers.'

Abby changed her mind a while later, when she'd finished tiptoeing around a room that made her feel as if she'd just stepped between the pages of a fairy tale and become some kind of princess and was getting on with the business of unpacking her clothes and the bag of new toiletries she'd purchased in Inverness. She didn't understand.

Oh, she could understand why Euan hated Christmas, with the sad memories it must invoke, but that didn't explain why he came here, year after year, to take part in a celebration that could only be heart wrenching. Was that for Maggie's sake? Or had it started because he could take care of other sick children when he could no longer care for his beloved sister? Was that why he'd chosen to become a doctor? And why hadn't Maggie said anything about his mother?

It was more than mere curiosity. Abby's heart had been well and truly captured by imagining Euan as a serious, young boy, living here in this astonishing castle, wanting to protect the little sister he adored but being all too aware of the cloud of fear that hung over the whole family. She wanted to hear his story so much it was all she could think about but it had to be his choice to tell her. Forcing him would only be cruel.

About as cruel as the way she'd gone on and on about how much she loved Christmas. By wearing that stupid elf headband. By the way she'd practically labelled Euan as the enemy who was out to stifle any seasonal joy. A Grinch. The more she thought about it, the more it made Abby cringe inside.

She wanted to apologise.

No, it went a lot deeper than that, actually.

What Abby wanted was to try and make Christmas just a little more bearable for Euan McKendry. What a gift that would be, if she could give him even a moment or two of the kind of real joy she always found. It would be a gift for Maggie, as well. One for herself, in fact, because Abby's heart was still aching for that little boy who'd loved his baby sister that much. A young person

who'd had to deal with another huge loss in his life probably only a few years down the track. And for the man
Euan was now, whose courage was seriously impressive. Okay, so he was trying to protect his own heart by
turning his back on the magic of Christmas and hiding
behind grumpiness, but here he was, brave enough to be
taking part, yet again, in a celebration of the season like
none other Abby had ever heard of.

If there was something she could do to make the next
few days at least more bearable, if not actually enjoyable, then she would be grabbing the opportunity with
both hands.

Why was Abby smiling at him like that?

As if his company, heading outside through the kitchen
door at the back of the castle, at nine o'clock, as the sun
finally rose above the mountains the next morning, was
all that she could have wished for.

Maybe he should have said 'no' to his grandmother's
request after breakfast this morning. Except it had been
more of an order than a request, hadn't it?

'The first children aren't scheduled to arrive until
much later this morning so you've plenty of time,' she'd
said.

'For what?'

'I was thinking about what Abby said at dinner last
night.'

'What about?' She'd certainly had plenty to say and
she'd given no indication that she found Euan's lack of
contribution to the conversation annoying. And he had
to admit that, not only was she a born storyteller, it had
been no hardship to listen to her cute accent.

'Mistletoe. I had no idea it might not grow in New

Zealand like it does here. Fancy never having seen it except for a picture on a Christmas card.'

'She hasn't missed much. It's just a parasite. I've never understood why it became associated with kissing.'

'Someone told me it has to do with fertility,' Maggie said. 'Or celebrating life, perhaps. Because it stays green when the trees lose all their leaves in winter so it's very obvious.'

Euan grunted. 'It's not the only strange Christmas tradition, I suppose. I wonder how many people used to break teeth on the silver coins that went into the plum pudding?'

Maggie wagged her finger at him. 'Don't try and change the subject. I told Abby I need some mistletoe for decorations and that you'd take her to find it. She's in the boot room finding some wellies her size.'

'I'm sure Duncan has far more idea of where to look—it's not as though it's a common thing up here. I've got a lot to do, Gammy. I want to make sure we're well stocked in the clinic.'

'Duncan's gone into Inverness to get replacement bulbs for some of the outdoor lighting. The effect of the sleigh moving up on the ramparts will be ruined with that gap in the sequence.' Maggie was all but pushing Euan in the direction of the boot room that lay between the kitchen and laundry areas at the back of the ground floor. 'I know exactly where some is growing. Do you remember that old, old apple tree that's beside the lake? Near where the rowboat is?'

So, here they were, their waterproof boots leaving deep footprints in the pristine snow of the paths that led through the kitchen gardens and then across a wide expanse of lawn to approach the edge of the forest.

And Abby was smiling at him.

A moment later, however, she had stopped dead in her tracks with a gasp and she clutched his arm with her hand.

'*Oh...*'

The sound came out with a cloud of mist from Abby's breath, which Euan found himself watching as if he'd never seen the phenomenon before. He was also aware of how acutely he could feel the touch of her hand on his arm, despite the layers of his woolly jumper and puffer jacket and her thick, woollen gloves.

'*Look...*' The instruction came with another cloud of mist.

Euan had to shade his eyes against the shafts of sunlight now filtering through tree tops to the edges of the forest in deep shade and it took a slight movement to see what had caught Abby's attention so completely. It was a small group of fallow deer, just standing at the moment, staring back at the humans disturbing their morning. The buck had a magnificent set of antlers and the hinds were just waiting for his signal before they turned and vanished into the forest with a flick of the black stripe surrounded by white on their tails.

'Did you *see* that?'

'Aye...' Euan found himself smiling. Who wouldn't, hearing the sheer joy in Abby's voice?

'I mean, it's not as if I haven't seen wild deer in the back country in New Zealand but...this is Scotland and there's a gorgeous forest and...and so much snow. And it's *Christmas* and...'

Abby stopped abruptly, biting her lip as her face suddenly changed to look, what...something beyond apologetic, perhaps?

'I'm annoying, aren't I? Sorry. I promise I won't say the "C" word again for...ooh, at least five minutes?'

Her expression was changing again, morphing into the kind of amused teasing he'd seen when Abby had learned that he called his grandmother 'Gammy'.

And he'd been correct in thinking that it was also charming. Her joy in things like Christmas and the snow and spotting wild deer was equally charming, even if it could be deemed somewhat childish. And...well...it was distracting, wasn't it?

For a little while, at least, it was making it noticeably easier to forget about that dark, sad cloud that was always ready to roll in when he was here at this time of year and that it was so much darker this year, what with Maggie's impending diagnosis hanging over them. Not only that, when Euan had opened his emails before breakfast this morning, he'd found information on the unexpected additional child who was about to arrive. The five-year-old girl, Lucy, wasn't simply a congenital heart disease patient. She had HLHS, like Fiona. It wasn't just a brother who was coming with her, either, but a big brother, Liam, who was ten years old. How could Euan be around these two children without seeing a potential mirror image of himself as a lad and Fiona when she had been the same age, which was probably her healthiest and happiest time ever? When life had held a promise he had actually started believing in. When he'd looked forward to Christmas as much as anyone else.

Euan led Abby along a forest path he'd been using ever since he could walk. There was sunlight reaching through the bare branches of the huge, ancient oak trees but it wasn't providing any warmth yet. A cheeky robin fluttered nearby and Euan knew, even before he slid a sideways glance at Abby, that she would be entranced all over again. As if she felt the glance, she turned her head and yes…her face was lit up with delight but she had her lips firmly pressed together so that she remained silent.

He almost chuckled out loud but, instead, followed Abby's example and pressed his own lips firmly enough together to prevent even a smile escaping. The fact that he actually had the urge to smile or laugh was distracting in itself. More than that, it seemed to have released some endorphins or something. Euan actually had a moment of feeling better than he had in quite some time. Who would have thought…?

It was obvious that Abby was making an effort to find something to talk about other than Christmas.

'So, I meant to ask…are you a specialist paediatrician? Or cardiologist?'

'No.' They were specialties Euan would never have considered devoting his career to. How much heartbreak would there be in spending your life working with families who were going through the kind of challenges he knew only too well? 'I'm just a GP,' he told Abby.

'It's never "just" a GP,' Abby said. 'There's an enormous responsibility in being the first person to pick up significant problems and manage them with appropriate referrals. Then there's the day-to-day management that comes back to you. You must need to dip into every specialty there is depending on the needs of your patients.'

Euan grunted. It was true. Amidst all the ordinary, and sometimes repetitively dull, tasks in general practice, there was the satisfaction of the detective work and the stimulation of acquiring new knowledge and skills.

'I might well end up being a GP myself,' Abby told him.

'Have you not already lined up a specialist hospital consultancy after the training you've just done? Back in New Zealand or here in the UK?'

Abby shook her head. 'I'm thirty-two. The career decisions I make now will probably determine what I do for the rest of my life so I decided I would take my time to be very sure of exactly what it is I want for my future.'

'But you must love working with children, yes?'

'Oh, yes…' Abby's smile was confirmation of the joy her work provided. 'In fact, that's the one thing I can be absolutely sure of. I want children in my life. And not just professionally, which is why a job as a GP could be perfect. Or maybe as a consultant part time, I guess. They're the kind of positions that would work well when I've got a few kids.'

Euan blinked. 'How many is "a few"?'

'At least six.' Abby was grinning now. 'I was an only child. Wonderful parents but nothing really got rid of that loneliness. When I played with my dolls or stuffed animals, I always gave them brothers and sisters. Even when I played with the button jar, I made families with a couple of big buttons and lots of little ones.'

Dear God, Abby was a nightmare. Exactly the sort of woman that Euan avoided at all costs. He had, in fact, politely ended more than one relationship in the past when he learned that a girlfriend saw motherhood as a priority in her future. Having his own child was even less appealing than becoming a paediatric cardiologist would have been. So why did imagining her as a small child, sorting buttons into families, make him want to smile again?

He could feel his scowl deepening. 'I suppose it's just as well there are people like you in the world,' he muttered. 'The human race would become extinct if everybody felt like I do about having children.'

At least they'd reached the halfway point of this expedition. In a few minutes, they could start heading back to the castle. Euan could see the old wooden rowboat that hadn't been used for years but hadn't been taken away because it looked so picturesque floating on the end of its long rope. Not that it was floating currently because it looked to be firmly wedged in the ice of Ravenswood estate's frozen lake. Abby was heading straight for the lake edge, looking as if she intended to try ice skating in her wellies.

'Careful,' Euan warned. 'I haven't checked it yet. It might look solid but it can have weaker spots, especially near the edges.'

'Isn't ice skating one of the activities available for the camp kids?'

'Aye. But that depends on what the ice is like. I'll make sure it's safe and mark any dodgy areas with safety cones. It's a very gentle ice-skating experience, anyway. Most of the kids aren't up for any strenuous activities.'

'Do you have ice skates for big people, too?'

Oh, man... That shine in those astonishingly blue eyes. You'd want to say 'yes' to anything, wouldn't you?

Euan just grunted instead. 'Let's get on with what we're here for. See that tree over there?'

'The really scraggly one? With the weird green birds' nests?'

'Aye. Those weird green birds' nests are the mistletoe.'

'No way... I thought they grew in, you know...circles.'

Euan could feel his face shifting into an expression of disbelief but then he saw the amusement dancing in Abby's eyes. Of course she didn't think the plant grew naturally in the kind of wreaths she'd seen on Christmas cards. This time, having unexpectedly fallen for the teasing, it was even harder to stop himself smiling. He could feel his lips twitching as he walked towards the tree.

'I'll do the climbing,' he told her. 'I started climbing this particular tree to get the apples when I was a wee lad so I know what I'm doing.' His sideways glance was deadpan. 'Trust me, I'm a doctor.'

It was working. Sort of.

He'd almost smiled properly that time.

Trying to win Euan McKendry's friendship as a first step to changing his negative view of Christmas was actually adding to Abby's enjoyment of her first morning at Ravenswood Castle. Waking up in the downy warmth of that amazing bed and then getting up to a delicious full English breakfast provided by Catherine the cook had been wonderful but what had come next was so much better. The icy chill of this morning air, the gorgeous deep snow, the spectacular red glow of the rising sun and the joy of seeing both the deer and that cute little robin. They would have been enough of a pleasure all on their own but watching Euan thaw even a tiny bit was giving her an internal warmth that was just delicious.

He might still have his protective barriers well in place but Abby intended to keep tapping until she found a weak spot—a bit like the way Euan probably tested the ice on this lake—and then she could put enough careful pressure on it to get through without causing any harm. Hopefully, with an invitation, even.

That was the plan, anyway.

She was learning more about him in the meantime. Realising that they were polar opposites in more ways than how they felt about Christmas. Abby couldn't imagine not wanting to have children. Although she was still totally focused on a career she was passionate about and loving the freedom to add adventure into her life like the extraordinary Christmas she was about to experience this year, becoming a mother was, in fact, the number one priority in her future.

Not that she was thinking about that right now, as she watched Euan climb into this gnarly old apple tree. She was watching the graceful movement of his body and the obvious strength in his arms as he pulled himself up, the focused expression on his face and then the delicate way he detached the rounded mass of greenery without damaging the branches that forked around it. Part of her brain was smudging what she was watching, apparently giving her the ability to time travel and see a small boy climbing this tree instead.

A happy kid who had no idea of what life was going to throw at him in the future or that it would hurt him enough to make him step back from living it to the full. Not even wanting a family of his own, even though he was having to face the prospect of possibly losing his grandmother in the near future. For a moment, Abby felt so sad that if the freezing temperatures hadn't been enough, her eyes would have been stinging anyway. She rubbed at her nose with her glove, suspecting it was both red and drippy.

'Here…catch, Abby.'

But the mistletoe didn't quite make it into her waiting hands because it snagged on some lower, outer branches. They were just a few inches too high for Abby to reach, even standing on tiptoes.

'I'll find a stick.'

'I can reach it. I'll just get this smaller one before I come down. Maggie's bound to have plans that need more than one weird bird's nest.'

Abby hadn't moved by the time Euan shimmied down from the tree only a minute later, with a smaller ball of mistletoe in his hands. His nose and cheeks were reddened by both the physical effort and the cold and he was breathing hard.

'You look like a dragon,' Abby told him. 'Puffing steam.'

'Hmph.'

She was getting used to that grunt that was clearly an important part of Euan's vocabulary. He reached over her head to unsnag the first mistletoe he'd harvested and, as it began to fall, Abby also reached up, to catch it. So she was looking up, with her arms above her head, as Euan looked down to see where the ball had gone. He was much closer than Abby had realised. So close that…

…that the moment suddenly froze.

She couldn't move. Euan seemed to be as still as she was. It was a blink of time but more than long enough for something to click into place.

It wasn't conscious. It had to be the result of a lot of things. Things like how excited Abby was to be here, in this spectacular place. The way Euan's story had captured her heart so firmly and her determination to try and do something to help him. The fact that, despite his outward grumpiness and the impression he wasn't that happy to have her here, there was a level of attraction that was the final catalyst for what Abby realised might be the perfect way to make this Christmas more enjoyable for this man.

She hadn't lowered the mistletoe and that was the perfect excuse for what she did next.

Abby stood on her tiptoes and kissed him.

She'd only intended it to be a friendly sort of kiss. A brief, under-the-mistletoe, Christmassy sort of kiss. One that wasn't going to be significant in any way.

But the instant her lips touched his, everything changed…

CHAPTER FOUR

IT WAS KIND of like walking along a beach, just a little too close to the waves. For most of the time, the sea was just the background to your walk on the sand, but every so often one of the waves would be a bit bigger and would flow over your feet and, for a moment, all you could think about was that wash of cool water and your connection to the mind-blowing depths and width of the ocean beside you.

Being in the castle clinic, for a medical meet and greet of all the children and their carers arriving for Camp Christmas, with Euan in the main consulting room and Abby in the treatment of the converted stable block, was kind of like the walk on the sand. The waves that he couldn't stop rolling too close to his feet at random intervals were the memories of that kiss.

Holy moly…*that* kiss.

That totally unexpected, uninvited, kiss that had been like nothing Euan McKendry had ever experienced in his entire life. The touch of Abby's lips on his own had been as if that extraordinary glow that shone around Abby Hawkins had been condensed into an energy and heat that was being directly transferred from one human to another.

From Abby to himself.

Sparks to a source of tinder-dry fuel he hadn't known existed within his mind and body. Or was it an alchemy of a mix of unknown chemistry that had produced something hitherto not even in existence for anyone? Abby seemed to have felt a similar reaction judging by the stunned silence in which they'd walked back to the castle, broken only by a brief, professional discussion about the questions to ask and baseline observations to take as part of the settling in process for the children when they arrived at the castle.

The kind of quick check up Euan was currently doing for Leah, a shy twelve-year-old who was a year past successful heart transplant surgery.

'You'll know the drill.' Euan smiled. 'This is just a quick check to give us some baselines so we'll know if anything changes over the next few days. I want to weigh you and have a listen to your lungs and heart. The usual sort of stuff.'

Leah nodded solemnly. So did her father, John, who had come as her carer.

'How are you feeling today?'

'Good.'

'Normal energy level? Appetite?'

Leah nodded. 'I had chips. On the train.'

Euan caught Leah's dad's gaze and he also nodded. 'She's been good,' he said. 'Very excited about coming to the camp. We both are. Leah's a bit nervous, too, mind you. The only holiday away from home that she's had pretty much in her whole life has been to go to hospital.'

'You're going to have the best time,' Euan told her. 'I promise. Come and jump on the scales for me.' He watched how cautiously the girl got up from her chair to walk across the room and then picked up her file to take a note of her weight. But something else on the page caught his attention first.

'No changes in Leah's medication since these notes were sent through?'

'I don't think so. Immunosuppressants, antivirals, the diuretics and that stuff for her stomach… I've forgotten what it's called…'

'Ranitidine,' Euan supplied. 'And there's a magnesium supplement listed here as well.'

'I've got them all in here.' John held out the plastic container he was holding. 'Sorted into days and times. Enough for well over a week.' His smile was embarrassed. 'I was a bit worried we might get snowed in when I saw the weather forecast.'

'They always manage to keep our roads clear enough to get through,' Euan reassured him. 'We've got a good supply of medications here, too, and the hospital in Inverness is not that far away. Try not to worry. We'll take very good care of Leah.'

Her father's anxiety might be partly why his daughter was lacking confidence, Euan thought. He'd bring that up in the meeting he was due to have with Maggie and Abby later today.

In almost the same moment as her name came into his head, Euan found himself distracted by another potential wash of remembering that kiss. Or maybe it was because he could hear a peal of laughter coming from the treatment room that was only separated from this consulting room by a sliding door that wasn't completely closed. Abby was having the pleasure of greeting Milo and was clearly enjoying meeting him and his mother, Louise, as she took his baseline observations.

It wasn't just the wash of a wave he needed to sidestep as Euan focused on his patient, recording Leah's weight and getting her to sit on the bed so that he could listen to her chest. This time, just for a split second, he was even more aware of the ocean behind the wave and, while he certainly wasn't going to allow himself to even think about it right now, he knew exactly where that enormous volume of water slotted into the simile he'd come up with. If the waves represented merely a kiss, the ocean was the unknown enormity of what *more* than kissing Abby Hawkins would be like. And, despite an obvious risk of drowning, Euan knew that the temptation would no doubt be totally irresistible. She might have initiated that kiss entirely by herself but he hadn't exactly been slow to respond, had he? He'd been lost, in fact, from the moment her lips touched his.

Through the disc of his stethoscope, he could hear the healthy *lub-dub*, *lub-dub* of a heart that was working perfectly well, its rate and rhythm within normal parameters.

'Sounds great,' he told Leah. 'I'm going to take your blood pressure now and then you and Dad can go and finish unpacking and explore the castle. I believe lunch is a bit of a picnic in the kitchens so you can go and meet Cath and all her helpers whenever you're ready. Are you going to come out to the pine forest this afternoon to watch us cut down the big Christmas tree?'

Leah shook her head. 'It's really snowy out there,' she said. 'It's hard to walk and...and I might fall over.'

Euan kept his tone casual. 'That's a shame. We've got a doctor here who's helping me look after everybody and she's a girl. Dr Abby, her name is, and do you know, she's the one who's going to cut down that tree? With a *chainsaw*. Don't know about you, but I can't wait to see that.'

Leah and her father had matching expressions of disbelief on their faces.

'I'll walk right beside you, if you like,' he offered, as

he wrapped a small cuff around Leah's upper arm to take her blood pressure reading. 'That way I can make sure you don't fall over.'

Even with the earpieces of his stethoscope in place he could still hear the laughter coming from the adjacent room. His patient's new heart might have a pleasingly normal rate and rhythm but he could feel his own skip a beat and speed up at the sound of Abby's laughter. This was another entirely inappropriate time to allow himself to soak in the memory of that kiss but it was easy enough to dodge that wave when needed. Would it be just as easy, Euan wondered, to *not* dodge it? To summon it, even, if he happened to need, say…a bit of distraction?

He'd been distracted earlier today for a moment or two, when Abby's joy in seeing those deer had made him smile. And again, when he'd been trying not to smile because of something she'd said or the expression on her face. Just being around Abby was a distraction all in itself but that kiss had taken it to a completely new level.

It could be useful.

It might even turn out to be a bit of a life-saver.

From starting out with quiet moments of magic, like seeing the deer as the sun rose to gild a winter wonderland and a kiss that had blown everything Abby Hawkins thought she'd known about kissing right out of the water, her first full day at Ravenswood Castle had spiralled into what could only be described as chaos.

Controlled chaos, for the most part, as people from the village, both employed and volunteers, streamed in to make the final preparations for the arrival of the children and their carers. There was a welcome committee headed by Maggie and excited children and their siblings who were impatient with administrative details like rooms to be allocated and luggage to stow and a check that any special needs were able to be catered for. A team of people helping Catherine the cook was providing refreshments and a rolling picnic style lunch that was being served in the kitchens and dining room. Both Euan and Abby were back and forth to the clinic rooms in the converted stable to match the children to their medical records and start the monitoring that would be routine for the next few days.

Abby was loving every minute of it. These weren't children with congenital heart disease who were sick enough to be admitted to hospital, because their condition had suddenly deteriorated or they were about to undergo major surgery, accompanied by frightened parents who were fearing the worst. These kids had all spent so much time in hospitals that it was a normal part of life, they were still facing challenges in their daily lives with essential medications or treatment, restrictions in what they were capable of doing and, for these children in particular, social or financial circumstances that added an extra layer of challenge, but the moment they arrived at the castle, those factors became simply a background. A nuisance that wasn't going to interfere with the joy of being here.

The introductory clinic appointments that were part of the settling in process for each child were unlike any clinical consultations Abby had ever performed in a hospital. She was almost literally bowled over by the enthusiastic hug she received from six-year-old Milo and they both made each other laugh. Abby loved the way Milo's whole face crinkled up so much with delight and Milo, well…she'd been right. He took one look at her elf headband and fell in love. He was wearing it himself that afternoon, on top of a woollen hat, when most of the children, bundled up against the cold, went on the expedition to the Scotch pine forest to watch the big tree being felled and choose the small seedlings for their own rooms. The only children who were missing were Callum, who was in a wheelchair and needed supplementary oxygen at all times, and the last-minute additions of Lucy and her brother, Liam, who hadn't arrived yet.

Abby was getting her wish to play with a chainsaw fulfilled. She was being assisted by a group of men from the village, who kept everybody at a safe distance and used ropes to guide the fall of the chosen tree that was at least ten feet tall, and any one of them could have wielded that heavy chainsaw with far more ease than Abby but they made it seem as if they'd never seen it done so well and they led the cheer from everybody watching as the tree toppled. These men had done it many times before and had a flatbed truck ready to take it back to the castle courtyard to be installed and decorated.

The small wilding pines that the children then chose for their rooms only needed a pruning saw to harvest and Milo was one of several children who were keen to try and do it themselves. Abby saw Euan offer a saw to Leah, their heart transplant patient, but the older girl shook her head shyly and clung to her father's hand. Abby left Milo's mum, Louise, to supervise her son with a saw and walked over to join Leah and Euan.

'Would you rather try a chainsaw, sweetheart?'

Leah's jaw dropped and Abby laughed. 'Just kidding. Not that you couldn't use a chainsaw if you wanted to one day but it's a bit safer to start off with a saw like that.'

She pointed to the one Euan was holding, still smiling as she lifted her gaze to his face. They were due to meet later, when the children would be busy making decorations for their trees, to discuss the first appointments and flag any concerns they might have, but they'd been so busy so far that she'd barely seen Euan since they'd come back from their mistletoe gathering this morning. Since that slightly awkward walk back to the castle when neither of them seemed capable of saying anything about what had just happened.

About that kiss…

Little wonder, then, that it was the first thing that crossed Abby's mind as she found those stormy, grey eyes watching her and she knew, she absolutely knew, that it was exactly what Euan was also thinking about. The flicker of sensation deep in her belly exploded into something that was every bit as astonishing as that kiss had turned out to be.

Wow…

Who knew that physical attraction could be *this* potent?

Abby had to look away very quickly. She didn't want Euan, or Leah's father for that matter, getting any hint of what had just flashed through her mind or body. How unprofessional would that be? Euan seemed just as keen to escape. He handed the pruning saw to Abby.

'Why don't you get Abby to show you how it's done?' he suggested to Leah.

Abby could tell that the girl was going to shake her head again so she smiled encouragement. 'How 'bout I start it off for you? That way it'll be easy-peasy.'

'So, did she actually use the saw herself?'

'She did. She needed a bit of hand holding, mind you. She's quite timid, isn't she?'

'Her dad's cautiousness doesn't help. I suspect they've made things harder for each other over the years.'

'He almost dived in and took the saw himself when I held it out.' Abby nodded. 'But I gave him a look.'

Euan's lips twitched. 'Poor man. He didn't stand a chance, did he?'

Abby ducked her head to hide her own smile. This was better. Any awkwardness in the wake of this morning's kiss seemed to have finally evaporated.

'He carried her little tree back for her instead. Leah's busy making coloured paper chains and glittery stars to hang on it now. Did you find anything that we'll need to watch in her physical assessment?'

'She's on quite a few medications, as you'd expect, but her dad's on top of dosages. All her baselines were within normal parameters.'

Abby could feel him watching her, even though she had her gaze on the files she was holding, and it gave her an odd sensation. As if she were dancing—in a floaty, white dress in the middle of a summer forest—instead of sitting here having a professional discussion about young patients.

'I was joking,' Euan said, quietly, a moment later. 'About you intimidating her father. You did well getting her to join in. I'd love to see her with a bit more confidence and enjoy life as much as possible. She's a very lucky girl to have got a transplant. There's far too many who never make it that far.'

Like Fiona? Had she been on a waiting list? Abby looked up but Euan was scanning another set of notes, a frown on his face, even though Leah had been the last child they needed to discuss. She found herself turning her head, to look at the wall in front of Euan's desk in this consulting room. A montage of dozens of photographs plastered the space and they were clearly past participants in Christmas festivities here at the castle.

There were children building snowmen, piled into a big cart that had sides added to make it look like a classic sleigh, ice skating on the lake and receiving gifts from a convincing looking Santa. Such happy photos. And so many different children. Maggie was in many of the images as well and there was one where she was cuddling a small girl with curly, red hair and a smile to rival Milo's in its contagiousness. Just looking at the photograph was enough to make Abby's lips curl. And then look back at Euan.

He looked disconcerted. Because she was smiling at him?

'What?' he demanded.

Abby's smile faded. 'Is that Fiona?' she asked. 'In that photo with Maggie? The little girl with that gorgeous smile?'

'How do you know about Fiona?' But Euan was shaking his head. 'Gammy's been talking to you, hasn't she?'

'She only told me that you had a little sister with HLHS.' *And that he had adored her...* 'She didn't really say anything else. She said it was your story to tell.'

Euan was staring at the wall himself now. He shrugged.

'It's not an unusual story,' he said. 'She had the first surgery—the Norwood procedure—at two weeks old, the Glenn procedure when she was six months and the Fontan just before she turned four.'

During her recent specialist training in paediatric cardiology, Abby had become very familiar with the complex, staged surgeries that could keep a baby alive when the left side of the heart had not developed normally and was unable to provide effective circulation. This clinical information that Euan was sharing was so matter-of-fact and overly concise, it was painfully clear that his very personal experience with the disease was not something he wanted to talk about. Abby simply nodded to let him know that she was listening. She knew there were no cracks in the ice to be felt in these first, tentative steps. If Euan wanted to change the subject, that was fine. And it seemed that he did.

'There was another child having the same surgeries at about the same time,' he told her. 'Wee Jamie. And he and Fi became the best of friends. They both got out of hospital near Christmas time after the Fontan and Jamie's mother was too exhausted—not to mention couldn't afford—to do anything special to celebrate. Fi saw her crying and wanted to know why. It was her idea to invite them to the castle for Christmas and that was how it all started. The Christmas camp for children just like her.'

'She was a special little girl,' Abby said softly.

'Gammy took the idea and ran with it, of course.' Euan was packing up the folders of medical notes. 'Every year, it got bigger and better with more children being invited and more people from the village becoming involved. Looking back, I think it was important because it gave her something she could control—and make as perfect as possible—when there were so many things that none of us could control that were such a long way from being perfect.'

Abby was sitting very, very still. Euan's words were calm. Casual, even, but there were undercurrents of emotion here that were huge. So heartbreaking that it wasn't a surprise that Euan was protecting himself by speaking as if it had happened to someone else. The addition of another quiet sentence did come as a surprise, however.

'Fi died when she was seven years old,' Euan said. 'While she was on the waiting list for a transplant.'

So Abby had been right in thinking that his comment

about how lucky Leah had been was significant. How devastating must that loss have been for a lad who would have been about fourteen or fifteen and probably coping with not only all the normal teenage stuff but the fact that he'd been the man of the family since his father had died, with three generations of his family that needed protection. Hardly normal teenage things. How strong had he learned to be because of that? Had that been when he'd learned to keep so much buried and locked away?

Abby had to swallow hard. Her heart had already been captured by Euan McKendry's story. Now, she could feel it properly breaking. He hadn't mentioned his mother, either, she realised, and the omission suggested that there was a story all of its own there. It was tempting to ask. To step onto a new patch of ice that might crack beneath her weight. Maybe it was just as well they both heard the quiet tap on the door.

It was Catherine. 'Mrs McKendry sent me to ask if you could both join her in the library if possible,' she told them. 'Those last two weans have arrived finally.'

Lucy Grimshaw was small for her age of five years. She was also one of the most beautiful children Abby had ever seen, with a cascade of bright red curls that reached her shoulders, piercing blue eyes in a pale, pixie face and a smile that reminded Abby of…

Oh, help… It reminded her instantly of that photo of Fiona. So did the hair colour. One glance at Euan's face and she could see the effort it was taking for him to keep his expression so neutral. Judging by the similar effort Maggie was making to hide her own concern, she was very well aware of the extra challenge this was going to present to her grandson. The scowl on Lucy's older brother Liam's face suggested that he was also picking up on the undercurrents. Either that, or he just wasn't happy at all about being here. The lad was sitting very close to his sister and he was quite tall and thin with a darker shade of auburn hair and freckles on his face. The scowl made Abby want to smile, partly because it made her think of what Euan would have been like as a child.

She was acutely aware of Euan behind her right now. He had to need some time to deal with this. Even a few more seconds before he was expected to participate might help.

'Hi, sweetheart.' She went straight to Lucy and crouched down in front of the little girl. 'My name's Abby and this is Dr Euan and we're going to be looking after you while you're here. We're so happy to meet you and your brother. It's Liam, yes?'

Liam wasn't returning even a hint of her smile. He wasn't even going to talk to her, apparently. It was Lucy who nodded in response to the query.

'And I'm Lucy.'

'I know.' Abby's smile widened. 'And do you know why you've come here to the castle?'

'Um... Judith said it was so me and Liam could have Christmas together,' she said.

'A really special Christmas,' Maggie put in. 'And we've got a special room ready for you and Liam to share but I'm guessing you're really hungry and tired after that big car ride.'

'I'm sure they're starving.' The young woman in the room had to be Judith, the social worker, who had brought the children. 'I didn't want to stop anywhere in case it was going to start snowing again and we got stuck. It's all been a bit stressful, to be honest. We got um...held up leaving Edinburgh.'

Catherine had followed Euan and Abby into the library. 'There's lots of nice things in the kitchen for your supper,' she told the children. 'You can choose sausages or fish and chips or spaghetti. And do you like chocolate pudding?'

She held out her hand and Lucy seemed happy to slide off the couch but then she stopped, turned, and held out her small hand to Liam. Clearly, she wasn't brave enough to go somewhere strange without her big brother. The glance between the children as he took her hand brought a big lump to Abby's throat.

'It's okay, Luce,' Liam said, so quietly Abby almost couldn't hear his words. 'I'll look after you.'

Maggie waited until the children had been taken out of the library to introduce Abby and Euan to Judith.

'Thank you so much for letting us come at the last minute like this,' Judith said. 'It's time out from rather a mess. Lucy and Liam have both been in foster care with the same family since their grandmother died but they just can't cope with the level of care Lucy needs. They said they'd keep Liam but...'

'Oh, no...' Abby didn't dare look at Euan. 'They can't be separated.'

'That's why we got held up leaving. Liam thought I was there to take Lucy to a new home. He locked them both into the bathroom.' Judith was looking as upset as Abby was feeling. 'The only way I could persuade him to open the door was to promise that nothing was going to happen while they were here at the castle but...what happens after Christmas will be out of my hands.'

'Let's not think about that for the moment,' Maggie said calmly. 'Let's just make sure that we give these two beautiful children the best Christmas they could wish for.'

Judith nodded, but her relieved expression vanished as she glanced at the screen of her phone when it began ringing.

'Excuse me... I'll have to take this.' She rushed towards the door as she answered the call. 'What did the doctor say?' they heard her asking. 'Is he all right?'

She was back a couple of minutes later looking even more stressed than before. 'It's my father,' she told them. 'I knew he was unwell earlier this afternoon and I had to leave it to my mum to take him to the doctor. That was when I was trying to get Liam to unlock that door...' Judith's face was alarmingly pale. 'That was Mum on the phone. She said he had a massive heart attack while he was in the doctor's waiting room and they rushed him to hospital but...but they think he might not make it and...'

'And you need to be there.' Maggie sounded calm and decisive as she got up from her chair and went to put her hand on Judith's arm.

'We can find someone to drive you.' Euan was also moving to offer support. 'I can take you to Inverness and we can arrange transport from there.'

'I can drive,' Judith said. 'It's only a few hours. But... I can't leave the children. And I can't take them to the hospital. And...and I don't know what to do...' She burst into tears.

It was Maggie who took charge. 'Dinna you worry, pet. You've brought these bairns to exactly the right place. There are any number of people here to give them all the love and care they both need.' It was her grandson's arm she reached out to touch this time. 'Isn't that right, Euan?'

Abby was watching his face as he caught his grandmother's gaze and, again, she was struck by the love between them. She was also caught by the sheer courage she knew it must have taken for Euan to turn and smile so reassuringly at Judith and she felt a squeeze on her heart that felt oddly like pride.

'That's right,' he said. 'We've got this. Now, let's get

you sorted with some food and a thermos for the journey and we can tell the children what's happening. Have you got enough petrol? I can arrange for Fergus in the village to open up his garage if it's needed.'

Maggie caught Abby's gaze as Euan and Judith left the room. The shared glance acknowledged what they both knew—that these two new arrivals that they were now to be taking total responsibility for meant that Euan would be facing memories that might be overwhelming.

It was also a shared pact. They were both going to do whatever they could to make it easier. For everyone, including little Lucy and her big brother who was carrying the weight of the world on his small shoulders.

And, there was something more. It felt as if Abby was somehow tapping into that love she knew existed between Maggie and her grandson. It felt as though Abby was being included in something very precious but, whatever it was, it had the ability to flow in both directions. She could give just as much as she was being given. Or maybe it was just hanging in the air in this remarkable place, as if the love from so many years of this woman's determination to help as many sick children as she could had seeped into the thick, stone walls of this castle.

Like magic.

The kind of magic that Abby had always known Christmas could provide.

CHAPTER FIVE

IT SNOWED AGAIN during the night and it was still snowing as the children and their carers tucked into one of Catherine's legendary breakfasts that was set out as a buffet in the dining room.

'It's a good thing that Christmas cookies are first on our list this morning,' Maggie announced. 'We're going to make and decorate gingerbread men and reindeers and stars and, while that's happening we'll get through our check ups with Dr Abby and Dr Euan. If it stops snowing, we'll be able to have some playtime outside and we can visit the farm animals and make a snowman, perhaps, and later on, we'll be writing our letters to Father Christmas, ready for our sleigh ride tomorrow to post them in the forest.'

She moved to where both Euan and Abby were waiting near the door to collect their first patients for their routine morning visit to the clinic.

'Could you check on Lucy first, please? I put Liam and Lucy into a room close to mine and kept the baby monitor on in case they needed someone in the night.'

'Did they?' Abby asked. She had already turned to look for Lucy amongst the children at one of the long tables. Euan followed her gaze to see Liam wiping what looked like egg yolk off his sister's face with one of the warm, damp cloths a helper was handing out. The way Lucy was laughing and trying to avoid the cloth didn't suggest that she was unwell in any way.

'No.' Maggie shook her head. 'But I think I got woken up a couple of times by Lucy coughing.'

Euan frowned. 'You're not sure?'

'Oh, I know I woke up. I'm just not sure if I actually heard her coughing or if I dreamt it. It had stopped by the time I was properly awake.'

Coughing at night could be an early symptom of heart failure. Something they'd both learned to fear when they heard Fiona coughing at night. Something he'd dreamt about himself, more than once, in the days before he'd learned how to shut things away in that locked space.

'I'll give her a thorough check.'

Abby spoke before Euan had a chance to say anything but he wasn't about to object. It was Abby who had the specialist training, after all, and he could find out what, if anything, there was to be concerned about when they had completed their morning appointments.

But it turned out that Abby wasn't sure either about whether or not there was something to worry about.

'Her baselines are all okay but I'm thinking we might need to adjust her dose of diuretics.'

'Oh? You worried about fluid retention? Increasing heart failure?'

'Her weight hasn't changed since her initial assessment but I could hear some lung sounds that aren't quite what I heard yesterday. Nothing as definite as crackles but her oxygen saturation is already at the lower end of what I'd be looking for. I don't know her well enough to know whether I need to be worried so it's just a gut feeling but I'm planning to watch her carefully.' Abby was smiling now. 'And Liam is obviously planning to watch us carefully. Maggie told me he was watching her like a hawk when she supervised bath time and getting Lucy to bed last night. She even got a lecture about how important it was to be very careful cleaning her teeth so that she doesn't get endocarditis.'

Oh…that released an unexpected memory. He'd known all the vocabulary when he was Liam's age as well.

'But I don't want to clean my teeth. It's boring…'

'You don't want to get bacterial endocarditis, either, so just do it, Fi.'

'You're bossy.'

'I'm your big brother. I'm just looking after you…'

There was a sudden concern to be seen in Abby's eyes. 'You didn't find any problems with the kids who came to you, did you?'

Good grief…how had she picked up so instantly on a flash of memory he'd barely had time to process? Euan was quite confident he wasn't showing anything in his expression but he tightened his mouth into a semblance of a smile, anyway.

'No. It's all good. Milo was sneezing a bit but I think that had more to do with all the flour on his clothing than having picked up a bug. He's an enthusiastic baker, by all accounts.'

It wasn't just the cookie baking that Milo had been enthusiastic about. His decoration involved using icing to glue on as many candy-covered chocolates as possible and he would have eaten them all if his mum hadn't intervened. He was just as excited about getting outside after lunch when it had stopped snowing and he chose Leah to signal, with his hands palm-upwards, making circles in the air.

'That's the sign for "play",' Abby translated. 'Milo wants you to play with him.'

Milo's smile widened until it looked as if it could reach both his ears. 'Pay,' he shouted. 'Pay...' He scooped snow up into his mittened hands and threw it into the air, his laughter such a joyous sound that everyone turned to watch. And Leah was laughing as well. She, too, scooped up snow and threw it up so that it showered down on both of them.

Euan stood to one side. He'd only come out to help with pushing Callum's wheelchair over the uneven brick pathways through the kitchen gardens and had no intention of joining in because they had plenty of helpers, but Abby was making a start on one of the giant snowballs they would need to make the body of a snowman. The new snowfall had obliterated the footprints that he and Abby had made yesterday on their way to the lake but that didn't stop Euan thinking about that walk and he knew what was lying in wait to ambush his brain if he didn't distract himself immediately.

'Are you warm enough, Callum? We can go back inside and watch through the window if you'd rather.'

But Callum shook his head. 'I want to stay.'

'I need some help,' Abby called. 'Milo...stop throwing snow and come and push. This is going to be the biggest snowball in the world.'

'Can I get out of my chair?' Callum begged. 'Can I, Mum? Please? I want to make a snowball too.'

Callum's mother looked at Euan and he had to look away from the shimmer of tears that acknowledged this might be the last time her son would have the opportunity to play in snow.

'I think we can manage that.' Euan carefully lifted the frail child, who was almost hidden under the layers of his warm coat and hat, earmuffs, scarf and mittens, making sure the tubing to the oxygen tank on the back of the wheelchair didn't get disconnected, and helped him shape some snow into a ball that he threw at his mother. The effort was enough to make him short of breath, but he was beaming as Euan put him back into his chair.

'Got you, Mum.'

'You sure did, baby.'

The bottom ball of the snowman was reaching epic proportions by then and several children were helping Abby to keep rolling it.

'Stop,' she called, but the children shrieked with laughter and kept pushing.

'No...*stop*...' The command in Abby's voice this time made everyone freeze and Euan could see that something wasn't right. It was Milo who'd tripped and fallen and now he was lying face down in the snow and wasn't moving. Euan knew what wasn't right, with the same kind of gut feeling that Abby had had about Lucy earlier. This was the unnatural stillness of someone who wasn't conscious.

Someone who possibly wasn't breathing.

He was beside Abby by the time she had turned Milo onto his back and tilted his head to ensure that his airway was open. Louise was only a step or two behind him.

'What's happened?' Louise knelt beside her son. 'Oh, God...is he breathing?'

Abby nodded. 'Yes.' She had her fingers against his neck. 'His heart rate is a little slow but it's picking up. I think he probably fainted.'

Which was a warning that the strenuous activity of rolling the huge snowball could have been too much for his heart to cope with.

'Let's get him into the clinic so we can check him out properly.' Euan crouched to pick Milo up and found that the little boy was waking up. For once, he wasn't smiling.

'Mum?'

'I'm here, darling. It's okay...'

Euan was bracing himself to pick Milo up from the ground without injuring his back but Milo made it much easier by reaching up to wrap his arms around Euan's neck and trying to get to his feet himself. By the time Euan was upright, Milo was clinging to him like a solid little monkey, hanging on tight with both his arms and legs. He felt increasingly heavy by the time Euan got to the clinic, having left the volunteer helpers and carers in charge of the snowman building, but it wasn't simply the weight that was becoming progressively harder to cope with—it was this intensely close physical contact with a child and he felt as if his heart were being squeezed even more tightly than his body. At least he could be thankful that it hadn't been Lucy who'd collapsed. She might be as light as a feather but Euan didn't even want to think about how it would have felt to carry her in his arms.

It was a huge relief to put Milo down on the bed in the consulting room and let Abby step in to start the assessment.

'Shall we get Mum to come and sit on the bed with you?' Abby suggested.

Milo nodded and cuddled up to Louise while Abby listened to his chest with her stethoscope.

'How long ago did Milo have the balloon dilation of the aortic valve?'

'Over a year, now. They did say that it might need to be done again but...but that if it wasn't enough, he might need another operation.'

'And this is the first time he's fainted?'

'Yes. He did have that episode where he got very short of breath not so long ago, though.'

Abby nodded, focused on what she was hearing and

trying to make the rest of her assessment no big deal for Milo.

'I'm going to put these sticky dots on your chest, now, sweetheart. And this little crocodile on your finger.' She opened and shut the pulse oximeter clip a few times. 'It doesn't hurt,' she promised. 'See?'

She put the clip on her nose and Milo laughed out loud, circling his hands in the sign for 'play'. He laughed again when she put the clip on his own nose briefly before shifting it to a fingertip and Euan heard his own chuckle escape. He also felt the weight he hadn't realised he was still carrying lift from his heart. By the time he and Abby were having a quiet lunch in the castle kitchen, to avoid the noise and busyness of the dining rooms, he could talk about what had happened with his normal and totally appropriate professionalism.

'I don't think it's an emergency by any means,' he said in response to Abby's query. 'I agree that it was a result of all that effort he was putting into pushing the snowball and, if he avoids that kind of strenuous activity, it's not likely to happen again. And it's not as if they're going to do any major investigations right before Christmas, like an exercise stress test or a catheterisation to get accurate pressure measurements above and below the aortic valve.'

'It's best that he goes back to the team who've been looking after him since birth for any of that.' Abby nodded.

'But I would quite like to get an echo done, just for peace of mind.'

Again, Abby nodded. 'Louise is putting a brave face on things but it's obvious that this has given her a huge fright. And made her realise that more open-heart surgery could well be on the cards. Milo could be picking up on that. He was quite subdued after his ECG. Even the elf headband didn't cheer him up.'

Abby looked as if she needed a bit of cheering up herself. She was using her spoon to stir the delicious vegetable soup Cath had provided for their lunch but seemed to have lost her appetite. Perhaps they all needed some reassurance so they could relax and enjoy the next few days.

'How 'bout I ring my friend in Inverness and see if they've got time to see Milo for an echo this afternoon?'

'Oh…that would be wonderful. Do you think they'll be able to see him?'

'I'm sure they will. We might have to wait a while but they all go out of their way to help any of our camp kids. I'll drive them in and we might even be back in time for dinner.' It was good to hear Abby's sigh of relief but what Euan really wanted was to see her smile again.

'I'll leave you to keep watch on everybody else for the afternoon. Are you going to write a letter to Father Christmas? And decorate the envelope, of course—that's obligatory. That way, you'll get to post it in the elves' post box tomorrow.' He lowered his voice to a secretive whisper. 'It's actually a big, old hollow tree in the oak forest that we cut a slot into. There's twenty years' worth of kids' letters inside that trunk.'

'What?' Abby was feigning horror. 'You mean the letters don't get to the North Pole?'

Euan's lips twitched. 'The sleigh ride is a camp highlight for the kids and we get some of the best photographs from it. Just wait till you see Bonnie and Scotch with their antlers on and bells all over their harnesses. It's quite a sight.'

The degree of pleasure that he had succeeded in making Abby smile was like an upward swoop on the emotional rollercoaster Euan seemed to be riding today.

'I can't wait. And, you know what?'

'What?'

'I think I will write that letter. There's something I'd love this Christmas.'

'What's that?'

'Can't say. If I tell, it might not happen. Christmas secrets, you know?'

'Mmm...'

But the way Abby was looking at him made Euan wonder if what she was wishing had something to do with him. Or maybe the wish was *for* him, which wouldn't be a surprise at all because he was beginning to realise how big a heart this woman had. How much love she had to give others. Maybe that was why she loved Christmas so much? Because it was a time to not hold back in showering the people around her with love? A bit of that squeeze had come back to enclose Euan's heart. That man who would father her six children currently had no idea how lucky he was, did he?

It was well after dinner time when Euan got back to the castle that evening. The usual buzz of getting all the children fed, bathed and into bed was well and truly over.

'How are you?' Maggie came out of the kitchen holding a couple of hot water bottles in bright woollen covers. 'How's Milo?'

'It's all good,' Euan assured her. 'We'll stop him doing anything too strenuous and there shouldn't be any more problems for now.'

'Oh, thank goodness. I was so worried.' Maggie didn't have to stoop far to give Milo a kiss. 'Are you hungry? Cath has got something in the oven for you all if you are.'

'We ate in the hospital cafeteria while we were waiting for the echo,' Louise told her. 'I expect Milo would like another one of his Christmas cookies but I'd better get this tired wee boy into bed and I might say goodnight as well. We've had a big day.' She reached into her shoulder bag. 'Something else we did while we were waiting...' She pulled out a large envelope. 'Someone was kind enough to make up a pack so Milo wouldn't miss out on the letter writing. I think posting the letter into that tree is his favourite part of camp.'

'Oh, lovely. Euan, can you take that, please? I've got to take these hotties up to Lucy and Liam. The box is in the drawing room. We'll do the list later, after everyone's gone to bed.'

In the end, however, Euan made sure that Maggie had taken some more painkillers and ordered her off to bed to rest and wouldn't listen to any objections. 'If you're not looking any better in the morning, it'll be you I'll be taking in to the hospital,' he warned her.

Maggie sighed. 'He's only saying that because he knows the sleigh ride is my favourite thing. All right... I'll go and get some sleep.' She put the box on the sofa between Euan and Abby and handed a folder to her grandson. 'You know what to do.'

He did. But Abby's jaw dropped when she saw him carefully open the first letter he took from the box.

'What are you *doing*?'

'Reading the letters. Oh, aye, I know about the Christmas secrets, but this is what we do.'

'Why?'

'So that we can try to make sure the children get something they've asked for.' Euan picked up the folder. 'The parents bring one gift, which is hidden away to go under the tree on Christmas Eve. We've got a list of what they are, so we don't double up on anything. Each child has a stocking that goes on their door handle and that's full of little treats that get donated. We also get funding from various charities and we use some of that to provide a gift that Santa gives them from his sack. That's Fergus, by the way, from the garage in the village. He makes a good Father Christmas, does Fergus.'

He unfolded the first letter. 'This is from Leah,' he told her. 'And what she wants most of all is a puppy. That's a no-no.'

'Because she's not allowed a puppy?'

'Because puppies are for ever and not just for Christmas,' Euan said. 'Besides, imagine the chaos on Christmas Day if we had puppies running around the castle?'

But Abby didn't smile back. 'So what will Leah get from Father Christmas, then?'

'A toy puppy.' Euan was making a note on a blank sheet of paper. 'And we'll have a word with her dad. If it's a possibility, he can tell her that there might be a real puppy down the track. Caring for a pet may be a good way for Leah to gain a bit of confidence.'

'Hmm.' Abby seemed distracted. She was peering into the box. 'You're not opening my letter,' she told him. 'And that's that.'

'Fair enough. The last time I put a letter in that box I knew I had to keep it a secret.'

'I'll look after this one.' Abby wasn't looking at him as she pulled an envelope from the box and put it to one side. 'Did you get *your* wish?'

Euan pretended he was also busy, reading the next letter, so he could ignore the query. 'Louise has written this for Milo and he's done the decorating. He wants a computer game, which will be easy. She'll give us his device and we can load the app.'

When some requests were already being provided, the shopping list got a question mark so that parents could be consulted about a surprise. There were no more requests for puppies and most were doable. Until the last.

'Oh...' It was Abby who was reading the letter. 'This is a joint request. From Lucy and Liam.' She looked up at Euan and he was shocked to see the tears filling her eyes. 'They just want to be able to stay together...' Her voice broke and a tear trickled down the side of her nose. 'Because...because they love each other.'

Euan found himself on his feet without conscious movement. He wanted to turn and head for the door and escape but...he couldn't go any further. He couldn't walk away from Abby when she was looking like this. When she needed comfort. Slowly, he sat back down again, shifting the box so that it wasn't between them.

'It's never easy, is it?' he said quietly. 'Being with these kids.'

Abby swiped the tear off her cheek. 'We can't make this one come true, can we?'

'No. But Maggie will have an idea of something special we can do for them. Maybe we can take a heap of photos and make books for them. Memories...'

'That's a lovely idea.' Abby sniffed, clearly trying to stem her tears. She was even trying to smile at him and Euan could feel a very odd squeeze in his chest at the way her voice wobbled when she spoke again.

'When was it?' she asked. 'That you wrote your last letter to Father Christmas? And what was it that you kept secret?'

Oh, damn...those tears were contagious, judging by the way his throat was constricting. And, while that part of his body was tightening up, another part felt as if it were cracking open.

'I was fourteen,' he said. 'And I asked for the same thing that Fi had asked for in *her* letter.' He had to stop and swallow hard. 'I suspect Maggie still has that letter somewhere.' Not that he'd seen it in more than twenty years, but it was still there in his mind as clearly as when he'd first opened that envelope. That picture of an angel and the careful letters of a seven-year-old.

> *Dear Father Christmas*
>> *Please can I have a new heart?*
>> *That's all.*
>> *Thank you very much.*
>> *Love from Fi*

'She only asked for one thing,' Euan whispered aloud. 'A new heart…'

To his horror, he could feel a tear rolling down his own face. Even more disturbing was the way that Abby threw her arms around him. No…what was doing his head in completely was how much he'd wanted her to do exactly that. To rediscover the kind of human comfort that he'd never sought as an adult. To offer that comfort as well, to someone else who was feeling sad.

He had no idea how long they simply sat and held each other but the fire had died down to glowing coals by the time he raised his head. Abby shifted as well and there they were, again, as they had been under the apple tree, so close that it would take no effort at all to kiss her. Even the thought of doing that made it irresistible. Euan wasn't even sure if he made the first move because it just seemed to happen and…dear Lord…it was even more un-believable than the first time. That softness. The taste. The warmth that was so much more than purely physi-cal. It was wrapping itself around his heart but stirring other parts of his body in a way he'd never experienced.

He'd never wanted to be with anyone this much. To be as close as it was physically possible to be.

It was Abby who said it, though, as they finally ended that kiss.

'Let's go to bed,' she said softly.

And, there it was.

The life-saver.

The most enticing way to step away from reality for just a little while. And, okay, he knew there was too much emotion involved, here. That, normally, he'd back off as far and fast as possible until he'd got his own head together. But...

But there had been too many downward swoops in to-day's rollercoaster. That reminder of how hearing coughing during the night could spark fear and how important a simple task like cleaning teeth could become. That look in Callum's mother's eyes as she got a glimpse into what they both knew the future held. That overwhelming experience of carrying Milo in his arms.

And now this. The comfort being offered in the wake of the hardest memory of all. That single request that Fi had made with total trust that the magic of Christmas could make it happen.

He'd wanted to believe, as well. He'd desperately needed that hope.

As much as he needed the comfort he knew that Abby could give him now. The comfort he knew he could give *her*.

As he got to his feet, he let his hand slide down Abby's arm until it caught her hand and, as he felt her fingers tighten around his, Euan knew without a shadow of a doubt that she wanted this intimate time together as much as he did.

* * *

There was definitely magic here, within the walls of this castle.

There was the glow of firelight and the twinkle of Christmas lights on the tree. The suits of armour in the entrance foyer were sporting red hats with white trim and pom poms and there were ropes of ivy and more sparkling lights wound through the stair bannisters and the balustrade above. There was even a wreath that Maggie had somehow found time to make from the mistletoe they'd gathered yesterday hanging beneath the enormous chandelier just in front of staircase.

Was that why Euan paused just there? Why he wove his fingers through Abby's hair to cup the back of her neck, holding her still while he kissed her again, with a thoroughness that drove any other thoughts from her mind—including how unprofessional it would seem if anyone saw them.

No one had ever kissed her like this. She'd never wanted to be with anyone like this. Was that because Euan McKendry was so completely the opposite of any man she would have considered to be her 'type'? That didn't matter a jot right now. This was about how she'd caught more than simply an echo of the kind of loss Euan had to be feeling. That scare of seeing Milo so motionless on the ground today. The sadness of knowing that Lucy, a child she had already fallen in love with, could be facing not only a limited future but that she might have to do it without the big brother she adored. To see Euan shed tears had been a point of no return, however. She could see through that grumpy façade so easily now. She could see the boy who'd been hurt so much he'd had to wall himself off to survive. The man who was still capable of that kind of love but too afraid to let it into his life. She could feel the whole weight of what he was facing for the next few days. Abby could also feel the ice of those barriers he'd built starting to crack all around her feet as she held his hand and climbed the stairs with him to her bedroom.

They walked silently along the hallway, past the closed doors that were offering them a safe passage to the room where the door could be clicked shut on something that could be kept completely private. Abby closed her eyes as she leaned on that door, her arms around Euan's neck as she stood on tiptoes to kiss him again.

He started to say something but she put her finger against his lips, smiling into his eyes as she tried to tell him, silently, that nothing needed to be said. That neither of them needed to overthink this in any way. This was a moment in time in which Euan could completely escape. That Abby was more than happy to go with him. She saw the moment when he took that first step into the delicious oblivion she knew they were going to find. When his eyes darkened and slowly closed as his lips covered hers, his hands sliding down her back to bring her hips in contact with the hardness of his body.

The tiny sound of need escaping Abby's lips got swallowed by Euan but he must have heard it because he moved his hand to stroke her skin beneath her clothes and then grasped the hem of her jumper to pull it up and over her head. And then his fingers were deftly undoing the buttons of her shirt and a sense of urgency became so strong that Abby had to let her own hands find Euan's bare skin and she, too, let everything else go to be completely in the moment. Being totally naked and cocooned in the feathery softness of that wonderful bed that was temporarily her own couldn't happen soon enough.

Never mind what she'd written in her private letter to

Father Christmas. This was going to be her gift to Euan this Christmas—the joy of human connection and comfort. Of desire and release.

And, tonight, maybe she needed it herself, just as much.

CHAPTER SIX

THIS HAD TO be up there with the best moments ever in Abby Hawkins' life.

To be snuggled up in faux fur rugs, with a small person to cuddle on her lap, and two of the biggest and most beautiful horses she had ever seen, with bells jingling all over their harnesses and clouds of steam puffing from their nostrils as they slowly pulled the enormous cartload of adults and children along a wide track through the oak forest and towards the lake.

Abby hadn't stopped smiling from the moment she'd joined the children in the farmyard as the final preparations were being made to the horses and sleigh. The castle's cow, Daisy, and the very friendly mob of pet sheep were watching the excitement through a fence and the donkeys, Joseph and Mary, had their heads over the half-door in their stable.

Euan had been helping to make sure the antlers were firmly secured to the horses' bridles when Abby had arrived and she hadn't been able to resist the pull to go to his side.

'They look so real,' Abby said. 'And super heavy?'

'They are real deer antlers.' Euan's face might be as serious as always, but there was a smile in his eyes as he spoke to her. 'They've been cleverly carved to make them lighter. It was Fergus's father that made them—more than twenty years ago now—when he was in his nineties, no less.'

Having made sure that Lucy was well wrapped up in her hat and scarf, Maggie joined them to reach up and stroke the nose of the horse that was towering above her. The way she didn't move when the horse snorted loudly and bobbed its head had made Abby smile even more. She was getting very fond of this feisty, small woman whom she could only hope would also be doing something remarkable in her nineties.

'Climb up,' Euan had instructed Abby. 'You can be Lucy's carer this morning. Maggie's going to sit up front and take the reins, as usual. I'll be walking, with Leah's dad.' He'd lowered his voice so that only Abby could hear. 'We're going to have a wee chat about puppies.'

So here she was, with Lucy on her lap and Liam sitting beside her in the back corner of an old hay cart that had been customised to look like a silver and white sleigh with runners that were low enough to almost hide the wheels behind them.

'Isn't this exciting? Are you warm enough, sweetheart?'

Lucy nodded. Like Abby, she couldn't stop smiling. She poked her brother. 'Have you still got our letter, Liam? I'm the one who's going to post it, aren't I?'

'Yep.' But Liam didn't even glance at the carefully resealed letter he had in his hands. He was staring through the trees beside him and then he pointed at something. 'What's over there?'

'It's a lake.'

'The one we get to go ice-skating on?'

'Yes. If it's safe enough. Dr Euan hasn't checked it yet. I think the skating is something we do on Christmas Day.' She gave Lucy another cuddle. 'How many sleeps is it now?'

'Two.'

'That's right. Two sleeps. Just as well we're getting our letters posted today, isn't it? I think Father Christmas is going to be very busy trying to get organised.'

This time, Liam did turn his head and the look he gave Abby finally dimmed her smile. Had it sounded as if she might be making an excuse for the non-delivery of their request? He couldn't know that she knew what he'd asked for in the letter he was holding but she felt as if he was blaming her for something. For being yet another adult that couldn't be trusted, perhaps? For perpetuating a myth that there was a Father Christmas who could grant wishes? Liam looked as if he knew perfectly well that any promises she might offer would be broken.

Was he already growing up to hate Christmas as much as Euan?

The boy didn't hold Abby's gaze long enough for her to try and offer any kind of reassurance, which was probably just as well because the only thing she could do was send a silent plea out into the universe that a miracle might happen and that these children could stay together for as long as possible.

Of course Abby knew that there was no Father Christmas in the North Pole but she did believe in miracles. In magic. A kind of magic that had nothing to do with fairies and wands, or wizards and spells, mind you. The kind of magic she had every faith in was about people caring and the amazing alchemy that could result in unexpected and beautiful things happening.

Abby let her gaze drift over the heads of the other children in the cart. Callum's wheelchair had been left behind and he, like Lucy, was wrapped in an incredibly soft rug, safe in his mother's arms. Milo was cuddled up beside Louise, laughing aloud with every jolt of the cart as it encountered tree roots on its path. There was Maggie on the front bench, with Leah sitting beside her, and Leah was helping to hold the reins, as Maggie called encouragement to the horses. Bonnie and Scotch were plodding steadily on and Euan McKendry was one of the people walking by their shoulders. For a long, delicious moment, Abby let her gaze rest on him.

She'd experienced some of the kind of that magic she believed in herself, only last night.

The trust Euan had offered her by making himself so vulnerable—coming apart in her arms, even—wasn't the most extraordinary aspect of the best sex she'd ever had, though. It was that this man, who'd so badly needed an escape from reality and ghosts from the past, could still care about her and that her needs were being met. To be such a generous lover. To be that gentle and sensitive and yet so astonishingly masculine at the same time. To control that strength in the height of passion and be so aware of his partner was the sexiest thing ever.

Her breath came out in a sigh that made Lucy look up, so Abby smiled down at the little pixie face that was so heartbreakingly gorgeous.

'Two sleeps,' she whispered. She didn't look at Liam again. Two days and two sleeps were a blip in time but maybe something good would happen. It wasn't beyond the realms of possibility that someone with a heart as big as Louise's might be found and be willing to open their home and heart to these two children.

Two sleeps until Christmas.

Three sleeps until Abby was due to leave Ravenswood Castle.

She found herself watching Euan again. Would he

need—or want—any more time out? Another…escape? *She* wanted it, that was for sure. If anything, the level of attraction she was feeling was snowballing, rather like that enormous stomach of the snowman she'd been in charge of creating before that scary incident with Milo yesterday. Given that it was already at a higher level than she'd ever felt in her life before, at least Abby could be confident that this physical desire wasn't going to become any more of a distraction. And that she could control it, when she needed to.

'There it is,' someone called. 'There's the tree.'

And there it was. A tall trunk that was the remains of a forest giant that had toppled long ago, with a slot cut into it at a level that a small person could reach if they stood on tiptoes. Around the base of the tree trunk was a collection of carvings. Big mushrooms with doors in their stalks and tiny elves in their gardens or workshops. It was a work of art that was enchanting. Surely even Liam couldn't be entirely certain that there wasn't a bit of magic involved in posting their special letters?

He did seem to be as captured as everybody else, including Abby. It was Liam who led Lucy by the hand to see the elven village up close and he was the one to lift his little sister so that she could post the letter. There was a professional photographer amongst the entourage on foot, snapping images of the occasion, but Abby had her phone out as well and the image she caught of Lucy's face as she slid that envelope through the slot was one she knew she would keep for the rest of her life. It wasn't just the glow of complete faith from Lucy that her Christmas wish was going to the one place and person who could make it come true, it was the expression of pure love on her brother's face as he watched her. The combination added up to something even bigger.

It felt like hope.

Abby was blinking back tears as she looked up from her screen to find Euan watching her and, for a heartbeat, that eye contact felt as intimate as anything physical that had happened between them last night. A wash of something astonishingly soft and warm rippled through Abby's body and, weirdly, that felt like hope as well, along with the certainty that their time together hadn't been a one-off. That they both wanted it to happen again.

The Christmas Camp programme was ramping up, which added pressure to finding the time to monitor all the children closely and deal with any medical issues without unduly disrupting their participation in activities.

On a personal level, Euan always found that he had to distance himself more and more from things that weren't medical as the anticipation built and there were specific activities he usually avoided like the plague. The Christmas themed dress up party at the castle tonight was one of those activities. So was the posting of letters in the elf tree. He'd gone along today, however, and while he'd told himself it was because he was keeping an extra eye on Milo and because he wanted to make sure Maggie wasn't doing anything that would make her pain level harder to manage, Euan knew that wasn't the whole story.

He'd gone on the sleigh ride because Abby had gone. Because he wanted to be close enough to be able to see her and talk to her. Because moments between and after the morning health checks hadn't been enough. Most of all, it was because he felt safe. It would only take a glance and he'd be able to tap into a distraction that could override any ghosts that were lying in wait for him. It would be no effort at all to remember what last night had been like. It would, in fact, be a pleasure to give in to the temptation to relive every touch. Every kiss. Every delicious stolen moment of being completely oblivious to the outside world. He'd been right in thinking that his attraction to Abby could be a life-saver and that had been when he'd only experienced what it was like to kiss her. Now he knew what it was like to fall into an exquisite, physical oblivion in her company and that had increased any distracting power exponentially.

To his astonishment, he had genuinely enjoyed the sleigh ride this morning.

And he was quite agreeable to Maggie's request that he got his bagpipes out for the period of time the children were warming up in the drawing room before lunch so that they could have a quick choir practice.

'As you will have seen on our programme, we go down to the village church for the carol service on Christmas Eve,' Maggie told everybody who'd gathered to soak in the warmth of the fire after their chilly outing to the forest. 'Euan pipes us in and we're carrying our candles and then the bagpipes fade away when we're at the front of the church and we start singing and then everybody else joins in.'

'Oh, that sounds lovely.' It was Ben's grandmother who spoke up. 'What carol will it be? We've been practising at home from the list ever since we knew we were coming to camp.'

'"The Little Drummer Boy". One of my absolute favourites.' Maggie beamed at everyone. 'Euan's going to play a little bit for you now, just so you know how loud it is. We don't want anyone getting a fright tomorrow night. Are you ready, Euan?'

'Aye.'

Euan already had already taken his set of bagpipes out of their wooden case. He had the bag under his arm and the drones on his shoulder. He lifted the blowpipe to his mouth.

'You can put your fingers in your ears if you need to,' Maggie called as he blew his first breath into the bag and the background base of the drones started to sound.

Even though he was on the far side of the enormous room, it was piercingly loud to be doing this inside and, as Euan increased the air in the bag to provide enough pressure to add the chanter notes of the song to the background, he saw Lucy, who was sitting on Abby's lap again, clap her hands over her ears. She looked as if she might be gleefully shrieking as well but he couldn't hear that over the sound of the Christmas song. Abby, along with many of the carers, were looking impressed but slightly overwhelmed. Liam's jaw had dropped and he was simply staring, mesmerised. And he wasn't covering his ears to try and muffle the sound.

Playing the bagpipes had been another kind of lifesaver for Euan all those years ago, when he'd been dealing with unimaginable loss, but he only used this instrument when he was at the castle these days and that wasn't nearly often enough. It was fortunate that he could play this song, and many other Christmas carols, from memory. It only took one verse and a chorus to knock any rust off his skills and that was enough to be doing inside for now. Maggie and her helpers, including Muriel with her small, portable keyboard, were ready to fill the silence by leading the singing from the children. Euan watched for a moment as he silenced the pipes.

Maggie was looking pale, he thought. And tired. Whether she liked it or not, he was going to take her over to the clinic and check her blood pressure and other vital signs and find out exactly how much pain she was in and any other symptoms she could well be hiding. He found himself sighing as he laid the pipes back in their case. What was going to happen when Maggie was no longer here? Would he even come to the castle at all? Would these wonderful old pipes that his father and his grandfather before him had played stay in their case and never be heard? His grandmother had never pushed past his reluctance to discuss his inheritance but the fact that this could be the last Christmas camp ever at Ravenswood Castle was another level of pressure that was ramping up.

Time could well be running out.

The savoury smell of the hot pasties Cath was serving for lunch was all the more inviting after the fresh air and excitement of the morning's expedition.

'Cornish pasties. Yum.' Abby lifted Lucy onto her chair and left another clear for Liam.

'Och, no.' Cath shook her head. 'These are Forfar bridies, lass. There's no potatoes in these so they're much tastier. There's homemade tomato sauce there, too, if you like it.'

Abby liked it very much. So did Lucy. What was threatening to spoil her enjoyment, however, was that Liam's chair beside her was still empty.

'He's taking a long time to wash his hands. Will you be all right for a minute while I go and find him, Lucy?'

Lucy nodded around a mouthful of bridie, a big smear of sauce on her chin, but Abby still paused as she left the dining room to let Maggie know she'd left the little girl to eat the rest of her lunch alone.

There was no sign of Liam in the foyer. Euan was there, however, and he looked far from happy.

'What's happened?'

'My bagpipes have vanished.'

'What? Where were they?'

'Right there, in their case.' Euan pointed at the empty wooden box on an ornately carved sideboard near the doors to the drawing room. 'I had something I wanted to do in the clinic and I've just come back. Who would have taken them? And why? One of the children, do you think? To play with them?'

Abby shook her head. 'They went to wash their hands straight after the singing practice. And then we all went to the dining room. Everyone was starving by then.'

Euan had to be hungry himself and Abby had the strongest urge to see him tucking into one of Cath's wonderful bridies but she could see that he was upset. There were tight lines around his eyes and dark shadow within them.

'They were my father's,' he told her. 'And my grandfather's before that. They're not a toy.'

No. They were something very precious but she'd already known that, hadn't she? The way the hairs on the back of her neck had prickled when she'd heard the first notes of the bagpipes had told her that and Euan's body language as he'd stood there playing had been…well… that had also touched something very deep in Abby.

'Oh…' She pressed her fingers to her mouth. 'Liam hasn't come in to lunch. That's why I've come out. To find him.'

It wasn't hard to put two and two together.

'Where would he go?' Euan's scowl was ferocious now. 'And what's he doing with the pipes? I thought he *liked* hearing them. He was one of the only bairns who didn't put their fingers in their ears.'

'There must be a million places to hide inside this castle,' Abby said. 'Let alone outside it.' She bit her lip. 'He wouldn't go far away from Lucy, though. Maybe he's gone to the only place he's ever alone with her?'

'His room?'

Euan was already heading for the sweep of the staircase, his face tightening with what looked like anger. Abby raced after him, hoping desperately that they weren't going to find those heirloom bagpipes damaged in any way. She'd seen Euan annoyed. She'd seen him walk away from things that he didn't like, but she'd never seen him lose control due to anger. Liam might need protection. *Euan* might need it himself.

She was moving so quickly as she went through the door of the children's bedroom that she bumped into Euan's back because he'd stopped as soon as he'd entered the room. He was standing very still, staring at the enormous bed that Liam and Lucy were sharing. Liam was sitting in the middle of the bed. He was clearly trying to hold the bagpipes the way he'd seen Euan holding them earlier and he had the pipe for blowing in his mouth but the ungainly instrument looked far too big and it had a life of its own, with the pipes rolling off Liam's shoulder as Abby watched.

Liam was staring back at Euan and he looked terrified—as if he knew that he was about to be severely punished. Abby wanted nothing more than to go to his side. To put her arm around him and offer support but she knew this was between Liam and Euan. She knew that Liam would have to face up to being told he'd done something he shouldn't have. She could only hope that Euan wouldn't be too hard on him. What Euan actually did, however, took her breath away.

He went and sat on the edge of the bed. He was looking at his hands, rather than directly at Liam, when he spoke.

'So…you fancy learning to play the pipes, do you, lad?'

Liam said nothing. He was hanging his head, staring

down at the bagpipes he'd taken, and Abby had never seen him look more miserable.

'It's not an easy thing to learn. I started when I was about your age…and it was something I wanted to do because I missed my daddy and these were *his* pipes so they were very special to me.'

Oh… That lump in Abby's throat was enough to block her breathing. Like the way she had been able to time travel and see a happy young boy climbing that apple tree beside the lake, she could see a slightly older and very different boy now. One that was aching for his daddy and trying, too soon, to fill his shoes. A courageous boy, now a man, who had a direct connection to another boy who was struggling with what life was presenting. And that raw emotion in his quiet words was touching a deep part of her soul. This was the real Euan, wasn't it? The one that was normally kept so well hidden.

This was a man who protected himself by growling at the world to keep people at bay but he was offering a door in those barriers to this boy. And this was a boy who was so unhappy that he was unwilling to trust or respond to anyone. Except that he was slowly turning his head now, so that he could look up at the man sitting on the end of the bed.

'The thing is, you don't learn by what you're doing now. That's like jumping into the middle of a lake before you've learned to swim a bit closer to the shore. When you start to learn the pipes, you play what's called a practice chanter. Same as this bit on the pipes…' Euan touched a part of the instrument '…but it's smaller and easier—like a recorder. I could show you mine if you like?'

Abby's heart was melting and, as she saw Liam's slow, shy nod, she found herself edging backwards so that she could leave this man and boy together. She needed a moment to herself, anyway, because it was in that moment that she realised there was far more than simply an irresistible physical attraction between herself and Euan McKendry. He might be the total opposite of someone she could see in her future but that hadn't stopped it happening, had it?

She was falling in love with him. So fast and so hard there was no chance of stopping it happening and it already felt as if her heart were about to break into a million pieces because it was too full. And, maybe, because it was the first time she'd felt *this* strongly about anyone and it was only going to last—*could* only last—until she left Ravenswood Castle, which meant there could be heartbreak ahead.

Only three sleeps away.

CHAPTER SEVEN

'YOU DISAPPEARED.'

He'd noticed? Even when he had been so clearly focused on dealing with a rather significant development in Liam's visit to the castle? Abby was aware of a frisson of something that felt curiously like...hope? She kept her tone carefully casual, though.

'I could see that Liam was ready to have a serious man-to-man talk about bagpipes. And I could see that you had it all in hand.'

Euan's glance acknowledged her unspoken approval for the way he had handled the incident of the borrowed bagpipes. Then he frowned. 'Your cheeks are very pink.'

He touched one very gently with the back of his fingers. 'And very cold.'

They must be almost frozen, Abby thought, because the heat coming from that light touch was so hot it was scorching. Euan blinked, as if he'd felt it as well.

'Have you been outside?'

'I went out to the stables.' Abby found a bright smile, confident she wouldn't reveal any of the emotional overload that had sent her off to find a quiet spot to get her head together. But, just in case, she offered an excuse for anything that might slip past her guard. 'I think I'm in love with Joseph and Mary. There's something about donkeys, isn't there?'

'Hmph…' Euan's grunt—and the way he looked away from her—suggested that he was back within his own defensive walls. 'They might deserve their place in a nativity scene, which is what Christmas is really about rather than the commercial circus we've since created, but I think Maggie went a wee bit overboard in naming them.'

A commercial circus? Oh, yeah… Euan was definitely well over that deeply personal moment he'd had with Liam.

'It's more than that. They're such gentle creatures. Serene, even. Just standing beside them can make you feel kind of peaceful.'

Thankfully, they'd made Abby feel a lot more in control, anyway. Okay, maybe she *was* falling in love with Euan but it didn't have to be a disaster at all. She could actually embrace it, knowing that it was only going to last a few days and then she could tuck it away. In the same place that she'd filed youthful crushes on movie stars or pop idols, perhaps, where nothing could ever come of it but it was rather delicious to play with. Mind you, she'd never gone to bed with any movie star or pop idol, had she?

'Ah…there you are, Euan.' Maggie was walking towards them. Slowly. A little unevenly, as if she was leaning to one side.

'Are you limping, Gammy?'

She shrugged. 'Maybe a little. Did you finally get some lunch? And what about Liam?'

'Don't change the subject. Are you hurting? I thought you were looking poorly earlier. Come over to the clinic with me so I can have a look at you.'

Maggie shook her head firmly. 'I've got far too much to do. We're just getting the children all settled for quiet time with a movie and stories so they won't be too tired for the party this evening.'

'You need quiet time too. There's plenty of helpers here. They can do whatever needs to be done and you know you only need to ask. Where are you off to now?'

'I'm on my way up to the attics on the south side, in the servants' quarters over the kitchens, and, I must admit, I wasn't looking forward to all those steep stairs.' There was a gleam in Maggie's eyes that made Abby want to smile. Even at this age and unwell, she was a woman who knew how to get what she wanted.

'What on earth do you need to go up there for?'

'The dress ups. We got the boxes of decorations down a couple of weeks ago but the party costumes got forgotten.'

'You shouldn't be climbing unnecessary stairs, let alone lugging heavy boxes.' Euan glanced over his shoulder as if he was hoping a helpful volunteer would be wandering around but the only other person here was Abby and his outward breath sounded exasperated. 'I'll get them,' he said. 'But only if you go and put your feet up for a while, Gammy. And take your pills. If you're still sore when I come back, you're coming over to the clinic with me and no arguments. Or I'll call Graham and drag him out from the village to give you a piece of his mind about not taking good enough care of yourself.'

Maggie's outward breath was a rather satisfied one. She ignored the warning and smiled at Abby instead.

'Euan could take you with him up to the attics,' she said. 'He'll need some help with all those boxes. I know there are parts of the castle we keep closed off because it's just too big to look after it all, but you'd like to see a bit more of the parts that are open, wouldn't you, pet?'

'I really would.' Abby nodded. She smiled at Euan. 'Can we go now?'

They had to go past the kitchens to get to the back stairs that led to the old servants' quarters and the attic above them and the enticing, savoury smell floating into the hall was irresistible.

'I do believe I can smell bacon. And I'm starving. I didn't get any lunch.' Euan veered into the kitchen. 'Catherine, you wouldn't be cooking some pigs in blankets, now, would you?'

The cook laughed. 'They've been your favourite since you were a wee laddie. Here…' She pointed to a tray on top of one of the ovens. 'You can have a taste. We're just starting to do the cooking for tonight's party.'

As always, the tiny chipolata sausage wrapped in crispy bacon made the most delicious mouthful ever. Euan picked another up by its toothpick to offer it to Abby and, without thinking, he held it up to her mouth and then watched closely as she delicately took the sausage off the toothpick with her teeth and lips, closing her eyes almost instantly in the sheer pleasure of the taste.

His own pleasure of seeing Abby enjoying something he was so fond of himself gave Euan an odd feeling— as if it was something he could be proud of, which was ridiculous. And that it was something he wanted to do again. And again. Which was disconcerting on top of being silly. But, when Abby swallowed her mouthful and then opened her eyes to meet Euan's gaze, anything odd about what he was feeling vanished. The kick of physical desire was easy to recognise. And even more irresistible than the lure of Cath's cooking.

'That was *so* good…' Abby licked her lips.

It was just as well there was a large team of people working in the kitchen or he might have given in to the almost overwhelming desire to kiss her senseless, right here, right now—especially when he was pretty sure he might be seeing a similar desire in Abby's eyes. Then it occurred to him that as soon as they left the kitchen, they would be heading for a part of the castle that would be completely deserted, which was the only incentive he needed to break that eye contact and get moving.

'Thanks, Cath. You're a legend.'

Euan helped himself and Abby to another sausage that they ate as he led the way past tables where trifles and jellies, sandwiches and savouries and all sorts of other party food were being created. He took Abby to the staircase that led to the old servants' quarters and then an even narrower one that went up into a vast attic space.

A space that was crowded with old furniture and cobwebs, strange items like a dressmaker's dummy and a spinning wheel and many, many boxes full of things like books and vinyl records and toys and tea sets. Abby was wide-eyed as she looked around the dimly lighted space.

Any plan to steal a kiss had to be put aside, Euan decided, because Abby was far more interested in this treasure trove of discarded possessions.

'How on earth did anyone get those brass bed ends up those stairs? And, good grief—is that a *harp* over there?'

Euan shook his head. 'It's a nightmare I've been avoiding for a long time.'

'What is?'

'What to do about clearing this place when it comes time to sell the castle.'

'Sell?' Abby looked bewildered. 'Why would you do that?'

'There's no one other than me to inherit this place when…' Euan didn't want to finish his sentence. He didn't want to think about what was hanging over their heads this Christmas. That it could be Maggie's last.

'The boxes with the dress up costumes should be easy enough to find,' he said crisply. 'They get brought out and put back every year. Goodness knows why, when there's any number of empty rooms in more convenient places. I think my grandmother just likes to do things the way they've always been done. Have a look inside just to make sure we're not carrying anything downstairs that we won't need.'

Abby was quiet as she followed the direction he took towards a stack of cardboard cartons and he had the feeling she knew perfectly well why he'd changed the subject so abruptly. She could probably guess why he would never want to live here again or take on the running of this castle because she knew exactly how devastating the memories were. She'd seen him cry, for goodness' sake, and nobody had *seen* him cry since his daddy had died when he was seven.

Remembering that moment brought a rush of what were flashes of feeling rather than any coherent thoughts. Like the way he'd felt when Abby had thrown her arms around him when she'd seen those tears. When she'd quietly held him for as long as he'd needed it. And when she'd touched him later, as if she not only could anticipate what it was that he craved but that she wanted nothing more than to provide it.

And now, she was allowing the conversation to drift and let him escape what was too hard to think about before he was forced to.

'Traditions are important,' Abby said, as if that had been what they'd been discussing all along. 'Especially

Christmas traditions. And I have a new one now, thanks to you.'

'Oh?' For a crazy moment Euan thought she might be referring to their time together last night. It couldn't possibly become a Christmas tradition for either of them when their lives were going to head in completely different directions, probably on opposite sides of the globe, in a couple of days but, just for a nanosecond, he couldn't help thinking that kissing under the mistletoe or making love to Abby Hawkins at Christmas time would be a tradition that nothing could beat. Making love to her at any time of the year would be a gift…

Abby sighed happily as she crouched to open the top of a large box and check its contents. 'Yep. It won't be Christmas for me from now on without those pigs in blankets. I'm going to have to find out exactly how Cath makes them. Oh…' She lifted what was on top of the box. 'How cute is this?'

She stood up to hold a brown onesie with a white bib against her body. 'Darn. I think it's too small for me. Look, it's even got a hood with ears and antlers. Oh… oh, yes…' She dived back into the box. 'This is definitely me.'

She was slipping her arms into the elastic loops that were attached to a pair of angel wings. Then she folded the reindeer onesie and put it back into the box that she picked up. 'Where does it go?' she asked Euan.

'Put it over by the top of the stairs for now. We'll stack everything there before we start moving them. That way we shouldn't leave anything behind.'

He watched her walk past him towards the staircase, the single bulb hanging above her making those wings glimmer. Shiny, golden wings on either side of the fall of that magnificent mane of golden waves. Euan's fingers tingled as he remembered the way they'd buried themselves in that silky softness and he found himself taking in a slow, deep breath as he remembered the scent of her hair. His gaze was still fixed on Abby as she put the box down and turned back.

'What? Have I put it in the wrong place?'

'No. That's fine.'

Abby's eyebrows were raised in a silent question as she came closer.

'I was just thinking,' Euan admitted, 'that you suit those angel wings. When I first saw you in that pharmacy in Inverness, with your long, blonde hair and blue eyes, you looked like the kind of Christmas angels that people love to put on top of their trees.'

Abby's eyebrows went even higher. 'Coming from you, when we both know what you think of Christmas, I'm not sure that's a compliment.'

'Oh… I can assure you that it is.'

Abby was still walking towards him. She was close enough to touch. Close enough to kiss. All those flashes of feeling that Euan had just been aware of seemed to be coalescing into something bigger. Something so huge that it was more than disconcerting. This was alarming. He knew what big feelings could do to you. He'd made sure he'd never let it happen again. When he lost his beloved grandmother, that would be the end of it. There'd be no more people who'd been given his heart and were part of his soul. He'd be entirely alone in the world. Safer from emotional trauma than he'd ever been in his life.

The way he was feeling in this moment, however, was a threat to that safety. Part of Euan wanted to take a step back but it was too late. Abby was right in front of him, smiling up at him as she stood on tiptoes, offering him that kiss that had been hanging in the air from several steps back. And, like the way he'd thought she could see right through him, it seemed like she could sense his alarm.

'I could be a Christmas angel,' she said softly. 'Which would make me the absolute opposite of a Christmas puppy.'

It was Euan's turn to look bewildered.

'Because you can have me.' Abby was smiling now. 'But not for ever—just for Christmas.'

The light brush of her lips again his made Euan want to sink into a real kiss. The kind of kiss they'd shared last night so many times. The kind that made the outside world disappear. He was starting to feel safe again. What did it matter if he was thinking weird things about wanting more time with Abby so that he could do things to make her happy? It was never going to happen. They had a couple of days to share and that would be that.

'I know you don't believe in it.' Abby's lips were so close to his own that he could feel the movement of her words. 'But I think this is a bit of Christmas magic. Something that we're both going to remember every Christmas time for the rest of our lives.' He felt her breath now, as a sigh against his lips. 'I think remembering might become another tradition for me. You know, like pigs in blankets.'

And that did it. It wrapped up whatever it was between them as a physical pleasure in the same way that eating something delicious was. You could choose to do it, or not. You could indulge on special occasions. It was never going to control your life or be some kind of threat. It was safe, that was what it was. In a few days, Abby would be getting on with her life. She would no doubt head back to the land of sunshine and beaches for Christmas. She would find that man who was going to be the father of all those children he would never want himself. But she would remember the magic of her Christmas in Scotland.

Her Christmas with him.

It was almost a duty, wasn't it? To make that memory the best it could possibly be?

The angel wings were in the way of sliding his hands around Abby and pulling her body against his own while he kissed her senseless but maybe it was better this way, anyway—cupping her chin gently with one hand and threading his other hand under her hair to steady the back of her head—because kissing someone senseless required a bit of effort.

The responsive pressure of Abby's lips and the way they parted to allow the tip of her tongue to meet his made it very clear that this gorgeous woman was up for the challenge. The way Euan's thoughts were evaporating so that he was falling into this kiss to the exclusion of anything else made him wonder if he was the one who was going to end up senseless instead. Then he heard the tiny sound of bliss that came from Abby and he let go of any anxiety.

They were both heading in exactly the same direction.

And Abby had been right. It *was* a bit of magic.

CHAPTER EIGHT

ON THE MORNING of Christmas Eve, Abby was taking just a little longer with the children's medical checks. She didn't want to miss anything that might mean someone could miss out on the excitement of the building anticipation later today or the early hours of the big day itself.

The blue tinge to Callum's lips was a concern but, sadly, it was normal for him now. Abby increased the rate of oxygen being delivered through his nasal cannula and had to be satisfied when the saturation level went up even a little. There was no worrying change to his weight or heart rate or any other signs or symptoms that might indicate a worsening or imminently dangerous level of heart failure.

'Thank you for taking such good care of Callum,' his mum said to Abby as she wheeled his chair out of the treatment room. 'We're so happy to be here. And he just loved dressing up as an elf at the party last night. I've got photos that we're going to treasure for ever.'

'I know.' Abby gave her a hug. 'I'm collecting some of those myself.'

Like the one of Liam helping Lucy post her letter to Father Christmas in the forest. And one she'd taken last night, when she'd caught Euan sitting on a window seat in the corner of the drawing room, well away from the main entertainment being put on for the children and guests from the village. He'd had a *whole* plate of pigs in blankets on his lap, no doubt nicked from the buffet spread in the dining room. Not only that, but he'd been sharing the profits from his crime with Liam, who was sitting beside him. They were both watching what was going on and no doubt Liam was keeping a close eye on Lucy, but it was the matching expression on their faces that had prompted Abby to take the photo. That deep scowl. That look that said they might be doing their duty and turning up but they weren't about to let themselves enjoy this party. It had made Abby smile but then catch her breath as she felt that rush of heart-squeezing warmth that was as golden as those angel wings that she had been wearing in the attic and that Lucy had chosen to wear for the party. It was the feeling of love, that was what it was.

She'd paused to take a slow breath when she looked at the photo she'd just taken because something else was so obvious in the image. Maybe it was just the similar expressions but they looked so alike they could be father and son. What a shame he never wanted to have any children of his own, she thought, remembering how brilliantly Euan had handled the incident of the vanishing bagpipes, which could have made Liam's stay at the castle an ordeal that might confirm his mistrust of any adults for many years to come. He would have made an amazing father.

Milo also passed his check up this morning with flying colours. He'd been dressed up as a snowman last evening, which was a bit ironic after the fright he'd given them all while building one, but that black top hat had suited him perfectly and he'd made everybody laugh, himself most of all, by lifting it from his head and replacing it every time someone looked at or spoke to him.

'Did I see you eating two jellies at the same time?' Abby asked as she recorded his weight. 'Red *and* green?'

Milo grinned at her and rubbed his belly and Abby had to return the smile. 'They were good, weren't they?'

'He was asleep the second his head hit the pillow,' Louise told her. 'All that excitement. I don't know where Maggie finds all that local talent. Who knew that the butcher was so good at making balloon animals?'

'Mmm.' Abby had her stethoscope against Milo's chest now so had an excuse not to respond but the truth was she'd barely noticed the balloon reindeers being produced. The whole party had been a bit of a blur, to be honest, because, after that time in the attic with Euan, and those mind-blowing kisses, Abby had been in such a state of anticipation about what she was quite confident was going to happen later that night that it was the main memory she'd been left with. Especially given that what *had* happened later last night had entirely lived up to those ridiculously high expectations.

Not just on a physical level. The touch and response of that oh, so private conversation between lovers and the joy to be found in both the build up and the ultimate release had been equally one of emotion, at least for Abby. She was quietly sure that it had been something more than purely physical for Euan, too. Why else would he have held her as she slept until the early hours of this morning, when he'd finally slipped out of her bed to go back to his own room?

Abby hadn't gone back to sleep. She had lain in that wonderful old bed and realised she was missing him already. She knew this couldn't last. She'd been completely sincere when she'd told Euan that the pleasure of indulging the astonishing attraction they had discovered between them was just for Christmas and not for ever, but she knew she had offered that reassurance because she sensed he was about to run—to repair all those defensive barriers of his and to even try to add an extra layer of safety.

Good grief…this was a man who'd convinced himself, decades ago, that opening his heart to anyone was a path straight to unbearable emotional distress. And, while Abby might be someone who was simply passing through his life briefly, she also represented his worst nightmare—a woman who couldn't wait to start creating as big a family as she possibly could and who loved celebrating every aspect of Christmas as much as his grandmother did. Abby had recognised that Euan was the total opposite of anybody she would consider suitable as a life partner and that had to work both ways. Which meant that she was the equivalent of a 'bad girl' for this taciturn and no doubt normally extremely well-behaved Scotsman.

She rather liked that idea.

What Abby didn't like was the change she found in Lucy, who was her last patient to check. The little girl was so pale but still found a gorgeous smile for Abby when Maggie brought her over to the clinic. She was still wearing the angel wings and pretty, white dress that had been her party costume.

'I'm an angel,' she told Abby.

'You are the most beautiful angel ever.'

'Liam said I couldn't wear them because it wasn't the party any more.'

'And I said she could keep them,' Maggie said. 'And wear them whenever she wants to. I'm not sure how happy Liam was about that, though.'

'He doesn't like dressing up much, does he?'

'He doesn't like pretend,' Lucy agreed. 'He says it makes real too hard.'

Abby and Maggie exchanged a glance that was a silent conversation in an instant. The wisdom of a child and the sadness that Lucy's brother already found life so hard.

'But I love pretend,' Lucy added. 'I want to be a princess, really. But now I love being an angel, too.'

'Well, let's pop you on the scales, Princess Lucy.' Abby held out her hand. 'I want to see how much you ate at the party.'

Not that food had anything to do with the increase in Lucy's weight. Or the crackling sounds in the base of her lungs or the fact that her blood oxygen levels had dipped overnight.

'I'm not happy,' Abby told Euan a short time later, when she went back to the castle and went over the details of her examination with him. 'I've already increased her diuretics to get rid of that extra fluid and we could maybe give her a bit of supplementary oxygen, which might well be all that's needed, but I'd be a lot happier with some more information. I'd like to know what her ventricular function and blood flow is looking like and what her ejection fraction is. Most of all, I'd like to be able to rule out a complication like a thrombosis.'

She broke off abruptly as Maggie came into the foyer with Lucy, who immediately dropped Maggie's hand and ran towards Abby, who swept her up into her arms for a cuddle, taking care not to squash the angel wings. Even with that short burst of energy Lucy was a little out of breath and Abby caught Euan's gaze as she held the little girl close.

'I know it's Christmas Eve, and probably impossible, but could you find out whether your friend could organise an echo and even an MRI if it's indicated?'

'I'll ring him and find out. I'm happy to take her into Inverness if they can make it happen.'

'You'll need to take Liam with you as well,' Abby said. 'He would be distraught if Lucy was taken off to hospital without him.'

Catching Maggie's gaze now, Abby realised that it had to be obvious she was going to be worried sick herself. It had to be just as clear how tightly Lucy was clinging to her. Was she aware that people were worried and wanted to both offer and receive comfort? Abby pressed a kiss to those gorgeous red curls. Lucy was the sweetest child she'd ever met. How could anyone spend time with her and not fall completely in love?

'You'll need some help with two children and a hospital appointment to juggle.' Maggie's expression was impossible to read. 'Take Abby with you.'

'But that would leave you without a doctor available.'

'Graham will be happy to come to the castle,' Maggie responded. 'He can deal with any emergency and call for extra help if it's needed. Plus, it'll give him a chance to lecture me at the same time. Oh…' Maggie turned her head as she began to walk away with the kind of step that advertised the need to organise something. 'You can do me a favour while you're in town. Just a couple of last-minute things on my shopping list. If all goes well, you could have a treat for lunch, perhaps, and let the children see what's going on in the high street on your way home while you sort that out for me.'

The echocardiography room might be very dim to allow the images on the screen to be more easily interpreted but Euan could read the expression on Liam's face all too well. Maybe he should have suggested that he waited outside with Liam while Abby and his friend Mike, the cardiologist in Inverness, watched the Doppler ultrasound examination of Lucy's heart.

Except that it had been all too easy to read what was going on in his head then, as well. Too easy to imagine that this was himself at ten years old, about to be separated from his sister while she had a test that could be frightening or painful.

So they all went in. Abby was holding Lucy's hand and making sure the little girl stayed as still as possible as she lay on the bed, wearing the angel wings she'd refused to take off.

'I'm an angel,' she'd told the technician. 'Angels can't take off their wings.'

'Of course they can't, darling. I knew that.'

Abby's eyes were glued to the screen now where colours and shapes shifted and changed and her conversation with the cardiologist was calm and quiet.

Euan and Liam stood to one side and they were far enough away for anything they said to not interfere with the examination.

'Have you seen a Doppler ultrasound test before, Liam?'

A jerky head shake was the only response Euan got. He could actually feel how tensely this lad was holding himself.

'It doesn't hurt. That device the technician is using is called a transducer and it can send and receive sound waves. It can see blood moving because the movement changes the pitch of the reflected sounds.'

It could also detect blood that had stopped moving completely and become a dangerous clot, which Euan knew was top of the list of Abby's concerns. Not that he was about to let Liam know that. The small voice beside

him was a welcome distraction to even thinking about
unwanted complications for Lucy.

'Is it like what dolphins use?'

'Bit more like bats than dolphins but it's kind of complicated. I'll try and explain later if you want.'

Liam shrugged and lapsed into silence, which meant
that Euan could hear what Mike and Abby were saying.

'That's a good apical four-chamber view.'

'It's looking good. I hope we're not wasting your time.
Seems like the change we've made to Lucy's diuretic
therapy is already clearing any extra fluid that was interfering with her oxygen uptake. I just…wanted to be
extra sure.'

'It's not a problem. I'd feel the same way.'

'Can we get a right ventricle ejection fraction from
end-systolic and end-diastolic volumes?'

'Of course…'

Everybody was focused on the shifting colours and
shapes on the screen as the technician worked.

'What are the different colours?' Liam whispered to
Euan. 'Is red good or bad?'

'The red is the blood that has oxygen in it and the blue
is the blood where it's all used up so it needs to go to the
lungs and get some new oxygen.' But Euan could sense
that Liam was lost already and he could feel something
like a kick in his gut. Had nobody ever sat down with
this boy and explained exactly what was wrong with his
sister's heart?

Maybe he'd known too much himself but it had helped.
So had being included in discussions and treated like an
extra adult in Fi's support team.

'You know that a normal heart has two sides?' he
asked Liam. 'The right and the left?'

'I guess.'

'And with people like Lucy, the left side doesn't grow properly and it can't pump blood around the body so things need to be switched around. The blood gets sent to the lungs in a different way and the good ventricle can take over the job of pumping the blood with the oxygen in it to all the places it needs to go. I've got some good pictures somewhere. I could find them for you.'

Liam nodded. 'Okay.'

He could tell him, Euan thought. About Fiona. Tell him that he understood what it was like for Liam because he could remember how lonely it was to feel as if he were the only boy in the world with a problem this big. Except he didn't know exactly what it was like, did he? He hadn't had to be forcibly separated from his sister while she was still alive. He'd been allowed to be involved every step of the way with her care. He'd been allowed to love her with every breath he took.

It was his turn to lapse into silence as the examination continued. He tuned in to what was being said and it was obvious that they were all happy with what they were seeing. The blood flow was exactly as it should be and the amount being ejected from the heart with every beat was within an acceptable range to allow for Lucy to be engaging in normal activities. The tricuspid valve was functioning well and there was no sign of any clots in the vessels, heart chambers or lungs.

Mike shook Abby's hand as the examination was completed. 'I wish we had someone with your training available here,' he told her. 'I'd love to do that course you've just finished but there's no way I can get away from here for something like that. Not when we're short-staffed as it is.'

'Thank you so much for fitting us in on Christmas Eve. It's such a relief to know that Princess Lucy is good to go.'

Mike ruffled Lucy's curls. 'Merry Christmas, Princess.'

'Can we go now?' Liam asked. 'You said we could have burgers for lunch.'

'I did,' Euan agreed. He caught Abby's gaze. 'If that's okay with you?'

'Are you kidding? I *love* burgers.' She was bundling Lucy into her pink coat. 'Let's go. We've got those messages to do for Maggie, as well.'

'So...did that burger live up to expectations?'

'It was *so* good.' Abby beamed at Euan. She reached for a couple of stray, now-cold French fries and ate those as well.

Euan shook his head. Only Abby Hawkins could look this happy about being in a fast-food restaurant, eating junk food, amongst the absolute chaos of last-minute shopping in the main street of Inverness. Very close to the pharmacy where their paths had crossed for the first time, in fact, in what now seemed like a life-changing moment in time for Euan McKendry. He knew that there were some things he'd never see in quite the same light again. Like long blonde hair. And golden angel wings like the ones Lucy was still wearing, one a little bent after she'd been lying on it at the hospital, as she let Liam push her on the swing in the restaurant's play area.

She *was* a wee angel. Euan watched as Lucy tipped her head back to grin at her big brother as he let go of the swing. He could hear her laughter even through the infernal din all the other children were making in this overcrowded space and it was pulling him back to how he'd felt wondering about whether to tell Liam about *his* sister. How it felt as if the pull into the past was getting too strong. Too fraught with painful memories that were shifting and changing, like the images of Lucy's heart

on the screen, but these were somewhere very deep in
Euan's heart. The sooner they got out of here, the better.

'We should go,' he said to Abby. 'I just need to pop into
the bagpipe shop for something and we can head home.'

Home...

Funny thing, given that he hadn't lived at the castle
for nearly two decades, but it really did feel like that was
what they would be doing when they left. Heading home.

'I'd like to go back to that pharmacy.' Abby seemed
to be making an effort to keep a straight face. 'I seem to
have misplaced my elf headband.'

Euan wanted to shake his head again but, instead, he
let his mouth curl into a bit of a smile. He'd hated that
headband with such a passion, hadn't he? And yet, that
was something else he'd see differently from now on
because Abby had shown him that there was a place for
silliness at Christmas. For smiles and laughter and joy
that was safe enough to take pleasure from because you
knew it was temporary. Just for Christmas.

'Oh...' he said aloud. 'We need to get that toy dog. For
Leah. Come on, let's get cracking. I think there's a store
down the road that has lots of toys.'

Abby buttoned Lucy into her warm, bright pink coat,
cleverly shifting the elastic loops of her wings so she
didn't have to take them off. Then there were the woolly
hat and mittens, which took extra time because a cuddle
was needed. Euan and Liam had put their puffer jackets and hats on and were waiting near the door where an
older woman was clearing a table and wiping it down.
She paused to watch Abby and Lucy join them and she
gave them all a misty smile.

'You have the most adorable children,' she told them.
'And I hope you have such a happy Christmas.'

Abby looked startled for a moment and then almost guilty as she realised they'd been taken for a family. She avoided Euan's gaze as she smiled brightly back at the woman.

'You too,' she said warmly. 'Merry Christmas.'

'I'm an angel,' Lucy told her.

'That you are, pet.'

Euan just grunted. So did Liam.

But something caught in his chest as he held the door for Abby and the children to go out ahead of him. Something so big it was impossible to breathe around. This was like the fantasy of letting himself get as close as he had to Abby, wasn't it?

But this was an even bigger fantasy. Of a whole family, including Abby.

But just for Christmas.

And that made it okay for Euan to tell Abby to take the children with her to the pharmacy to find another elf headband and they would meet at the toy shop in ten minutes or so. He would go to the bagpipe shop alone, to find a book of simple tunes for a learner to play on a practice chanter. He might have a look at the chanters they had available as well, because Liam would not only need one of his own after he went home, a child-sized one would be easier. He would make sure he found some time later today to give the lad another lesson, too, because Euan knew that the busier he kept himself, the better, because it filled the spaces where things he didn't want to think about could sneak into his head.

Oh, *man*…

That look on the woman's face when she'd told them

they had the most adorable children. When she'd assumed that they were a family.

Abby already knew that she had fallen in love with Euan and that it was just a few days of living a fantasy but this had just taken it to a completely different dimension. *This* was the real fantasy. Not just a gorgeous man and amazing sex and a Christmas to die for. This was what Abby had been searching for. This feeling of family. She was with a man she was in love with and children she'd also fallen for.

And yes, she still knew perfectly well that it was the last thing Euan would want and had to carefully avoid even catching his gaze, but Abby intended to hang onto this feeling. To memorise it perfectly, because then she would recognise it when she found it again. If she was lucky enough to find it again.

The pharmacy had sold out of elf headbands but there was a halo that was the finishing touch Lucy needed for her angel impersonation and the joy on Lucy's face earned a grateful glance from Liam. He almost smiled but grunted instead and it was so like Euan that Abby not only had to fight the urge to pull him close for a hug, she also had to blink back tears.

They got back to the castle a bit after two o'clock, after a somewhat rushed visit to the toy shop, when the rest of the children were settling in for the quiet time after lunch. Like last night, they all needed to save their energy for something special that evening—this time for the carol singing in Kirkwood's picturesque stone church in the village.

Maggie seemed very happy to see them back, to hear the good news about the results of Lucy's examination and collect the shopping they'd done for her, but there was something that didn't feel quite right. When Abby had tucked

Lucy into bed for a nap, promising to come back and check on her soon, she hurried back down the stairs having come to the conclusion that Maggie was hiding something.

She found Euan coming out of the drawing room.

'Is Maggie in there?'

'No. She's not in the kitchens, either. She's probably in the library.'

Abby held his gaze. 'So, you felt it, too? She's hiding something, isn't she?'

'I just spoke to the GP, Graham. He said he'd rung about the results of her biopsy, hoping they might have come back.'

Abby's heart sank like a stone. 'And they have?'

'Apparently so. He wouldn't tell me, though. He said that was my grandmother's business.'

Their shared glance became a pact. They were both going to find out what was going on. Maggie was in the library, sitting behind a huge desk in one corner of the book-lined room. Euan and Abby kept moving until they were standing in front of it but, as Abby waited for Euan to ask the question, she realised that he was scared stiff and her heart broke for him. He didn't want to know the answer, did he, in case it meant the beginning of the end?

Abby moved sideways. Just enough for her hand to be touching Euan's and, as if it was an automatic response, his fingers curled around hers. It was Abby who cleared her throat carefully.

'We've heard that you've had some news about your biopsy,' she said quietly. 'Would you rather talk to Euan alone?'

Maggie blinked and then her face softened as she let her gaze settle on her grandson. 'Oh, lovie. I'm sorry. I'd almost forgotten about that news. And it's good. The tumour's not malignant. I'm going to need surgery as soon as possible in the new year but... I'm not going to die. Well, not just yet, anyway.'

Abby's hand was being gripped so hard her fingers were going numb. It was very revealing that Euan could hide such an emotional response by speaking so calmly.

'That *is* good news, Gammy. The best Christmas gift I could have wished for.'

Abby extracted her hand from Euan's so that she could go to the other side of the desk and throw her arms around Maggie. She had tears in her eyes, and so did Maggie, but the difference was that Maggie was looking anything but happy.

'What is it?' Abby asked, frowning, as something that Maggie had said earlier clicked into place. 'What was it that made you almost forget about such amazing news?'

'Judith rang.' Maggie had to pause and take a deep, shaky breath.

'Oh, no... Has her father died?'

'No. In fact, he's doing better than expected after surgery. That's not what she called about.'

'What is it?'

Maggie closed her eyes for a long beat as she started speaking again. 'They've found a new foster home for Lucy. Someone who's had a CHD child in the past and knows exactly what they're signing up for. It sounds perfect.' She opened her eyes but avoided looking up and her voice was still strained. 'A woman who lives right beside a beautiful beach but only a few minutes from a hospital that has a specialty paediatric cardiac unit. And she breeds Shetland ponies and...and...'

'It does sound perfect,' Euan said.

'But it's not, is it?'

Abby's question was more a quiet statement and Maggie shook her head in agreement. 'She can't—or won't—

consider taking Liam. Apparently she fostered a boy about his age once and it was a bit of a catastrophe. I've said that he's a wonderful lad and just needs the reassurance that he can stay with his sister. It's possible that a meeting could be arranged, but…'

'But that's not really going to help, is it?' Euan's breath came out in a heavy sigh. 'And why would he try to pretend that he won't make any trouble? He has good reason not to trust anyone.'

'We can't tell him,' Maggie said. 'Not yet. Let them at least have a Christmas Day they can remember as being together and happy.' She brushed away a tear from her cheek. 'It might well be their last one.'

Abby straightened as she caught a movement from the corner of her eye. Her head turned sharply towards the door, in time to see someone stepping back.

'Liam? Is that you?'

But the figure had vanished. Abby exchanged an alarmed glance with Euan.

'I sent him to find the practice chanter in my bagpipe case,' he said, the frown lines deepening around his eyes. 'I was going to give him a lesson while Lucy had her nap. He might have come looking for me.'

'How long do you think he was there?' Maggie sounded as horrified as they were all feeling. 'How much could he have heard?'

Euan's voice was grim. 'If he heard any of what we were saying, it would have been too much. I'd better go and have a talk to him.' He turned on his heel to leave.

'And I'll go and check on Lucy,' Abby said. But she paused to give Maggie another hug. 'Are you okay?'

'Those poor wee bairns.' Maggie wiped her eyes. 'They remind me so much of Euan when he was a lad.

And our wee Fi, of course.' The sadness in her eyes as she looked up at Abby was unbearable.

'We can't let it happen,' Abby said. 'There must be something we can do to stop them being separated like this.'

But Maggie shook her head. 'I'd adopt them myself in a heartbeat,' she said. 'But I know they wouldn't consider me. Not at my age and with the health issues I've got ahead of me.' The strength that Abby had sensed in this woman from the moment she'd met her seemed to be fading away. 'Lucy needs someone a lot younger than me to be her mother.'

'She needs to be with her brother, too. She needs Liam as much as he needs her.'

And Abby needed to go and stand in that bedroom door and just watch the little girl sleep for a moment. Or to tiptoe into the room and leave a butterfly's kiss on those curls. In the end, however, she did neither of those things. Seconds after she went up that grand staircase with its bannisters woven with Christmas decorations, she was running back down. Euan was moving almost as fast as he came out of the drawing room.

'I can't find him,' Euan said. 'And nobody's seen him.' He held his hands up in a gesture of helplessness. 'This place is so big. He could be anywhere…'

Abby's mouth was so dry it was hard to speak. 'Lucy's gone, too,' she told him. 'Her bed's still warm but… it's empty…'

CHAPTER NINE

EVERY AVAILABLE ADULT was called in to help with the search. Catherine the cook simply turned off the ovens and abandoned the sponge cakes she'd been baking for afternoon tea. Ben's grandma and Ruth were left in charge of all the children who were engaged in quiet activities in the drawing room and Callum's mum was watching over a few sleeping children including her own. Every other parent, caregiver and volunteer helper dispersed all over the castle and outbuildings in a commendably short space of time.

'Should we call for more help?' Maggie asked anxiously. 'Like the police?'

'Not yet,' Euan said. 'But you could call the Kirkwood station and let them know what's happening so they're on standby. If we haven't found them within an hour, we'll be in trouble. It'll be starting to get dark by then and we'll need to activate an official search and rescue with dogs, maybe.'

In the meantime, they needed to cover as much ground as they could.

'Where should we go?' Abby watched Maggie head outside, already talking on her phone, presumably to a member of the local police force. 'Somewhere that isn't being covered already.'

'Let me think for a moment...' Euan found it easy to put himself in Liam's place. He could imagine himself at ten years old, desperate to stop anyone taking his sister away from him. He could guess where he might go to hide in this vast, old house as well, but then he had the advantage of knowing pretty much every square inch of it.

'One thing we can be certain about,' he said to Abby, 'is that Liam won't be heading anywhere that he'd think an adult might be. So he's not likely to go to the stable conversion where the clinic is even though we've still got people checking there.'

'He might have gone to the stables where the animals are, though. Lucy loves those donkeys.'

'That's where Gammy's gone,' Euan reminded her. 'I'm going to head up the back staircase first. It's lucky that we've got areas closed off and locked in other parts of the castle, but there are all those old bedrooms as well as the staircase up to the attic that it's easy to get to and it would be the kind of place I would have gone at his age.'

'I'm coming with you.'

Euan didn't argue. There was no point in sending Abby off in another direction because she didn't know the castle layout as well as he did. Besides, they all knew how attached Lucy was to Abby. If the little girl was going to respond to anyone's call, it would be Abby's. And, on a selfish note, Euan wanted her company. Because a fear he thought he'd banished for ever was beginning to surface and he really didn't want to be left without the escape of being able to distract himself.

It took several minutes to open all the doors to small, disused bedrooms and bathrooms in the rabbit warren of the old servants' quarters and there was no sign of Liam or Lucy. It was another minute or two to get back to the staircase that led up to the attic and, the moment they got up there, they could sense the emptiness of the space.

'Lucy? Are you in here, sweetheart?' Abby's voice echoed in the vast area. 'Lucy? *Liam...?*'

She caught Euan's gaze as the echo faded into a dense silence. And then she held the eye contact for a heartbeat longer. Was she having the same flash of remembering what had happened the last time they were alone in this space? Those heady kisses? That silent pact they'd made to make the most of the magic they'd found together because it was only ever going to be for Christmas? Not that it mattered now. Nothing mattered except to find Liam and Lucy. That they were safe.

Euan turned away from the intense scrutiny he'd been giving the attic space even though his gut had instantly told him it was empty of everything except junk and dust.

'They're not here.'

'Let's go downstairs again. Maybe someone else has found them.'

Euan shook his head. 'I've got my phone. Maggie would let me know.'

His grandmother was probably feeling as sick as he was at this turn of events. If only they hadn't been talking about the children. If only Liam hadn't overheard the plan to destroy the part of his world that mattered the most. If only he and Maggie didn't know exactly how scared Liam had to be feeling right now, knowing that the worst was going to happen and that he had absolutely no control over it.

It was instinctive to head to where Maggie was searching. Just to touch base and make sure that she was coping. Even with the immense relief of knowing that Maggie didn't have a malignancy that could have meant she had very little time left, she was still unwell, in pain, and facing major surgery. At nearly eighty years old, she really didn't need this extra stress. It was hard enough having these two children here, like small ghosts of their own pasts. That something terrible could happen while they were here at the castle was...well, it was unthinkable.

Euan pulled open the massive front door. Again, he had one of those unwelcome flashbacks that were entirely irrelevant right now. This time, it was the shock of opening this door to find the Christmas angel from the pharmacy on his doorstep. Wearing that ridiculous headband with the elf on it, the joy of the season still shining in her eyes.

There was no joy in her voice behind him right now.

'Oh, no...'

He spun around. 'What?'

'Lucy's coat. I left it on that table when we got back. With her hat. It's not there.'

They stared at each other for a long moment, as the horror sank in that their search area might be expanding exponentially. That they might have hypothermia to add to any concerns for the children's safety because it was beginning to snow again. Just a gentle drift of flakes but it could get heavier at any time.

'There'll be footprints,' Abby said. 'In the snow. And...' She closed her eyes as if summoning a memory that could be important. 'There's only one path that Liam knows about—the one we took in the sleigh, to go to the letter box tree.'

'Get your coat.' Euan's instruction came out in a snap of urgency. 'And hat. I'll meet you in the kitchen garden.'

Only a minute or two later and they were off on their new search, buttoning their jackets as they moved. It was hard to tell if there were any fresh footprints in the snow after the activities of building the snowman and the sleigh ride and the marks that were there were already being softened by new flakes, but Abby's guess as to where Liam might have taken his sister was as good as any to go on and there were already other people fanning out from the castle in different directions.

They raced past the snowman with his carrot nose and forked branches for arms and hands and into the forest, following the same track the sleigh had taken. Was it only yesterday he'd been walking this path, alongside Leah's dad, talking about how looking after a dog could give her both companionship and confidence? He'd surprised himself by enjoying the outing, hadn't he? And Abby had looked so happy up there in the sleigh with Lucy snuggled on her lap and Liam hunched beside her.

'What were you and Liam talking about in the sleigh yesterday? He was pointing at something.'

'He could see the lake through the trees. We were talking about going ice skating but that we didn't know if it was safe enough yet.' Abby cupped her hands around her mouth. 'Lucy,' she called. '*Liam?* Please come out. *Please...*' She bit her lip, turning her head to scan in all directions. 'Lucy's coat is so bright. Surely we'd catch a glimpse through the trees, even if they were trying to hide.'

Euan stopped in his tracks.

'What is it?'

'The rowboat.'

'Out on the lake? Near the mistletoe tree? What about it?'

'It's big enough to hide in if you're small. It's about the only thing out here that is.' Without thinking, he held out his hand and Abby took it with no hesitation at all. They didn't even need to speak to know exactly what they were both thinking and they both began moving in the same instant, running through the trees, taking the quickest route to the lake that they could. Euan could feel the warmth of her hand even through two layers of woollen gloves. More than that, he could feel the same desperation he had, to find these two children before anything terrible happened. It felt almost as if he were looking after Fiona all over again. That this was *his* responsibility.

There were footprints at the edge of the lake in snow that hadn't been trampled by many feet. And they were too small to have been made by the wellington boots he and Abby had been wearing on their mission to gather mistletoe.

'Liam?' Euan's voice seemed to bounce off the expanse of ice in front of them. It sounded loud. And angry? He tried to soften his tone. 'Where are you?'

'Lucy?' Abby's voice also rang out like a bell. 'Where are you, princess? I need a cuddle.'

And then they saw it. A flash of pink as a small hand gripped the edge of the rowboat. A head popped up over the side and Lucy was smiling at them.

'We're hiding,' she said. 'It's a game. *Ouch...*' Lucy looked down. 'Don't pull me, Liam. I don't like it.'

Euan stepped out onto the ice. He got three steps in before he heard the loud crack and when he looked down, he could see a deep crack and smaller fractures spreading like a spider's web. He put his arm out to stop Abby coming onto the ice.

'Stay there,' he told her. 'It's not safe.'

'I'm not as heavy as you are. It might be okay for me.'

That wasn't a risk Euan was prepared to take. The urge to protect Abby was far too strong to ignore. He didn't want to risk falling into the lake himself, either, or creating holes that would endanger the children. He could spread his weight by lying down and rolling, or sliding towards the boat, and he might be able to bring Lucy back that way, but would Liam come back without a struggle? He knew all too well how desperate this lad was feeling. He also knew what was most important to him and maybe he could use that to get them both to safety.

'Talk to me, Liam,' he called. 'I need you to help us get Lucy back to somewhere warm. It's far too cold for her out here.'

Liam had to be lying on the bottom of the boat to remain invisible. His voice was clear enough, however. And it was angry.

'We're not coming back.'

'I want to go back.' Lucy was trying to stand up. 'I'm cold, Liam. And I'm hungry.'

'We can't go back, Luce.' Liam was speaking more quietly now.

'Why not?'

'We just can't.'

Euan exchanged a glance with Abby. At least Liam hadn't told Lucy what was going to happen after Christmas. If he did, they would have two distraught children to deal with. Abby would be just as upset, he thought, noting how pale and strained her face was.

'Liam?' It was Abby who called this time. 'I know what you're worried about and…it's not going to happen.'

Euan's jaw dropped. What was she doing?

'I won't let it happen,' Abby said firmly.

Euan closed his eyes as his heart sank. When he opened them again, Liam was sitting up in the boat, his gaze fixed on Abby.

'Really?' he asked. 'Do you promise?'

No…but Euan didn't say the word aloud. He couldn't be the one to shatter the hope he could see on this boy's face. The hope he could actually feel inside his own chest even though he knew it wasn't based on anything real.

Surely he could trust that Abby wasn't about to make a promise she couldn't possibly keep? To give Liam even more hope that would only make the inevitable all the more devastating?

But his trust was obviously misplaced.

'I promise,' Abby said.

Okay…maybe the promise was a little premature because Abby hadn't done her homework yet but that didn't make it any less genuine. She *was* going to do whatever she could to make sure that this brother and sister stayed together.

The moment she'd seen Lucy's head bob up over the side of that rowboat and had seen the smile that was already imprinted on her heart for ever, something came together and she just *knew*. That trip out with the children this morning had let her know that she'd found exactly what she wanted in life, in that feeling of family that being with Euan and the children had given her. She'd known all along that being with children was going to be a huge part of her future, both professionally and personally. She'd also known that she'd know what felt right when she found it. She'd learned to trust her instincts in matters such as this.

She had found it. And her heart was telling her it was the right thing. But it wasn't just any children, was it?

It was *these* children. Liam and Lucy. A damaged boy and a little girl who needed to cram a lifetime of love into who knew how long? Abby loved them both. With all her heart.

She loved Euan as well, but that was a completely different kind of love. And he didn't need saving.

Well…he actually did, but nobody could help him if he didn't want to be saved. And, right now, he was look-

ing as if he didn't even want to be anywhere near Abby.
He was looking...furious?

He was keeping it hidden, mind you, as he talked Liam
into getting out of the boat and then lifting Lucy onto the
ice. He coaxed Lucy into walking alone. 'You're as light
as a feather,' he told her. 'It's quite safe.'

Lucy tiptoed across the ice until she got close to Euan.

'Go to Dr Abby,' he said. 'She's going to look after
you.' Even his tone was so neutral Abby could tell it was
being used to disguise what he was feeling. Maybe he
was hiding it so well, he couldn't even see it himself.

But Lucy didn't continue on to where Abby was standing. She stayed where she was and smiled at Euan as she
held her arms up.

You'd have to have a heart of stone to resist that plea
but was Lucy aware of the hesitation before she was
picked up? Or that Euan's face was definitely like stone
as he walked towards Abby and transferred Lucy into
her arms? He didn't even meet Abby's gaze.

'Your turn now, Liam,' he said, turning his back on
Abby. 'But if you hear the ice cracking, you need to lie
down, okay?'

Why was Euan so angry? Was he afraid that she would
expect him to be a part of the lives of these children as
well? Was it too much of a pull back into the past for
him? She could still hear the sadness in Maggie's voice.

*They remind me so much of Euan when he was a lad.
And our wee Fi, of course...'*

Abby could understand that. And it might break her
heart to know that she'd never see Euan again, but she
could live with it. After all, she hadn't expected anything
more from him than this magical few days fate had somehow decreed they could have together.

What she couldn't live with would be turning her back

on Liam and Lucy. Again, she could hear an echo of Maggie's voice.

'Lucy needs someone a lot younger than me to be her mother...'

She'd have Maggie on her side, she was quite sure of that. And, somehow, she was going to make this work. She had to, because she'd made a promise and she wasn't going to let Liam grow up to be like Euan and believe that Christmas was about promises that got made and then broken.

'I think it's a wonderful idea. Exactly what I would do if I was you, Abby.'

'It's a daft idea,' Euan snapped. 'Totally impractical.'

'For whom? Me?' Abby folded her arms. 'Isn't that something I get to decide for myself?'

Euan, Abby and Maggie were back in the library. This time, the door was not only firmly closed, Catherine the cook had been tasked with keeping the children in the kitchen and making their afternoon tea of hot chocolate and cookies last until someone came to get them.

'Do you not think I'd feel partly responsible if you throw away your career after an impulsive decision you make when you're in *my* home?'

'Why would I be throwing away my career?' There was a flash of defiance in Abby's eyes. 'Women with children can work as well as raise kids these days, you know. And I've already told you that having children in my life is important enough for me to work around the commitment. I could be happy working as a GP.'

'Oh...' Maggie's sigh was pure hope. 'We so need a new GP in Kirkwood.' Then she shook the distraction away. 'But we can talk about that later. As for you, Euan, this isn't really your home any more, is it? It's mine. You haven't lived here since you went to medical school. You don't even like coming back for Christmas, do you? You just do it because you think it's what I want.'

'That's not true.' Except that it kind of was—he just didn't like it to be spelled out. And it wasn't the whole truth. He did it because he loved his grandmother. It was a shock to hear the criticism that was almost anger in her voice. Gammy had never spoken to him like this.

'I'll support Abby in any way I can to foster and adopt these bairns,' Maggie continued. 'Whether or not she wants to take over from Graham. They can all live here. With me.'

Euan let out a careful breath. 'You can't do that, Gammy.'

'Don't tell me what I can or can't do, Euan.' Maggie raised her eyebrows. 'Last time I looked, this is my life, what's left of it.'

'Exactly. There won't be very much left of it if you take on a problem like these children.'

'Have I ever told you what you should do with *your* life?' Maggie was on her feet now, all five foot nothing of her. 'Have I said you should come and live here in the home that you grew up in that will be yours one of these days? No… I haven't. And I wouldn't, so don't you be doing it to me.' She was walking towards the door now but she paused before pulling it open to fire another volley over her shoulder. 'Or, heaven forbid, I could have told you that you should have let Graham retire years ago by coming home and being the GP that our village so badly needs. But did I do that? No, of course I didn't. Because I love you and because you're an adult and you get to make your own decisions.' She was halfway out of the door now but she raised her voice before slamming it shut behind her. 'Even if they're the *wrong* decisions.'

Abby was looking as shocked as Euan was feeling. Or maybe it was awkwardness that she had been drawn into family tensions that had been buried for decades. Tensions that had nothing to do with her. Except they did now, didn't they? And maybe Abby had just realised that she had triggered this unprecedented confrontation.

'I'm sorry, Euan,' she said. 'I didn't mean to cause trouble between you and your grandmother.'

Euan just stared at her. There was such a mix of feelings going on in his head that it was too hard to find any words. He was upset that his grandmother was so upset. He was worried about her. He was worried about Lucy and Liam and…and, yes, he was worried about Abby as well. Maybe it had been an unwise choice to get so close to someone who was so different they would never be able to understand him but that didn't mean he didn't care about her. A lot more than he was comfortable caring for anyone. Enough that he couldn't let her throw her chance of a happy future away.

'You do realise how crazy this is, don't you? That you think you can swoop in like some guardian angel and fix the lives of two children you only met a couple of days ago?'

Oh, help…that reference to her being an angel had been a bad idea. It made him remember their first meeting. Worse, it made him remember how he'd felt when he saw her wearing the angel wings in the attic. About wanting to make Abby happy. Wanting to have more time with her. As much time as possible…

It was a catalyst to make the turbulent emotions he was grappling with unbearable and there was only one way out of this. To open that mental door, shove everything inside and slam it shut, the way Maggie had just slammed the library door shut. The easiest way to find the strength to do that was by harnessing a new emotion.

Anger.

'You actually made a promise to Liam and Lucy that you *were* going to fix their lives. Do you have any idea how unlikely it is that you're going to be able to keep that promise? I don't care how good your intentions might have been, to make a promise like that…a promise you probably can't even keep…it would be unforgivable at any time but…to do it at *Christmas*? When you knew they'd written that damn letter saying that was their Christmas wish? How *could* you?'

'I don't happen to think it's that unlikely.' Abby lifted her chin. Aye, she was really defiant now. And he had to admire how determined she sounded. 'I think that they'd see a paediatrician with specialist cardiology training as an ideal carer for Lucy. And I have support from someone who would make it even more of a family situation for them. I might just take up your grandmother's incredibly generous offer to live here.'

'You cannot do that.' Euan's face had frozen so hard he could barely get the words out.

'What? Live here at the castle with Maggie? Give up a career as a specialist consultant to be a GP? Become a mother to two children who need to be together more than anything else?' Abby was controlling her voice so well, her words were quiet but it was obvious she was as angry as Euan was feeling. 'Give everything I've got to love them as much as they deserve to be loved?' Her voice finally wobbled. '*All* of the above?'

'It would destroy you.'

'How can you be so sure about that?'

'Because, as we both know perfectly well, Lucy's not going to live for ever.'

Abby shook her head, dismissing his words. 'None of us are going to live for ever,' she said. The look she was giving Euan seemed almost one of pity. 'If you take the attitude that you're not going to love someone—or let them love you—because it's going to hurt when it's over, then…then you're not really living at all.' Abby looked as if she was going to follow Maggie's example and walk out on him. And yes, she was continuing to tell him what she thought as she turned away. 'I'm more than prepared to risk the heartbreak of loving,' she told him. 'Because that's the only way to find the joy.' She shook her head again. 'I feel sorry for you. You're never going to feel that joy again, are you?'

'It will destroy you,' Euan said again. 'Like it destroyed my mother.'

That stopped her. She turned back. Blinked. Took a long, slow inward breath.

'Tell me,' she said quietly. 'What did happen to your mother? Why does nobody talk about it?'

'Maybe it was one tragedy too many. Or maybe we feel responsible in some way.' Euan shrugged as the words he had never intended to share fell like stones into the air between them. 'My mother took her own life. The year after Fi died.'

'Oh…my God…'

The look he was getting now was more than one of pity. It was the look of someone who was shocked and hurting on his behalf. Someone who cared about what had happened to him and who he was. Someone who cared far too much.

'Oh, Euan… I'm so, so sorry…'

He couldn't let Abby continue to look at him like this, with tears beginning to make her eyes shimmer. She couldn't be allowed to care about him like this. Because he couldn't accept it. He didn't want those kinds of feelings in his life. And he knew he could control them. God knew he'd worked hard enough for too many years not to have learned how to do that. Already, they were back through that door and all he needed to do was make sure it was firmly shut. It wasn't Abby that was going to walk out on this conversation. To walk away from whatever closeness they had generated between them in the last few days.

It was Euan.

And that was exactly what he did.

CHAPTER TEN

ABBY COULD FEEL the distance growing between them with every step that Euan took as he left the library, and that distance wasn't simply physical. He was pulling down the shutters. Making sure that any chink she had found in his emotional barriers was being rapidly repaired.

The worst thing was, she couldn't blame him. Not at all.

Discovering the reason that nobody talked about Euan's mother had been so shocking she'd had no idea what to say. Or do. And then, as she watched him leave, Abby realised that she had already said and done far too much. It might have been totally unintentional but she had reopened old wounds for both Euan and his grandmother. Deeper wounds than the ones she had known about that had been caused by the tragic deaths of both Euan's father and his beloved little sister. A dark wound that must, at some level, have felt like an abandonment to a grieving teenager.

For a long, long minute and then another, Abby simply stood there alone in the library, as a pain like nothing she was familiar with grew in her heart until it felt heavy enough to be pulling her down. She had hurt Euan and Maggie but she was also feeling a pain that felt very personal because, although it had been such an astonishingly

short space of time, instinct was telling her very firmly
that she had found her own family in Ravenswood Castle.

She had met two children who had completely captured her heart. A tradition of celebrating Christmas in
a way she could have happily embraced herself for as
many years as she had ahead of her. A man that she just
knew she could have loved for the rest of her life. And
an amazing grandmother who was everything Abby had
always aspired to be. A strong, brave woman who was
so generous, so compassionate that she had endless love
to share. Abby finally stirred herself to go to where she
knew Margaret McKendry was likely to be. She was in
need of a smidgeon of that love for herself right now.

Maggie was in the kitchen, as expected, sitting at the
enormous, old, scrubbed pine table with a cup of tea in
front of her and a small girl, with curly red hair, half
asleep on her knee. Liam was sitting at the table as well,
a plate with a half-eaten gingerbread man on it in front
of him. Abby could see instantly that there was something different about him but it took a heartbeat to realise what it was.

He wasn't scowling. Or avoiding eye contact. He was,
in fact, looking directly at Abby as she came into the
kitchen. A steady look that was all too easy to read. He
might not believe it was actually going to happen but he
was trusting Abby to keep the promise she'd made. She
knew how big a deal this was. If she broke that trust, it
would most likely never be offered again. To anyone.

An already heavy heart had just got even heavier.
When Lucy held her arms up to offer Abby a cuddle, it
was too much of a mission to blink away the tears in time
as she stooped to press her face against those soft curls
for a kiss. And, of course, Maggie noticed.

'That grandson of mine.' She made a 'tutting' sound

of sympathy as her gaze met Abby's. 'He's gone off by himself again, hasn't he?'

'Mmm.' Abby couldn't trust herself to say anything more. She sank into the chair beside Maggie. Even being this close to the older woman was making her feel a little better—as if strength came as a bonus with that understanding and love.

Maggie didn't say anything more, either. Instead, she cuddled Lucy. 'Do you know what the other children are doing at the moment?'

'No.'

'They're making stockings. Do you know what stockings are?'

Lucy shook her head.

'I do,' Liam said. 'They're really big socks.'

'They are,' Maggie agreed. 'Special red socks, these ones. You know our Cath who cooks all our food? Well, her mother has some friends who have a knitting circle and they work hard to knit these stockings and collect things that they help the children sew onto them to make them pretty. And then they embroider your name on them and you can keep them for ever. That's what's happening in the drawing room at the moment.'

'Aren't you supposed to hang them somewhere like on a door handle?' Liam asked.

'Absolutely.' Abby nodded.

'We hang them on the fireplace in the drawing room,' Maggie told him. 'It's big enough for everybody's stockings.'

'Do they have presents inside them on Christmas morning?'

'They most certainly do.' Maggie nodded.

Lucy's eyes were very wide. 'What sort of presents?'

Again, that steady gaze of Liam's was on Abby. 'Maybe the sort of presents that you ask Father Christmas for when you write a letter,' he suggested.

Maggie blinked, catching Abby's gaze as they both acknowledged the plea behind his words.

Lucy was sliding off Maggie's lap. 'I want to make a stocking,' she said. 'Please?'

Maggie smiled at Liam. 'Do you think you could take Lucy into the drawing room? The knitting ladies will be very happy to help you both make a stocking if you want. Dr Abby and I have a few very important phone calls that we need to make.'

Liam suddenly looked a lot older than his ten years as he nodded slowly. It felt as though he understood that those phone calls would be how Abby was going to be able to answer his plea and keep the promise she'd made. As if he knew, all too well, that his and Lucy's futures could well rest on the outcome of discussions with authorities.

'Come on, Luce.' He held out his hand. 'I'll look after you.'

As soon as the children had left the library, Maggie put her telephone on speaker mode and made their first call.

'Judith? It's Maggie McKendry here. I hope your father is still improving?'

'He is. Thank you. I'm so glad you called, Maggie. I've been worried about calling you with that bad news about Liam and Lucy earlier. I just wish I could do something.'

'You know what?' Maggie smiled at Abby as she spoke. 'Christmas is all about making wishes come true, isn't it? I think we might be able to work together to make one happen to change that bad news into something rather miraculous.'

The tears that Maggie was brushing away as they fell were melting Abby's heart and it took only another shared glance for the bond that was forming between them to feel strong enough to be invincible. They both loved Liam and Lucy and would do whatever they could to keep them together.

And they both loved Euan McKendry. Abby couldn't tell Maggie that she now knew the dreadful secret about his mother because she'd caused enough grief already in reopening old wounds. But Maggie knew he'd taken himself off again and she was clearly aware that he would be using his time alone to repair his emotional barricades. They might have both been shut out of trying to help him get through something that was overwhelming but they could support each other. And Euan, when or if he got to a point when he would allow them to get closer.

'I'm aware that we're running out of time today,' Maggie continued, 'but you'll know exactly who we need to talk to and it would be such a gift to all of us if we could at least get an agreement in principle today. Do you remember Abby who was here when you brought the children to the castle?'

'Of course. She's lovely. I could see that Lucy warmed to her straight away.'

'It was mutual,' Maggie said. 'And it's grown to a very special bond. I've got Abby here with me now, Judith, and what we want to try and make happen is to not let that bond get broken. Between Lucy and Abby but even more between Lucy and Liam. And I'm behind it a thousand per cent. I can be sure that the whole village of Kirkwood will be behind it.'

'Oh, my…' They could hear Judith's intake of breath. 'I think I can guess what you're going to say but tell me everything and I'll do whatever I can to help.'

* * *

The Christmas stockings had been finished, with a child's name embroidered on white trim at the top and the rest decorated with knitted snowflakes and Christmas trees, stars and baubles along with tiny golden bells. They'd been hung from the mantelpiece over the huge, open fire in the drawing room and were quite the distraction for a final carol singing practice before everyone got ready to be ferried down to the village church in a convoy of volunteer's cars.

Lucy's angel dress was looking distinctly grubby after the game of hide and seek in the old rowboat, and the wings were even more droopy, but she was still determined to wear them.

'You'll need warm tights on under that dress, sweetheart,' Abby told her. 'And you'll have to have your pink coat on top. There's more snow out there tonight and it's very, very cold.'

'Can I still wear my wings?'

'Of course you can.' Abby had to give her another cuddle and she met Maggie's eyes over the top of those soft, red curls. 'It's the best night of all to be wearing angel wings.'

They were still waiting to hear back from the person who had the power to make their own Christmas wish come true but everyone, starting with Judith and then stepping up through the Social Services administration levels, had been cautiously optimistic.

'We'll get back to you as soon as we can,' they'd said. *'But with it being Christmas Day tomorrow you'll understand that we can't make any promises about how quickly that will be.'*

'You go and get yourself ready,' Maggie told Abby.

'I'll finish getting this poppet into her coat and wings and hat.'

Abby nodded. 'I won't be long.' She paused beside the door. 'Have you seen…? She paused and then bit her lip as Maggie shook her head.

Abby went into her room and began to change her clothes. She'd brought two dresses with her to the castle— a red one that would be perfect for Christmas Day and another that wasn't seasonal but it was one of her favourite dresses ever and it was lovely and warm, being a dark blue, wool knit with folds of soft fabric that reached the top of her long boots. It even had a hood so she wouldn't need to add a hat. She had warm tights to wear under it, as well, just like those Lucy would be wearing under her angel dress. Abby brushed her hair but left it loose and then hurried to find her coat so that she was ready to join the excited children and carers who were gathering in the foyer.

She put on a bright smile as she went downstairs but she was sadly getting used to her heart feeling too heavy. Abby had been looking forward so much to the carol service in the old, stone village church this evening, with Euan playing the bagpipes to lead the children in and Maggie had been sure that he'd turn up in time.

'He's never missed a single Christmas Eve,' she'd told Abby between two of the many phone calls they'd made that afternoon. *'Not since the very first time when it was just our Fi and wee Jamie who wanted to sing a carol.'*

'What did they sing?'

'"We Wish You a Merry Christmas".'

The wry smile they'd shared had said it all. That this Christmas was in danger of not being as merry as any of them might have wished.

But Maggie was there, now, at the bottom of the stairs,

in the midst of a group of people that she'd brought together to have the merriest Christmas that she could create and she had a bright smile on her face, too. Abby
was suddenly quite confident that she could give her
best this evening, no matter what. Because Maggie was
here. Because this remarkable woman had found a way
to create joy despite the many challenges that life had
thrown at her.

And because Abby believed the words she'd thrown
at Euan this afternoon—that the only way to find the joy
was to risk the heartbreak of loving. And there was so
much love, right here, with Liam standing beside Maggie, holding his little sister's hand.

'Come with us,' Maggie said. 'Fergus has brought his
car to take us to church.'

They gathered again at the rectory right beside the old
church where the pastor's wife would tell them when the
village congregation was gathered and ready for the children to be led in. In the absence of the traditional piping
in, Muriel was going to fill the gap and play 'The Little
Drummer Boy' on the organ.

The candles didn't have real flames, but the glow of
the small lights was enough to be charming in the darkness of a snowy, Scottish evening. They lined up near
the arched doorway. Callum, in his wheelchair, was supposed to be first but Milo was too excited to stay behind
him and nobody minded. The pastor's wife peeped into
the church where silence had fallen and she was about to
beckon them in, when the silence was broken.

Not by any of the waiting children. It was a sound
that came from around the corner of the church. A sound
they all recognised because they'd heard it before, in the
drawing room of Ravenswood Castle, no less. The squeak
and drone of a set of bagpipes being primed to respond

to the piper. The setting of the base notes that the tune of the song would dance on top of.

As the first notes of the song became clear, the piper stepped around the corner of Kirkwood's church and came towards them, the pipes under his arm and a soft drift of snowflakes overhead.

Abby had known that it would be Euan McKendry— from that first deep sound that sent a thrill right into her bones. A sound that encompassed the rich history of this northern country along with the mystery of a proud man who kept too much, too close to his heart and intended to keep facing life alone.

Yes, Abby had expected to see the man she was so in love with. What she hadn't expected to see was that he would be wearing formal, Scottish attire. A kilt with a background that was dark green and a long swathe of the same tartan draped over one shoulder and fastened with a big, silver brooch. Long white socks and black shoes and even a leather sporran that hung from his hips with a chain.

Even more unexpected was the way Abby's heart felt as if it had stopped. That the whole world stopped turning for that missed heartbeat, as she realised that, no matter how much love she had around her, her life would always have an enormous Euan-shaped gap in it if he wasn't close to her.

She'd never experienced a feeling of being in love like this. Surely something powerful enough to make her wonder if the world really had stopped spinning for that moment couldn't be purely one-sided?

Following Milo's example, most of the children were putting their fingers in their ears as Euan walked slowly past and into the church. Lucy buried her face against Liam, who put his own hands over her ears. Abby didn't cover hers. If anything, she stood a little straighter and waited for the moment she knew would come—when Euan would meet her steady gaze. He was about three footfalls away when he did and he held her gaze until his next step put her behind him. Abby could see that he was at one with the music he was playing, using it as a shield from the outside world. But she could also see that he *saw* her.

And that she wasn't wrong in believing that she wasn't the only one captured by a love like no other. Maybe Euan wasn't ready or willing to admit it but that certainty that it was there was enough for Abby for the moment. Enough to bring a smile to her lips and a shine to her eyes as she sat with the children in the prettiest, stone church and sang the Christmas carols she'd known and loved all her life.

It was enough to keep her smiling as she got caught up in the happy chaos of getting all the children back to the castle and given supper and then the excitement of putting some hay out for the reindeer, mince pies for Santa and a last, lingering look at the magic of all the fairy lights adorning the grand, old castle. It took a while to settle the children into bed, of course, but they all knew the sooner they were asleep, the sooner the joy of Christmas Day would begin.

After the children were tucked up and sleeping, the adults had more work to do. The special gifts from families were placed under the Christmas tree in the drawing room. Stockings were filled with small treats and toys and a sack was stuffed with the extra things that Fergus, in his Santa suit, would distribute after Christmas dinner. Parents and carers took a couple of small things, like books and games, to put under the little trees in everyone's rooms. With a bit of luck, they told each other, it might mean they could catch a few minutes of extra sleep in the morning.

It was getting close to midnight when Abby wrapped her last parcel and put it into Santa's sack for Lucy—a fluffy toy donkey she'd managed to secretly buy, along with the dog for Leah, because it would remind Lucy of the donkeys she loved at Ravenswood Castle. And how easy had that been? A shared glance with a secret message—the kind parents no doubt became experts in—and Euan had distracted both the children by taking them to watch an animated display of Santa's elves in his workshop on the other side of the toy shop. Good grief…had it only been early this afternoon? So much had happened today.

So much had changed.

She hadn't expected to see Euan helping with any of these Christmas Eve activities but it was surprising that she hadn't seen him anywhere in the castle since they'd come back from the church. Come to think of it, she hadn't noticed him at all in the bustle of getting children into cars before they could get too cold or the road could become too covered in snow. She'd been in doctor mode at that time, as well, watching every child carefully and speaking to the carers to make sure they were coping with the stress that excitement could bring.

Maggie had needed watching as well. She was very clearly tired and in pain by late in the evening after the children had been settled and Abby made sure she had taken her painkillers and then sent her to bed as soon as they were having an obvious effect.

'You need to get as much rest as possible,' Abby had told her firmly, a couple of hours ago. 'It's the day we've all been waiting for tomorrow and…it's *your* day.' She wrapped her arms around Maggie. 'The day you've created every year for so many years, to bring happiness

to so many people. You're amazing, do you know that?'
She kissed Maggie's soft cheek. 'I love you so much.'

'Oh...lovie... I wish it was true. I wish I *could* bring
happiness to everyone. Or at least happiness that will last
longer than just one day. Especially to you, right now,
because if anyone deserves to be truly happy, it's someone with a heart like yours.'

Euan also deserved that kind of happiness, Abby
thought, as she finally headed towards her own room in
the closing minutes of Christmas Eve. And they'd found
it, hadn't they? At least for a while. This last couple of
nights together had taken them somewhere that was as
far away from any sadness and memories of suffering
and loss as anyone could get. They had found a place
that only they could be. A language no one else in the
world could speak and the joy in that communication
had been astonishing.

Would he let her get that close again? The look he'd
given her, as he'd walked past her at the church, had
sent a silent message that strongly suggested he wanted
to let her come that close. But was he still angry with
her? Enough to deny them even one last night together?

She went past the door to her own room and on to the
end of the hallway to the side of the house where she
knew one of the towers of this magical castle would be
shaping the walls of Euan's bedroom. She tapped lightly
on the door and then again, but she didn't want to dis-
turb anyone else, especially Maggie, who wasn't that far
away, so, instead of knocking more loudly, she turned the
handle of the door and opened it carefully.

There was a lamp glowing on the bedside table. She
could see the round wall with a beautifully arched window with a stone sill that was deep enough to function
as a window seat. She could see a four-poster bed like

the one in her room, and a rich, Persian style carpet over the wooden floorboards. A fireplace was set but not lit. A door stood open to reveal an unoccupied bathroom. The covers of the bed had been turned down but it was empty.

The whole room was empty.

Any confidence Abby had of what she'd read in that gaze as Euan had walked past her playing his bagpipes evaporated and her chest tightened so painfully, it was impossible to take in a new breath.

It was Christmas Day.

And Euan hadn't come home.

CHAPTER ELEVEN

STONE WAS NOT the best material for a window seat in Scotland on a snowy winter's night. Abby had no idea how long she'd sat there, watching the swirl of flakes outside as she waited...*hoping*...that Euan would return. The cold was seeping further and further into her body and it felt as if it were finally reaching vital, internal organs.

Like her heart.

She could go and warm up by climbing into her own bed but what was the point when she knew there was no hope of getting any sleep? She would be too acutely aware that Euan wasn't sharing her bed, and lying there alone in the dark, missing him so much, would make it even harder to stop her thoughts going in directions she was determined not to let them go.

It would be so easy to sink into misery and start believing that this was going to be her worst Christmas ever. That the pain of heartbreak that was hovering like the darkest of clouds could spoil everything, but how stupid would that be? She'd come to Ravenswood Castle absolutely convinced that this was going to be her best Christmas ever—because she was going to spend it with children and that was what Christmas was all about. Children who needed the kind of care she was able to provide. The unexpected bonus of spending these special days in a castle that looked as if it were a fairy tale come to life was magical, and to be experiencing her very first white Christmas was the icing on an extraordinary cake.

None of those things had changed. If anything, they'd just got better. Way more significant. She'd found Maggie. And Liam and Lucy. And a place that felt achingly like the home she'd been searching for without realising it. She was taking steps to an unexpected but meaningful future that she hoped, with all her heart, would make this place, and these people, a part of her life for ever.

Was she going to let the fact that Euan didn't want—or, more likely, simply wasn't able—to be a part of this new future tarnish the joy of everything else?

No, she absolutely wasn't.

The stiffness from the chill in Abby's limbs began to wear off as she walked past her room, down the stairs, towards the kitchen where she had every intention of making herself a very large mug of hot chocolate. She'd also go hunting for some of Cath's delicious shortbread, she decided, because just thinking about it was enough to imagine the taste. As she reached the kitchen, however, and saw the thick flurry of snowflakes reflected in the light shining out through the windows, Abby remembered standing on that street in Inverness and being so tempted to open her mouth and stick out her tongue to try and catch some of those flakes to see what they tasted like.

It was enough to make her smile. To recapture some of the joy she'd feared she was losing and…what the heck? There was nobody around to see her behaving like a child so Abby let herself out of the back door into the kitchen garden, wrapping her arms around her body to stave off the cold. She tipped her head back and stuck out her tongue and found it was easy enough to catch snowflakes. They might be nothing more than semi-frozen water but they tasted exactly how she'd imagined they would. They were flavoured with magic…

Not that she could stand out here too long. It was time to put the kettle on and make a hot drink. But as Abby turned to go back inside she heard a very odd noise. Not unlike one of Euan's grunts when he didn't want to say anything but it was a lot louder and longer. Abby looked around the garden, softly lit by the lights she'd turned on in the kitchen, half expecting to see a fox, perhaps. Or a deer? The sound came again as she looked and she realised it was coming from the section of the old stables that was still being used for animals rather than the clinic. Where the horses and donkeys and other farmyard pets were kept in their warm stalls at night. Abby knew she had to go and check what was happening. She hadn't grown up on a farm without developing an instinct that was telling her quite clearly that something wasn't right, here.

There was a musty warmth behind the thick stone walls of the stables, with the smell of the animals mixed with the deep layers of fresh straw in all the stalls and pens. Abby turned on lights that only provided a few pools of illumination but, while some of the inhabitants stirred sleepily at the interruption, there was one stall that was clearly the source of the unusual sounds. Mary the donkey was rolling on her back when Abby opened the top half of the door. Then she got to her feet and paced around the space, stopping to arch her back and make another grunting noise.

'Oh…' Abby caught her bottom lip between her teeth. 'You're in labour, aren't you?'

She glanced at her watch. It was nearly one a.m. She couldn't go and wake Maggie when she'd been in too much stress when she wasn't well and was in so much need of as much rest as she could get. There was no point in waking anybody else, nor was there any need to call a vet unless there was a problem with the birth and there were no signs to suggest that might be the case at this point in time. Abby's experience of helping lambs and calves into the world, on the farm alongside her father, was more than enough to ensure she could recognise when or if things were not shaping up to go well.

On the other hand, she couldn't leave Mary to give birth alone, in case problems did develop, so Abby turned on a wall heater above the cleaning area with the sinks and buckets full of brushes and rags and cupboards full of stable necessities and positioned herself on the pile of nearby straw bales that allowed her to see into Mary's stall. There was a pile of old horse blankets in a wheelbarrow in this corner of the stables as well, so she took a couple of those, one to cover the loosely tied bales and give her a soft surface to sit on and the other to wrap around her shoulders to keep warm, because it was going to take a long time for that heater to make any real difference to the temperature inside these stone walls.

Abby had no idea how long a donkey's labour might take. Mary was restless, lying down often, only to get up and start pacing again. Joseph, who was in the neighbouring stall, seemed uninterested in what was happening, even when the first signs of the birth were obvious and the white membranes of the sac enclosing the foal could be seen under Mary's tail.

'I'm here,' Abby told Mary. 'I won't leave you alone. You're doing well.'

Knowing that a new life was going to appear very soon gave Abby another flash of that joy she'd thought was tarnished and she hugged that to her heart as she watched over the donkey. Mary was lying down again and the contractions were coming close together. Abby could see part of the front legs and hooves of the baby through the mist of the membranes. She pulled the blanket closer around herself, remembering icy spring mornings on the high-country New Zealand farm she'd grown up on, as she helped her father deliver lambs.

She'd never wanted to be a farmer herself, maybe because of that loneliness she'd been so aware of as an only child, so it was ironic, she realised, that here she was in the highlands of a country on the opposite side of the world, with a dwelling that was so huge it had whole wings closed up because there were too many rooms, and yet Abby had never felt less lonely in her whole life. There was so much love here she could feel it even being by herself out here in the stables in the middle of the night. Love that had everything to do with Maggie, who was the most extraordinary woman she'd ever met, and with Lucy and Liam, of course. And, even if it was never going to come to anything more, a huge part of that love—maybe most of it—had everything to do with Euan, from the courageous, loving boy he'd been to the proud but scarred man he was today.

Her breath caught in her throat at that point as she realised something that seemed suddenly so very clear. So simple. If only Euan could realise that it was letting that love, that was here in such abundance, *in* that could heal his heart, not shutting it out as he'd spent so much of his life trying to do to protect himself. She had to blink away tears then, and as she did so she could see that Mary was getting tired. Her legs were sticking out straight and she was arching her back with each contraction but her breathing was getting laboured and, when she tried to lift her head, she simply let it drop onto the straw again.

The foal's face was visible now, with its nose resting on the front legs.

Abby climbed down from the straw pile. Mary needed help. Maybe more help than Abby could provide alone but she didn't have to wonder where she might find that extra help from because, in almost the same instant as the thought was forming, she felt the brush of freshly cold air as someone opened one of the outer stable doors.

No…it wasn't just 'someone'.

It was the one person that Abby had been desperately hoping to see when she'd been sitting alone in his room, hours ago now.

'Euan…' Abby couldn't help herself. She had to go to him. As if she was perfectly confident he would want nothing more than to take her into his arms. She even held out her own arms so that she would be ready to wrap them around his neck as soon as she was close enough.

And…maybe this was her first Christmas miracle, because taking her into his arms was exactly what Euan did.

Oh…the shape of her as he took her into his arms…

As though it was filling every empty corner in his life.

That warmth. The scent of her hair. That feeling of the joy of simply being alive and not being alone.

Euan held Abby close against his own body. And she wrapped her arms around his neck in a gesture that was pure Abby—ready to give so much love. And maybe forgiveness, as well? He'd pushed her away and that must have felt like a totally undeserved rejection.

He pressed his cheek against her hair. 'I'm so sorry,' he said. 'I needed…some time…to get my head around all of this…'

To grapple with a flood of emotion that had been threatening to drown him for days now. Ever since he'd come home to what could have meant facing up to losing Maggie. To the usual battle his childhood home represented, of pushing ghosts back into the past where they belonged and the extra, unexpected challenge of coping with what seemed like a reflection of his own early life in Liam and Lucy. And, on top of that, to the irresistible pull towards a woman he'd believed was completely wrong for him and who could never be allowed to be a part of his life.

How wrong could someone be?

Abby was exactly what he desperately needed in his life if he was to keep feeling this…*whole*…

'I know.' Abby pulled back just far enough that he could see the depth of understanding in her eyes. And… miraculously, the love that was still there. 'It's okay… you're here now and…it's perfect timing. I *need* you, Euan.'

He tightened the band of his arms around her. 'I'm here.' He pressed a kiss against her hair this time and was about to tell her how much he needed *her* and how he would always be here but Abby pulled away.

'No… I *really* need you. For Mary.'

'Mary?' For a split-second Euan had no idea what Abby was talking about and then it clicked. They were in the stables. 'The *donkey*?'

'She's in labour. I think she's in trouble.'

Maybe Abby only needed him so urgently because of Mary but, for now, that was enough. She needed him and he wouldn't want to be anywhere else. He opened the lower door of the stall and they both went to the exhausted donkey lying in the straw.

'You hold her head and talk to her,' Euan said. 'I'll pull with the next contractions. The sooner this baby is born, the better.'

If it was even still alive. Euan could see the foal's head inside the broken membrane and there was no sign of life. He put some straw in his hands to help get a grip on the forelegs that had punctured the sac and, as Mary's legs stiffened again, he pulled, gently increasing the pressure as the contraction continued. Abby was lying in the straw with her arms around Mary's neck, applying some counter pressure and talking reassuringly to the jenny at the same time.

'It's okay, Mary. You're doing really, really well. Euan's here now and your baby's going to be okay too. Just one more big push...'

It took several more pushes and, when the baby finally slipped out, there were still no signs of life. Mary tried to lift her head to look at the foal but she fell back and lay there panting, almost as limp as her newborn.

Abby was on her knees, still stroking Mary's head but her gaze was fixed on the foal. Then she looked up to meet Euan's gaze and he could see the distress in her eyes. He could feel it himself. She thought it was hopeless, didn't she? Euan didn't say anything aloud, he just held her gaze a heartbeat longer, so that she could know what he was thinking.

I can't promise a happy ever after but I can promise I'll do the absolute best I can... Every time...

He pulled away the shreds of membrane covering the foal's face to make sure the nose and mouth were clear and then he grabbed big handfuls of clean straw to rub its body and stimulate circulation. He could feel Abby watching. He could almost feel that she was holding her breath. Holding that huge heart of hers in her hands.

And then it happened. The foal twitched. The small chest expanded as it took its first breath and then its eyes opened. Mary could feel the movement behind her and, this time, she managed to raise her head for long enough to see her baby.

'I'll bring the foal close enough for her to lick,' Euan said, gathering the long-legged baby into his arms. 'It's a girl,' he told Abby. 'And isn't she gorgeous?'

'She's adorable.' Abby's smile was joyous. 'I'm so happy she's okay. That you arrived just in time. I couldn't have done that on my own.'

Again, Euan wanted to tell her that he could always be here and that she would never need to be alone again, but so many years of practice in deflecting emotions made him retreat to safer, practical, things to say. 'We'll need to watch them both for a while, to make sure they've bonded and the placenta's arrived. Bring one of those blankets and we'll cover Mary until she's rested enough.'

'There's a good place for us to sit and watch,' Abby told him. 'Where I've been for most of the night, up on the straw pile. Close enough to help but far enough not to be interfering.'

A few minutes later, that was where they both were. Snuggled into a nest of straw. Euan pulled a blanket around their shoulders.

'It's not exactly clean but I think we've ruined our clothes anyway.'

'I don't care.' Abby's face was shining with joy again. 'Look…'

Euan had to make himself look away from her face as he felt a new rush of emotion that had nothing to do with the donkeys. Mary had rolled onto her stomach, with her legs tucked beneath her, and she was licking her foal from head to foot, including the pair of ears that this baby would need a lot of time to grow into.

'I think they've bonded,' Abby whispered.

Euan shifted his gaze back to her face and he was

smiling as he leaned in to kiss her. Slowly. Gently. The donkey mother and child weren't the only creatures to be sealing their bond here.

'Merry Christmas,' he whispered. 'I'm sorry I haven't got a gift for you.'

Abby's lips wobbled as she tried to smile back. 'Being with you is the only gift I need,' she said. 'I thought… I thought I'd lost you.'

'I nearly lost myself,' Euan confessed. 'I've been sitting in my car for hours and it felt like I was in a fight for my life.'

'And you were alone…' Abby touched his face. Such a gentle touch but it still conveyed exactly how much she cared.

'I think I had to be. There was so much that I'd shut away for so long because I didn't want to feel the pain that came with them and it needed to come out. So many things I needed to remember. And feel…'

'Like what?'

'Like my mother and her floaty dresses and all her bangles and how soft her hands were. I'll tell you all about her one day.' Euan swallowed hard. 'And I remembered how I'd watch Fiona in her bassinette. She wasn't expected to live at all but she was a wee fighter and I'd sit there and wait for her to open her eyes and I'd tell her to keep fighting. That I'd look after her. I'd watch her go blue and struggle to breathe but, every time, she'd get through and they gave her the first operation when she was three weeks old.' Euan was finding it a bit of a struggle to take a new breath himself. 'So, there I was fielding the punches and kicks that came with every memory and wondering how much pain it would take before it killed me. It took until I felt as exhausted as poor Mary down there but then…'

'What?' Abby had snuggled down to tuck her head in the hollow beneath his collarbone as he was speaking and her voice was a whisper against his neck. A warm puff of her breath and the tickle of her lips against his skin. 'Tell me…'

'I thought of you. No, that's not quite true. You were there all along—in my head. In my heart. But I'd been pushing you away. Ever since you'd told me that if I couldn't let love into my life I wasn't really living. That I'd never feel the joy. And then you'd asked me about my mother…'

'I'm so sorry.' There were tears in Abby's eyes. 'I had no idea…'

'Of course you didn't. We never talk about it. Because that's when I shut myself off from living. And that's what I was thinking about. That you were right. That I *was* actually scared of feeling that joy and… I might never have felt it again if it wasn't for you coming here. You give that joy so freely, Abby—that love. And you do it without hesitation even though it could mean that your heart will get broken again and again. You're prepared to do that for Lucy *and* for Liam, when you know how hard it might be, and that kind of courage is one of the things I love so much about you.'

One of the things…?

Love…?

Had Euan just told her that he loved her?

Abby had to tune in again to the soft words that were continuing.

'…and aye, it might have been painful, but I think you've brought me back to life, Abby Hawkins…' Euan's smile was wry as he looked down. 'I think I knew I was in trouble the moment I found you on the castle doorstep.'

'Oh…' Abby lifted her head so that she could meet Euan's gaze but she lost her words as she saw the way he was looking back at her. She could drown in the love she could see in the misty grey of his eyes. She needed to find more of the oxygen that seemed to be in short supply around here, and when she opened her mouth to take a gulp of air the words were there, after all.

'I love you,' she whispered. 'I love you so much, Euan McKendry.'

And this had to be her second Christmas miracle—that Euan had found a way forward. That, given time and care, his heart could really be healed.

And yes, maybe they still wanted very different things in their futures but, right now, that didn't seem to matter, because this was like the time they'd found together when they'd shut the bedroom door behind them. The place where they could just be. Where they could find the joy that was bright enough to banish any shadows.

'I love you,' Euan murmured, 'even more…'

One kiss led to another. Slow, gentle kisses and long, shared glances that held the promise of everything, including enough time to let it all fall into place. And then they simply held each other, tucked into the warmth of that nest of straw, until they drifted into sleep, their bodies so close it was impossible to tell whether it was their own heartbeat or each other's that they could feel. And it didn't matter, anyway, because being that close was all that either of them wanted for now.

'Oh…look… Can you see?' Maggie couldn't lift Lucy high enough to see over the stable door without it being too painful, so she opened it instead.

'It's a baby…' Lucy was awestruck. 'A baby *donkey*. A Christmas baby donkey…'

Liam had a tight hold of his sister's hand. 'Don't get too close, Luce. The mum won't like that.'

'Mothers do protect their babies,' Maggie agreed. 'Mary's very gentle but we won't ask to pat the baby just yet. It must have been born in the middle of the night, I think. She's all dry and fluffy already and look…she's having a drink of milk.'

But Liam wasn't looking at the foal. He was staring at the straw pile where something was moving under a blanket.

'Oh…' Again, Maggie's exclamation was heartfelt. 'So that's where you are. I came looking for you both, when Liam and Lucy wanted to open their stockings.'

She'd never seen her grandson looking so dishevelled. And Abby had straw in her hair and was blinking sleep from her eyes but she'd never looked so beautiful. Seeing the two of them, together, filled Maggie's heart with hope. If only they knew how much they needed each other.

'And I needed to find you, too. I got a message, late last night, after I was asleep so I only saw it this morning. A message from Judith.'

She could hear Abby's sharp inward breath as she realised how significant the next words she would hear would be. She saw the way her gaze flew to meet Euan's, as if she was looking for strength, and Maggie's heart gave a huge squeeze as she saw the way he was meeting that gaze and the way his fingers were curling around Abby's as he took hold of her hand. It was so obvious that he was letting her know that he was there for her. That what she was hoping for was just as important to him.

That he loved her…

'It's been approved,' she said quietly. 'There's interviews and paperwork to be sorted, of course, but, in principle, everybody's on board.' She took a deep breath, looking down at Lucy and then across to Liam before looking back to Abby. 'I thought you'd like to tell them yourself.'

It was Liam that Abby focused on. 'You know what this means, don't you?'

Liam shrugged. 'Maybe…'

'It means that we're both going to take care of Lucy. Together. And, if I can, I'm going to adopt you both.' She held out an arm towards Lucy. 'Is that okay, sweetheart? Can I look after you and love you and be your mum?'

Lucy didn't have to speak. Her answer was obvious by the way she let go of Maggie's hand to start scrambling up the pile of straw and into Abby's lap for a cuddle.

'So…we're going to stay here?' Liam sounded dubious. 'At the castle?'

'If that's still okay with Maggie. Otherwise we'll find a wee house of our own.'

'Don't be daft,' Maggie said. 'Of course you're going to stay here. I want to be part of this family.'

'Me, too.'

Maggie's breath caught. She could feel the tension in the way Liam was holding himself as well. Even Abby and Lucy had gone very still. They all turned to focus on the person who'd just spoken with such sincerity.

Euan…

It was Lucy who broke the stunned silence.

'Are you going to be my daddy, then?'

It was Liam who answered. 'That would only work if they got married. Him and Dr Abby.'

'That's true.' Euan nodded.

'And you can't get married.' Liam shook his head. 'Not unless you really love someone.'

'That's also true,' Euan agreed. 'But you know what?'

'What?'

Maggie was holding her breath as Liam asked the question she also wanted the answer to.

'I do. I really, really love Dr Abby.'

'Me too.' Lucy wound her arms around Abby's neck to cuddle her, but Abby was looking past that cloud of red curls to hold Euan's gaze.

'And I really, really love Dr Euan,' she said.

'So…' Liam was almost scowling as he stared at them both. 'You're going to get married, then? And we're going to be your kids? For ever? Even if you have kids of your own?'

Euan held Abby's gaze for a heartbeat longer before he shifted it to let it settle on Liam. Long enough for Maggie to see that there were no barriers between Abby and Euan now. That the possibilities for their shared future seemed without limits. They might well have their own bairns. They might even carry on with Ravenswood Castle's Christmas camp for sick children, but they were going to trust each other and take it one step at a time.

Euan's smile for Liam gave the impression of offering a pact. 'How 'bout we get used to being a family first and then we'll talk about getting married? But I promise you, we're not going anywhere. This is home now, okay?'

Liam nodded slowly. He was watching Euan begin to climb down from the straw. Maggie could sense that Liam was close to tears as the news that he and Lucy were not going to be separated began to sink in. She put her arm around his shoulders and drew him close to her side.

'It's about time we went inside, don't you think? I do believe there are some Christmas stockings to open.' Euan touched Liam's shoulder as he drew close enough and lowered his voice. This was a man-to-man communication but Maggie could still hear it. 'Lucy might need her big brother's help to climb down. That straw can be a bit slippery.'

Maggie could feel the way Liam's shoulders straightened and her heart filled with pride as he went to look after his little sister. She already loved this lad with all her heart. The thought that she could well have many years ahead of her, after she got that pesky surgery out of the way, to win Liam's trust and hopefully his love filled her with as much joy as the knowledge that Abby and Euan had, without doubt, found the person they were meant to be with. Their life partner. A soul mate.

You only had to catch a glimpse of the way they were looking at each other to know that they were both the happiest people on earth right now. But so was Maggie, come to that. This was the first time she'd ever seen Liam smiling as well and Lucy... Maggie was feeling even more misty. Abby had probably lit up whole rooms with her happiness just like Lucy when she was a little girl because she was still doing it now. The love that was filling this ancient building in this moment was, in fact, well...it was nothing short of a Christmas miracle, that was what it was.

'I had a feeling that this was going to happen.' Everybody was looking at Maggie as she wiped away a few happy tears. She turned to lead them all back to the warmth of the castle. Into their home. Everybody would be up by now and the celebrations would be well under way. She could imagine the excited faces of children who still believed in the magic. She still believed in that magic herself—who wouldn't after what had already happened so early on this special day? A glance over her shoulder showed Lucy holding Liam's hand on one side and Abby's on the other. Abby's free hand was being held by Euan.

They looked like a family.

They *were* a family now. And Maggie was blessed to be a part of it.

She was just thinking aloud but her words were loud enough for everyone to hear.

'This is going to be the best Christmas *ever*.'

* * * * *

COMING SOON!

We really hope you enjoyed reading this book.
If you're looking for more romance, be sure to
head to the shops when new books are
available on

Thursday 23rd December

MILLS & BOON

Coming next month

SECRET FROM THEIR LA NIGHT
Julie Danvers

Last night was just a fluke. It doesn't have to mean anything. It doesn't have to be a slippery slope back into old patterns. She'd simply had a moment of weakness, brought on by loneliness and old memories, and she'd given in to temptation. With time, she could forgive herself for that. But first, she needed to find her shoes.

Ah. She spied the pointed toe of one ballet flat poking out from beneath the bed. She gathered up her shoes, not bothering to put them on. Her own room was only a few floors away, and it was early enough that the halls were still empty. She turned the doorknob; the door creaked as she opened it, and she slowed so it would open quietly. At least she hadn't lost her silent creeping skills.

As she stepped out, Daniel turned over in his sleep, and her heart rose in her throat. His snores paused, and for a moment she was certain he'd woken up. But then she relaxed as his breathing returned to a slow, even pace. He really was very attractive, with his dark, tousled hair and his barely shaven stubble. But great hair or not, she needed to put last night behind her. Daniel, fun as he had been, represented a past she had tried her best to forget, and the past was where he needed to stay.

One brisk shower later, Emily was back in professional mode. She took a cab to the convention center and found the right conference room a few moments before orientation was scheduled to begin. She was the last one into the meeting, but only just; a few other stragglers were still hanging their jackets when she arrived. She took the last seat available, next to a dark-haired physician who turned to greet her.

Her stomach dropped.

His brown eyes widened.

Emily was completely tongue-tied, but somehow, he was able to speak.

"Dr. Daniel Labarr," he said, holding out one hand. "I do believe we've met."

Continue reading
SECRET FROM THEIR LA NIGHT
Julie Danvers

Available next month
www.millsandboon.co.uk

JOIN US ON SOCIAL MEDIA!

Stay up to date with our latest releases, author news and gossip, special offers and discounts, and all the behind-the-scenes action from Mills & Boon...

 millsandboon

 millsandboonuk

 millsandboon

It might just be true love...